KEEPING GUARD

SANDRA OWENS

carina
press

carina
press®

Recycling programs
for this product may
not exist in your area.

ISBN-13: 978-1-335-40184-7

Keeping Guard

Copyright © 2021 by Sandra Owens

All rights reserved. No part of this book may be used or reproduced in
any manner whatsoever without written permission except in the case of
brief quotations embodied in critical articles and reviews.

This is a work of fiction. Names, characters, places and incidents
are either the product of the author's imagination or are used fictitiously.
Any resemblance to actual persons, living or dead, businesses,
companies, events or locales is entirely coincidental.

This edition published by arrangement with Harlequin Books S.A.

For questions and comments about the quality of this book,
please contact us at CustomerService@Harlequin.com.

Carina Press
22 Adelaide St. West, 40th Floor
Toronto, Ontario M5H 4E3, Canada
www.CarinaPress.com

Printed in U.S.A.

This book is dedicated to our military heroes, those women and men who put their lives on the line to protect our country and our freedom, sometimes making the ultimate sacrifice.

KEEPING
GUARD

Chapter One

"He's a stray someone tied to our gate a few nights ago."

Noah Alba, Double D—or sometimes just DD—to his SEAL teammates, stared at the fifty pounds of wiggling animal. "Are you sure it's actually a dog?"

The thing looked more like something put together all wrong. Wiry fur stuck up and out at odd angles and had to be about a dozen different colors. There was more fur on his furiously wagging tail than on its body. The oddest parts of the animal were the two different colored eyes, one blue and one brown. There was intelligence in those odd eyes, though, an alertness that Noah liked.

His friend and former teammate laughed. "Actually, no."

A year ago, Jack Daniels—Whiskey to the team—and his dog had come home to Asheville, North Carolina. When he learned that his arm and shoulder were permanently damaged, he'd started Operation K-9 Brothers to train therapy dogs to be companions to their military brothers and sisters who were suffering from PTSD.

Noah was both proud and impressed with what his friend had accomplished, but the last thing he wanted was to be around people and dogs. Former teammate included. The only reason he didn't do a vanishing act was because his commander had ordered him here. If he left, he'd be AWOL. He'd fucked up his life enough without getting charged with a serious crime.

"He's yours to work with while you're here," Jack said.

"Oh, hell no." The last dog he'd been around was dead because of him.

Jack put his hand on Noah's shoulder. "Yes, and that's an order, DD."

Noah pressed his lips together to keep from telling him what he could do with his order and the dog. What had his commander been thinking by sending him here, and not only that, but also ordering him to report directly to Whiskey? Hell, Jack wasn't even in the navy anymore.

"You'll work with me every day on training him while you're here. You also need to give him a name."

The ever-simmering rage inside him burned hotter. "You're making a mistake trusting me with a dog."

"I disagree."

Noah slipped his hand into the pocket of his jeans, his fingers wrapping around the pair of dice he always carried. They'd belonged to his father, a reminder of everything he refused to be. All he had to do to remind himself that he was not his father was to touch the pair of dice. Throughout his life, he'd touched them thousands of times, and it always worked, always led him to find the calm in his soul that made him not his father. To be the kind of man his mother would have been proud of.

For the first time since he was a boy, his rage didn't go from boiling over back to simmering when he touched them. "I need to go somewhere for a while."

"Take the dog with you."

Noah hated the knowing look in Jack's eyes, like his friend knew he was losing it and understood. Maybe he did. Jack had appeared three nights ago at their home base in Virginia Beach, announcing that he was taking Noah home with him. Noah had told him to go to hell.

"You have two choices," Jack had answered. "Come with me or tell our commander you refused to obey an order. Makes no never mind to me which you pick."

Noah knew his friend and teammate was there to save him, and that made him antsy. He didn't want to need saving, had never expected to be the one his SEAL brothers had to worry about. He had his shit together. Nothing could be as bad as what his boy-self had survived, right? Or so he'd thought until his mistake caused the team's dog and their translator to be blown up.

Noah took the dog with him…as far as his temporary apartment. The ants weren't just crawling under his skin, they were biting. He couldn't be near a dog right now. Every time he looked at the thing, he saw his team's dog.

After giving the dog time to do his business, Noah took him inside. "Here's the thing, dog. I don't own this place, so don't chew on the furniture or pee on the floor." Unable to think of anything else the dog needed to know, he left the creature to his own devices.

He ended up on the Blue Ridge Parkway, his rental car pointed in the direction of the waterfall Jack had taken him to yesterday. After hiking down to the bottom of the falls, Jack had said, "This is a good place to come when you feel like you're about to lose your shit."

He'd glanced around. "If you let it, you can find a few moments of peace here."

"Speaking from experience?" Noah had asked.

"I've spent quiet time here, especially after I first came home." He smiled. "Before I met Nichole."

That was another thing. Jack had gone and fallen in love. Noah never thought he'd see Whiskey look at a woman with sappy eyes. Nichole was great, and she'd even seemed disappointed when Noah said he was going to find an apartment to rent while he was here.

He didn't think Jack was happy about that, either—he'd prefer to have him where he could keep an eye on him. Understandable, since Noah had been falling down drunk when Jack arrived to collect him.

After Noah swore there'd be no repeat performance—all the booze he'd poured down his throat hadn't wiped his memory clean, anyway—Jack helped him find a lease-by-the-month place. He'd moved in right away, grateful that he hadn't had to sit around with Jack and Nichole last night and pretend he was enjoying himself.

If Noah had to be around people twenty-four-seven, he was going to climb out of his skin.

Peyton Sutton wasn't supposed to hear her fiancé telling his best man that he was only marrying her because her father had promised him a share of her family's brewery. The share that was supposed to be hers.

The rat bastard. She'd only overheard the conversation because she'd gotten last-minute cold feet and wanted to talk to Dalton, needed him to assure her that they were both ready for a lifelong commitment. Turned out he was more committed to her father than to her.

After she graduated from college, her father had dangled a carrot in front of her. Do this and a share in the company will be yours one day. Do that and the entire company will be yours one day. She'd jumped through hoops doing this and that, trying to please him. Like saying yes when Dalton asked her to marry him. Dalton was Elk Antler Brewery's chief financial officer, the son her father had always wanted, and marrying Dalton would make Gerald Sutton happy with her.

Well, to hell with both of them.

She gathered up the skirts of the princess wedding gown she'd grown to hate. She was done with trying to please her father.

From the time he'd let her hang out at Elk Antler Brewery, she'd been fascinated by the process of making beer. She'd been thirteen the first time he'd brought her there, pointing at the corner where she could do her homework. It was supposed to be punishment for not getting a perfect score on her math test.

That day had been far from punishment and set the course of her life. She spent her afternoons at the downtown brewery, supposedly doing her homework, but anytime her father was in a meeting or out of the building, she was learning how to make beer instead. Her father's brewmaster had taken a liking to her, and over the years he'd shared his knowledge, his love of brewing, and his recipes. She could step into his shoes and no one would notice.

She'd returned home with degrees in business and marketing and went to work for her father. Pleasing him was impossible—even with bringing in more business with tours and events—but she'd kept trying anyway.

Until today.

She was over it. He'd made her a promise that he obviously had no intention of keeping. The long hours she'd put in, the heart she put into the brewery, the jumping through hoops for him apparently meant nothing.

"Where is she?"

Peyton stilled at hearing her father's voice. If he found her, he'd convince her to go through with the wedding.

With the voluminous skirts of the gown gathered up, she headed in the opposite direction. She didn't have a plan since it hadn't for a minute occurred to her that she'd sneak out on her own wedding.

Three hundred and twenty-nine guests were seated in the country club ballroom waiting for her to walk down the aisle in a matter of minutes. They were sure going to be in for a surprise when the bride didn't appear. Avoiding the ballroom, she scooted into the banquet hall. The staff setting up for the reception all stopped what they were doing to stare at her. She nodded at the bartender, snatched two bottles of champagne, and almost laughed at his wide eyes.

"You never saw me," she tossed over her shoulder as she headed for the door leading to the parking lot. She should be in tears, crushed, heartbroken...blah, blah, blah. Weirdly, what she felt was free.

Outside, she paused for a moment, and as she breathed in the pine-scented mountain air, the heavy weight that had settled on her shoulders ever since Dalton had put an engagement ring on her finger lifted, carried away by the breeze. As much as she wanted to luxuriate in the feeling of freedom, she needed to go before someone found her. But where to?

Her car wasn't here since she'd arrived with her father in the limo he'd rented. She spied Dalton's silver

Mercedes parked near the main entrance and headed for it. Wasn't her fault he'd once shown her where he'd hidden a spare key remote.

She cringed at the Just Married someone had written on the rear window with white shoe polish. Couldn't be helped. She needed a getaway car, and Dalton's was her only choice. After retrieving the key, she unlocked the door, got in, put the champagne bottles on the passenger seat, and then spent minutes she didn't have getting the skirts of the stupid gown inside so she could close the door.

The next time she planned to get married, she was wearing one of those slip wedding dresses. Much easier to escape in if need be. She glanced in the rearview mirror, saw her father and Dalton walk out of the building, and hauled ass.

With no direction in mind, she drove around, and at the entrance to the Blue Ridge Parkway, turned on her blinker. What she really wanted to do was go home, get out of this ridiculous dress, put on her jammies, and then plow her way through the champagne.

Or go to the brewery and make beer. Getting lost in recipes, that was her peace place. Where all her troubles floated away. But she couldn't do either of those things. Home and the brewery were the first places her father and Dalton would look.

She needed to find somewhere she could think, make a plan for where she'd go from here. After her stunt today, she doubted her father would welcome her back to the place she loved above all else. Oh, he probably would if she went back and married Dalton, but that was so not happening.

Peyton blinked away the tears that threatened at the

thought of never setting food in Elk Antler Brewery again, tears from losing something she loved…and that was not Dalton. Not good to bawl her eyes out while driving. Along with a place to consider her future, she needed somewhere she could have a good cry in private.

After driving along the Parkway for a while, she saw a sign announcing a waterfall. No other cars were in sight in the parking lot, and she decided it was the perfect place.

She parked in the lot, grabbed the two bottles of champagne, then headed for the trail. She stopped and eyed the steep path down. No way was she going to manage that wearing white satin heels without falling and breaking her neck. She kicked them off. The sheer white stockings the bridal shop consultant said she had to wear soon followed. They were her first ever stockings, and she hated them as much as the dress.

Even barefoot, going down was tricky in a gown consisting of more material than all the clothes in her closet put together. A squirrel clinging upside down to a tall pine tree chattered at her as she passed. "Yeah, yeah, I'm not having a good day, either."

She almost slipped when she stepped on a mossy rock, and, forgetting she had a champagne bottle in her hand, she grabbed hold of a rhododendron branch. The bottle rolled and bounced down the trail. Thankfully, it didn't break. She needed that champagne.

"Well, that wasn't a piece of cake," she muttered after finally making it to the waterfall with both bottles intact. Speaking of cake, she should have snatched some of her wedding cake while she was at it since she hadn't eaten anything all day because her stomach had been in knots.

The dress her father had paid a small fortune for was torn and dirt streaked. He wasn't going to be happy about that, but she wasn't happy with him, either, so they were even. She headed for a boulder with a flat surface. She tried to climb up it, but that proved impossible when wearing a million yards of...whatever the dress was made of. Fashion and fabrics weren't her thing. Clothes were a necessity, something she had to put on before she could appear in public. And right now, there was no public, and she wanted on top of that boulder. She deserved to be up there after knowing her actions would cost her the only thing that mattered to her.

So...it was a struggle, but she finally got the hated gown off. Irritated with the stupid thing, she tossed it to the side with more force than she'd intended.

It tumbled down the embankment, landing in the waterfall pool.

"Oops." Who knew a dress that heavy could travel so far?

Free of the gown, she climbed up to the top of the boulder, giving thanks that it wasn't winter, when she'd be freezing her bottom off wearing only a sexy white corset that she *had* wanted to wear. She'd imagined that Dalton would finally look at her with desire in his eyes when he saw her in it, spicing up their sex life.

Although brewing beer and creating events that brought beer lovers to Elk Antler Brewery was her jam—or had been—she wanted to experience how it felt to be truly wanted by someone.

She was, as far as she'd gathered, the result of a one-night stand between her parents. The mother she only vaguely remembered had dropped her off at her father's when Peyton was four years old, then had disappeared from her life. Her father had kept her, but she'd never been sure he'd been happy to have her. That uncertainty was the reason she'd spent her life until now trying to please him…so he wouldn't give her away like her mother had.

All good reasons why the champagne should go straight down her throat. She managed to pop the cork on one of the bottles. The cork shot up before arcing and falling into the pool to join her wedding gown.

"Cheers to me." She lifted the bottle to her mouth as tears rolled down her cheeks for what she'd lost today.

Chapter Two

There was only one other car parked on the dirt-packed lot at the entrance to the falls, a silver Mercedes with "Just Married" scrawled on the rear window. Shrugging off his curiosity, Noah locked the doors of his rental and headed for the trail, hoping Jack was right and a bit of peace that would quiet the ants awaited him at the bottom.

Noah paused at the top of the trail going down, frowning at seeing the white heels, one upright and the other on its side. A pair of white stockings were draped over a nearby bush. He glanced back at the silver Mercedes. Was he going to stumble on a bride and groom, and what the devil were they doing here of all places?

He almost turned around to leave, but curiosity got the better of him. If he discovered them getting it on—a distinct possibility considering the bride was shedding clothing—he'd discreetly disappear. Going down in stealth mode, he reached the bottom of the trail, stopping dead in his tracks when a woman said, "Cheers to me." He blinked and then blinked again.

A woman wearing nothing but lacey white panties, a white corset, and a veil attached to a tiara was perched on a boulder, a champagne bottle held up to her mouth as she chugged the contents. He scanned the area, searching for the groom. Something white floating in the pool caught his eyes, and after staring at it for a minute, he realized it was a wedding dress. The hell?

His gaze returned to the woman. Had she done away with her groom? Was the man in the pool under her dress? He wasn't sure what to do, but one thing was for sure. This woman—whoever she was…a murderer?— had him forgetting his own troubles.

She still hadn't noticed him, and he took the opportunity to observe her. A lacy veil topped the black hair that fell around her shoulders and down her back, and the corset did a mighty fine job of displaying her breasts. Her long, firm legs were splayed over the rock as if she had no modesty.

Of course, she thought she was alone, and realizing he was no better than a Peeping Tom, he debated leaving or making his presence known. But what if she had offed her groom? Was that why she was crying? The last thing he wanted to do was get involved in someone else's mess, so he decided a dead groom wasn't going to be his problem. When he got to the top of the trail, he'd call Jack, tell him what was going on, and let him decide what to do.

Besides, he wasn't fond of brides. He'd almost had one of those once. His had walked out on him the day before their wedding after telling him that he loved his SEAL team more than her. That wasn't true. He'd loved her as much as his teammates.

Brides couldn't be trusted, especially a killer bride who chugged champagne to celebrate her groom's demise.

Time to do a disappearing act. He took a step back,

but his movement caught her attention before he could slip away. She lowered the champagne bottle and stared at him. Blue eyes the color of the sky above, he inanely thought.

She tilted her head as she studied him. "Are you going to kidnap me?"

"Wasn't planning on it."

"Oh." She sounded disappointed.

"Sorry. I didn't mean to disturb you. I'll be going now."

"You don't have to. Just ignore me."

Like it was possible to ignore a beautiful woman wearing nothing but a corset. "That's okay. Probably best if I go."

She lifted a foot and stared at it. "My feet are dirty."

"I see that." Weirdest conversation ever.

"You want some champagne?" She held up the bottle, showing him the label. "Only the best will do for my father."

"No, thanks." If he stuck around and drank with her, his luck, he'd end up arrested as an accomplice to murder.

"I'm a runaway bride."

He didn't know what to say to that, but he definitely had thoughts. Like, there you go, just more proof that brides can't be trusted. Then another one…at least that meant there wasn't a dead groom under that wedding dress. That one was definitely a relief. And why was she only wearing a corset and veil, and her dress floating in the pool?

"Do you need some help?" he finally said, hoping she said no.

"Yeah, with this champagne. It's not good to drink alone, you know."

He did know that, not that it stopped him. Why wasn't she afraid of him? She picked up a second, still-corked bottle, and held it out to him. "You can even have your own if drinking out of a bottle my mouth has been on bothers you."

His gaze fell to said mouth. Negative. He'd have absolutely no problem putting his mouth anywhere hers had been. *Situation dire!* Time to retreat. He didn't do brides, even ones with sky-blue eyes and lips made for kissing.

"Come on. Don't be a stick in the mud." She waved the bottle like it was a red cape and he was the bull.

Apparently, he was a bull because his feet took him to the edge of the boulder. "Why aren't you afraid of me?"

"Should I be?"

"No, but you can't know that."

She shrugged. "I figure the universe can't be meaner to me today than it already has. And if it is, not sure I have it in me to care anymore." She tipped the bottle up, chugging down more champagne like a pro.

As much as he wanted to leave, knew he needed to put this woman and her problems behind him, he couldn't bring himself to go. Not when tears were pooling in her eyes and her lips trembled. Somehow, he knew she was trying hard not to cry in front of him.

So, despite hating brides, crying women, and champagne, he took the already opened bottle from her and brought it to his mouth. She was right. Daddy did go for the best. First time he'd actually liked the taste of champagne.

"You can't stay down there if you're going to drink with me." She patted the space next to her.

Obeying, he pushed himself up. As they passed the bottle back and forth, he tried to imagine telling Jack that he'd spent the afternoon at a waterfall, drinking top-shelf champagne with a runaway bride who was wearing only a corset and veil. His friend would laugh his ass off, not believing a word of it, then say, "Good one, DD."

"You want to hear my sad story?" she said after about five minutes, her words now a little slurred.

Not really. He was already on sad story overload, but he shrugged, letting her decide whether or not to share. He was a little curious, though.

"The man I was supposed to marry doesn't love me," she said, then peered up at him with those pretty eyes of hers.

"The woman I was supposed to marry didn't love me enough." That was what he'd finally settled on after Avery had called off the wedding. She had loved him, he was sure of that, but she'd needed all his attention on her, and that was more than he could give her.

"She was a runaway bride, too?"

"Not exactly. She called it off the day before the wedding." Why was he sharing his shit with a stranger?

"Oh, I should have done that, but I didn't know."

"Know what?" He took the bottle from her and set it behind them, hoping she wouldn't notice. She was buzzing pretty good already. Much more, and he'd have a sick bride on his hands, and that he definitely did not want.

She waved a hand in the air, almost slapping him. "Doesn't matter. I don't think my father loves me."

"I know mine doesn't."

"My mother gave me away."

"Mine died." What was he about? It wasn't that he was trying to one-up her, but he didn't like her being sad, and maybe if she knew she wasn't the only one bad stuff happened to it would help.

"That's terrible. What happened?"

"My father killed her." Right, he needed to shut up and stop sharing.

"Oh my God, really?"

"Old news. Tell me something good about yourself," he said, needing to get this conversation away from his life story.

Instead of answering, she burst out laughing, laughed so hard she fell back on the rock. Yeah, she was buzzing all right. She was also more temptation than he'd ever endured, lying there in her sexy corset, her breasts almost spilling out, her tiara tilting to the left, and her black hair a sharp contrast to the white veil spread out over the boulder. A disheveled princess. Even the mascara streaking down her cheeks didn't take away from her sexiness.

He tore his gaze away. Yep, he should have turned around, gotten in his car, and hightailed it away at seeing the shoes and stockings at the top of the trail. He didn't even know her name, and she was getting under his skin. One positive, though. The ants had stopped biting.

"Care to share the funny?" He couldn't help grinning at the absurdness of it all, and that in itself was a minor miracle. After what had happened on deployment, he was sure he'd never smile again.

Her hands flew out to her sides, and this time she did hit him, but at least it was on his arm and not his face. "We've just shared our life stories, and I don't even know your name. How weird is that?"

"Pretty weird, and it's Noah."

"I like that name." She glanced at where her hand was still on his arm. "Oh, I hit you. I'm so sorry."

Well, that was a delayed reaction. "No problem."

"So, Noah, I'm Peyton. Nice to meet you." She pushed up, then held out her hand.

"The pleasure is mine." With a million guesses, when he'd gotten up this morning, he'd never have seen himself sitting on a rock with a barely clothed runaway bride while shaking her hand.

"I brew beer, really great beer."

"Okaaay."

"You asked me to tell you something good about myself, and that's it."

She was giving him whiplash. "I happen to like beer."

"That's good. I couldn't like a man who didn't." Her gaze fell on her left hand, and she frowned. "You want to know something?"

"What's that?"

"I never liked this ring. Don't you think it's gaudy?" She waved her fingers in front of his face.

He supposed *gaudy* was a good word for it. *Flashy* worked, too. "Got a lot of diamonds."

"Go ahead. You can say it. It's ridiculous." She pulled it off and without hesitation, tossed it in the pool to join her wedding dress. "Oopsie," she said, then giggled.

"Did you really just do that?"

"Appears so. Now where'd you hide that bottle?"

The sound of voices coming down the trail caught his attention. "We're about to get company." He glanced at the corset that was barely containing her breasts. Whipping his T-shirt over his head, he said, "Put this on."

"Why?"

"Because you're next to naked?"

"Is that a question?"

This girl. "Put on my shirt, Peyton."

"I like how you give orders. Are you that bossy in bed?"

He could be if she wanted. He also needed to stop thinking of her and bed in the same sentence. He was a mess. She was a mess. The two of them combined… he didn't even want to think of what kind of implosion that would be.

Instead of arguing with her—which would still be going on when whoever was almost at the bottom of the trail arrived—he said, "Arms up."

Like a good girl, she obeyed. He almost wished she hadn't since her obeying him went right back to thinking of her in his bed and him giving her orders that got them both hot and bothered. *Shut that thought right down, douchebag.*

He got his T-shirt on her, the hem thankfully reaching her midthigh when two men walked into view.

"Crap," she muttered, then grabbed his face and kissed him.

Chapter Three

Peyton panicked when her father and Dalton appeared. How had they found her? They were going to take her back to a wedding she refused to participate in, and she did the first thing that came to mind. She kissed Noah.

How that was going to keep them from taking her, she wasn't sure, but...okay, wow! If Dalton had ever kissed her back like Noah was doing, she would be married right now and not a runaway bride.

"Peyton Sutton, you have a lot of explaining to do," her father said.

Didn't she always? And you know what? She was so tired of it. She'd proven herself over and over, and yet, instead of recognizing that she knew beers and had so much to offer, he would never give her the same respect as he would have if she'd been a boy.

"Why the devil are you kissing that man?" her father yelled. "Why are you wearing his shirt?"

Because you'd really be freaking out if I wasn't. She pulled away from Noah's lips—although she wouldn't mind kissing him a lot longer—and put her mouth next to his ear. "Please don't let them take me."

He looked at her with deer-in-the-headlights eyes,

like he was trying to compute how he'd gotten from dis-
covering a runaway bride to kissing that bride.

"Please," she said again.

"Copy that," he said too softly for her father and Dalton to hear. He put his arm around her shoulders and
pulled her next to him.

Her father glared at Noah. "Whoever you are, you
need to step away from my daughter."

"I can't do that, sir, unless she wants me to." Noah
tilted his head and peered down at her. "Do you want
me to?"

"We haven't finished drinking all the champagne,
so no."

When he laughed, it sounded rusty, like he wasn't
used to that particular emotion. "She doesn't want me
to step away, so I guess I'm not going to, sir."

"That's my daughter, and I'm taking her with me.
She has a wedding to attend."

"I'm not getting married today." Why wasn't Dalton
fighting for her? If he loved her, he would, right? Instead, he stood behind her father, letting the man who
wanted a son more than a daughter fight his battle.

Her father's expression was one of disappointment.
What else was new? "You've embarrassed me in front
of three hundred guests, Peyton. Let's go. We can explain your behavior away."

So, he was disappointed in her. Story of her life.
"I don't care about any guests, but you're my father.
Shouldn't you care about my happiness?"

"Of course I do. Which is why I'm going to fix this
mess for you."

And still Dalton hadn't said a word. Did he even care
that he'd seen her kissing a stranger? When her father

headed for her, she knew he meant to grab her and take her back to the venue he'd picked for her wedding. She moved behind Noah.

"He's going to force me to go back with him and get married," she said.

Noah glanced back at her, his eyes softening in a way that made her want to melt at his feet. "Not on my watch, he's not." He picked her up and tossed her over his shoulder, causing her to screech.

The screech was only because he'd surprised her. Her body draped over him and her face about eye-level with his butt—the best butt she'd ever had the pleasure of having her eyes on—wasn't such a bad place to be.

Noah patted her leg. "You sure about this?"

"Roger dodger," she said, then giggled at the ridiculousness of her day. "Don't forget my champagne."

He leaned over and hooked his fingers around the necks of the two bottles. "Got 'em."

As Noah marched past her father and her no-longer groom, she said, "You know, Dalton, if you'd ever gone caveman like this on me, I might not be your runaway bride. Too bad, so sad for you."

Noah's laugh vibrated through her girly parts, the ones that just happened to be pressed against his chest. She was very pleased with herself over that because she had the impression that he didn't laugh much.

He carried her up the mountain as if he were out for a morning stroll without the weight of her body decorating him. How could he do that without gasping for air?

Go ahead, girl, and swoon. Just get it over with.

She had no idea who he was, but she did know that he had stepped up and protected her when he had no reason to. If he was a local, she should probably tell him that her father could cause him all kinds of trouble, and she would do that…as soon as she removed herself from his superpower. Because he did have one, and it was the power to make her go all tingly. She'd always wondered how it felt to tingle because of a man. Now she knew.

Her father and Dalton scrambled up behind them, but even with carrying her, Noah was going up the trail twice as fast as the two of them.

"Put her down right now, or I'll call the police and report a kidnapping," her father said.

"I'll deny it, so don't bother." Wow! If she'd known how good it would feel to stick up for herself, she would have done it a long time ago.

She half expected Noah would drop her like a hot potato at her father's threat, but instead, he picked up his pace. Gosh, the man was strong. With her father's and Dalton's arrival, she hadn't had much of a chance to appreciate his chest and count those abs—were they a six or an eight pack?—when Noah had taken off his T-shirt, but she'd had a glimpse, and oh boy. Highlight of her day.

When they reached his car, he set her on her feet, reached into his pocket, and pulled out a car remote. After he got the passenger door open, she scooted inside, and he handed her the two champagne bottles. He jogged around to the driver's side. Her father and Dalton made it to the top of the trail as Noah tore out of the lot.

Peyton giggled as she waved at them. She felt like she was in a B movie, racing off in a getaway car. What an absurd day! Maybe it was because of the champagne that she wasn't freaking out, but right now, all she wanted to do was laugh.

"Glad someone's amused." Noah glanced at her. "I assume that was your groom with your father?"

He was obviously far from amused, and that sobered her. He hadn't asked to land smackdab in the middle of her trouble, and he didn't deserve whatever her father decided to do. Because he would find a way to punish Noah. Gerald Sutton didn't tolerate disobedience.

"Yes, that was him."

"Interesting that he had nothing to say. Does he let Daddy do all his talking for him?"

She shrugged "Mostly." It was somewhat embarrassing actually. Dalton hadn't even tried to fight for her, even when a shirtless, buff to the hilt stranger threw her over his shoulder and carried her away. She'd only known her rescuer maybe an hour, yet she somehow knew he wouldn't have stood by and watched some strange man take off with her. "He's the son my father never had. If I married Dalton, then he would actually be family."

"You never said what happened to make you decide to be a runaway bride, and I don't really care, but did you want to marry Dalton before he did or said something to change your mind?"

"I thought I did. It would have made my father happy."

Noah grunted at hearing her answer. "Seems like Daddy should be more concerned with his daughter's happiness than his own."

The way he said *Daddy* sounded derogatory, and her first reaction was to defend her father, but the words wouldn't come. Tears stung her eyes. Had she convinced herself that she loved Dalton because it would make her father happy? From the time her father had made it known that a match between her and Dalton would please him, she'd gone along with the idea. Dalton had been attentive and charming, and they shared an interest in the brewery. So what if he didn't make her heart go pitter-patter? They respected each other—or so she'd thought—and that was important in a marriage.

Noah was right. A father should care about his daughter's happiness. Sure, he had let her come to work for him, had let her institute her events, had allowed her to brew beer alongside Eddie, and had even let her name some of the beers. Yet, he'd never given her a word of praise when she'd brought in more customers or for any of her accomplishments. Dalton, though, could do no wrong, even though he'd never shown any interest in learning the art of brewing beer, of loving Elk Antler the way she did.

That had been okay. She'd been learning the business, and one day, she'd have the coveted share of the brewery he'd promised her. Her father had encouraged the match with Dalton, and now she was realizing that she'd fallen in with the plan because it was what her father wanted.

All her life, she'd tried to please her father. A little girl he'd never wanted had been dumped on him. She could only be thankful he'd kept her, but the fear always lurked that one day he'd get tired of her like her mother had.

Blessed God above, she'd been a fool her entire life, hadn't she? She would never have the unconditional love of the man she called a father. Her eyes were finally open, and it was about time. Almost more—and maybe not even almost—she mourned the loss of Elk Antler over knowing she'd ruined her relationship with her father.

"Where am I taking you?" Noah asked.

"Um…" She couldn't go home, not yet. Not until she was strong enough to stand up to both her father and Dalton. She was getting there, but she wasn't there yet.

She could go to a friend's house if she had one of

those in Asheville. Her two best friends had been her college roommates, and both lived in other parts of the country. Because of the hours she'd put in at the brewery, she basically didn't have a life outside of Elk Antler. Her friends here were more like acquaintances, and she couldn't think of a single one who would welcome her and the problems she'd bring with her.

That was another thing she'd correct now that her eyes were open. Along with finding a new job, she'd make real friends here. Girlfriends who cared about her. She especially wanted some of those.

"You don't have a place to go, do you?"

"No," she whispered. "The first place they'll look for me is home."

The last thing Noah needed right now was a tempting woman with problems and no place to go. "You do know that you are an adult and can make your own decisions, right?"

"You don't understand." She turned her face to the window, and he was afraid she was going to cry. "I can go to a hotel."

He managed not to sigh. No, he didn't understand, but he couldn't just dump her off at a hotel, especially barefoot and only his T-shirt covering her corset. He'd been keeping an eye on the rearview mirror, and the black Mercedes that he'd noted in the parking lot that had to have belonged to her father was several cars behind them. Following that car was the silver one she'd driven to the falls.

The speed limit on the Parkway was turtle slow, but he'd been pushing it a little. Unfamiliar with the road, he wasn't sure how well it was policed, and he didn't want to get stopped.

"Is the silver Mercedes yours?"

"No, it's Dalton's. I borrowed it."

"Borrowed, huh?" He still didn't get the boyfriend. The man hadn't said a word to her, and although curious what the deal was, he was already more involved than he had any wish to be.

"I wasn't going to keep it, so yeah, borrowed. How do you think they found me?"

"Does he have OnStar or some kind of app that can locate his car?"

"Fudge. I never thought of that. Yeah, he does."

She went silent again, and he glanced over at her. "You're going to chew your finger off."

"Nervous habit." She dropped her hand to her lap. "I'm sorry, Noah. I'm sure the last thing you wanted to do was to have to rescue a crazy runaway bride."

True that. "Never said you were crazy." Might have thought it a time or two since coming across her.

The exit from the Parkway came up, and as soon as he was on the public road, he picked up speed. He wanted to quickly lose the two Mercedes without ending up in a chase. At the first intersection he came to, he turned right, then left at the next one. He wasn't familiar with the area, wasn't sure how to find his apartment from where they were, but he'd worry about that once he was sure he'd lost her father and boyfriend.

After making several more turns and not seeing either car behind them, he pulled into the parking lot of a grocery store. He stopped in a space where he could see the road.

"Why are we stopping? Do you need groceries?"

"No. Need to put my address in the GPS. Watch the road and tell me if you see your father or boyfriend pass by."

"He's not my boyfriend. Not any longer. Why do you have to put your address in the GPS. Don't you know where you live?"

"Not exactly."

Her finger went back in her mouth. He was sure she had questions about that, but he chose not to enlighten her. The less she knew about him, the better. He'd already shared more than he wanted back at the waterfall.

"Oh, God," she muttered. "You're a runaway bride serial killer traveling the country in search of prey."

"Busted." Damn this girl for making him laugh. He didn't deserve to laugh, and he especially didn't deserve to have a beautiful, sexy woman sharing his space.

"You are kidding right? I mean, I was just joking around."

At least she'd stopped trying to gnaw off her finger. "Yes, Peyton, I'm kidding."

"I knew that. Would you please tell me where we're going?"

He could tell she was starting to get worried, and he had no desire to add to her stress. "My place."

"Not sure that's a good idea."

According to the GPS, they were about ten minutes away from his temporary apartment. "Listen, you said you can't go home, and you can't go to a hotel. Not dressed like you are. I promise you're in no danger from me, and we're just going to go to my place long enough to make a plan. Okay?"

Hopefully, he could convince her to go home.

Chapter Four

"You don't have much stuff," Peyton said as she stood in the middle of Noah's living room, her gaze taking in the bare walls. There were no knickknacks on the coffee and end tables, not a thing that gave her a clue about the man who'd rescued her.

"Just moved in."

Where were the boxes filled with his stuff? The apartment was small, the living room and a tiny kitchen in view, and then a hallway that she assumed led to a bedroom and bathroom.

A dog barreled into the room, heading straight for Noah. At least, she thought it was a dog, but that was questionable. Ignoring it, Noah took a few steps, which put him in the kitchen. He set the champagne bottles on the counter.

"Want some water?"

"Do you have any green tea?" She could really use a cup of calming hot tea.

He looked at her as if she'd asked for a serving of bird brains. "Do I strike you as someone who drinks green tea?"

"No, you strike me as someone who drinks the blood of wombats." When he snorted, she put her hands on her hips. "How am I supposed to know what you drink? You could just say, 'No, Peyton, I don't have any green tea.'"

"No, Peyton, I don't have any green tea. That better?"

"Much." It was obvious he didn't want her here. It wasn't like she'd asked him to take her home with him, but she was sorry she'd involved him in her mess all the same.

He leaned back against the counter. "Yes or no on the water?"

Finally, she was getting a good look at his chest and abs, the question of whether they were a six- or an eight-pack answered. Lordy! Eight it was. Even with those abs—the likes of which she'd never before had the pleasure of viewing—he wasn't overbuilt. Yes, he had muscles, but they fit his body perfectly. Yummy was the word that came to mind, and she had a strong urge to lick her lips.

"Peyton?"

"Hmm?"

"Eyes up here."

She jerked her gaze up to see him pointing at his face, and heat traveled up her neck and into her cheeks. "Sorry, what?"

"Two things. Do you want a glass of water? And secondly, don't look at me like that. It puts ideas in my head."

She so wanted to know what those ideas were. For a girl who'd never had a man have *ideas* when he looked at her, she suddenly felt cheated. Good gosh, she was twenty-six years old. At some point, shouldn't at least one man have had ideas about her?

It wasn't fair. She'd had a boyfriend in college, but he'd been a gamer, more interested in his games than her, and sex with him had been about as exciting as shelling beans. Okay, she was being her silly self, but it was almost true. At least Dalton had been an improvement, but he had never blown her mind. She wanted her mind blown. She wanted a man to have ideas about her.

Now, Noah? She'd bet her favorite beer recipe that he could curl her toes, and she really, really wanted her toes curled. *Seriously, Peyton?* She slapped her forehead. What kind of woman fantasized about another man on her wedding day? Okay, a wedding that didn't happen, wasn't going to, but still…

"I can't decide if I want to know what all is going through your head or not."

She focused back on Noah. His arms were crossed over his very, very fine chest. "You really don't. Why do you have a hummingbird tattoo?" It was on his chest, right over his heart. It didn't seem like a guy kind of tattoo, but if there was ever a man who could wear a silvery blue hummingbird on his skin and still be manly, it was this one.

"Just do."

Okay, hummingbird tattoos were off limits, which only made her all the more curious what the story was. It wasn't easy, but she forced herself to keep her gaze on his face. She'd been so busy admiring his abs that she hadn't noticed how pretty his eyes were. They made her think of the copper color of a rich amber beer.

The dog sitting at his feet whined. "Go away, dog," he said.

She frowned. "That's not a nice way to treat your dog. What's his name? Or is it a her?"

"Not my dog." He glanced down at it. "It's a boy. What would you name it?"

Wow! The man rescued runaway brides and stray dogs? "I don't know. Lucky because he's lucky you rescued him?"

"Didn't have anything to do with that."

She waited for him to explain, but when he didn't, and the dog whined again, she said, "Maybe he needs to go out."

"Guess I better do that before he pees on the floor." He picked up a leash from the counter, clipped it on the dog's collar, and then walked out the door.

Okay then. While he was gone, she went in search of the bathroom. The first door she came to was a bedroom, and she peeked inside. A duffel bag was on the unmade bed, and…nothing else of a personal nature. Did he even live here?

The man was a mystery, and that made her uncomfortable. But even though she didn't know why, she sort of trusted him anyway. He'd helped her when he didn't have to. He hadn't done anything to make her apprehensive of him, but it would be best to get her act together so she could go back home.

Who was he? He could be anyone…a drug dealer, a man hiding for some nefarious reason, an undercover cop, or maybe he was in the witness protection program. She shook her head. Her imagination was running away with her.

She found the bathroom and shrieked when she glanced in the mirror. "Good gravy, Peyton. You look like…" She wasn't even sure what. Black stripes of mascara ran down her cheeks from when she'd cried. Her eyes were bloodshot, the skin around them puffy, and for goodness' sake, she still had on her veil. How had she not realized that?

After removing the veil and washing her face, she borrowed the comb on the counter and worked the tangles out of her hair. What she really wanted was a nice, hot shower, and as tempted as she was to use Noah's, she thought that was taking his hospitality too far.

By the time she returned to the living room, Noah was back inside. His gaze swept over her. "Feeling better?"

"Some. Why didn't you tell me I had mascara running down my face?"

"Didn't notice."

She rolled her eyes. "Yeah, right." He sat on the sofa, and she perched on the opposite end. "Thank you again for helping me get away. I'm sure it wasn't how you planned to spend your day."

"Can't deny that, and you're welcome."

"You'd probably like to send me on my way, so—"

"Thought you said you couldn't go home right now."

"I guess I was overreacting." She wasn't, and as soon as he dropped her off, she'd put on some clothes and then check herself into a hotel. But she couldn't do that until she got her purse, which was at home with the luggage she'd packed for her honeymoon.

"Are you sure about that, Peyton?"

Noah asked himself what he was about. She'd offered him exactly what he wanted…take her home and forget he ever walked down to that waterfall and found himself a runaway bride.

After a moment's hesitation, she said, "Sure, why wouldn't I be?"

"Tell you what. Why don't you stay here tonight?" Did he really just say that? "Take the time to figure out whatever you need to before having to face your father and DG." His mouth was carrying on as if his brain had no opinion in this.

"Who's DG?"

"Dumb Groom." At least that got a grin from her. She'd been silly at the waterfall, and he kind of missed that side of her.

She frowned as she glanced around. "Stay here?" Her gaze landed back on him. "Are you sure you're not a murderer?" Her eyes widened as if she hadn't meant to say that.

He snorted. "I wondered the same thing about you."

"Why would you think I was?"

"Thought maybe the unfortunate bastard was floating in the pool under your wedding dress."

"You really thought that?"

"Seemed a possibility, considering."

"That's hilarious. It's amazing you didn't skedaddle."

He should have. "Believe me, doing that had its appeal."

She grinned, then a giggle slipped out, and then she fell back on the sofa and laughed with abandon. Although he didn't know what was so funny, he liked the way she laughed…all out and lusty. It was actually impressive that she could find things that amusing on the day she was supposed to get married and instead ended up almost naked at a waterfall, two bottles of champagne in tow.

"Are you sure you don't want to repair things with your fiancé?" He wasn't sure she'd thought all that had happened through, didn't want her to wake up in the morning and regret she hadn't tried. He still didn't know exactly why she'd run from her wedding, wished he wasn't curious to know the reason. Maybe she'd caught her dumb groom kissing the bridesmaid. That would explain her running.

She waved a hand in the air. "Pfft. DG is so far in my rearview window that I can't even see his headlights anymore." Tears popped up in her eyes. "And so is life as I knew it."

The woman was giving him whiplash. She went from giggly to teary in zero to sixty. He supposed it was to be expected considering the emotional ups and downs she'd had today. Or this was her normal. He also wished he wasn't curious about that, too. What was she like when not playing the role of a runaway bride?

"Want to talk about it?" *Brain to mouth...shut the fuck up.*

"This is the kind of thing you're supposed to talk to death with your bestie, but I don't have one of those."

"If you did, what would she say?" He'd never talked anything to death and wouldn't know where to start.

"That DG had only been using me to get what he wanted. Seems my father promised him my shares of the business if he married me. The shares that were supposed to be mine. I heard him telling his best man that a few minutes before I was supposed to walk down the aisle, so I left." Anger glinted in her eyes. "My father will never forgive me for the stunt I pulled today, so I lost that anyway. Maybe I should have married DG. At least I'd still have a job."

"Would that job be worth marrying a man who was using you?"

"No. Maybe. I don't know. Elk Antler is...was basically my life, so now I have nothing."

"You said at the waterfall that you knew how to brew good beer, and I wondered about that." A sexy woman who put her all in it when she laughed and who brewed good beer? What wasn't to love there? Her DG was a fool.

"Didn't believe me, did you?"

"I figured you meant you brewed beer in your kitchen with one of those do-it-yourself kits."

She made a huffing noise. "Little do you know. I'm a master brewer."

A sexy female master beer brewer? Now there was every man's fantasy. "From what I understand, this area is known for its microbreweries. Seems like it would be easy to find another job."

"Probably. It's just that Elk Antler Brewery is family. I've worked doggone hard to earn my place there, to one day have it passed on to me. It's not fair."

"Sometimes life isn't fair. My team has a saying that might apply. Suck it up, SEAL, and move on."

Her eyes widened. "You're a SEAL?"

Damn his mouth to hell. He was going to glue it shut.

Chapter Five

"Really? An honest-to-God SEAL?" Peyton said. *Wow!* That did explain his most excellent eight-pack. His eyes shuttered, and she had the impression he hadn't meant to let that fascinating tidbit slip. "Am I not supposed to know that? Is it one of those, if I tell you, I'll have to kill you things? I swear on my favorite beer recipe, I won't tell a soul."

"Yeah, now I have to kill you."

"You're kidding now, right? Right, Noah?" Of course he was. SEALs didn't just go around murdering runaway brides. Not that she'd ever heard, anyway. Come to think of it, they were a secretive bunch. Other than being aware they existed, what else did she know about them? Absolutely nothing.

He chuckled. "Of course I'm kidding." A sly smile appeared on his face. "Probably."

"If you kill me, you'll never get to sample the best beer in the world."

"That'll do it. You and your beer are now under my protection."

And who better to have as a protector than a SEAL? He was probably going to regret saying that, because now an idea was brewing. Ha! She was a brewer of beer and ideas. The silly thought made her giggle.

"Now what's funny?"

"This whole day," she said, not ready to hit him up with her plan before having it all worked out. The first step would be accepting his offer. "I've been thinking, if you meant it, I would like to stay tonight—" she patted the seat cushion "—right here on this comfy sofa."

"You can have my bed."

"No way, and that's not up for discussion. I'm smaller than you, and I'll be perfectly comfortable." Besides, it would be weird to sleep in his bed. "Do you actually live here?" From all appearances, he was only passing through.

"For the time being."

"Well, that explains everything," she muttered.

He glanced at the dog, then stood. "I need to find a grocery store and get the dog—"

"Lucky."

"Get some dog food and something for dinner. I assume you don't want to go out to eat?"

She eyed her filthy feet. "Too dirty and not really dressed for going out." She held her feet up. "Plus, I don't have any shoes, and I'm quite certain you won't have any that fit me."

"Not likely. Why don't you take a shower while I'm gone? I'll give you a clean T-shirt to put on."

"Thank you, that would be really nice." She was past ready to get the stupid corset off.

"What would you like for dinner?"

"I'm not picky. Anything you feel like having. Something easy like sandwiches, maybe?"

"Copy that," he said, then disappeared down the hallway. A few minutes later, he returned. "I put some stuff on the bathroom counter for you to wear. I'll pick you up a toothbrush. Anything else you need?"

A whole list of things—including some clean underwear—but she didn't think he'd be appreciative of that request. She narrowed it down to the two most important. "A brush and deodorant. Any feminine brand is fine."

He nodded, then headed for the door.

"Noah."

"Yeah?" He glanced over his shoulder.

"Thank you. For everything."

He dipped his chin, then as he left, she could have sworn he muttered something about remembering the glue.

"Well, Lucky, it's just you and me now. What's your story?" The dog gave her a pitiful look, then went to the door Noah had walked out of and stared at it as if willing the man to return. "He does kind of grow on you, doesn't he?"

Since Lucky refused to tell her Noah's secrets, she headed for the bathroom. Noah's duffel bag was still open on the bed. She was sorely tempted to peek at the contents, see if there were clues to the man. "You will not snoop," she admonished herself.

In the bathroom, she found the T-shirt he'd said he'd left her, along with a pair of sweatpants. The man was a mystery, all right. She'd been wallowing in her own misery and buzzing on champagne, and she hadn't paid all that much attention when he'd revealed some things about him that she'd wager he hadn't meant to.

As she showered, she tried to remember their conversation, and she sucked in a breath as his words came back to her. He'd said his father had killed his mother, right? He must have. That wasn't something she could make up off the top of her head.

How old had he been? Surely, his father had gone to prison for that. What had happened to Noah? She wanted to know everything about him, but she sensed that it would be easier to pull his teeth out than to get him to share his life story.

She dried off, glared at the corset that she'd hoped would make Dalton—no, make Dumb Groom look at her as if she was the most desirable woman he'd ever seen. That had been a foolish longing. She knew that now.

"There. That's where you belong, you piece of cow dung." She dropped the hated corset in the wastebasket, along with her dreams.

If she let herself think about the one thing she'd lost that did matter, she'd crumple to the floor, so she took Noah's advice and sucked it up. Maybe she'd find a job with a competitive brewery. Wouldn't that get her father's goat?

She pulled Noah's sweatpants up to her waist. When she let go, they fell down. Maybe he had a belt in his duffel bag. He would understand her rifling through his stuff to find something that would keep her from flashing her bottom, wouldn't he?

She found a belt, and she also found a small framed photo of a pretty woman and a boy she guessed was around seven or eight. She recognized the boy right away. *Oh, Noah. What a cutie you were.*

"Can I help you find something?"

Startled, she dropped the photo, then faced Noah. He stood in the middle of the doorway, his hands stuffed inside his jeans pockets. A storm brewed in his eyes as his gaze shifted from her to the photo that had landed on the bed instead of in his duffel bag and then his gaze settled back on her.

"Um…" She grabbed the waist of the sweatpants that had already drooped halfway down her bottom and pulled them back up. "I wasn't snooping. I swear." Okay, maybe a little. She glanced down. "They won't stay up, so I thought maybe you had a belt I could borrow."

And how old were you when you lost your mother? What happened to you after that? Oh, and one last question. I could use a hero. Will you accept the job?

Without a word, he strode to the bed, snatched his bag and the photo away from her prying eyes. He reached into the duffel bag, pulled out a belt, handed it to her, tossed his bag into the closet, and then shut the door. The photo he kept clutched in his hand.

Message received. Don't snoop. What she would never tell him was that her heart was breaking for the boy who'd lost his mother in the most horrible way. She had only known him for one day, but what she did know was that he'd hate her pity.

He left, again without a word, and when he returned, she was still frozen in place, wishing with all her heart that she hadn't abused his trust. Because she had. Her excuse of looking for a belt was merely to give her permission to snoop through his belongings.

"I'm sorry," she whispered.

Not replying, he tossed a plastic bag on the bed, then left again, Lucky trailing in his wake. Even the dog had given her a look of disappointment. She wished she could hide, but that would just make her a coward, so she pulled up the sweatpants, and as she put on the belt, she realized that they had a drawstring, and she didn't need a belt. That only made her feel worse.

She picked up the plastic bag, and when she saw the contents, tears burned her eyes. Not only had he bought her a brush and deodorant, but also body lotion, socks, and a pair of flip-flops.

"Oh, Noah," she murmured as she stared at his gifts.

Noah put the photo—the only one he had of his mother—in a kitchen drawer, making a mental note not to forget it was there. Like the dice always in his pocket that reminded him not to be his father, the picture of his mother was always with him, a reminder that there had been a time when someone loved him.

His father had been a man with a temper he couldn't control, a man who'd killed his wife after he'd gambled away the grocery money and there was nothing in the house to feed their son. It had been the last straw for her, and his father had gone into a rage when she'd told him she was leaving and taking Noah with her.

He'd been nine years old when he lost his mother, the only person in the world who'd loved him. When the cops had arrested his father, they'd searched him, and finding his so-called "lucky dice," they'd dropped them on the floor.

Noah had snatched them up when they weren't looking. Not that he'd wanted anything from the man he hated with a bone-deep fury.

After his mother's death and his father's arrest, he'd gone to live with his mother's sister. Although his Aunt Melody and her husband had been both kind and generous in taking him in, they already had five children.

He'd been a heartbroken boy lost in the middle of a crowd.

Money had been tight, his aunt and uncle's attention stretched thin with so many children in the house, and there had been a three-year difference between him and the two children closest to his age. The kids tolerated him, but that was the extent of it.

Because there wasn't an extra bedroom, a cot had been put in corner of the four-year-old's bedroom for Noah to sleep on. He'd kept his mother's photo under his pillow, and the only way he could fall asleep at night was with his fingers wrapped around the frame.

To find Peyton, a woman he barely knew, holding the one thing he owned that mattered to him, had hit him wrong. Even so, he'd overreacted, and he owed her an apology. She couldn't have known that no one but him had touched his mother's photo since the day she'd died. Why that mattered, he wasn't sure, but it did.

"I'm sorry, Noah."

He turned, then leaned back against the counter. "Apology accepted, but I owe you one, too. I overreacted, and I'm sorry for that."

"The woman in the picture. She was your mother?"

"Yes."

"She was very pretty."

No, she was beautiful, and not just in looks. She was kind and generous. She had a smile for everyone she met. Everyone had loved her. He remembered that.

"Will you tell me about her?"

"No." He couldn't talk about her to other people. Had never been able to. The one time he had tried to, when his aunt and uncle's pastor had attempted to get through to the boy who rarely talked, he'd cried so hard that he'd vomited on the man's shoes.

That had been the last time. For one thing, she was his and he didn't want to share her. He was also sure if he did, there would be a repeat performance. It was one thing for a boy to barf on someone, but a man? Not gonna happen.

"I don't remember much about my mother." She stared at her foot as she made a circle with her toes. "I'm not sure if that's a good thing or not. Mostly, I remember that when she'd have a man come see her, she'd give me a coloring book and crayons and tell me to stay in my room and be quiet." She shrugged. "I loved coloring, so I was okay with that. She yelled at me a lot, but I don't remember why."

At least he'd had a mother who'd loved him unconditionally. It didn't sound like the princess had a mother or father who gave her that. He didn't want his heart softening for her, but the damn organ did it anyway. That wasn't good. He already thought she was gorgeous and sexy as all get-out. Add a soft heart to the mix, and he'd be in trouble with this one.

Trouble was his middle name these days, and the last thing he needed was a woman in his life. Nor did she need a man with his baggage considering what all she was dealing with. Tomorrow he'd take her home, think about her for a few days, then he'd forget about her.

Whoever that was laughing in his head could fuck off.

"So…" she said when he didn't respond to what she'd said. "We're good now?"

"We're good. The grocery store had rotisserie chickens. I got one of those and some stuff from the deli. That sound all right?"

"Yes, that sounds perfect."

She was wearing the socks he'd bought her, and for some idiotic reason, that pleased him. He also liked her in his clothes. She shouldn't look sexy in sweatpants that she'd had to roll up the bottoms and in a T-shirt that almost swallowed her, but she did. Definitely trouble.

Tearing his gaze away, he found a knife to carve the chicken. Not having any idea what she liked other than her saying she wasn't picky, he'd bought mac and cheese, two kinds of pasta salads, and cans of corn and green beans. Then he'd gone a little crazy and decided she might like some ice cream later. And again, not knowing her preference, there were now three pints of assorted flavors in the freezer.

"Beer, wine, water, or green tea with your dinner?" Yep, he'd bought green tea for the first time in his life. He really needed to get her home and out of his life. If not, who knew what he'd be buying next?

"You got me green tea?"

"Uh-huh." By the smile on her face, you'd think he'd bought her a diamond necklace.

"Thank you. I'll have a cup later. What kind of beer?"

He was probably going to earn points he really didn't want for this, too. He opened the refrigerator, grabbed a bottle, and held it up. "This good?" Another smile that almost made him wish he'd bought anything but the Elk Antler Brewery beer. He was starting to like seeing her smiles too much.

"That's one of mine. I mean, I created it." Her smile faded. "I guess it's the last one I'll ever brew for Elk Antler."

Ah, hell. Now there were tears in her eyes. It was stupid not to realize the beer would remind her of what she'd lost. He put the bottle back in the refrigerator. "We'll have the wine. Unless you'd rather have water."

"Screw it. I want the beer."

"Atta girl." There was a glint of defiance in her eyes that he liked seeing, and a definite improvement over the tears.

Lucky finished the bowl of dog food Noah had put down, then ambled over to sit at his feet. Why the dog seemed to be gravitating to him, he didn't know, since he was doing his best to ignore it. Ignoring the woman wearing his T-shirt and sweatpants wasn't working so well, either.

Chapter Six

Peyton's home was a loft in downtown Asheville, one of the most diverse towns in the country. She loved living smackdab in the middle of the city. Restaurants were at her fingertips, and Elk Antler's original brewery was a five-minute walk. If they didn't have three other locations in the area, she wouldn't even have needed a car.

"So, this is it, my home." She glanced at Noah. It shouldn't matter what he thought, but for reasons she couldn't explain, it did. She was proud of her loft and the renovations she'd made to it. The building had once been a department store and had sat empty for years after the store had gone out of business. Now, the first floor was a merchant mall, with all kinds of small shops.

The space above the mall had been turned into lofts. She was on the third floor, and the view of downtown and the mountains beyond from her floor-to-ceiling windows was awesome, especially at night with all the lights.

"Nice. You moving out?"

Her gaze followed his to the boxes stacked alongside the wall. "I was. Now I'm not."

Dalton owned a lovely house in a gated community, and it had been understood that she would move in with him. It was just another thing she'd gone along with to make him and her father happy even though she hadn't been thrilled at the thought of living in a gated community where the houses were spread apart and no one knew their neighbor's name. She would miss the back deck and yard and the hummingbirds, though. It had been such a peaceful place to relax with a beer after work. Would he remember to change the hummingbirds' sugar water?

She loved living downtown. Loved the energy vibes, the restaurants, the shops, and the eclectic mix of people. She hadn't questioned her refusal to put her loft up for sale, but now she wondered if she'd subconsciously had her doubts about the marriage all along. When Dalton had insisted she list it, she'd stubbornly refused to do so until after they were married. At least she'd done something right.

"Well, I'll get out of your hair," Noah said.

"Um…would you like a beer or something?" She didn't want him to go, didn't want to be left alone to contemplate her mistakes and what she'd lost. And then there were her father and Dalton. She didn't doubt one or both would be banging on her door at some point, probably sometime today. There was also her plan that she wanted to talk to him about.

"It's nine in the morning, Peyton."

"Yeah, well, it's a start your morning with a beer kind of day, but if you're not an adventurous sort, I'll make you some coffee."

"Thanks, but there's somewhere I need to be."

"Oh, okay. Well…thanks for everything. I'm not sure what would have happened if you hadn't been there when my father and Dalton showed up."

He smiled. "You're welcome. Just be strong and re-member that you don't have to do anything you don't want to."

Easy for him to say. Also, that smile! Gracious, but it made her stomach feel like butterflies were hatching by the thousands. Before she begged him not to leave, she walked to the door and opened it.

He was a few steps from walking out when he stopped. "Where's your phone?"

"There in my purse." She pointed to the suitcase near the door with her purse on top. The suitcase was packed for a honeymoon trip to Napa Valley to tour wineries, what Dalton had wanted to do. She'd wanted to go to Germany and taste beers.

"Get it." When she retrieved it from her purse, he said, "Unlock it." Once that was done, he took it from her.

The way he was barking out orders, she almost sa-luted him, but then she got distracted when she real-ized he wasn't paying attention to her as he punched the keys on her phone. It was the perfect opportunity to do a little unnoticed drooling.

The man wore a plain white T-shirt and well-worn jeans like a boss. What she wouldn't give to explore all those muscles, to trail her fingers down his chest and explore those abs, the likes of which she'd never seen before and couldn't stop thinking about.

"My number's in your phone." He handed it back to her. "Don't call me, though, unless you're desperate."

Okay, then. "Exactly what falls under desperate? Just so I don't call you when I shouldn't. Not that I'm going to call you at all. But you never know what I might con-sider desperate that you don't. So, give me a list of—"

Oh God, he was kissing her!

"You kissed me," she said, stating the obvious when he stepped back, but that kiss, his setting all her nerve endings on fire, had her wanting more, more, more. He'd just updated her life goals, moving "get a whole lot of kisses from this man" to the top spot.

"It seemed the easiest way to make you stop talking. But I shouldn't have done that."

"You can kiss me again if you want." Like a hot kiss with tongue would work. That she had a thought like that with a man she'd just met…well, she hardly knew herself. But this was the new her, the woman who was going to go after what she wanted. And she wanted to feel tingly. Noah was just the man to make that happen.

"No more kisses." He backed toward the door. "Take care of yourself, Peyton."

"You're no fun." If she hadn't been looking at his mouth, she would have missed the slight twitch of an almost smile.

"Yep, that's me."

"Oh, wait," she called to him as he headed for the elevator. "I need to give back your clothes."

"Keep them."

And with that, he was gone. She sighed. Such a shame she'd never get to experience another Noah kiss. Even though it had only been lips to lips, she'd definitely tingled. That was a good sign, though. At least she now knew that she could tingle. It just had to be with the right man, and that definitely wasn't Dalton.

She closed then locked the door, which reminded her. Dalton had keys to her loft, and she needed to get the locks changed. The sooner the better. She didn't trust her father or Dalton not to pull a stupid stunt. Her plan had been to ask Noah to move into her guest bedroom for a week or so, until she was sure that her father and Dalton accepted that there wasn't going to be a wedding.

That was one reason she'd wanted to show him her loft, so he could see that it would beat living in that tiny apartment of his. She'd gotten up early and made him breakfast, hoping to sweeten him up, but he'd been a grumpy bear, and she'd known she'd get a hard no.

If the man slept, he might not start his mornings mad at the world. She'd woken up several times and could hear him moving around the apartment. When she'd come out to make him breakfast, he was standing at the living room window, staring out. Her good morning greeting had been met with silence.

The man had demons, and, more curious than she should be, she wanted to know what they were. She'd resisted the urge to wrap her arms around him and soothe his troubled soul, but oh, she'd wanted to.

When he'd refused a beer or coffee, she'd realized he would also refuse to temporarily move into her guest room, so it was on to plan B…whatever that was. If nothing else came from meeting Noah, she'd gotten a kiss, a taste of what was possible. Surely there was another man out there besides him who could make her tingly. She just had to find him.

Why the hell had he kissed her? It was a stupid move. Now he wanted more. But whatever. In a few days, he'd forget about her.

You sure about that, Alba?

He ignored the voice in his head.

As he pulled up to his apartment to pick up the dog, he realized he was singing Keith Urban's "Kiss a Girl."

That he was singing was a surprise, and not a good one. He'd stopped singing after getting the team's dog and Asim, their translator—a young man they all liked—killed. Although he'd never had aspirations to pursue a career in music, he had a good voice and loved to sing. But he didn't deserve to do something he enjoyed.

His guitar was packed away in its case for good. He'd intended to leave it back in his Virginia Beach apartment, but at the last minute, he'd grabbed it, along with his duffel bag. As soon as he walked into the temporary apartment, he put it in a corner of the closet where he couldn't see it.

The last time he'd had it out was the day he was giving Asim a lesson. Even after a dozen or so sessions, Asim's fingers were still clumsy on the instrument, but Noah had never seen anyone more determined to learn to play.

The next day, Asim and Snoop, the team's dog, were blown to bits by a bomb because of him. Because he hadn't done his job.

Noah buried his face in his hands, willing the movie constantly playing in his head to go away, but it was there. Every fucking minute of the day and night. Sleep was a thing to be dreaded. The nightmares were too real. He was drowning in guilt and sorrow, and there was no life ring to save him.

Operating on reliable intel, their mission had been to locate a bomb maker hiding out in a village. The hut where the target was supposed to be was empty, so the team spread out to search the other buildings. Noah entered a dusty room to clear it, only finding an old man too frail to get out of bed.

"I'm sorry, but I have to do this," he said, even

though he knew the elder didn't understand him. The man looked back at him with humiliation and hate in his eyes. "I'm sorry," he said again as he pulled the cover down so he could search the elder for weapons or a bomb.

After completing his search of the man and the room, he called for Asim to interrogate the man. "See if you can get him to tell you if our target is actually still in the village and where he could be hiding," he told Asim. "I'm going to see if anyone else has found anything."

He went outside, his gaze scanning the area for his teammates. Snoop—his nose to the ground—was heading toward the mud house he'd just left. Snoop disappeared inside. Noah frowned, his stomach twisting. Had he missed something? When Snoop didn't come right back out, Noah ran toward the hut. Before he reached the door, an explosion knocked him to the ground. He rolled over, and when he looked back at the house, all he saw was devastation.

"Sweet Jesus," he gasped. He pounded the ground with his fist. "Fuck. Fuck. Fuck." This was his fault. How the hell had he missed a bomb?

Dallas Manning, his teammate and best friend, ran up to him. "You okay, Double D? The hell happened?"

"My fault." He leaned over and retched as those two words raced through his mind over and over. *My fault. My fault. My fault.*

After clearing the debris, the team found a third body that turned out to be the bomb maker. They also found a hole under the old man's bed where the bomb maker had been hiding.

"How the fuck you miss that, Alba?" his commander said at the briefing. "Did you even look under the bed?"

"Yes, sir." He had looked and had swept his hand across the floor as far as he could reach. What he hadn't done was call one of his teammates in to help him move the bed so a thorough search could be made. The majority of beds in these poor villages were pallets on the floor, and that the elder was on a heavy wooden bed should have raised his suspicions. Instead, he hadn't wanted to disturb an elderly sick man more than he had to. Now that man was dead, along with Asim and Snoop. The bomb maker he couldn't care less about, but the others would be on his conscience until the day he died.

"Why didn't he blow me up?" Noah asked.

"We'll never know, but my guess is that he hoped he wouldn't be discovered," his commander said. "Then when Snoop came in and alerted to the bomb, the motherfucker set it off."

My fault. My fault. My fault.

Back at their base camp, Noah had closed the case holding his guitar and hadn't played it since. His last memory of the guitar was laughing as Asim butchered "You Are My Sunshine." The instrument was a reminder of his failure, and he couldn't bear to take it out of the case and touch it again. He hadn't been able to leave it behind, though, and he figured a head doc would have a field day with that.

The ringtone from his phone penetrated the soul-stealing memories drowning him. He blinked several times, the fierce heat and choking sands of the desert fading away. Sweat poured down his face, and his breaths were ragged. How long had he been parked in front of the apartment, the car engine running while he relived the second worst day of his life?

He picked his phone up from the cup holder, seeing

Jack's name on the screen. He didn't want to talk to Jack or anyone else right now, but if he didn't answer, Jack would come looking for him.

"Yeah?"

"Where are you?"

"At the apartment." He glanced at his watch. Damn, he was supposed to have been at Operation K-9 Brothers half an hour ago.

"What's wrong?"

"Nothing, man. Just getting a late start. Sorry."

"Don't bullshit me, Noah. I can hear in your voice it's not nothing."

He sighed. It was hell having a brother—because that was what the team was to each other—who knew when to call bull.

"Fine. I had a flashback. But I'm okay. See you shortly." He disconnected before Jack could answer, because Jack would say, "You're not okay." Then he'd tell Noah to take the day off. The last thing he needed was to sit around his box of an apartment and stare at the walls as they closed in on him.

He went inside, showered, dressed, collected Lucky, and headed for Operation K-9 Brothers.

"The dog—"

"Lucky."

Jack grinned. "You named him. Good."

"If you say so." He wasn't about to tell Jack that Peyton had been the one to name him. That would mean having to explain how he'd absconded with a runaway bride, a woman he'd never see again. That thought sent a pang of regret through him, but feelings like that were to be ignored.

His friend laughed. "Stop looking like you're sucking on lemons." He glanced at the dog pressed up against Noah's legs. "Lucky is yours to train, and it's obvious he likes you, so you both are off to a good start."

"I don't know about this. I don't even know why I'm here."

"Let's go sit for a minute." Jack headed for a bench under the shade of a tree.

Noah blew out a breath as he followed, Lucky trotting alongside him. Appeared it was time for a lecture on getting his act together. Whatever Jack thought being here and working with dogs would do, it wasn't going to work. Not only was he having nightmares *and* daymares about what happened, but the ones he'd had as a boy who'd watched his father kill his mother were coming back. It had taken him years to put those behind him, and he didn't know if he could do it again.

Refusing to make it easy on Jack, he kept silent after sitting on the opposite end of the bench. He loved Jack as much as he would love a blood brother, but he resented being forced to be here, to be within a mile of dogs, expected to face his demons, which was what this was all about. No one could help him. Not a dog, not Jack, not sharing his feelings.

"Here's the deal," Jack said. "I had nothing to do with your being ordered to be here, but I can help you." His gaze fell to Lucky, who had one paw resting on Noah's knee. "Lucky can help you. At some point, you're going to have to talk about what happened, but I'm not going to force that on you. You'll talk when you're ready."

"Or not at all."

"If you want to live the rest of your life miserable,

then yeah, not at all. But I don't think you do, even if you won't admit that to yourself."

An image of a black-haired, blue-eyed girl shimmered in his mind. Maybe if he could kill off his demons, he could see if something was there. But he deserved to be miserable, so miserable he would stay.

"I made an appointment for you to talk to a therapist."

Noah scowled at his friend. "Not happening."

"Yeah, it is, and that's an order from your commander."

"To hell with this." He tossed the end of Lucky's leash at Jack. "I'm outta here."

So he'd be AWOL. The hell if he cared.

Chapter Seven

After Noah left, Peyton unpacked her suitcases, then she got to work making a life plan. She had enough money in her savings to last seven or eight months, so that gave her breathing room to find a job. It had to be something to do with beer, preferably brewing it. Asheville was known for its microbreweries, so unless her father decided to blackball her with all of his colleagues, that should be doable.

Second on her list was to find a man who made her tingle. Sadly, that didn't sound all that doable. Every time she tried to imagine who that man might be, she saw Noah. That left her with mixed feelings about him. He'd shown her that it was possible for her to tingle, but then he'd walked out the door, taking her newfound tingles with him. If she couldn't find another tingle-making man, she was going to regret ever meeting Noah…what was his last name, anyway?

Other than learning that he rescued runaway brides, was a SEAL, had a dog he hadn't named and wouldn't explain why he lived in a temporary apartment, she knew nothing about him.

That wasn't exactly true. She knew he was a champion of damsels in distress. She also knew he had demons, ones that had him pacing the floor all hours of the night. He would do so much better if he was staying in her guestroom. Her loft had a good two thousand more square feet to roam. And if that wasn't enough, he could walk the streets of downtown. She would never do that in the middle of the night, but any bad person deciding Noah was easy pickings would be in for a surprise, and not a good one.

She also knew that as much as he tried to deny he wanted anything to do with Lucky, that wasn't true, even if he didn't realize it. She'd seen him several times rest his hand on Lucky's head, and she thought he felt some kind of calmness from the touch. It gave her a warm marshmallowly feeling that he let her name his dog.

Gah! Why couldn't she stop thinking about him? It was aggravating. But those abs! How was she supposed to forget what Noah—whatever his last name was— looked like without a shirt? And that kiss? She touched her bottom lip. Would needing another one fall under desperate enough to call him?

"Get your mind back on the important thing," she told herself. Like finding a job. She'd never had to job hunt and wasn't sure how to go about it. Should she just pop in at the various breweries, ask if they needed a beer brewer? Or maybe she should write up a résumé.

If they asked for references, what should she do? Her father sure wasn't going to give her one. Eddie would, but that would make her father furious, so she'd never ask that from him.

Her phone rang, her father's name coming up on the screen. She was going to talk to him at some point, but she wasn't ready yet. Half a minute later, her phone beeped, signaling that she had a message.

She wished she could delete it without listening, but what if he was calling because he realized she wouldn't be happy married to Dalton? "Fat chance of that," she muttered, but she brought up voice mail to hear what he had to say.

"Call me, Peyton. I don't know what's going on with you, but Dalton's heartbroken." She snorted. "Whatever made you do what you did can be fixed."

"Can not!" she yelled at the phone, disconnecting without listening to the rest of his message. Now she was mad. Did her father even care about her, about what made her happy? Had he ever? The answer was no, and she'd never understood why she couldn't please him, but she was over trying. In fact, she was so furious that she had things to say to him right now.

As Peyton walked through the lobby toward her father's office, and as her black heels tapped over the wooden floor, she rubbed her hands down the black pencil skirt, smoothing nonexistent wrinkles. She'd dressed in what she considered her power suit, a skirt, white blouse, and a black jacket.

Do not let him intimidate you into doing what he wants, she admonished herself as she approached her father's office.

Lydia, his assistant, smiled at seeing her. "There you are. He's expecting you."

"I don't know why. I didn't tell him I was coming in."

"He said to expect you."

"Really, he said that?"

At Lydia's nod, her steps faltered. Was she doing exactly what he expected? She almost turned around and walked out, but no. Just no. If she did that, she'd never have the courage to face him again. It was now or never.

She lifted her hand and knocked on her father's office door. She had to be strong, and that was just what she was going to be.

"Enter," he said.

After taking a deep breath, she opened the door. Her father studied her as she walked in. Because she spent a good portion of her days in the brewery, she normally wore jeans and a blouse unless she had a client meeting. Gerald Sutton was an observant man, and she knew he noticed her clothes and understood the reason for her power suit.

"If you're calling Dalton to come in here, I'll leave," she said when he picked up the desk phone receiver. This needed to be a conversation between the two of them, nor did she want him and Dalton to gang up on her.

He dropped the receiver. "Don't you think he's owed an explanation?"

"Yes." She sat in the chair across from his desk. "But you and I need to talk first." It shouldn't hurt that he didn't ask how she was, since he rarely did, but there it was. Would that longing to believe that he cared about her enough to show concern, even if it was only a hint that he loved her, ever go away?

From the time she'd come to live with him, she had told herself that he loved her. Of course he did. She was his daughter. She'd always made excuses for him. He hadn't expected to have a young child dumped on him without notice, and he could have refused to take her in. Because he did, she'd always felt grateful that he'd given her a home, but there was resentment she tried to keep buried that a child shouldn't have to feel grateful to a parent for doing the right thing.

It was a hard pill to swallow, but it was time to accept that she was simply an obligation, that he didn't love her. Maybe he didn't know how. She'd often wondered why he'd never married, but that wasn't the kind of thing he would discuss with her. He was a good-looking man, and she knew he dated, but he never stayed with one woman for very long, never brought anyone home to meet his daughter.

"Explain why you ran out on your wedding, leaving Dalton standing at the alter in front of your guests. Do you know how embarrassing that was for him? For me?"

"I'm sure it was, and I'm sorry." That wasn't true. "You know what, I'm not sorry. I'm not in love with Dalton, but I liked him well enough. Although I think I would have eventually regretted it, I would have gone through with the wedding because it would have pleased you."

"And the reason you didn't?"

"I overheard him telling Ron that you promised him shares in the brewery if he married me. Those were my shares, Dad. You promised me." The hurt that he would do that to her was still as painful as when she'd heard Dalton telling his best man why he was marrying her. How could her father do that to her?

"And the problem is? The shares will stay in the family when you and Dalton marry."

She counted to ten, then to twenty before replying. He'd skipped right over the fact that she wasn't in love with Dalton. Why didn't he want her to be happy? Why did he think it was okay to promise her something, and then betray her?

"The problem is you promised me shares in the brewery, and now you want me to marry a man I don't love and give him my shares." Tears burned her eyes, and she willed them away. She would not cry.

"Why don't you love me?" She hadn't meant to ask that question even though she'd wondered all her life why she didn't have her father's love. The only answer she could think of was that he resented having a child dumped on him.

"Where's all this coming from, Peyton?"

So, he wasn't going to answer, not that she was surprised. She swallowed past the lump in her throat, and needing to leave before she cried, she stood. "I'm done here."

As she walked to the door, she tried not to hope that he would stop her, maybe tell her that he did love her, but all she heard behind her was silence. She told herself not to look back, but she couldn't help it.

When she was twelve, she'd walked into his home office, and he'd been staring at a photo with the saddest eyes she'd ever seen. As soon as he noticed her, he'd put the picture face down on his desk. She'd asked what he was looking at, wanting to know what was making him sad, but he'd refused to answer. Several times after that, she'd searched for the photo, never finding it.

That hurt, whatever caused it, was in his eyes now. She took a step toward him. "Dad?"

He blinked, then shifted his gaze to her. "Just go, Peyton."

So be it. She would go because her heart couldn't take any more of his rejections.

Noah wasn't sure why he ended up back at the waterfall and with the dog in tow. Jack must have let go of the leash, because the damn thing had raced after him, jumping in the car when he'd opened the door.

"I met the prettiest princess, sitting right up there on top of that boulder," he told Lucky. Had that been only yesterday? Seemed like years ago. "She was something else." And now he was talking to a dog. Maybe he should see a therapist.

Lucky pulled against the leash, trying to get to the water. It was probably against the dog training rules to let him do what he pleased, but since for all intents and purposes, Noah was officially AWOL, what did rules matter?

He followed Lucky to the edge of the water, and both of them stared at the wedding gown still floating in the pool. Lucky growled. It did look like a ghost, just floating there, so he didn't blame the dog for being suspicious.

Seeing the gown led his thoughts to Peyton. Was she okay? When he'd put his number in her phone, he purposely hadn't sent it to his phone so he wouldn't be tempted to call her. Because he knew he would be. Now he was sorry. He just wanted to know that she was all right.

Since he knew where she lived, he could stop by, tell her he was checking on her. Although, if Jack had reported him as being AWOL, the navy would soon find him, and he'd go to prison, never knowing if Peyton was safe. He didn't even know if she was worried about being safe.

"We need to go," he told Lucky. He had to stick around and make sure Peyton didn't need to make a desperate phone call. Unless karma had decided not to give him a break, Jack would wait a day or two before reporting him missing. If going back meant he had to learn how to train Lucky for a brother in need—that wasn't at all a bad thing—and if he had to haul his sorry ass to a therapist he'd refuse to talk to, then that's what he'd do.

Why had he used that word, almost guaranteeing she wouldn't admit she was desperate and call him, no matter how much she needed to?

He doubled-timed it up the trail with Lucky at his heels. The first place he had to go was back to Operation K-9 Brothers. He was as certain as he could be that Jack wouldn't report him. At least, not yet, but he had to make sure.

As soon as Noah opened the door, Lucky jumped into the car, parking his butt on the passenger seat. "I guess you're stuck with me, dog. Not sure how lucky that makes you." Noah heard Peyton's voice in his head admonishing him for not using the dog's name and sighed. "I mean Lucky."

With his tail wagging like a flag in a hurricane, the dog tried to cross the console. "No, you can't sit in my lap while I'm driving." Noah pushed him back. "You don't have any respect for personal space, do you?"

Lucky tried to climb on his lap again. "Dumbass dog. Get back in your seat." He lowered the passenger side window halfway, and that did the trick. Lucky stuck his head out the window and kept it there the rest of the way to Operation K-9 Brothers.

He found Jack hosing down a kennel. "Need help?"

"Yeah, you can clean the last three. Put Lucky in this one while you work." He stepped out of the kennel, handing Noah the hose. "I've got some paperwork

I need to get done. When you're finished, we'll put the dogs back in their homes."

Noah glanced around. "Where are they now?"

"In the playpen."

"They have a playpen?"

"Yeah. I give them a little time together to play each day while I clean their kennels."

After Jack left, Noah put Lucky in the just cleaned kennel, then started hosing down the next one. The sooner he got this done, the sooner he could check on Peyton. Or maybe he should stay out of her life. The last thing she needed was a screwed-up man who had nothing to offer. Not that he was looking for a relationship, he was just worried about her. Needed to know she was okay.

Lucky had his nose pressed against the fence, watching Noah's every move. "Nice place, huh?" He didn't know what training therapy dogs involved, but Jack had a topnotch operation going. The individual kennels were large, with the concrete part under a roof for shade, then a grassy area giving the dogs plenty of room to roam around. Each kennel had dog beds on frames, lifting them about a foot off the floor. The food and water bowls were attached to the kennel fencing. He assumed that helped keep ants out of their food.

He'd thought Jack would get on his ass for taking off, but he hadn't said a word. Noah wished he had, getting the lecture he knew was coming over with. What magic his commander thought being here, cleaning kennels, would accomplish was a mystery.

Soon, he would have to return to his team, and just thinking about another deployment woke up the biting ants. What if he made another deadly mistake? That would be the end of him.

Hello, darkness...

"Stop it," he muttered when the words to Simon and Garfunkel's "The Sounds of Silence" streamed through his mind. His team got a kick out of his always coming up with a song that fit any situation, and he'd had fun doing it. Not so much anymore.

At the same time he finished cleaning the kennels, Jack returned. "I'm suspicious of your perfect timing," he said.

Jack chuckled. "You should be. Let's get the dogs back in their homes, then we'll spend some time working with Lucky."

Still nothing about him taking off earlier. Noah eyed his friend. Was he doing that on purpose, waiting for Noah to bring it up? If so, Jack was going to have a long wait.

They got the dogs back in their kennels, then Noah, with Lucky on his leash, followed Jack to a large fenced in area. "How's a therapy dog different from a service dog?"

"Good question. Service dogs are trained to perform tasks that their handler can't do. Pick up things, open doors, things like that. A therapy dog is trained to provide emotional support. They go to places like hospitals and retirement homes, and spend time with people. In our case, though, we're training them for our brothers and sisters, and they'll provide that support for a specific person, especially ones suffering from PTSD."

"Okay, but what if a person needs a dog that can do both those things?"

"And some do. We'll do extra training when necessary."

"What does it cost to have a therapy dog?"

"Nothing, and I'm hoping to keep it that way." Jack glanced around him, and Noah could see the pride in his eyes at what he'd accomplished. "It's all about sponsorships to cover the cost, and I work hard to keep the money coming in. Not my favorite part of all this, but most of our brothers and sisters can't afford the cost of one of these dogs. I don't want that to keep them from getting the help they need."

Jack had found his calling, and Noah envied him. The man they'd loaded into a helicopter, not sure if he would live, had created a new life that gave him purpose. Add to that he'd found Nichole. During the little bit of time Noah had spent with them, it had been obvious that they loved each other.

"How'd you meet Nichole?"

"That's a funny story. I'll tell you over a beer later," Jack said, grinning.

Noah bet it wouldn't beat how he'd met Peyton. Not that anything was going to happen with her. And not that he was going to share his funny meet story because he was never going to see her again, a decision he made at seeing the way Jack grinned when thinking of his fiancée. Noah didn't have it in him to make a woman happy. He didn't know Peyton well, but he did know she deserved a man who could make her smile.

"The first thing you need to remember is that these dogs aren't pets," Jack said. "That includes Lucky. They're not military dogs trained to go to war, but they are working dogs with a job to do."

"Got it." That worked for him since he had no desire for a pet.

"You will be taking him home with you each night—"

"Why can't he stay here?"

"Because during the time you spend training him, you're his handler."

"Do the other dogs go home with their trainer?"

"Some do, some don't, but that's not important to you. You and Lucky are a team. When you're working with him, you need to be focused, so put all the shit going on in your head aside. I know that won't be easy, but learn to do it. If you think that's impossible, remember this. We're SEALs. Discipline is our middle name."

"What if I can't?" The shit in his head was always there, like it or not. Although, his dark thoughts had left him alone when he was with Peyton.

"You can, and you will. That reminds me. You have an appointment with a therapist Friday morning. You can explain then why you took off this morning."

It was only by calling on all that discipline Jack spoke of that Noah didn't walk away again.

Chapter Eight

"Does your father know you're asking me for a job?"
Kenneth said.

"I haven't specifically mentioned applying to you,
but my father is aware of my reasons." She wished she
had it in her to lie. "You're aware of my reputation and
qualifications, Kenneth. I'd be an asset to your brewery."

"So, that's a no? I'm sorry, Peyton. As much as I'd
like to offer you a job, no can do. I don't have any desire to deal with Gerald when he finds out you're working for me. Sorry."

"Well, thanks anyway." Not.

That was what she got for having Sutton as a last
name. The microbrewers all knew each other, and Gerald Sutton had been a fixture in the industry in Asheville for close to thirty years. Like Kenneth, they all
knew who she was.

There were more breweries on her list to try, but
she'd listed them in the order of the ones she'd most
like to work for. After walking out of Mountain Top
Brewery, she took a pen from her purse and crossed
out number seven on her list.

As much as she didn't want to leave Asheville—it
would break her heart to have to leave the city she loved

so much—when she got home, she'd research other towns well-known for their microbreweries. Places where the Sutton name did not put fear in the eyes of the cowards she'd talked to so far.

Okay, not that she blamed them. If she owned a brewery and Peyton Sutton came calling, asking for a job, she'd say a hard no, just like all the ones she'd visited so far. Because…Gerald Sutton.

So, where did that leave her? Continue down the list or wave a white flag? She'd visited the best ones, the ones she'd hoped might want a master beer brewer working for them enough to not be afraid of the repercussions. Because every damn one of them knew she could brew beer with the best of them.

Could she work for any of the breweries farther down on her list? She could put them on the map, make their good beer amazing. She just knew it. Or, maybe it was time to break away from her father. Go someplace where she could make a name for herself without his influence. What to do?

If she left Asheville, she'd never see Noah again. Not that she expected to, but there was always a chance it could happen. His mouth on hers as he kissed her popped into her mind. She wanted to kiss him again, and then some more. What if he was the only man in the world who could make her tingle? If so, that was just sad, since she would never see him again.

Thinking about a hot SEAL and his tingly kisses wasn't going to solve her job problem, though. She scanned the rest of the names on her list. No more today. She just wasn't up to it.

On the way back to her loft, she stopped at her favorite Vietnamese restaurant and got an order of pho and spring rolls to go, along with a bowl of beef and vegetable noodles. If she did end up moving, it had to be somewhere that she could live downtown with easy access to the restaurants and shops.

But she didn't want to move.

"Hey, Joseph," she said at seeing the man in his usual spot on the sidewalk.

"There she is." A smile appeared on his weathered face. "How's Miss Peyton today?" he said, picking up his beat-up guitar.

"Great." That was always her answer, and usually, she was. The disabled vet had enough problems without hearing about hers. "What are you going to play for me today?"

"See if you can guess what this one is."

It was a game they played, and because after brewing beer, music was her jam, she usually guessed right. For that reason, he delighted in trying to stump her. He never sang, so she had to come up with the song title from just his playing the guitar.

When he finished, she grinned. "That was 'Killing Me Softly With His Song.' One of my favorites."

"I thought for sure I had you with that one. You're too young to remember that song."

"No way. Roberta Flack is awesome." She took the noodle bowl out of the to-go bag and gave it to him. Then, like she always did, she dropped a five-dollar bill in his cup.

"Thank you, Miss Peyton. You have a nice day."

"You take care of yourself, Joseph."

"I'll do that."

When she'd first met him, she'd tried to bring him food every day, but he'd refused to have any part of that.

"Not your charity case, Miss Peyton," he'd said. So, after some intense negotiations, they'd agreed that she could occasionally bring him something and he would play a song for her. That had evolved into the guess-the-name-of-the-song game, one they both enjoyed.

As for the five dollars she dropped into his cup four or five times a week, when he'd fussed about that, she'd told him to get over it. When he'd still resisted, she'd held the bill up, and then had let it go to blow away with the wind.

"That's your two choices, Joseph," she'd said. "It either goes in your cup, or I give it to the wind."

"Guess in the cup then, but I don't have to like it."

She'd laughed. "Thought you'd see it my way." She'd never figured out why he didn't want to take her money when it didn't bother him that other people dropped bills or coins into the cup.

"You're a stubborn one, Miss Peyton" had been his only comment on the matter.

As she headed for her loft, she thought about that long-ago remark. If ever there was a time to be stubborn, it was now. To keep the life she loved, to stay in the city of her heart, and to keep the loft she adored, all she had to do was find a job. If that meant continuing down her list, even to the last one—a place she really didn't want to work at—so be it, because she was going to stubbornly refuse to move.

You could start your own brewery.

Huh? Where the devil had that thought come from? Crazy as it was, as she rode the elevator to her floor, her heart beat faster at the idea. Could she? It had never occurred to her to do such a thing since she'd thought she would always brew beer for Elk Antler, and that when her father decided it was time for him to retire, the brewery would be hers. But what if?

Excited about the possibility, she'd start researching the cost of doing it as soon as she finished her lunch. Could she even get a bank loan? What would rent run for a downtown building? And equipment, that wouldn't be cheap. Then there was the inventory—the grains, yeast, bottles, and other stuff. It was probably a pipe dream, but dreams didn't cost anything. What would she name her brewery?

Beer names these days were crazy cool and the bottle labels outrageous. It wasn't going to be easy to come up with an awesome brewery name that wasn't already in use. She discarded names as she unlocked her door. When she stepped inside her loft, she came to a dead stop. Dalton stood at one of her windows, looking out.

"Still feeding your friend?" He turned and raised his eyebrows. That was one of his idiosyncrasies that she hated, those eyebrows going up when he thought she'd done or said something stupid.

Joseph's corner was visible from her windows, and if she'd known Dalton was watching them, she would have sat her butt down on the sidewalk and spent another hour with her friend. Dalton had never come out and said so, but his body language always indicated that he disapproved of her giving Joseph money or bringing him food.

Well, screw him. She'd be friends with whoever she wanted, feed whoever she wanted, and give money to whoever she wanted. "Why are you here?"

"I'm here to save you from yourself." He gave her an indulgent smile. "What's gotten into you?"

"Not you, that's for sure." Because she had trouble

being mean, she about bit her tongue off to keep from telling him that he'd never made her tingle like a certain sexy SEAL.

"Don't be a witch, Peyton."

Witch? The name of her maybe brewery flashed right in front of her eyes. *Wicked Witch Brewery* was perfect. She laughed. "Well, turns out you're good for something anyway."

He frowned. "What are you talking about?"

"Nothing. I'm fixin' to eat my dinner, so goodbye." She headed for the kitchen.

"Fixing to?" He shook his head. "Do you know how ignorant you sound when you say that?"

"Don't care." She set her to-go bag on the counter, then strode back to him and held out her hand. "I want the keys to my loft back."

"Don't you think I'm owed an explanation? Why did you disappear from our wedding? And who was that man you were at the waterfall with? Are you having an affair?"

She wished she was having an affair with Noah. "You're right. You do deserve an explanation. You don't love me, so I'm not going to marry you."

"Of course I love you." He crossed his arms over his chest and scowled. "Where's this ridiculous notion coming from?"

"From you. I heard you, Dalton. You told Ron that you were marrying me because my father promised you shares in the brewery." She held out her hand again. "I want my keys, and then I want you to leave."

Anger flashed in his eyes. "No to both. We're going to settle this today, and then we are going to get married. I'm thinking a quick trip to Vegas will work just fine."

"Listen carefully. I. Am. Not. Going. To. Marry. You. Not today, not tomorrow, not ever. Give me my damn keys."

He grabbed her arm. "Wrong." He dug his fingers into her skin. "Now *you* listen carefully. We are getting married, so stop acting like a spoiled brat."

"You're hurting me." She tried to pull her arm away, but he gripped her harder. What was wrong with him? "You're scaring me, Dalton." This wasn't the carefully controlled man she'd known. This man with the cold, hard eyes was a stranger, and she had a revelation. He'd always controlled his temper around her, and suddenly she knew, just knew that would have changed had she married him.

"And you're trying my patience."

She was never more thankful that she'd overheard his confession to his best man than she was at this moment. "You're delusional." She yanked her arm away, and then ran and locked herself in her bathroom. If she stayed in there long enough, surely, he would leave.

Then she'd call the locksmith again and demand that he come change her locks immediately. When she'd called yesterday, he'd scheduled her for Friday afternoon, the soonest he had open. If he couldn't make an emergency call, she'd find someone else.

"Peyton." Dalton knocked on the bathroom door. "Open the damn door."

"If you don't go away, I'll call the police."

He laughed. "Go ahead. What will you tell them? That you're having a spat with your fiancé? You think they'll care?"

Luckily, she hadn't set down her purse when she'd put her lunch on the counter. It was still hanging from her shoulder, and her phone was in it. Was he right? He hadn't hit her, had just grabbed her arm. He'd probably convince the police that it was nothing more than a minor argument.

Noah had said she could call him if she was desperate. Well, she was.

Chapter Nine

"Nichole drunk dialed you?" Noah said.

Jack grinned. "That she did. Not that she meant to. She thought she was calling someone else. It's going to make a great story to tell our kids."

"If she doesn't kick your ass to the curb for ratting her out."

"Never happen. I keep my girl too happy for her to ever leave me."

"Bragging there, Whiskey."

Jack chuckled. "Just saying."

They were sitting on Jack's back deck. Noah wondered what his friend would say about how he'd met Peyton, and he was tempted to tell Jack, but something held him back. He wasn't sure why he wanted to keep her a secret. Maybe it was because he couldn't stop thinking about her, and if he talked about her, Jack would sense there was more to it than just a funny story.

"She still thinks she's on the job, doesn't she?" he said, lifting his chin toward Jack's dog. Dakota was perched on the top step leading down to the yard, her alert gaze sweeping the area around them.

"Always. She's not real happy there aren't any bad guys to bite these days."

They both chuckled. Dakota had saved Jack's life by pushing him back seconds before an IED exploded. The bomb had still seriously wounded both of them, but here they were, still breathing. Noah would forever be grateful for that.

"He already thinks you're his," Jack said.

"Who thinks what?"

Jack dipped his chin at Lucky. "Your dog."

"Not my dog." He jerked his hand away when he realized he'd been combing his fingers through Lucky's fur. "Where's Nichole?" he asked before Jack could talk about the healing power of dogs.

He wasn't going to drink the Kool-Aid. A dog wasn't going to help him sleep at night, wasn't going to take away his nightmares. He was the reason a good dog was dead, and he was done with dogs.

"In her studio. As soon as she finishes glazing the bowl she's working on, she'll join us." He glanced at Noah's empty cup. "Want some more coffee?"

"I'm good." Jack was drinking a beer, and Noah would love to have one, but he'd decided to try and limit his drinking to one glass of liquor or one beer a day. If that was all he was going to have, he'd prefer to have it at night. Sometimes it helped him sleep. Sometimes not.

His phone buzzed, alerting him to a text message. He picked it up from the table next to him.

Dalton's here and won't leave.

"I have to go," he said, standing.

"Where?"

He glanced at Jack. "To rescue a damsel in distress."

"Explain."

"Later." He'd told Peyton not to call him unless she was desperate. Until he could get to her and assess the situation, he couldn't know if she really was in danger, but he wasn't taking any chances.

Jack stood. "I'm coming with you."

"Not necessary." He was perfectly capable of dealing with Dumb Groom.

"Still going. Just let me tell Nichole."

"Fine. But you have three minutes. Can Lucky stay here?"

"No. Wherever you go, he goes."

"You're a pain in the ass, you know that?"

Jack laughed as he jogged down the steps, Dakota chasing after him as he headed to Nichole's studio. Noah clipped Lucky's leash to his collar. "Let's go see your friend." He wondered what Peyton was going to think when he showed up with both Jack and Lucky.

In his car, he started to call Peyton but paused. Maybe there was a reason she texted instead of calling, like she didn't want her ex to know she had help coming. He clicked on messages and typed.

On the way. U ok

Locked myself in the bathroom. My elevator code is 4349 Text me when you get to my door.

"In the back seat," he told Lucky when he saw Jack approaching. On second thought, he wasn't sure what the situation was. What if he decided he needed to stick around to make sure her ex stayed gone?

"Listen," he said when Jack opened the passenger

door. "I don't know what the deal is, so why don't you follow me in case I decide to stay for a while?"

Jack studied him for a moment. "Okay, but you need to tell me what's going on."

"When we get there."

"Where are we going if I lose you?"

"Don't know the address, but it's downtown. The building has a mall on the first floor with lofts above."

Jack nodded. "I think I know it. I'll be right behind you."

When he shut the door, Lucky stuck his nose between the front seats and whined. "Fine. You can have your seat back."

At the waterfall, Noah had studied Peyton's ex as he stood behind her father, silently watching. If the man loved her, he should have been upset to see her with a bare-chested stranger and her in that stranger's shirt. Hell, if that had been him, he would have had a whole lot to say. There probably would have been fists involved.

What kind of man didn't blink an eye at seeing his fiancée almost naked in the presence of another man? The answer to that was one who didn't give a damn about her other than the gains marrying her would bring him. Noah blamed her father as much as the ex. If what Peyton said was true, and he had no reason to doubt her, her father had betrayed her. He was pretty sure that had hurt her more than losing a fiancée.

When he reached downtown, he watched for the landmarks he'd memorized when he'd left her, and after only one wrong turn, he found the garage where he'd parked when he'd brought her home.

"What's the situation here?" Jack asked after they'd both parked and were headed for the exit.

"Her name's Peyton. Don't know her last name. I met her yesterday at that waterfall you took me to. She's... ah, she's a runaway bride." He glanced at his friend to see his reaction.

Jack came to a dead stop. "Tell me you're yanking my chain."

"Nope," he said, not stopping. He could still see her ex's cold, calculating eyes as he watched her. The douchebag was no match against him, but he was capable of hurting Peyton. If he had, Noah was going to make him sorry.

Jack jogged, catching up with him. "And we're going to save your runaway bride because?"

"Because her ex-fiancé is there, and she's locked herself in the bathroom."

"She's afraid of him?"

"Appears so."

"No one hurts a woman on our watch," Jack said.

"Copy that."

"Peyton, you have exactly one minute to come out before I kick the damn door in."

Was he serious? Were her shares of Elk Antler really worth forcing her to marry him?

The door crashed open. She screamed.

"Damn it, Peyton, you're being ridiculous." He grabbed her arm when she tried to become one with the wall. "So your father promised me shares in the brewery. Why is that a problem? We'll just be keeping it in the family."

"Let go of me. I'm not going to marry you."

"Yes, you are." He dragged her to the living room. "You can pack a bag, or I'll do it for you. Either way, by tomorrow night, we'll be married."

"No! I'll scream bloody murder to anyone who'll listen."

He shook his head as if she was nothing more than a naughty child. "You really don't get it, do you?"

"Get what?" She tried to pull her arm away again, but that only made him dig his fingers deeper into her skin.

"Your father's dying. His wish is to see you taken care of."

"You're a lying toad. He's not dying. He's not!" How could he say something so horrible? If that was true, her father would have told her. Wouldn't he? She was so furious at Dalton's lies that she stopped thinking and let the rage take over. She pulled her arm up, lowered her mouth to the fingers that were going to leave bruises and clamped her teeth down on them.

"Bitch." He jerked his hand away from her teeth, but she saw the droplets of blood bubbling on his skin.

Good. Her phone vibrated on the floor where she'd dropped it when he'd grabbed her. Noah? *Please let him be on the other side of her door.*

"Noah," she screamed.

Her front door splintered, and two of the most furious-faced and intimidating men she'd ever seen rushed in. One was Noah, but before she could reach for him, Dalton pulled her against his chest.

"You!" Dalton said, his gaze on Noah.

Lucky rushed past Noah and his friend, his tail wagging as he tried to get to her. Noah picked him up, handing him to the other man. "Hold him while I deal with this asshole."

"What is this, a garden party?" Dalton snarled.

"Let her go." Noah took a step closer. "Do it now before I make you, and believe me, you don't want that."

Dalton tightened his hold on her. "So, you are fucking him."

"You're disgusting." Why had she ever agreed to marry him? Noah's eyes were growing icier by the second, and his hands were fisted at his sides. She was pretty sure he'd like to plant those fists in Dalton's face. "You're outnumbered here, Dalton. You really should let go of me."

He put his mouth next to her ear. "This isn't over," he said, then pushed her so hard that she fell to her knees.

Faster than she'd ever seen anyone move before, Noah had him backed up to the wall, his hand wrapped around Dalton's neck. "You touch her again, come anywhere near her again, you'll wake up in the hospital. You hearing me, you worthless piece of shit?"

When Dalton remained silent, Noah's friend said, "I'd answer him before he decides to make good on his threat."

"I hear you," Dalton ground out.

Noah dropped his hand from Dalton's throat. "Good. Now get out."

Wow! Not that she approved of violence, but was it wrong to think Noah in warrior mode was about the sexiest thing ever? Dalton glared at her as he walked past with Noah following him out, and she was afraid she hadn't heard the last of him.

Lucky tried to wiggle out of the other man's arms. "Hey, sweet boy." She'd never expected to see Noah or his dog again, and she couldn't stop her happy grin.

"Hey," the man with Noah said, his eyes dancing with amusement.

She laughed, surprised she even could. "I was talking to Lucky."

"And here I thought you were sweet-talking me. I'm Jack, by the way."

She waved her fingers. "Nice to meet you, Jack."

He held out his hand and helped her up. "You okay?"

"Yeah." Except for her left knee. She'd hit it pretty hard on her wood floor. It was throbbing, but if she told these guys, they'd probably haul her off to the hospital for X-rays.

Noah came back in and walked right up to her. Hot doggity, was she ever glad to see him again, and not just because he'd sent Dalton packing. "Hi," she said kind of breathlessly.

"Are you really all right? I heard you grunt when your knee hit the floor."

"I don't grunt."

"You so did."

"Did not." She loved that he was trying not to grin, but she saw his lips twitch. "You might be able to scare the bejesus out of DGs, but you'll not win the did, did not game with me, so give it up, boyo."

"Did you just call me a boy?"

She knew that'd get his goat, and she smirked when his eyes slitted. "If I did?" Now she was daring him to do something. What, she wasn't sure, but her vote would be for him to shut her up again with a kiss.

"Fire," he said, the eyes that were pure ice when focused on Dalton now hot enough to melt butter.

"Fire?"

"Yeah. You're playing with it, and you're going to get

burned." His gaze lowered to her arm, and he frowned as he touched the bruise already turning purple. "He hurt you."

"A little, but I'm okay."

"I have questions," Noah's friend said.

She'd forgotten he was there.

"You can go now, Whiskey," Noah said, not taking his gaze from her.

"Negative. Who's DG?"

Peyton giggled. "Dumb Groom. That's what Noah calls him."

"After seeing the way he treated you, I'd call him worse than that. Were you really a runaway bride?"

"Yep. And I think it was the smartest thing I've—"

Noah put his finger over her lips. "Go away, Jack."

"On one condition. The two of you come to dinner tomorrow night."

"No," Noah said.

"Okay," she said at the same time.

"Good. Nichole will want to meet you."

Noah groaned. "What? You going to adopt her, too?"

She scowled. "You don't think I'm adoptable?"

He scowled right back at her. "Did I say that, princess?"

"No, but it sounded like you implied it." She didn't know why it was fun to rile him up. Maybe because when he was sparring with her, that haunted look in his eyes dimmed.

"I never imply. When I have something to say, I'll say it."

"Well bless your heart, sugar."

His friend chuckled, but she kept her gaze on Noah. Noah's eyes narrowed. "For?"

Jack outright laughed. "He's from Maine, Peyton, so that went right over his head. Valuable intel, Double D. When a Southerner blesses your heart, chances are that they're insulting you without straight-out calling you a jackass."

"That so?" Noah said. "I might be a jackass, but you're damn sassy."

"Humph." Oh, yeah. There was that sign of life in his eyes she wanted to see. And why did Jack call him Double D?

"Humph? What the hell does that mean?"

Another chuckle had her glancing at Jack, who was watching them with a grin on his face. He handed Noah the end of Lucky's leash. "I'll leave y'all to battle this out. Come over around five and we'll have a few drinks before dinner."

"Maybe," Noah said.

"We'll be there," she said.

Chapter Ten

This woman! Noah swiped his hand through his hair. "Sassy and bossy."

"Well, aren't you just precious?"

"You're insulting me again, aren't you?"

"A little."

Humor flashed in those pretty blue eyes, and he ordered himself not to grin. What was it about her that made him feel alive inside? His urge to grin faded when his gaze fell on her arm again. He pulled his phone from his pocket.

"Hold your arm out."

"Why?"

He sighed. "Just do it." The bruise was already turning a deep purple. He took several pictures, then dropped his phone back into his pocket. "If you show these photos to the police, they'll arrest your ex for domestic abuse."

"I just want him to go away."

"Not sure that's going to happen, princess."

She shrugged, then bent over when Lucky nudged her leg with his nose. "I missed you, sweet boy."

Noah wondered if she'd missed him a little. She laughed when Lucky tried to lick her face, and as they loved on each other, an unfamiliar longing grew inside him. He didn't want it, this feeling she stirred up inside him. So what if he was jealous of his…not his. If he was jealous of a damn dog.

"Why does Jack call you Double D? If that's your bra size, I'm impressed."

"Funny. It's what my team calls me because I always have a pair of dice in my pocket."

"They must mean something to you," she said, her attention still on the dog.

"Just a reminder of what not to be."

"Yeah, how so?"

She was a sneaky one, tricking him into telling her more than he'd ever told any of his SEAL brothers. His teammates didn't know that his mother had been killed by his father. He never talked about the old man or the reason for the dice, had never told a soul why his fingers sought the dice when he was tempted to act in any way like that bastard.

"Noah?" she said, looking up at him when he didn't answer her question.

"It's probably best if I go." Before he laid his pitiful life story out for her.

"You told me at the waterfall that your father killed your mother. Do the dice have anything to do with that?" she said, her attention back on the dog. "I think they do if they're a reminder of what you don't want to be…or maybe who you don't want to be."

How the hell had she connected the dots? To keep from kissing her again to shut her up, he walked to the window and stared down at the people walking by. Exactly what was he about here?

"Noah?"

That soft voice wrapped around him, offering…

what? He didn't have a clue. There was only one thing he'd like to have from her, and that was to get lost in her body for an hour or two. Then he'd leave and never return. But she wasn't a woman a man could walk away from. She was a woman a man would want to wake up with in the mornings, go to bed with every night, to make a life with. That made her dangerous.

He'd see to her broken door, and then he'd leave and never come back. But was she safe? Her ex wouldn't come back today, but what about tomorrow? He turned toward her. "You should tell your father about the stunt your ex pulled today."

She unclipped Lucky's leash from his collar, then stood, walked to the kitchen, and filled a bowl of water for the dog. Noah stuffed his hand into his pocket and wrapped his fingers around the dice. The ingrained protective side of him didn't want to walk out that broken door, leaving her defenseless. He was messed up, though, and had no business adding her troubles to his.

"Are you ignoring me?"

"No." She left Lucky in the kitchen lapping up the water. Stopping a few feet in front of him, she said, "Will you be my person?"

He blinked. What in the world did she mean?

"That sounded better in my head than hearing me say it." She blew out a breath. "I was out interviewing all morning, and my feet are killing me in these shoes. I'm going to go change, and then I'll explain, okay?"

"It's your show, princess." It was a shame she was losing the shoes. He allowed himself a few seconds to imagine her wearing nothing but those heels while her legs were wrapped around him.

"Enough of that," he muttered. While she was changing, he studied the door. The lock was broken, and the wood around it splintered. It really needed to be replaced.

He called Jack. "Hey, you know anyone who can make an emergency visit to replace Peyton's door today?" He could do it, except that would mean a trip to Home Depot or wherever, but he wasn't going to leave her alone with a broken door.

"Actually, I do. I meant to call him before I left but got sidetracked by the entertainment."

"Entertainment?"

"Yup. Watching you and Peyton was like being at a comedy show."

Since Noah couldn't deny that, he kept silent. The woman was amusing.

"So, what's the deal with you two?"

"There is no deal." Because he wouldn't allow it.

"Uh-huh. Not sure this is a good time for you to get involved with someone."

"Not having this conversation." Next, Jack would want them to have a slumber party and paint each other's toenails while sharing their love life.

"When you're ready to have it, let me know. In the meantime, I'll have Dell call you about the door. Have measurements ready to give him."

"Copy that." He disconnected before Jack decided to continue his Dr. Phil impersonation.

Peyton walked back in, and damn. He was going to spend his sleepless night debating which was hotter: Peyton in nothing but those sexy heels, or a barefoot Peyton with cherry red toenails and legs that went on forever. She'd changed into white shorts and a sleeveless blue silky-looking top that perfectly matched her eyes.

Want her. Want her right now, the million-year-old caveman ancestor embedded in his brain said. At the moment, he wished he was that caveman so he could haul her back to his lair without getting slapped silly.

"I need your measurements." It didn't take more than a nanosecond for his brain to register what he'd said. When had his mouth gotten so stupid?

She stilled, looked at him, and blinked. "Tell me you didn't just say that."

"Of your door. You need a new one."

Her gaze sifted from him to her door and then back to him. The sexiest smile he'd ever seen in his life— and he'd seen his fair share—appeared. "There are a lot of things I need, and I think you can help me out with most of them."

That he could. "Do you have a tape measure?" He was proud of himself for asking that question instead of the one he wanted. Like…how would you feel about a few hours of playtime?

Peyton put her hands on her hips. "Think again, buster. You are not going to measure me." She knew why he wanted the tape measure, but it was just too much fun messing with him, especially when her reward was that fish-mouth impression he was doing now.

"You…you…" He huffed a breath.

She fluttered her eyelids. "Me?"

"You're impossible."

"Not really." For him, she could be all kinds of possible. It really was weird that she trusted him, considering she'd only met him yesterday. She'd probably been a fool to let him haul her away from the waterfall, but in her defense, she hadn't been thinking clearly what with being a runaway bride and all.

There were things she'd like to get from him, like another tingly kiss, but at the top of her list was his agreement to hang out for a while in her guest bedroom. Dalton had warned her that this wasn't over. That meant he still planned to marry her regardless of her telling him that wasn't going to happen.

Before today, she'd never considered Dalton dangerous, but now she did. Having a SEAL bodyguard seemed like a good idea, but how to get him to agree? What did she have to offer that would get him onboard with her plan? She could brew him the best beers he would ever taste, or—

He snapped his fingers in front of her face. "Tape measure. You have one?"

"Yes. You want it?" She hid her grin when he let out an exasperated sigh.

"Would you please get it?"

"Only because you said please." She got the tape measure out of a kitchen drawer. After giving it to him, she returned to the kitchen. Her soup was cold now, so she transferred it to a microwaveable bowl. While he was measuring the door, she gathered the fixings for grilled cheese sandwiches.

Wasn't the way to a man's heart through his stomach? If she fed him, maybe he would be agreeable to hanging around for a few days. His phone rang, and she listened to him give the door measurements to someone and then answer questions about the door and hardware.

Lucky sat at her feet, watching her every move. She wished she had some dog treats for him. "Can dogs have cheese?" she asked him. He barked what she guessed was a yes. Not sure if cheese would mess up his stomach, she broke off a corner from a slice of sourdough bread instead. "Here you go." She laughed when he scarfed it up. "Didn't your mama ever tell you to chew your food?" His only response was to look at her with hope for more in his eyes. "One more piece, then that's it."

By the time Noah finished his call, she had the grilled cheese under the broiler, along with the spring rolls, and the soup heating.

"Jack's friend will be here in about an hour with a new door."

"That's great." She hadn't mentioned Dalton kicking in her bathroom door. She'd deal with getting that replaced herself. Noah and his friend had done enough already, and she was about to ask Noah for more. "You want one of my amazing beers for dinner or something else?"

"Dinner?"

She slid the grilled cheese sandwiches from the oven rack onto a cutting board. "You know, that thing you do with food where you put it in your mouth?" She pressed her lips together to keep from laughing at his exasperated expression. If she wasn't careful, one of these times teasing him, she was going make his eyes cross.

"I know what dinner is." He leaned his side against her kitchen island. "Why are you making it for me?"

"Because I feel like it?"

He shook his head. "Try again."

Drat. He was on to her. "Because I'm hungry, and it wouldn't be polite to eat in front of you?"

He shook his head again, only slower this time, which strangely put even more emphasis on his rejection of her excuse. "If you're answering in the form of a question, then you're still not giving me the real reason."

Oh, he was smart. "Fine. I want to talk to you about something, and I figure you'll be more open-minded on a full stomach."

"Does this have to do with that nonsense about me being your person?"

"Not nonsense," she muttered. "Do you want a beer or something else?" She cut the grilled cheese in halves, put them on plates, along with the bowls of soup. There were two spring rolls, and she gave them each one.

"A beer's fine."

She gave a mental fist pump. He was going to sit down and eat with her. "There are several choices in the fridge. Pick which you want, and one for me." She'd already set out placemats and silverware on the island, and she carried the plates over.

"This is really good," he said after taking the first bite of the grilled cheese.

"That's because it's sourdough bread and has three kinds of cheeses in it, sharp cheddar, Havarti, and goat cheese. That's nothing. Just you wait until I make you my famous grilled cheese with bacon and tomato."

"You're not going to be making me more dinners."

She ignored that comment since she planned to have him around for a few days. "Unfortunately, I didn't have a tomato on hand tonight, and I didn't feel like cooking bacon. You wouldn't think a tomato would be good on grilled cheese, but you'd be wrong. Every person I've ever made it for—"

"Princess?"

"Hmm?" She never would have thought she'd like a man calling her princess, and although he probably intended for her to take it as an insult, she heard the softness in his voice when he said it. He probably didn't even realize that.

"No tomatoes on my grilled cheese."

She saluted. "Copy that." She'd heard him say those two words a few times. And there was a minuscule upturn of his lips before he flattened them back to his trademark scowl. Getting an almost smile out of this man was almost as satisfying as creating a new beer.

By the time she finished her soup and half her sandwich, she was full. Dropping the other half of her grilled cheese and the spring roll on his plate, she picked up hers. After loading her plate and silverware in the dishwasher, she cleaned up the kitchen while covertly watching Noah finish his dinner. He seemed to really enjoy it, and that made her happy.

Dalton would have turned up his nose at such a simple meal. Her ex never talked much about his childhood, but from the few things he'd let slip, she knew he grew up poor. The one time she'd made him the sandwich, he'd refused it, saying he'd eaten a lifetime's share of the damn things.

Noah picked up his empty plate and bowl and brought them to the sink. "Thanks. That was good."

"You're going to like it even better when I make it for you with bacon and tomato."

His gaze landed on her, and he narrowed his eyes. "No. Tomato."

At least he wasn't still saying she wouldn't be cooking for him. She picked up her half-full bottle, noting that he still had some left in his. "Let's finish these in the living room." It was time to convince him to agree to her plan, and she was nervous.

She sat on the sofa, tucking her legs under her. He

walked to the window and looked out. Since she could appreciate his fine body without him noticing, she took advantage. He wasn't as big as his friend Jack, not quite as muscled, but he was perfectly formed. His dark blue T-shirt stretched over broad shoulders, his hips were lean, and his legs long.

All that was as sexy as all get-out, but it was his forearms that snagged her attention. She didn't know what it was about men's forearms, but they did it for her, and Noah's were perfect. She wanted to trail her hands over them, to feel the strength of those muscles. Even better, she'd love to have them wrapped around her.

"You ready to tell me what's going on in that pretty head of yours?"

He thought she was pretty? A thrill gushed through her, and she couldn't help her grin. Maybe his thinking that would help get his agreement to her plan, but she refused to talk to his back. "I will when you turn around."

A soft sigh escaped him as he faced her. A questioning brow went up, but he kept quiet. He could be quite intimidating when he wanted. Like now with his lips pressed together and his eyes already hardening, as if he was preparing to say no to whatever was about to come out of her mouth.

She almost chickened out under his relentless stare, but she had to at least try. Although her goal was to have him act as a bodyguard for a few days, she couldn't deny that she wanted more time with him. And just maybe, he would kiss her again.

"Okay, here's the thing." She wished she wasn't so nervous, afraid he was going to give her a big fat no. "I think Dalton's lost his ever-loving mind. He's decided I'm going to marry him whether I want to or not. And believe me, I don't. He said we were going to Vegas. I got away from him and locked myself in the bathroom. He kicked the door in, and—"

Noah made a growling sound deep in his throat as he strode out of the room.

"Uh, I wasn't finished," she informed the empty space.

Chapter Eleven

Noah stared at Peyton's broken bathroom door. Rage filled his chest, boiling his blood. He was transported back to the day he and his mother had locked themselves in the bathroom in an attempt to stay out of reach of his father's fists.

It hadn't worked. The old man had kicked the door in. He'd dragged both of them out, him by his skinny boy's arm, and his mother by her hair. It was only one of many times his father had let his drunken rage loose before one day crossing a line that couldn't be uncrossed. That had been the day Noah's mother died at the hands of the man who was supposed to love and protect her.

That was a fucking joke.

"Noah?" A warm, soft hand pressed against his back. He blinked, his mind returning to the present. He didn't know Peyton's ex, didn't know what the man was capable of, but if he kicked in doors to get to a woman afraid of him, left bruises on her body, and was willing to force her to marry him, he was not a man to be trusted.

"What do you want from me?" He was afraid he knew the answer.

"Come with me." She slipped her hand around his. He shouldn't like her hand in his so much. She took him across the hall, into what was obviously a guest room since there were no personal effects of hers.

"Nice room." He was even more certain he knew what was coming.

"It's almost as big as that little apartment you're staying in." She let go of his hand, walked to the window, and looked out. "You can see the hog statues from here."

He joined her at the window. Sure enough, there were two hogs on the sidewalk. "The question begs to be asked. Why hogs?"

"In the mid–eighteen hundreds, Tennessee hog farmers brought their hogs to market here, drove them right through downtown."

"That had to be messy."

She laughed. "I would imagine so. Anyway, the statues commemorate that."

Delaying tactics. He waited her out.

"So." She glanced around. "What do you think of this room?"

"It's nice." Nicer than any bedroom he'd ever slept in, but he kept that fact to himself.

"There's a bathroom attached."

"Hmm."

She put her hands on her hips. "Are you being dense on purpose?"

"I have no idea what you're talking about, princess." He liked that fire flashing in her eyes.

"And here I thought you were smart," she muttered.

He snorted.

"I'm offering you a place to stay that's a palace compared to that box you're currently in."

"So, let me get this straight. The princess wants

the warrior to move into her castle and what? Slay her dragons?"

"In a nutshell, yes."

He'd intended to insult her, but her grin said he'd failed. "No."

She blinked her pretty blue eyes as if his answer was a complete surprise. "No? Just like that?"

Lucky ambled into the room, glanced from them to the bed, and then jumped up on it. He lay down, rested his chin on his paws, and leveled his gaze on them.

"Lucky likes it here."

"Then he can stay." That would work just fine. He could tell Jack he'd found a good home for the stray, and then he'd be free of having responsibility for the thing.

"I don't understand why you'd rather stay in an apartment not much bigger than a walk-in closet when you could be here. I'll even keep you supplied with free beer and food. There're all kinds of good restaurants nearby, and a lot of interesting shops. You look like you work out, and there's a gym right here in the building, or plenty of sidewalks if running is your thing. I don't know why or for how long you're in Asheville, but you'd save money staying here. Of course, Lucky's welcome, too. I'll even walk him for you, and—"

"No."

"—you can have complete control of the remote, even if all you watch is sports. I do like NASCAR and baseball, but not—"

He sighed, then kissed her, since that seemed the only way to shut her up. As he had the first time, he waited for her to slap him, and rightly so. Instead, she melted against him, her mouth soft and welcoming.

This was why he couldn't stay near her. The woman

was entirely too much temptation. When she put her hands on his chest, and the heat from her palms seeped through the material of his T-shirt, his brain forgot he only meant to give her a quick kiss to make her stop talking. He slid his arms around her back, drawing her against him.

He wasn't a man who fell into bed with a different woman every night. He wasn't a monk, either. He'd kissed his fair share of women but kissing Peyton Sutton could too easily become an addiction and a complication he didn't need. His brain came back online, and he pulled away.

It was only because of his discipline and physical training that he wasn't inhaling and exhaling air like he'd just ran ten miles with fifty pounds of gear on his back. Not her, though. Her chest was heaving, and that he'd had that effect on her sent satisfaction rolling through him.

No lie. He'd be safer walking through a minefield than being anywhere near this woman. "I gotta go." As far away from her as he could get.

"Oh, okay."

He didn't like the disappointment in her eyes, as if he'd failed her, but he couldn't stay. Even the discipline he'd learned as a SEAL was no match against this woman.

"Knock, knock," a man called out.

"That's the man here to fix the door." Noah took advantage of the interruption to walk out of the room before he decided it was a good idea to kiss her again.

It didn't take long to install the new door, and when Noah showed Dell the bathroom door, he promised to come back first thing in the morning to replace it.

"You can pay me tomorrow," Dell told Peyton when she asked what she owed him.

After he left, Noah said, "Your door's fixed and you have new locks. You'll be all right." But what if she wasn't? "You have my number. The same goes. Use it if he bothers you again." He called himself a fool for leaving that offer on the table, but it was the only way to get his feet to move.

"He's going to be a problem, but I won't call you."

That should make him happy. He wasn't happy. "Why is he so determined to marry you?"

"I don't really know, other than he wants the shares of Elk Antler my father promised me. He claims my father is dying, that my dad just wants to see me taken care of."

"I'm sorry about your father, but maybe he just thought he was doing what was best for you?" As for the ex, there had to be more to his determination to marry her than just shares in a brewery.

"Dalton's lying. My father would tell me if he was sick."

"Are you sure about that?"

She nodded. "I would know if something was wrong with my father. Dalton's just trying to scare me. He's not going to give up, Noah."

Ah, hell. Those blue eyes were looking at him with so much hope. Another minute and he was going to be agreeing to anything she wanted. "I really need to go."

"What about Jack's invitation to dinner tomorrow night?"

"Feel free to go. I'll text you his address."

"Will you be there?"

"No." If he had to, he'd chain himself to his bedpost

to keep from showing up at Jack's while she was there. "You want the dog?" Jack probably wouldn't be happy he gave the mutt away, but he'd deal with it.

"Why would you give away your dog like that?"

"I told you, he's not my dog." He didn't like the way she was frowning at him, as if she found him lacking, which he was. She just didn't know how far down he'd fallen. If she did, she wouldn't be offering him a bed in her pretty room.

It was time to go. Noah ignored the weird pang in his chest that grew with each step he took away from her. By the time he reached the door, his feet felt like they were encased in cement blocks, making it almost impossible to walk out.

For her sake, he had to. He was in a bad place, and dragging her down with him wasn't an option. He opened the door, and Lucky shot through ahead of him. "Hey, you're supposed to stay with her." Lucky looked up at him with those two-different-colored eyes, his tongue hanging out the side of his mouth, and his tail swirling like helicopter blades.

"You'll need this," Peyton said, tossing him Lucky's leash.

Before he could reply, she closed the door, and he heard the click of the lock. "Guess she's done with both of us."

Lucky whined, apparently not happy about that.

As he crossed the street, headed for the garage and his car, he glanced down at the thing he still wasn't sure was a dog. One blue eye and one brown eye stared up at him, and Noah had the feeling Lucky was disappointed in him.

"You're not the only one," he told the dog. There was a long list of people he'd let down.

He was steps away from entering the garage when he noticed a homeless man sitting on a blanket at the corner. His eyes were closed, and he was strumming a guitar. The man was good, and Noah recognized the song, "Imagine" by John Lennon. What got his attention, though, was the other man standing over him... Peyton's ex.

Noah stopped, his instincts kicking in. The homeless man was clearly ignoring whatever her ex was going on about. Noah didn't like that Dalton was in the area. She'd said he lived in a gated community, so that wouldn't be in downtown Asheville.

"We need to do a little recon," he told Lucky. "Stealth is the name of the game. You got that?"

Enough people were passing by that Noah was able to come up behind Dalton without the man being aware of him.

"Look, I'm offering you a hundred dollars. That's more money than you make in a week sitting here on your lazy ass. All you have to do is call me when she leaves."

The asswipe wanted to spy on her? Lucky growled, and Noah assumed the dog was picking up on his tension. Not wanting Dalton to know he was there, he took a few steps back.

The homeless man kept playing, ignoring Dalton, but he opened his eyes, his gaze going straight to Noah. He lifted a hand, gave Noah a salute, then closed his eyes and continued playing. Had the man recognized that Noah was military?

Noah backed away. If he was smart, he'd cross the street, get in his car, and put Peyton and her problems in his rearview mirror. He had his own issues to deal with, and he wasn't doing such a good job of that. Obviously, he wasn't smart because a few minutes later, he was knocking on her door.

She had a peephole, and he stood in front of it, making sure she could see his face. As soon as the door opened, Lucky gave a happy bark.

"Noah?"

"We need to talk."

She stepped back, then dropped to her knees, letting Lucky shower her with kisses on her chin. You'd think it had been days since they saw each other, not just minutes. As she leaned over Lucky, her hair cascaded around them like a black curtain. He wanted his hands tangled in that hair. For the first time in his life, he was jealous of a dog. He walked in, dropped the leash, then closed the door and locked it.

After she and the dog finished their lovefest, she unhooked his leash and stood. "Talk about what?"

"Is your offer of a room still good?" What the hell was he doing?

"Depends. Why the change of mind?"

"Your ex. He just offered a homeless man money to spy on you."

Her eyes widened. "Joseph? He wouldn't do that." She rushed to the window.

"You know the man?" He followed her to the window. Dalton was gone, but had he gotten the man to agree?

"Yeah, he's my friend. I need to go talk to him." She disappeared down the hallway and returned a minute later with a pair of flip-flops. She dropped them to the floor, slid her feet in them, and then grabbed the key to her new door from the counter.

Lucky tried to follow them out, but Noah pushed him back. "Stay."

"How do you know Dalton offered Joseph money?" she asked when they were in the elevator.

"Heard him."

"So you what? Decided to play hero after all?"

"You really need to get it through your head, princess. I'm not a damn hero."

Surprised by the anger in his voice, Peyton pressed her back to the elevator wall. Why had that made him mad? She couldn't figure him out, but she wanted to. What had put that haunted look in his eyes? Why was he living in a temporary apartment? He'd said he was a SEAL, so why wasn't he out doing whatever it was SEALs did?

She hadn't expected to see him again, so she was happy, yes, but also shocked when he'd returned. If he was going to be around for a few days, maybe she could learn his secrets. And if she was really lucky, she might get a few more tingly kisses.

"Why are you smiling?"

"Huh?" She wasn't about to answer that question. Thankfully, the elevator door opened, and she marched out. Noah stayed at her side, and she glanced at him. He was scanning the area around them, and she'd never seen a man so alert and aware of his surroundings. She'd seen pictures on the news of soldiers in their camouflage uniforms, and she just bet that he looked darn sexy in his.

"Guess this one, Miss Peyton," Joseph said as soon as she reached him.

The song sounded familiar, but she couldn't place it. It didn't happen often, but occasionally, he stumped her. "Ah…"

"It's 'Trouble' by Ray LaMontagne," Noah said. Then he muttered something she didn't catch.

"What's that?"

He smirked. "Just making an observation."

"Are you implying I'm trouble?" She bumped her arm against his. "If so, you'd be wrong. I'm as tranquil as a cat taking a nap in the sun."

He snorted.

With a grin on his face, Joseph segued into "What's New Pussycat," and she glanced at Noah. Her heart stuttered at seeing the hint of a smile. If he ever gave her a full-on smile, she'd likely need oxygen.

"What did Dalton want?" she asked Joseph when he finished the song.

Joseph set his guitar aside. "Aren't you supposed to be married to him now?"

"Yeah, well, that didn't happen."

"Never did like that man. He isn't good enough for you, Miss Peyton." He turned his attention to Noah. "And who might you be?"

Noah held out his hand. "Noah Alba. You play a mean guitar, man."

She appreciated the respect Noah showed her friend. The more she was around Noah, the more she liked him. Despite the hard outer shell he showed the world, she was beginning to think he had a soft heart. She wanted to know everything about him, especially why his eyes always looked sad.

"Lucille here—" Joseph rubbed a gentle hand over the guitar's neck "—she gets me through the low times."

"May I?" Noah asked, gesturing to the guitar.

"I don't let Lucille cheat on me with just anybody,

but I have a feeling about you, Noah Alba." He picked up the guitar and handed it to Noah.

Peyton figured Noah knew how to play because of the guitar case she'd seen in his bedroom, but she hadn't been prepared for what he could do with Joseph's beat-up guitar. "Wow, just wow," she exclaimed when Noah finished playing Stereophonics' "Bust This Town." Talk about playing a mean guitar!

People clapped, and so absorbed in Noah's playing, she was surprised to see that a crowd had gathered. Almost as if he'd forgotten he was on a public street, Noah's gaze darted around them. His face blanked, he handed the guitar back to Joseph, and then he walked away.

What just happened?

Had he played that particular song on purpose, like did he wish he could bust this town, maybe bust her? She wanted to chase after him, ask him all her questions. But first, she had to know what Dalton was up to.

"That man has demons," Joseph said.

It sure seemed like he did. She tore her gaze away from Noah's receding back. "He said he heard Dalton offering to pay you to keep tabs on me. Is that true?"

Joseph's lips curled in disgust. "It is, but his money's no good with me, Miss Peyton. I told him that."

"Thank you. You're a good friend." To please her father, she'd accepted Dalton's proposal before really getting to know him, but her eyes were open now. She shuddered to think if she hadn't overheard him minutes before their wedding, she would be married to him now.

After saying goodbye to Joseph, she headed for her loft. She wanted to know why Noah had walked off the way he had. What did his demons have to do with playing a guitar?

Chapter Twelve

Why had he touched that guitar?

Noah leaned his back against the wall and stuffed his hands in his pockets. He stared at Peyton's locked door, wishing he could get in and close himself in the guest room before she came back. She would want to know what happened, but no way was he talking about it.

For a few minutes, he'd forgotten that not playing a guitar was his punishment for his tragic mistake. It didn't matter whether it was his or someone else's. He hadn't known just how much he would miss his guitar. That instrument was his go-to when he was stressed or lonely or angry. Putting his fingers on the strings and letting the music take him away calmed him. It was his Xanax.

He was angry that he'd forgotten because those few minutes of having a guitar in his hands again reminded him of what he'd been missing. He'd almost gotten used to not turning to his guitar when a storm was brewing inside him. Now, he had to start over. He was pissed about that.

The elevator door opened, and his…*the* princess stepped out. If he was smart, he would walk right past her, get in that elevator before the door closed, and remove himself from her life. He'd be doing them both a favor. The door closed while he stayed attached to the wall. Looked like he wasn't so smart.

She stopped in front of him and put her hand on his arm. "Are you okay?"

No. He was not. Funny thing, though. Her fingers were warm on his skin, and the volcano inside him ready to blow cooled down a little. Strange how that worked, her warmth cooling him.

Still, he needed to be alone, locked in his room where her concerned eyes weren't trying to see into his soul. He wouldn't share his ugly secrets, especially with her. Peyton was sunshine, and he wouldn't allow the dark inside him to kill her light.

"Can you open the door, please?"

Hurt flashed in her eyes. "Sure."

Already he was disappointing her. He wanted to tell her that that was what he did…hurt people. It seemed only fair to warn her, but the words wouldn't come. As soon as she unlocked the door, he headed for the guest room. Lucky raced circles around him, excited to see him.

Damn dog. As much as he wanted to hide, he had to take Lucky out before closing himself in for the night. He grabbed the leash and hooked it on Lucky's collar.

"I'll walk out with you," Peyton said.

"No, I'll only be a few minutes." There was that hurt in her eyes again. Maybe it was good that she was learning that all he did was hurt people.

"Okay. You hungry? I can make us a snack."

"Thanks, but no." He walked out. As he waited for the elevator, she ran out. She was going to ignore his wishes? The simmering volcano grew hotter.

"You might need this." She handed him a plastic baggie.

Puzzled, he stared at it. "For?"

She rolled her eyes, as much as telling him he was stupid. "If he poops, you need to pick it up."

Right. He was stupid. "Thanks." The elevator opened, and he took the baggie. Without another word, he stepped inside. The door closed, and as he rode down, he called himself every vile name he could think of. He was acting like a jerk, and she didn't deserve that. An apology was in order, and he'd do that when he returned.

Lucky did his business, and ten minutes later, he was back in the loft. Peyton was nowhere in sight. Her bedroom door was closed, and he paused. He raised his hand to knock then dropped it. He'd apologize tomorrow.

If he was going to stay here for a few days, he needed his duffel bag. He considered going to get it, but he didn't want to leave Peyton unprotected, and he couldn't be around her tonight. He was too much on the edge to be around anyone.

He'd thought he was doing okay until he'd touched that guitar, losing himself in the music. Then clapping had sounded in his ears when the last note had faded, and he'd been horrified to see a crowd had gathered. If they knew what he'd done, they would have turned their backs on him instead of cheering him on.

Stretched out on the bed, he stared at the ceiling. He didn't have to sleep to see those few minutes that were seared into his brain. All he had to do was close his eyes, and it was there, his own personal horror movie playing behind his eyelids. As if that wasn't enough, when he finally succumbed to sleep, the nightmare came, with one addition that hadn't actually happened. In his personal hell, Asim looked straight at him with accusing eyes, and then the bomb exploded. So, he resisted closing his eyes for as long as possible.

He didn't deserve to play his guitar or anyone else's, didn't deserve the pleasure or the escape the instrument brought him. He'd forfeited the right to lose himself in the peace playing it gave him.

His eyelids grew heavy, slid closed. Asim looked at him with those condemning eyes. Noah jerked up, his scream dying in this throat. Lucky put his paws on the bed and whined.

"What?" There was concern in the animal's expression. Even the dog knew he was messed up. If he was still at the temporary apartment, he'd get in his car and drive somewhere, anywhere. But he couldn't leave Peyton unprotected. Getting up, he stepped quietly down the hallway in his bare feet.

In the living room, he turned on the TV, muted the sound, and flipped through the channels until he found a baseball game. Restless, he roamed the living room. "Wow," he murmured when he stopped in front of her bookcase. The shelves were filled with vinyl albums. In the middle of the bookcase was a turntable. She was just as obsessed with music as he was. Didn't mean anything, though.

He returned to the sofa and tried to watch the game, but the ants were biting, so he dropped to the floor and counted his way through a hundred push-ups. Then he started over.

Peyton heard low grunts and wondered what Noah was doing. Since she slept in only her underwear and a soft camisole, she slipped on the leggings she'd worn earlier and a T-shirt over the camisole. She eased her door open and crept down the hall.

Lord above and all of heaven's saints, the shirtless man doing push-ups on her floor, sweat glistening on his back, was the hottest thing she'd seen. Ever. She wanted to lick him. She wanted to press her fingers over those bulging muscles in his shoulders and arms. She just wanted. Period.

He had on jeans, but that was all. Would he agree to lose those if she politely asked? She had never been so close to perfection in a male, and it didn't seem fair if she couldn't touch him. Maybe get some more tingling kisses.

Just thinking about having her hands on him made her sigh with longing. She hadn't meant to make a noise, but apparently she had, because he stilled with his face an inch from the floor. He rolled into a sitting position with the grace and fluidity of a gold medal gymnast.

"Peyton?"

"Hmm?" He wasn't even breathing hard. How long had he been at it? Ten push-ups torturing her body like that and someone would have to scrape her off the floor.

"Did I wake you?"

"No." She waved her hand. "Carry on. I'll just quietly sit here." And commence drooling. She plopped down on the sofa.

"I'm done."

Well, drat. He eyed the hallway, and she was sure he wanted to close himself up in his room again. She didn't want him to, so she said the first thing that came to mind. "Will you tell me why you have a hummingbird tattoo?" She was still curious about that.

Ignoring her question, he stretched his neck, rotating his head in a circle, then went to the window. Even from across the room, she could feel the tension rolling off him. She chewed on her bottom lip, then made her decision. If ever there was a man who needed someone to care about him, it was this one.

The only reason she knew he was aware of her coming up behind him was the way he cocked his ear toward her. When she was close enough to smell his musky scent, she drew in a deep breath.

"I stink," he said, his voice gruff.

"No." He didn't. He smelled like all man, and it was intoxicating. She put her hands on his shoulders and pressed her thumbs into the hard knot at the base of his neck. He stilled, and when he didn't push her away, she massaged the muscles in his shoulders.

"Gosh, Noah, you're tighter than a frog's butt, and that's watertight." She felt like she'd won the lottery when he huffed a laugh. Then he lowered his forehead to the window, and she knew he was shutting down again. Not on her watch.

"Full disclosure, I don't really know if a frog's butt is airtight. There are a lot of things I don't know, but I do know this. You're running from something, and if you want to talk about it, I'm a good listener. Sometimes I even give good advice. But you don't have to talk about anything if you don't want to. It's entirely up to you. It's a proven fact, though, that bottling up the bad stuff hurts the soul." She moved her finger back to the knot at the base of his neck. "That's why you're as tense as a boy about to ask a girl he has a crush on to the prom." She hated it when she rambled, and she was definitely doing that, but she couldn't seem to stop. "Were you

nervous the first time you asked a girl out? I doubt you
were. You probably had girls falling all over you." She
would have definitely been one of those girls. "How old
were you when you had your fist kiss? I was—"

Before she knew what was happening, his mouth was
on hers. She was beginning to suspect that this was his
way of shutting her up, and if so, she had a whole lot
more to say if it got her these amazing tingles invad-
ing her body.

When he'd kissed her before, it had only been mouth
on mouth, but this time, his tongue slid between her lips,
and every thought in her head was obliterated. Nothing
existed in the world, nothing mattered but this man and
what he was doing to her.

He slid his hands down to her hips and pulled her
to him. She slipped her hands around his neck, needing anything and everything he was willing to give
her. He plundered—that was the only word for it—
her mouth, lighting her body on fire. She whimpered,
wanting more.

"No," she said when he pulled away. "Don't stop."

"You need to stop making me kiss you." He scowled
at her, and then he walked away, disappearing into the
guest room, shutting the door behind him.

"Not in this lifetime," she muttered. She fully intended for there to be more kissing. And hopefully,
other body-tingling stuff.

Peyton slapped her hand over the clock, shutting off
the blaring alarm. She hated mornings and usually hit
the snooze button five or six times before rolling out of
bed and stumbling to the bathroom. She was slipping
back to sleep when her eyes popped open.

Was that coffee she smelled. And bacon? How could she forget the sexiest man alive was sleeping in her guest room? Suddenly wide awake, she scrambled out of bed. Ten minutes later, wearing a pair of red shorts and a black sleeveless top that tied at the waist, she walked into the kitchen. Her smile faded when she found it empty.

A plate was on the warmer, and she peeked under the paper towel covering it. A dozen or so slices of perfectly cooked bacon were on the plate. "Like bacon much," she murmured. He'd also made a pot of coffee, and she poured a cup.

Coffee in hand, she walked down the hallway, stopping at the open guest room door. The bed was perfectly made, and she wondered if he'd even slept in it. Where was he? Lucky was missing, too, so Noah was probably out walking his dog.

The doorbell chimed, and she went to the door and peeked out the eyehole. Seeing it was Dell with her bathroom door, she let him in.

"This will only take a few minutes," he said.

"I really appreciate it." True to his word, he was done in fifteen minutes. After she paid him, he left. She went to the living room window. "There you are." Noah stood next to Joseph, the two of them seeming to be in a serious conversation. They talked for another few minutes, and then Noah and Lucky headed her way.

Taking advantage of the chance to study him, her gaze roamed over him. One thing she noticed was his alertness. She'd bet he was aware of every person around him. If Dalton was lurking nearby, she didn't doubt Noah would know. That made her feel safe.

He moved with a confidence she'd never seen in a man before, and as his long legs ate up the sidewalk, power radiated from him. "You're one sexy boy, Noah Alba." He looked dang good in jeans and a T-shirt that did nothing to hide one fine body.

Seconds before he entered the building, he looked up at her, and she realized that he'd known she was watching him. He didn't smile, just kept his eyes locked on hers until he disappeared from sight.

She fanned her face as she let out a long breath. Not sure what his mood would be this morning, she decided to finish the breakfast he'd started. It would give her something to do instead of attacking his body as soon as he walked in the door, although that would be her preference.

What did she want? She considered eggs, but that didn't excite her. "Pancakes," she said at seeing the box in her pantry. By the time Noah arrived, she had a pan heating on the stove, and was stirring the mix.

Lucky ran to her as soon as Noah unclipped his leash. She kneeled, laughing when he tried to lick her face. "Good morning, you sweet thing." She glanced at Noah. "Good morning to you, too."

He grunted something that sounded like "Morning."

Okay, grumpy Noah was still in the house. "Dell was here and replaced my bathroom door."

"Good."

"How about pancakes to go with all that bacon?" She stood and lifted an edge of the paper towel covering the bacon. "Are you going to eat all that?"

"One can never have enough bacon." He snatched two pieces, broke off the end of one, and handed it to Lucky. The dog scarfed it up, then lifted begging eyes to Noah.

"That's it for you, dog."

She flicked a finger against his arm. "His name's Lucky."

"He couldn't care less what I call him."

Now he was just being ornery. "Well, I care." She was on to him. By refusing to use the dog's name, Noah was keeping the animal at a distance, not wanting to get attached. "Why do you have him if you don't want him?"

"Good question. Ask Jack when you see him."

"I'll do that." She looked forward to dinner tonight. Maybe she'd learn more about Noah from his friends.

His phone buzzed, and he put it to his ear as he walked away. While he was talking, she made pancakes. Because she had an open floor plan, she couldn't help hearing his side of the conversation, and she guessed he was talking to his friend, Jack.

"I'm going to have to bring her with me," he said.

She glanced over to see him looking at her. Bring her where with him? He didn't appear very happy, and she wondered if he regretted agreeing to stay here. Sometimes she was impulsive, and this was one of those times. No doubt the last thing he wanted to do was follow her around while she tried to find a job.

"Bring me with you where?" she asked when he finished his call.

"To Jack's dog training place."

"No can do." She set their plates on the table. "What do you want to drink? I have juice, coffee, and milk."

"You don't have a choice." He crossed to the coffee-pot and poured a cup.

"Excuse me?" She put her hands on her hips. "You're not the boss of me."

"Wrong, princess." He picked up a handful of bacon

and wrapped two pancakes around the slices. "Be ready to go in twenty minutes," he said as he walked out of the kitchen with Lucky on his heels.

"Hey," she yelled, but he kept going. She followed him down the hallway. "I'm talking to you." He closed the door in her face. She banged on it. "Noah, open the blasted door."

"Fifteen minutes now," he said from the other side. "I'd suggest you change into some old jeans, and if you have an old pair of running shoes, those would be best."

"I'm not talking to you through a closed door." Silence. "You really are a jackass!" The blasted man chuckled. If he thought she'd fall in line like a good little soldier, he had another think coming. "I have things I have to do today." She opened the door. "Like find a…"

She forgot what she was going to say.

Chapter Thirteen

"You're naked."

Noah glanced down at himself. "Not true." He still had on his boxer briefs. "Another few seconds, and you would've gotten an eyeful." Her gaze roamed over him, and if she didn't stop looking at him like that, she was going to see physical truth of just how much he wanted her.

"Ah…" She blinked like someone coming out of a trance.

"I was about to jump in the shower. Want to join me?" He lifted a brow, daring her.

"Ah…" Her cheeks turned pink, and she stepped back. "I'll just go change."

"You do that, princess." After she shut the door behind her, he glanced at Lucky. "Do me a favor. If I so much as touch that woman again, bite me in the ass."

Peyton Sutton was proving to be dangerous to his sanity. Why was he even attracted to her? His life was one of deployments, dangerous situations, and training. Rinse. Repeat. Any woman wanting a ring on her finger was to be avoided at all costs.

Peyton wasn't a woman a man walked away from. She wasn't a one-time thing, and he wasn't a man who stayed. But he did like that sassy mouth of hers. Who knew he'd find that a turn-on? And the way she blushed? Made him want to discover where else she turned pink.

All those were reasons he should walk right out her door and put her in his rearview mirror. He would, too, if Joseph hadn't told him that Peyton's ex had shown up early this morning and doubled his offer for Joseph to spy on her.

So he'd stick around for a while. He'd make sure his runaway bride didn't end up married against her wishes. As soon as that mission was accomplished, he would do her a favor and get out of her life.

Until then, he'd have to be her shadow. He needed to stop at the apartment and get his duffel bag on the way to Jack's dog place, and he made a mental note not to forget the picture of his mother that he'd put in a kitchen drawer. It wouldn't be so bad having Peyton hang out for the day. She could play with the puppies while he did whatever Jack had in mind for him.

"What did you say this place is?" Peyton asked when he parked in front of the dog kennels.

"Operation K-9 Brothers. Jack trains therapy dogs for our brothers and sisters in need."

"When you say brothers and sisters—"

"Our fellow military personnel, especially those suffering from PTSD." He reached over the seat and clipped the leash on Lucky's collar.

"That's really awesome. And you're a part of this?"

"Temporarily apparently."

"What does that mean?"

They hadn't talked on the drive over, and suddenly

she gets chatty? Explaining why he was here wasn't going to happen. He exited the car. Lucky squeezed between the seats, following him out. Peyton got out and jogged up next to him. Too close. He could smell her scent, something fresh and citrusy. Made him think of summer days and sunshine. Light to his dark.

He sidestepped, putting distance between them. What was he even doing here? Spending his days with dogs wasn't going to magically fix his head. Why his commander thought it would was a mystery.

Jack walked out of the office. "Good morning, Peyton."

She gave Jack a warm smile. "Morning. It's good to see you again." She glanced around. "Noah told me what you do here, and I have to say that's really awesome."

"Would you like a tour?"

"Very much. How many dogs are you training? How long does it take before one's ready to go to someone? Where do you get the dogs from? I know about therapy dogs, but I've never met one." She eyed Lucky, who seemed to be hanging on her every word. "Oh, is Lucky a therapy dog? I guess I have met one then."

Noah resisted the urge to kiss her into silence. Talk about training…in two days, she'd trained him to kiss her whenever she talked too much. He glanced at Jack, who was grinning like a fool as he listened to her. Noah didn't like that. Not that he was worried his friend would make a move on her. Jack was totally in love with Nichole.

Her rambles belonged to him, though. And if that wasn't the stupidest thought he'd ever had, he didn't know what was. The two of them wandered off, Peyton asking her endless questions, barely waiting for an answer before she was on to the next one.

Instead of tagging along, he headed for the nearby stone bench. Lucky jumped up and sat next to him. The dog watched the two as Jack walked Peyton past the kennels.

"You like her, huh?" Lucky glanced up at him, then turned his attention back to Peyton. When she and Jack disappeared into the building that housed a new litter of puppies, Lucky whined.

"Yeah, I like her, too, but that's my problem." He really had to stop kissing her, because every time he did, he wanted more. "Bad timing. You know what I mean?" And now he was talking to a dog that he'd wanted nothing to do with.

How had his life gone south so fast? He took the pair of dice from his pocket and stared at them. Justin Alba had always sworn they were his lucky dice and wasn't that a joke since the man had to be the worst gambler in the world. He was always broke, but Noah couldn't count how many times his father swore the next big win was just around the corner.

What was actually around the corner were the people his father owed money to because of his gambling. Another thing Noah had lost count of was how many times they'd moved in the middle of the night, each new place worse than the last.

He'd once told his mother that he wished she'd never married his father. "Then I wouldn't have you," she'd answered, and he knew she meant it. Knowing now that she'd died at the hands of his father, he would gladly give up his existence for her to live again. And to have never met Justin Alba.

All this reminiscing reminded him that he hadn't returned his brother's call from five days ago. He needed to do that before Clint decided to pay a surprise visit. He wouldn't put it past his rich half brother to do that.

Until four years ago, he hadn't known he had a brother, one the same age as him. When Clint had tracked him down, Noah had been so enraged that another woman had been pregnant with his father's son at the same time his mother was that he'd told his brother to get the hell out of his life.

Clint was a stubborn bastard, though, and despite the initial verbal abuse Noah had rained down on him, he kept coming back until Noah surrendered, tired of fighting him. The first year of their relationship had been uncomfortable...for him, anyway. Nothing seemed to bother Clint. The brother he hadn't wanted had wormed his way into Noah's life, and now he couldn't imagine not having him there.

Still, when his life had fallen apart, he'd ignored Clint's calls, not able to face being a disappointment to his brother. But it was time to man up. He'd call him soon. Jack walked out of the building alone, and Noah slipped the dice back into his pocket.

"She's going to play with the puppies for a while," Jack said, stopping in front of Noah. "You ready to do some work with your dog?"

"Not my dog, but since I don't seem to have a choice, let's do this."

"There are always choices, Noah. If you don't want to be here, leave."

"Don't fancy ending up in the brig." Although it was damn tempting to walk away, just disappear to wherever.

"Then drop the frown and attitude, brother. I know

you don't believe me now, but give me a week with an open mind, and I promise you, you'll start feeling better about yourself."

Doubtful. How was he supposed to feel better about himself after what he'd done? But unless he was willing to go AWOL, he was stuck here until Jack and his commander decided he had his act together. "Fine. You got your week."

"Good." Jack squeezed Noah's shoulder. "And try smiling once in a while."

"Anything else, like shooting rainbows out my ass?"

Jack laughed. "That happens the second week you're here."

"Oh, joy," Noah muttered.

"Before we start, I want to go over a few things." He took a seat next to Noah on the bench. "Some things to remember. Your tone of voice, eye contact, touch, and facial expressions are all important in training a dog."

"Okay." He wasn't the team's dog handler, but he'd sometimes watched Striker work with his dog, and before him, Jack.

"Old-school training was to punish a dog to correct unwanted behavior. Don't ever do that. We'll reward them for good behavior, for doing what we want, for accomplishing a task. Always remember that Lucky will pick up on your emotions, the good and the bad ones. If you're anxious or upset, he will be, too. As you work with him, you'll learn his signs, the ones that will tell you if he's paying attention, if he's tense or confused about what you want from him. He'll tell you those things by the position of his ears, the tilt of his head, what his tail is doing. He wants to please you. If you're centered, he'll be centered."

"Centered? I don't even know what that means anymore." Much less how to achieve it.

"You were always one of the most centered on the team, so it's there." He tapped Noah's chest. "You just have to find it again, and you will." He stood. "Ready for your lesson with your dog?"

Not his dog. "Sure."

"Today was fun," Peyton said as they walked Lucky before leaving for dinner at Jack's house. They'd come home to shower and change clothes. When Noah had clipped the leash on Lucky's collar to take him out, she'd tagged along without asking. If she had, she knew he would have refused her company.

"Good."

"The puppies are so cute. Jack said he'd teach me some things he does in their early training. Isn't that cool? Did you know he plays all kinds of music over the speakers in their room? It gets them used to different kinds of noises. I would have never thought of doing that. Eventually, he'll get them used to really loud things like firecrackers and guns. He does that so if someone's out with their therapy dog and say a car backfires, the dog won't panic and try to run away."

She paused, waiting for a response or even better, a kiss, but all she got was a grunt. He'd been in silent mode since leaving the therapy dog place. If it was Dalton acting like this, she'd be wondering what she'd done or said wrong. Whatever was going on with Noah, though, had nothing to do with her. It was weird that she knew that, considering she barely knew the man.

"Was Jack in the navy with you? How does he know so much about dogs?" Maybe if she asked questions, she could get him to talk.

"Yes, and he was the team's dog handler, trained by the navy."

Okay, that was the most he'd said since leaving Jack's, so questions were the way to go. "What was your job?"

"Whatever I was told to do."

She poked his arm. "That answer's really helpful, Mr. Mysterious." He almost smiled, she was sure of it. "Are you still in the navy?"

"Yep."

"You're a joy to talk to, you know that?"

"If you say so."

"Does that mean you won't be staying in Asheville?"

"Correct."

She doubted he'd want to hear that made her sad. They paused when Lucky decided to water the hog statue. "Guess he doesn't have a high opinion of pigs. Speaking of, do you like barbecue? We have some great places for ribs and pork sandwiches. I could take you for barbecue tomorrow night. Do they put coleslaw on pork sandwiches where you're from? I always thought that was normal until a friend from college came for a visit. She'd never heard of such a thing. Where in Maine are you from, anyway?"

Yes, he was kissing her! Right there on the street in front of anyone walking by. That excited her, and wasn't that weird? He had his hand on the back of her neck, holding her still while his mouth took possession of hers. The way he held her felt possessive, and mercy, did she ever want to be possessed by this man.

"Peyton!"

The harsh voice cut through her haze. Noah's mouth lingered on hers a few seconds more, and then he lifted his head but kept his eyes on hers. She saw the question in them. Did she want to talk to Dalton? Not even, her eyes answered. He gave a curt nod, and with his hand still on her neck, he led her away.

"I'm talking to you, Peyton."

Lucky looked back and growled. She and Noah kept walking. There was nothing left to say to Dalton, so why couldn't he leave her alone? She was glad Noah hadn't felt it necessary to get in a pissing battle with Dalton, and that told her something. There wasn't a doubt in her mind that Noah could be badass when he wanted, but he didn't feel the need to prove it. That impressed her...like she needed anything more to be impressed with him.

"So you don't care that your father's dying?" Dalton called. "Are you really that cold of a bitch?"

Noah squeezed her neck. "Keep walking, princess."

But she couldn't. She turned. "Stop lying. It's not true and you know it."

"Are you sure about that?" He glanced from her to Noah, then back to her. "I need to talk to you. Alone."

"Not happening," Noah said, his voice surprisingly calm.

"He's right. You have something to say to me, say it, then get out of my life and stay out."

Dalton glared at Noah, and when he turned his gaze to her, she could see him battling his rage. She'd come within minutes of being married to this man, and it would have been the worst mistake of her life. It deeply hurt that she'd lost her place at the brewery, but it was a price she was willing to pay.

"Your father is dying. I'm not lying about that."

"Stop saying that. If that's true, he would have told me."

"He doesn't want you to know." Dalton stepped

closer. "He wants to make sure you're taken care of, and I'm the man to do that."

Beside her, Noah snorted. She grinned at him. "I know, right?" He winked, and it was like they had a secret. Something big fluttered in her chest, a condor maybe.

"We're going to be late for dinner if we don't head out soon," Noah said.

"Then let's go." She turned her back on her ex, hoping he'd finally get the hint and give up.

"I think you should go see your father," Noah said as they rode the elevator up to her loft. "You need to make sure Dalton really is lying, and you also need to tell your father he's stalking you."

"I'm going to see Dad in the morning, but I'm not sure I'd call it stalking—"

"He's stalking you, Peyton. If he keeps it up, I'm going to have to hurt him. I don't think you want me to do that."

"I don't. This isn't your mess, and I don't want to see you get in trouble." She put her hand on his arm. "Maybe you should go back to your apartment and forget you ever met me." That was the last thing she wanted, but she really didn't want him in trouble because of her. She thought he was on leave because something happened that was so bad that it kept him from sleeping.

"No thanks. I've gotten used to the finer digs you offered, princess."

"Well, just don't get in trouble because of me, okay?"

"Yes, ma'am."

"I brought you beer that I brewed," Peyton said after she was introduced to Nichole.

"You brew beer?" Jack said. When she nodded, he glanced at Nichole. "Sorry, babe, but I'm going to have to leave you for Peyton."

"No problem, but I get custody of the dogs."

"Well now, we need to talk about that."

"Nope. Beer or dogs. Your choice."

"You're just cruel, babe."

Peyton loved their banter, and the mischievous gleam in Nichole's eyes. Although she'd just met the woman, she knew she was going to like her.

"Peyton's actually a master brewer," Noah said.

"How cool." Nichole took the bag Noah was holding and peeked inside. "I just assumed he meant you brewed beer as a hobby." She pulled one of the bottles out and read the label.

"I brought an assortment. That one's Elk It Now. It's a heavier beer with hints of hazelnut coffee and spice notes. Noah tried it last night and really liked it." Peyton took another bottle out of the bag. "This one is Island Affair. It's a light citrus-flavored beer."

"Oh, I have to try it. I love the fun names."

"Yeah, the trend in naming craft beers is to go funky. We get the whole crew together when we have a new beer and start throwing out the silliest names we can think of. We have a blast."

"I can imagine. Let's take these babies out to the back deck. We have time to chat a little before dinner." She wrapped her arm through Peyton's.

"Hey," Jack said. "Aren't y'all forgetting something?"

Nichole glanced over her shoulder. "Yeah, a bottle opener. Grab it, will you?"

"I was referring to me and Noah," Jack muttered.

"Such fragile egos," Nichole whispered, making Peyton laugh, and looked back again. "While you're at it, see if you can find our ice bucket to put these in."

"Yes, ma'am. Anything else, ma'am?"

One thing Peyton really liked about Jack and Nichole was the way they seemed to enjoy teasing each other. It was fascinating to observe a couple who were clearly in love. That was the kind of relationship she wanted. One where there was mutual respect, laughter, and love. She decided then and there that she wouldn't settle for less.

Chapter Fourteen

"What's up with you and Peyton?"

Noah leaned back on the counter while Jack filled a bucket with ice. "Nothing's up with us." That wasn't literally true. He was *up* anytime she was in the vicinity. Kissing her definitely wasn't helping, and he needed to cut that out. That was proving easier said than done, though.

"Where'd you sleep last night?"

"In a bed." What was with all the questions?

"Not the one in your apartment." Jack's gaze zeroed in on him. "I stopped by last night. You weren't there."

Noah sighed. "When did you get so nosy?"

"When you became mine to worry about." Finished filling the pot, Jack set it on the counter. "She's a beautiful woman, and she seems nice. A good person."

"But?" He knew where this was going, and he couldn't disagree. Still, he was getting pissed. What he did or did not do with a woman wasn't any of Jack's concern.

"There's always a but, yeah? This one is, are you in the right frame of mind for a relationship? Or are you just looking for an affair?"

"I have no intention of messing around with her. She asked me to camp out in her guest room for a few days until her ex gets the message that she's done with him. I agreed, and that's all I'm doing." And kissing her, but he'd keep that to himself. Besides, he wasn't going to do it again. *Or she could be the one worth getting your head screwed on straight for.* He needed to put a stop to that kind of thinking *and* the kissing. Done with this conversation, he picked up the ice bucket, then walked out.

The girls were stretched out on chaise longues. "Ice delivery." He helped them put the bottles from the bag into the ice.

"Thanks," Nichole said. She glanced up at Jack when he walked up. "You bring the opener, babe?"

"Don't need one." He took the bottle she held and twisted off the cap.

"I'm impressed." Peyton looked at Noah and flirtatiously fluttered her eyelashes. "Are you manly enough to do that, too?"

"For you, princess, I'll slay dragons." Where the hell had that come from? Jack snorted, and Nichole was watching them with a curious gleam in her eyes. He didn't like it.

He twisted the cap off, and after handing the bottle back to her, he perched on the deck railing, about as far away as he could get from her. Jack grabbed a bottle, then settled on the lounge chair next to Nichole.

"You want a beer?" Peyton asked.

"Sure."

"What flavor?"

"I'll stick with the Elk It Up. That's one of Peyton's creations," he told Jack and Nichole. Peyton gave him a soft smile, and he wished he could take the words back. He didn't want her soft smiles. *Liar.*

Three dogs raced onto the deck, two going to Jack

and one to Nichole. Jack leaned over and put a hand on each of their heads. "We have guests, so be on your best behavior."

"What pretty dogs." Peyton held out a hand to the one next to Nichole.

"That one is Rambo," Jack said. "He belongs to Nichole." He tapped the Belgian Malinois on the head. "This is Dakota. She's the head honcho of the bunch." He moved his hand to the other dog. "This goofball is Maggie May. She's a kleptomaniac, so guard your stuff around her."

"You're making that up," Peyton said.

Nichole shook her head. "No, she really is. She'll steal anything that catches her fancy."

"She stole one of my shoes the night I was here," Noah said.

Peyton grinned. "That's funny."

"Where's Lucky?" Jack said.

"At Peyton's." He'd left him behind because he needed a night without a dog shadowing him. Jack could shoot disapproval his way all he wanted. He focused on Peyton, who was laughing at something Nichole said.

Damn, she was pretty. It wasn't just her sky-blue eyes and long, inky-black hair, nor a body he itched to explore, that called to him. As much as those attributes appealed, it was her inner light that drew him in, that he longed to touch. He thought she could help him heal, but he had nothing to offer in return. All he could do was take, and he wouldn't do that to her.

As he perched on the railing, listening to the three of them talk, his gaze stayed on Peyton. Every emotion showed on her face and in her eyes when she talked. Her hands were never still. If he didn't know better, he'd think she'd been friends with Jack and Nichole for years.

The sun was setting, he was surrounded by people he liked, particularly one of them, and the conversation was interesting and sometimes funny, especially when Peyton got going. It was almost too easy to think life was normal, that he had possibilities. He wanted that to be true, but it wasn't.

"What about you? What's your superpower?" Peyton said, looking at him.

"Superpower?" His thoughts had drifted, and he tried to run their conversation back through his mind. He didn't have a clue what they'd been talking about.

"Yeah. Jack can touch his nose with his tongue, which is impossible for most people. Nichole can wiggle her ears, and I can tie a cherry stem in a knot with my tongue."

"You can do that?" What else could she do with her tongue?

Jack snorted, letting Noah know he was aware of where Noah's mind had gone.

"I can. So, what can you do?"

"He can sing the alphabet backwards," Jack said when Noah didn't answer.

Peyton clapped her hands. "Do it."

Only because he couldn't bring himself to refuse her, he started singing. It was a trick he'd won money on every time someone bet he couldn't do it. When he finished, she clapped again. "That was cool."

It was a silly thing, but making her happy made him…well, happy. He wasn't sure he was okay with that, this good feeling, but he'd examine that later. For tonight—and only tonight—he'd lock his demons away and enjoy the company.

"The weird thing is," Jack said, "he can't speak the alphabet backwards."

No one believed him, so he had to prove it. Then the others tried, and Peyton got so tripped up on the letters that she dissolved in giggles, laughing so hard that she had the rest of them laughing at her.

For the rest of the night, he allowed himself to have a good time without feeling guilty. It was a gift he wasn't expecting.

"I love your friends," Peyton told Noah when they returned to her loft. She wanted to tell him that she'd also loved seeing him enjoy himself. His smiles and laughter tonight had been a beautiful thing to see.

"They're good people."

She smiled. "Yeah, they are." Lucky was bouncing around them, excited they were home. She kneeled, giving him a hug and chin scratch.

"I need to take him out."

She glanced up at Noah. "I'll go with you."

"You don't have to."

"I want to." Already, he was reverting to gloomy Noah, and she wanted to beg him to please stay happy. She wanted to know what had put that haunted look in his eyes, but he wouldn't tell her, so she didn't ask. What she could do was be a friend, and everyone needed a friend, even when they pretended they didn't.

"You never told me where in Maine you're from," she said when they reached the sidewalk. That seemed a safe enough question, and she was curious to know everything about him. With each passing minute, he was retreating into himself while she was growing more desperate to keep him from shutting her out.

"No place you would have heard of."

"What's the closest town I'd recognize?"

"Bar Harbor."

"That's on my bucket list. If I ever get to go there, I'm going to eat lobster for breakfast, lunch, and dinner." When he didn't respond, her nerves kicked in. "With lots of butter. You can't get a really good lobster here in the mountains, so I don't bother. I did go to a restaurant in Charleston once that had Maine lobster on the menu. I had a two-pound one and ate the whole thing. Can you believe that? They put one of those bibs on me, and I had butter all over my hands and face. Dalton said I was embarrassing him. He—"

Yes! He was kissing her. His hand was behind her neck again, and he caressed her skin with his thumb. He hadn't done that before, and talk about tingles. That circular motion he was making with his thumb sent goose bumps down her back.

If he could do something new, then so could she. She slid her hands around his neck, praying he wouldn't push her away. He didn't. He circled her back with an arm, pulling her against him. There was no place she'd rather be. When he deepened the kiss, her body hummed in response. How did he do this to her? Make her hum, tingle, and get goose bumps? It was too much. It wasn't enough. If she could ever get him in her bed, she might not survive it, but she'd sure like to find out.

"What was that?" Noah said, breaking the kiss. He scanned the area around them.

She wanted to drag his mouth back to hers. "What?" Then she heard it. A woman was crying, begging someone not to hurt her.

Noah handed her Lucky's leash, then strode away. Pulling at the leash, Lucky whined, and Peyton let the dog tug her along. A narrow alley ran between two buildings, and Noah disappeared around the corner. When she came to the entrance to the alley, Noah glanced back at her.

"Stay there."

"Okay." Lucky wanted to go with Noah, so she held tight to the leash.

Halfway down the alley, a man stood over the crying woman. "You think you can walk away from me, bitch? I say when it's over."

Peyton gasped when the man hit her. He was so intent on yelling at the woman, that he didn't notice Noah coming up behind him. The man was big and mean looking. Afraid Noah was going to get hurt, Peyton wanted to call him back.

Noah stopped inches from the man's back. "You touch her one more time, and I'm going to show you how it feels to have a fist in your face."

The man spun, and Peyton slapped her hand over her heart when she saw the rage in the man's eyes. She searched around for a cop, but there wasn't one in sight. Why hadn't she brought her phone so she could call the police? Knowing it would distract him, she bit down on her bottom lip to keep from calling out to Noah.

"You need to mind your own business, dude," the man said.

"I'm making it my business, asshole." He glanced at the woman cowering against the wall. "Does it make you feel manly to pick on a woman half your size?"

Why was Noah taunting him? The man was bigger, and his arms bulged with muscles. She couldn't tear her gaze away from Noah. He stood as still as a statue, as if a huge woman beater wasn't worth the blink of an eye. Never had she seen a man so deadly calm, yet so menacing. She was looking at a warrior, a man trained to conquer his enemy.

Her worry for him eased. Did the man not get that Noah was daring him to come at him? She still wished a cop was around to put a stop to this madness, but she knew in her heart that Noah wasn't someone to be messed with. Unfortunately, the horrible man didn't seem to grasp that. He grinned as he fisted his hands.

Even though she believed Noah could win the fight, she still worried that the man could get lucky. When the man lunged at Noah, Lucky growled and jerked the leash out of her hand. The dog raced down the alley with his teeth bared. Before she could call him back, Noah had the man on his back. It happened so fast that even though she was watching, she couldn't say how he'd done it.

Lucky had his mouth clamped around the man's ankle. "Get him off me." The man kicked his free leg at the dog.

"Don't hurt him," the woman screamed.

Really? She was worried about the jerk after he'd hit her? Peyton ran down the alley. She grabbed the end of the leash and pulled. "Lucky, come here, boy." The dog gave one last shake of the man's ankle before letting go and coming to her. He sat next to her feet, still growling as he kept his gaze focused on the man.

"Baby, are you okay?" the woman said, kneeling near the man's head.

"What's wrong with you?" Peyton wanted to shake some sense into her. "He was beating you, and you're worried about him? Your lip is bleeding, and you're going to have a black eye. You should be calling the police and sending him to jail."

"She's right," Noah said, stepping away from the

couple. "He'll do it again. Probably wasn't the first time he's hit you, right?"

The woman glared at him. "Go to hell."

"You should be thanking him," Peyton said. "He saved—"

"Save your breath, princess." Noah wrapped his hand around her elbow. "Let's go."

There was no emotion in his voice, and his face was blank. It was as if he'd completely shut down.

At the end of the alley, she glanced back. "Shouldn't we call the police or something?"

"No."

She lengthened her stride to keep up with him. "But what if he hits her again?"

"He will."

"Then we shouldn't leave her with him."

"What do you think we should do? Kidnap her? Drag her away against her will?"

"I think we should call the police." He stopped so suddenly that she was several steps ahead of him before she realized he wasn't next to her. She faced him, and where before his face had been a blank slate, he now looked tortured.

"We could do that, but she'll bail him out as soon as they let her. Then he's going to be even angrier, blaming her for the reason he had to spend the night in jail. She'll pay for that at his hands, but she'll blame herself and forgive him." He started walking again.

It struck her then why his expression looked so tortured. She caught up with him. "Was that how it was for your mother?" she softly said.

"Until the day he killed her."

"Noah." Her heart broke for the boy who'd lost his

mother at the hands of a man who should have loved and protected them both.

"Don't."

"Don't what? Feel sad for you? Wish it hadn't happened?" She knew he wanted her to shut up, but she couldn't. Her heart hurt for him, and she didn't know how to pretend it didn't. She slipped her hand in his, and for a few seconds he didn't respond, then his fingers tightened around hers. "My father keeps a distance between us, but he's never laid a hand on me, or anyone for that matter. I can't imagine what it does to a child to see the man who's supposed to love his mother hurt her."

They stepped inside the elevator to her loft. "I think a part of you blames yourself, thinking you should have protected her. But you were just a boy, no match against a grown man. Did he ever hit you?"

"Shut up, Peyton." His mouth landed on hers and stayed there until the door opened on her floor. He lifted his head and stared down at her, turbulence in his eyes. "You drive me crazy, woman."

"Well, anytime I do, feel free to kiss me." The man was holding a lot of heavy stuff inside him, and that wasn't healthy. He'd never be happy if he didn't forgive himself for his imagined sins.

It wasn't only the death of his mother weighing him down—she didn't think so, anyway. He was on leave from the navy for something, and that was the thing she thought was keeping him from sleeping at night. If he kept everything bottled up, eventually he was going to explode. She decided it was her job to keep that from happening.

How could she get him to talk to her?

Chapter Fifteen

Damn woman. She was like a pesky little termite, burrowing into the wood until it was dust, exposing the secrets hidden behind the walls. He'd already told her too much, and for a moment, when she'd slipped her hand in his, he'd wanted to tell her everything. To just let it all out, to trust that maybe in all her words there would be ones that would show him the way out of his personal hell. But he hadn't, thankfully.

Admit the real reason, dickhead.

Okay, so there was that. He couldn't bear the thought of seeing her look at him with disappointment in her eyes, or worse, disgust. Jack didn't even know the full story, and he, more than anyone, would understand that things had a way of going south in the sandbox. If he couldn't admit his failure to Jack, he sure couldn't bare himself to Peyton.

He should move out, go back to his little box of an apartment. And he would if her ex wasn't hanging around. He'd seen the man tonight trying to hide in the shadows across the street from her building. Noah hadn't told her, not wanting to upset her. That was wrong, though. She needed to know so she'd keep a vigilant eye out, and he'd do that in the morning.

They returned to her loft and he closed himself up in his room before she started talking again and he'd have to kiss her to silence her. It wasn't that he didn't like to hear her talk. He did…too much. He could listen to her for hours on end, not that he'd ever tell her. And kissing her? That could become an addiction if he let it.

After holing up for a few hours, the ants were biting. He had to get out of this room. By now, Peyton would be asleep, so it would be safe to come out. Lucky got up from his dog bed as soon as Noah opened the door.

"You don't have to follow me around, you know." Apparently, the dog didn't know that since he trailed along. That was another thing he didn't want to admit. He was beginning to like having Lucky around, and the dog didn't talk a mile a minute like a certain other person.

Funny thing, though. All her talking kept his mind from wallowing in regrets and wishing he could turn back the clock. He'd thought he wanted silence, but she was proving him wrong.

What he really wanted was to slip into her room, crawl into bed with her, and lose himself in her sweet body. Being near her and trying to keep his hands off her was a new kind of torture. Not that he'd succeeded in the hands-off part since he kept kissing her. But that had to end, because another time or two and he wouldn't stop with just kissing. The willpower to resist her was close to nonexistent as it was.

"Would you like a cup of tea?" the woman filling his head said as she walked out of the kitchen, a cup in each hand.

He was slipping. He should have been aware she was nearby. That lack of awareness was how one got a knife in the back or a bullet between the eyes. Or how a woman he couldn't get out of his head could sneak up on him.

"I don't drink tea."

"This is special tea. It's got a splash of whiskey in it. Maybe it will help you sleep better."

Nothing was capable of that. "Why are you up?"

She gave him a shy smile. "Because I knew you would be."

Definitely a burrowing termite. Maybe not a flattering image, but it was how he was beginning to think of her. He should hate it—her worming her way into his heart—but he didn't. His SEAL brothers loved him and had his back, but when was the last time someone actually took care of him? That question had an easy answer. His mother, a long time ago.

She held out the cup. "Drink the tea, Noah."

"Yes, ma'am." And that pleased smile of hers...he wished he could take a picture so when he returned to his team, he could look at it and remember the night she'd stayed up with him because she knew he couldn't sleep.

"Come sit." She sat on one end of the sofa, curling her feet under her.

He took the opposite end. "You should be in bed." *With me.* Not that he'd ever allow that to happen, but a man could dream.

"Not really sleepy. I can't stop thinking about that woman. Why does she stay with a man like that?"

"Could be she has no place else to go." His mother hadn't. His father had made sure of that. "Or she doesn't have any money. Or he's made her afraid to leave him."

"Were those the reasons your mother stayed?"

"All of them." He sipped the tea, welcoming the burn of the whiskey as it flowed down his throat. She'd been generous in the pour.

"She never tried to leave?"

Maybe it was that they were sitting in the dark, with only the downtown lights filtering through the windows, or maybe it was the whiskey, or it was just her, but for the first time since it had happened, he wanted to talk about it.

"She tried once, the night he killed her." Even though she still had no place to go, no money, and she was afraid of her husband. He emptied the cup of tea down his throat. Peyton didn't say anything for once, and in her silence, he talked.

"He came home drunk after gambling away the grocery money again. There was no food in the house to feed me, and I guess that was the last straw. She told him she was leaving. He told her she wasn't going anywhere, and no way in hell was she taking me away. Not sure why that mattered since he didn't give a shit about me."

Still, she didn't talk, but she handed him her cup. Why that simple gesture made his damn eyes burn, he didn't know. He swallowed more of the whiskey-laced tea. Now that he'd started this, he had to get it all out.

"I tried to stop him, but he was a big, mean son of a bitch. He knocked her across the room, and she hit her head on the doorframe wrong. Broke her neck. You know what he did?"

He didn't wait for an answer, because of course she didn't. "He fucking cried. 'Baby, wake up,' he said. When she didn't, he got mad all over again, yelling that it was her fault while he went about destroying everything he could get his hands on. I called 911 and begged them to send an ambulance to save my mom." Tears were falling down his cheeks now, and he swiped his hand over his face.

He reached into his pocket and pulled out the pair of dice, dropping them on the coffee table. "These were his so-called lucky dice." He snorted. "They were about as lucky as throwing rocks in the wind."

"If they were his, why do you carry them?"

The question finally breaking her silence was a good one. "To remind me to never be him."

"You could never be him, Noah. You know that, right?"

"That's one of the few things I know." Even though his mother wasn't here to see the man he'd become, he'd never dishonor her by being anything close to his father.

"Where is he now?"

"Prison. He tried to claim that it was an accident, that she tripped and fell, but I testified against him." The scariest day of his life, facing his father in that court-room. "Between my testimony and his extensive record, all the times the cops were called because he'd beat her, along with some other things he'd previously been arrested for, he got life." Hearing that sentence was the first time he'd felt safe from his father.

"Good. What was your mother's name?"

"Darcy." He liked that she asked that, but he didn't like the tears he saw pooling in her eyes. "Don't cry."

"I can if I want to."

How did this woman make him smile when he least wanted to? And how did she keep surprising him, like now when she scooted across the sofa and settled on his lap?

He looked down at her. "Hello there."

The little termite burrowed into him. "Hi."

"What are you doing?" Besides sending him dangerously close to stripping off their clothes and literally burrowing into her.

"You needed a hug, and I'm giving you one."

"My mom loved hugs." He'd forgotten that. "She'd say, 'Here comes the hug bug.' I pretended to hate it, but she knew I didn't. She'd hug people that she knew in the grocery store."

"She sounds like she was a wonderful person. I'm sorry you lost her."

"Me, too. I have a brother…a half brother. We're the same age. Turns out his mother was pregnant at the same time as my mother." Someone had sliced open his brain and all his secrets were spilling out.

"Are you close to him?"

"I am now. I didn't know about him, but he knew about me." He trailed his hand over her back, liking touching her. "When he tracked me down, I didn't want anything to do with him." He chuckled. "Clint's a stubborn one, though. Kept coming around until I got tired of trying to push him away."

"I'm glad you have him, that he's a part of your life."

"So am I." He wasn't sure how she'd ended up straddling him, but she was going to feel his erection in about five seconds. "You need to get off me, princess." Before he forgot she was off limits.

"What if I don't want to?"

"Do it anyway."

Peyton didn't want to move. He'd finally opened up to her…not about everything, but more than he'd wanted to, she thought. If she pushed, she could probably get what she wanted, but he'd regret it, and she'd lose all the ground she'd won. He wasn't ready for her. Not yet. She wasn't normally a patient person, but he was worth waiting for.

He'd asked her to get off him, though, so she would respect that. "I'm hungry," she said as she moved away. "And I have just the thing. Don't go anywhere."

While she put together the snack, she considered how she could get him to talk about why he was on leave from the navy. Whatever it was, keeping it bottled up wasn't going to help him.

Noah stared at the tray, and then lifted his gaze to hers. "This is a little more than a snack, princess."

"Told you I'm hungry." She didn't have a sweet tooth, but cheese? Sign her up. Along with slices of two kinds of cheese, she'd added tart green grapes, thin slices of prosciutto, and stoneground crackers. She picked up one of the two bottles of beer and handed it to him. "This is a dark lager, one of my own recipes. It's darn good, if I do say so myself."

He took a sip of the beer, then another. "Damn good."

"Told ya." Warmth spread through her at his simple praise.

"Not Grandma's Tea," he said, reading the label. "You name this one?"

"No, one of our bartenders came up with that one." She picked up a slice of cheese and popped it in her mouth. "Gotta pee. Be right back." She walked off to his chuckle.

On the way back, as she passed his room, she glanced in, then stopped at seeing his guitar case leaning against the wall. On impulse, she got it and took with her it back to the living room.

She set the case on the sofa next to him. "Will you play for me?"

"No." He picked up the guitar case and walked out of the room. Lucky scrambled up and trotted after him.

She cringed when she heard his bedroom door close. What was his deal? She'd been stunned by how great he was when he'd played Joseph's guitar. He'd lost himself in the music. The moment he'd finished and opened his eyes, though, it was as if he was in pain. Whatever was going on with him was tied to his guitar, which was puzzling.

She'd wondered if something had gone wrong on a mission, but he wouldn't have his guitar with him then, would he? The more he doubled down on keeping his secrets, the more she was determined to get him to talk. Her appetite gone, she carried the tray to the kitchen. After covering the tray with plastic wrap and putting it in the refrigerator, she headed to bed.

Unable to fall asleep, she thought of and discarded ways to get Noah to open up to her. There was no easy answer, so she decided she'd just be his friend and hope that was enough.

The next morning, there was no Noah to be seen. His bedroom door open, the bed made, and his duffel bag on the chair by the window. Where was his guitar? She took several steps toward the closet, then stopped. She'd invaded his privacy enough.

So, breakfast, and then she needed to go see her father. Dalton had to be lying. Her dad wasn't sick, but she needed to hear it from him. She made a pot of coffee, then decided the cheese, crackers, and grapes from last night would make a great breakfast.

Noah returned with Lucky while she was eating. "Good morning." She smiled but didn't get one in return. He was grumpy again. Whatever. If he wanted to be a grumpball, not her problem. "I need to go see my father this morning. You don't need to come with me. I'll be fine."

After unclipping Lucky's leash, he filled a dish with dog food. That done, he poured a cup of coffee. He was ignoring her, and that irritated her. "Look, I'm not sure what I did wrong last night, but I'm sorry. If you don't want to talk to me, that's fine, but you can at least—"

"You have nothing to be sorry for." He sat across the table from her. "There are things I'm just not going to talk about, and why I won't play my guitar is one of them, okay?"

"But you play so beautifully, I don't understand—"

"Drop it, Peyton. There's nothing for you to understand. As soon as you're ready, we'll go see your father, then I need to head to Jack's. You'll be coming with me."

"But…"

Coffee cup in hand, he walked out.

"…I need to find a job." Only Lucky was still there to hear her, and he had nothing to say about that. "Your daddy is very bossy, you know that?" Lucky barked. "I take that as a yes."

She covered the tray, then put it back in the refrigerator. "Guess I better get dressed before bossy man decides to do it for me." Although, she wouldn't so much mind that. Better yet if he undressed her.

Normally, she wore jeans to the brewery if it wasn't a day for a client meeting or an event because she'd be brewing beer. But today, she needed to be strong and face her father with confidence. So, the power suit again it was.

As she dressed, she couldn't stop wondering why Noah wouldn't touch his guitar when how much he loved playing was obvious.

"Here goes nothing," she said.

Noah leaned against the wall outside her father's office. "I'll be right here."

She purposely left the door open because she wanted him to know she wouldn't keep secrets from him. Maybe he'd get the message, but probably not. Her father glanced up from the computer screen when she walked in.

"Hi, Dad."

"So you've finally come to your senses?"

"In what way?" Why was her heart pounding so hard? This was her father, the man who'd raised her. She shouldn't be so nervous that her knees had turned to jelly. Before her legs betrayed her and she face-planted to the floor, she lowered to the chair in front of his desk.

"Did you know Eddie went on strike?"

That wasn't an answer to her question, but what? "Because?"

"Said he wouldn't come back to work until you did."

She laughed. God bless that old man. There had been times when he'd been more of a parent to her than her own father. With Eddie's belief in her, and his taking a stand on her behalf, her nerves settled.

"It's not funny. He said he's ready to retire, but you're the only one he'll turn over his brewery to. Like it's his brewery and his decision."

"Well, without him, you've got no beer." Or without

her, but if her return was dependent on marrying Dalton, she definitely needed to continue her job search.

"You need to come back, and then he'll stop his foolishness."

"And you won't expect me to marry Dalton?"

By the expression on his face, one would think she'd just said she was going to dance naked through downtown Asheville. "Dalton loves you, Peyton. He's worried about you. He said you have that man from the waterfall living with you. What in the world is going on with you?"

If Dalton was in front of her right now, she'd punch him in the nose. She stood, dropped her hands to his desk, and looked her father in the eyes. "Dalton does not love me. All he wanted was control of Elk Antler." That was what she'd decided, anyway. She'd thought about his behavior a lot since becoming a runaway bride, and why else was he so determined to get his hands on her shares?

"Don't be ridiculous."

"Why do you think I ran away from my own wedding? He told his best man he was marrying me for my shares of Elk Antler. And you know what else your precious Dalton did? He let himself into my home, and when I locked myself in the bathroom, he broke the door down. Told me we were going to Vegas and getting married whether I wanted to or not." She banged a fist on his desk. "And then he lied and said you were dying, and me marrying him was your dying wish."

She waited for him to deny it, but he wouldn't even look at her.

"Dad?" Her knees buckled, and she sank down on the chair. "Oh, God. It's true, isn't it? When were you going to tell me?"

"After you were married." He finally met her eyes. "I wanted to see you happy and taken care of."

If she hadn't just learned her father was dying, she would be angry. "I'm perfectly capable of taking care of myself. But that's not the important thing right now. Talk to me. What's wrong, and what are we doing about it?" She was… She didn't even know which emotion to grab hold of. Shocked? Afraid? Hurt that he hadn't told her before now? Terrified he would die never having loved her? As long as he was still living, she had hope that the day would come when he'd learn to love her. Tears burned her eyes, threatening to run over. She willed them back. If ever her father needed her, needed her to be strong for him, it was now.

He blew out a breath. "It's lung cancer."

"But you don't smoke."

"Lung cancer doesn't always care if one smokes or not."

He couldn't die. She wouldn't let him.

Chapter Sixteen

Noah had been surprised that Peyton had left the door open, and he shamelessly eavesdropped on their conversation as her father told her about his treatment. When her voice trembled, he pressed his feet to the floor to keep from going to her.

A man came around the corner, and he stared into the face of her ex-boyfriend. The man was headed for the office, and Noah stepped in front of the open doorway. "You can't go in there."

Dalton scowled. "What the hell are you doing here?"

"Making sure you stay away from Peyton."

"Get out of my way."

"No. You need to leave Peyton and her father alone right now." He didn't want to cause a scene, but if he had to physically carry the man away, he wouldn't hesitate.

"What's going on here?"

Noah glanced back at Peyton's father. "Your daughter doesn't want this man near her, so I'm making sure he stays away from her."

"Gerald, this man threatened me. You need to call the police if he doesn't leave," Dalton said.

Her father stepped around him. "You're the man from the waterfall."

"Yes, sir. Noah Alba." He held out his hand, not expecting her father to take it, but he did.

"I'm Gerald Sutton. Explain what's going on."

"What's going on is this man—"

"I'm asking him," Sutton said, shooting a glare at Dalton.

"As Peyton told you, she doesn't want to marry him, but he's harassing her, so she asked me to be her bodyguard for a few days." *Her person.*

"That's a lie," Dalton said.

"So you didn't break down her bathroom door when she locked herself in because she was afraid of you? You didn't threaten to force her to marry you? You didn't grab her so hard that you left a bruise on her arm?"

"This is ridiculous. Don't listen to this man, Gerald."

Noah opened his phone and brought up one of the photos he'd taken of her arm. He handed Sutton his phone. "I tried to get her to call the police, but all she wants is to be left alone."

Sutton lifted his gaze from the phone and stared hard at Dalton. "You did this to my daughter?"

"I would never hurt her. I love her. He probably put that bruise on her."

"Dad, everything Noah said is true." Peyton pushed her way past him, coming to a stop in front of Dalton.

Noah was hard pressed not to scoop her up and carry her away from the bastard. He managed to resist, but as soon as he could get her out of this damn place, he'd take her to Jack's and turn her over to the puppies. Then she'd smile again.

"How dare you blame Noah for something you did." She poked Dalton in the chest. "For the last time, I am not going to marry you."

Sutton put his arm around his daughter and pulled her back. "You're fired, Dalton. Effective immediately."

Noah decided he might like her father after all.

"You can't be serious," Dalton said. "This is all just a misunderstanding."

"I couldn't be more serious. And putting a bruise on my daughter's arm is not a misunderstanding. Collect your personal effects and then leave the building. Now." He lifted a chin at Noah. "Go with him and make sure he doesn't take anything that doesn't belong to him."

"Yes, sir." And he'd do it with pleasure.

"You're going to regret this, Gerald."

"I have regrets, but this isn't one of them." He put his hand on Peyton's back and ushered her into his office, closing the door behind them.

Dalton glared at him. "This is your fault."

"Whatever." The man would blame everyone but himself for what just happened, and Noah had no inclination to set him straight. "You heard the man. He wants you gone. You have ten minutes to walk out the door before I physically carry you out."

"You're going to be sorry you messed with me."

Doubtful. "Nine minutes now." He followed Dalton to an office down the hall. Positioning himself just inside the door, he watched the man pile personal items on the desk. When he unplugged a laptop, Noah took a wild guess. "That's not yours." That got him a death glare, but Dalton dropped the cord. When he opened a filing cabinet, Noah shook his head. "Nice try, but any folders in there belong to the company."

Noah noticed a box pushed up against the wall with beer bottles in it. Samples maybe? He walked over, removed all but one of the bottles, then dropped the box on the desk. "Put your junk in here. And to show that I'm a nice guy, you can keep the beer. I figure you could use it after losing your job and the girl." He almost snorted at the nice guy comment.

"Fuck you."

Noah glanced at his watch. "Two minutes if you want to walk out of here on your own."

Dalton snatched up the box. "You think you can just waltz in and take away everything I've worked for? Not gonna happen, pal."

"I see you anywhere near Peyton, and you'll regret it. That's not a threat, *pal*. It's a promise." He had a bad feeling that the man was desperate, and desperate men got stupid.

He followed behind Dalton to the parking lot, then stood outside until his car disappeared from sight. "Okay then. That was fun." For real.

"I expect you back to work first thing tomorrow."

Peyton would have been overjoyed to hear that, and her father firing Dalton, if she hadn't gotten the worst news of her life. "You know I'll be here. But you have to promise not to shut me out of what's going on with you."

"I don't want you worrying about me."

"You've got to be kidding me." How could he possibly think she wouldn't worry about him? "I mean it, Dad. There's no way I'm going to let you go through this alone. I want to go with you to your next doctor's appointment."

"Peyton—"

"Don't Peyton me. You've never let me in, not really. There's always been a wall between us, and I don't understand why. But that changes as of today."

A smile played on his lips. "Does it now?"

"Yes, and maybe someday you'll explain that wall to me."

"Maybe I will." He picked up his phone and pulled up his calendar. "My next doctor's appointment is Monday at two."

"Good, and don't you dare go without me." Relief spread through her that she'd won this battle. Now all she had to do was win the battle for his life.

"Now tell me about this Noah Alba guy. How did you meet him?"

"At the waterfall." How to explain Noah? She doubted her father wanted to hear that she wanted to jump Noah's bones, so she'd leave that part out.

"You didn't arrange to meet him there?"

"No!" That was what he thought of her, that she'd meet another man on her wedding day? "He came down when I was there. I'd never seen him before in my life."

"Yet you brought a strange man home with you?"

That did sound bad, she'd give him that. "He's been nothing but honorable toward me." Did tingly kisses count as honorable? She decided they did. "He's a Navy SEAL, and after Dalton pulled his stupid stunt, I asked Noah if he'd be my bodyguard for a few days. Since I'm sure you're wondering, he's staying in my guest room."

"Why is a SEAL hanging out in Asheville? Last I heard, there's not a navy base here."

"He's on medical leave." Was he? He'd never said exactly what kind of leave he was on, but for her father's benefit, that would do. "He has a friend here he's spending time with. Jack was his teammate before he left the navy. Now he trains therapy dogs. You should let me take you out there sometime. It's pretty awesome what he does."

"I'll take you up on that." He tapped his fingers on his desk, and she knew that look. He was thinking something through. "Bring your…bodyguard to dinner tonight."

"Why?"

"A man I don't know is living with my daughter? I think I need to assure myself that he's what you say he is, an honorable man."

Now he wanted to start playing daddy? A part of her resented that he had never taken an interest in her life or friends before now, but the part that had always wanted his attention was okay with it. More than okay.

"What time?"

"Six."

"We'll be there." Hopefully, Noah would agree.

"You okay?"

Peyton shrugged. "Yeah. No." They'd stopped by her loft to pick up Lucky and so she could change clothes. Now they were on the way to Jack's dog place. Noah had let her brood in silence until now, and not up to talking, she appreciated that.

"I'm sorry about your father, princess. I really thought Dalton was lying."

"Me, too. God, I wish he had been." She buried her face in her hands. She wouldn't cry, not now. That would happen later tonight when she was alone in her bed.

He put his hand on her knee and squeezed. "Cancer doesn't necessarily mean a death sentence. There's all kinds—"

"He's not going to die! Don't even imply that's a pos-

sibility." She'd just yelled at him, and all he was trying
to do was comfort her. "I'm sorry. You didn't say anything wrong. It's just…it's just…" She didn't have the
words to explain how scared she was.

"That you're afraid."

"Yes," she whispered. So afraid. For the first time
since she'd been dropped off to her father as if she were
nothing more than unwanted baggage, she had hope
that she meant more to him than a daughter he'd never
wanted. He'd said that maybe he would tell her why
he'd built a wall between them, and she really needed
to understand the reason.

"Your dad surprised me," Noah said. "I was prepared
not to like him, then he went and fired your asshole ex.
I have to respect that."

That had surprised her, too, because Dalton had always been the son she was sure her father wished she'd
been. "I don't know what to think anymore."

"Maybe don't overthink it?" He came to a stop in
front of the kennels. "He loves you, princess. I don't
know what the deal is between the two of you, but I do
know that much."

"He wants us to come to dinner tonight."

"No. You need time alone with him, so you go, but
I'm not a dinner with a girl's father kind of man."

She wanted to punch him. Or kiss him. Either thing
would give her the satisfaction she needed right now. "I
told him you'd be there, so you will be there."

"You shouldn't make plans that involve me without
talking to me."

"Get over yourself, Noah." She unbuckled her seatbelt. "I know something awful happened to you, and

I'm sorry for that, but the world doesn't revolve around you. We have to be there at six."

Not giving him a chance to refuse, she exited the car and headed straight for the puppy nursery. The puppies all yipped, rushing to her as soon as she stepped inside the room. This was what she needed…puppy love. She sat in the middle of the floor, and they bounced around her, begging for her attention.

She tried to put everything out of her mind except for the puppies, but she couldn't help thinking that she wasn't being fair to Noah. All he'd signed up for was the role as her bodyguard. Dinners with her father weren't in his job description, and she'd been wrong to make plans on his behalf.

He wasn't her boyfriend. Not that she wouldn't like if it he was. She totally would. But other than spine-tingly kisses—and those were only to hush her—he'd shown no interest in her. Sad, that. She needed to apologize and tell him he didn't have to come with her to dinner.

Besides, some one-on-one time with her father would be good. For the first time since she'd come to live with him, he'd been almost warm toward her. Now that the door seemed to be open, she wasn't going to let him slam it shut in her face.

"Nope, not going to happen."

At hearing her voice, the puppies swarmed her, and she fell to her back, letting them cover her with their wiggling bodies. They all tried to lick her face off, making her giggle. For a few minutes, she'd let herself push aside thoughts of her father and Noah, and then she'd go find Noah and apologize.

Chapter Seventeen

"I want to test his reaction to noises," Jack said.

"Why?" Noah glanced over at the puppy building. He'd been an ass to Peyton, and he needed to tell her he was sorry. She'd just learned her father was sick, and he should have been more understanding. Instead, he'd made it about him.

He realized Jack had stopped talking. "Sorry, what?"

"I said we need to know how he'll react to loud noises, like firecrackers, thunder, sirens, trucks backfiring. Things like that." Jack crossed his arms over his chest. "Are you even listening to me?"

"Hold this." He handed Jack the end of Lucky's leash. "Be right back." He headed for the puppy building. Until he got right with Peyton, he wouldn't be able to pay attention to whatever Jack was trying to teach him.

The inside of the building was bright, and dog toys were scattered over the floor. Right in the middle of that floor was Peyton on her back, a wiggling mass of puppies crawling all over her while she hysterically laughed. Her black hair was spread around her head, and sweet Jesus, her T-shirt was pushed up to just below her breasts, exposing the creamy white skin of her stomach. He wanted to put his tongue on that skin, wanted to know how soft she would feel under his fingers.

Something inside his chest expanded, making it hard to breathe. She was beautiful. Of course, he already knew that, but he hadn't *known it* known it. Not like this, where he was struck with a longing he'd never experienced before. Not even with the woman he was once supposed to marry.

He was in dangerous territory. She deserved so much more than he knew how to give at this time in his life. It was better to leave her mad at him. He'd hang around for a few days, make sure her ex left her alone, and then he'd get out of her life. With that decision made, he turned to leave.

"Noah?"

So much for sneaking out. "Yeah?"

"I was coming to talk to you." She pushed the puppies away, and then came to stand in front of him. "You're right. I shouldn't have made plans without talking to you first, and I'm sorry."

"'Sometimes sorry just ain't good enough.'" At the hurt in her eyes, he wanted to punch himself in the face.

"Blake Shelton's 'I'm Sorry,' but you're a jerk, Noah."

He caught her hand when she tried to walk away. "You're right, I am. That slipped out. I have…used to have a song thing. A kind of parlor trick, I guess. I can…could come up with a song for every situation. Ask Jack if you don't believe me. When you said you were sorry, I guess out of habit that song popped into my head and I spoke without thinking." And that was entirely too much talking.

"Oh, okay, but why are you saying you used to? Seems like you can still do it."

"Not anymore." He realized he was still holding her hand, and he reluctantly let go. "I came in here to apologize to you for the way I talked to you in the car. I'll go with you to dinner tonight."

She studied him for a moment, then said, "But you really don't want to."

"You got me there." He brushed a lock of hair away from her cheek before he realized what he was doing. "Still, I'll come with you." A calculating gleam appeared in her eyes, making him nervous.

"I'll make you a trade. You don't have to come if you'll kiss me whenever I want you to."

Huh? What the devil was she up to? Not that he minded kissing her...not at all. "What do you want from me, Peyton?"

"I don't expect anything from you except for tingles."

"Tingles?"

"Yeah, I've never had them before you kissed me. I want more." She trailed a finger over his bottom lip. "Lots more. From you."

"Never?" No man had ever made this incredible woman tingle? But he had? Something that felt a lot like satisfaction filled him.

"Until you, no. The first time you kissed me, it was like I finally got it, what the big deal was. So, I want more. And I mean more than just kisses. I think you could do a lot more for me than my vibrator. I don't expect romance and roses. You won't tell me why you're on leave from the navy, but I know you'll have to go back. I'm not going to fall in love with you or hope for a commitment. Seems like that would be a good arrangement for both of us. You have access to my body in exchange for tingles…and, Noah, I want tingles that make me see stars. I want to know—"

There was nothing to do but kiss her. Any more words out of her mouth and he'd be lowering her to the floor and giving her those tingles she wanted while a dozen puppies tried to participate in the fun.

She nestled into him as if she belonged there. He slid his hands down to her hips, pressed his fingers into her skin, and rolled his hips against her, letting her know what she was doing to him.

"Noah."

That whisper of his name against his lips was almost his undoing. He almost didn't care if they gave the puppies a show, but grasping the thin thread of control he still possessed, he broke the kiss. Before anything more could happen between them, he needed to be sure she meant what she'd said. He could give her those tingles she wanted, could make her body sing, but that was it.

He cupped her cheek and traced her bottom lip— damp from his kiss—with his thumb. "We'll talk about this later, princess. Right now, I have to get back to Jack before he comes looking for me." He brushed his mouth over hers, then forced his feet to take him away from her.

If he was smart, he wouldn't even consider agreeing to what she wanted, but he didn't want to be smart. Not with her, not when she looked at him with those sky-blue eyes shimmering with desire.

For the next few hours, he'd get his mind on his lessons with Lucky. As soon as Jack said they were done, all bets were off. He had a few lessons of his own for Peyton, but first they'd talk. As long as she could assure him she had no expectations beyond the pleasure they could give each other, he'd show her how it could be between a man and a woman.

"You've taken to wearing lipstick now?" Jack said, smirking.

"Shut it." He swiped a hand over his mouth, and when Jack laughed, he hooked his leg behind Jack's, putting his friend's ass on the ground. That resulted in a round of wrestling. Thinking it was a new game, Lucky joined the fray. He managed to pin Jack, laughing when Lucky covered Jack's face with slobbery licks.

"Is this a new type of training?"

Noah looked up to see Nichole staring down at them. "As soon as your boyfriend cries uncle, I'll give him back to you."

She bent over, putting her face near Jack's. "Need some help, babe?"

He grinned at her. "Watch and learn." With that, he flipped over, scissored his legs around Noah's, and pinned Noah.

Noah glanced at Nichole. "I let him do that so he would appear manly in front of you."

She slapped a hand over her chest. "So manly I'm going to swoon on the spot. When you boys are done playing, I brought lunch."

"You're the best," Jack said.

Her eyes softened as she smiled at him. "For you, always."

"I'm going to get sugar overload from the two of you." Noah rolled away from Jack and then stood. "Peyton's here. Is there enough for her, too?"

Nichole nodded. "Yep. Jack told me she was here when he called earlier."

"Great. I'll go get her."

"We'll be over there." She pointed at a picnic table under the shade of a tree.

"Be right back." Lucky followed him. "You could have stayed with Jack." When he reached the building, he stopped. "You can't come in here." Lucky stuck his nose to the crack in the door and wagged his tail. "You smell the puppies, huh? Sit." Damn if the dog didn't sit. "Good boy. Stay."

He slipped into the building, closing the door before Lucky could follow him in. Peyton must have worn the puppies out. They were all conked out, some next to her and three on her lap. She glanced up at him and smiled. There was that weird feeling in his chest again.

"Hey. Nichole's here, and she brought lunch."

"How nice." Peyton eased the puppies in her lap onto the floor, then pushed up. All she'd been able to think about after Noah had kissed her earlier was that he'd agreed to talk about…well, having a fling she supposed. She'd never had a fling before, and the idea excited her. Mostly because it would be with him, but a part of it was also because it was outside the norm of her behavior, and she was ready for a little fun.

Lunch with Noah's friends was entertaining, and she was able to push aside worry for her father for a while. Noah and Jack seemed to enjoy going at each other, their digs and insults making her and Nichole laugh.

"Are they always like this?" she asked.

Nichole chuckled. "You should see them when the whole team's together. It's like being in the locker room of fifteen-year-old boys."

"Hey," Jack said. "I resemble that remark."

Noah threw a pickle at him. "She nailed it. Fifteen

is about your maturity level. Since you left the team, I haven't had to check my bed for snakes."

"You didn't," Nichole said, her wide eyes on her boyfriend.

"It was just a little green snake." Jack smirked. "He screamed like a girl."

"I willingly admit to that. The damn thing crawled up my leg," Noah said. "I got him back, though."

"What did you do?" Peyton was fascinated by this new side of Noah. His voice wasn't laced with sorrow and there was laughter in his eyes.

"I put itching powder in his underwear."

"My balls will never forgive you," Jack said.

Peyton lost it, laughing so hard she got hiccups.

"You okay?" Noah patted her back. "Don't pass out on me, princess." He put his mouth close to her ear. "We got plans later."

"Before we go home, I need to take Joseph dinner," Peyton said after Noah parked his car in the garage. *Home.* She really liked saying that to him.

But she couldn't let herself think of him being a part of her life. She'd told him she had no expectations beyond a physical relationship, and she'd keep her word. He'd said they needed to talk, but maybe he'd made a decision and by plans, he meant he was agreeable.

The only thing tempering her excitement was her worry for her father. He hadn't said what stage his cancer was, and she hadn't thought to ask. It had to be in the early stages since he had annual physicals. She also wanted to know what treatment was planned for him, and she'd find that out at dinner. It really would be best if Noah didn't come with her so she could have a serious talk with her dad.

"In here," she said when they came to a bar and grill. "Joseph loves their cheeseburgers."

"You're a nice person, princess."

His compliment warmed her, but not as much as the hand he put on her back did. Dalton had never complimented her or rested his hand on her as if he liked touching her, and until now, she hadn't realized how much she had been missing.

"I'll wait out here with Lucky," Noah said.

"Be back in a few." While she waited for her order to be ready, she watched Noah through the front window, smiling when he leaned over and said something to Lucky while running his hand down the dog's back... the same dog he swore he didn't want any part of.

Noah could pretend all he wanted that he didn't care about anything, but the man had a soft heart. That was the only soft thing about him, though. Her gaze slid over his shoulders and the muscles that flexed as he bent down to pet Lucky. From there, her eyes traveled down, past a trim waist to the firm butt encased in a pair of well-worn jeans. She'd never been a butt person, believing her turn-on was a man's eyes, but then she'd never had Noah's behind to admire before.

"He's pretty hot," the waitress said as she set a to-go bag on the counter.

Peyton tore her gaze away from Noah. "Who?"

The girl grinned. "The man you're drooling over. Is he yours?"

She wished. "He's just a friend."

"Uh-huh." The girl shook a finger at her. "We don't

eat a man up with our eyes when he's just a friend, and you were eating him alive."

Peyton laughed. "I totally was."

"Well, here's to getting lucky tonight," she said after Peyton paid.

"Uh, thanks." She smiled as she walked out. One could hope, right?

Joseph picked up his guitar and started playing when they stopped in front of him.

"I know this one." She glanced at Noah. "Do you?"

"Yep. It's 'Two Is Better Than One' from the band Boys Like Girls."

"Who sang it on their album?" Other than Joseph, she'd never met anyone who knew songs like she did, and it was pretty cool that they had that in common.

"Taylor Swift." He bumped his arm against hers. "You're going to have to try harder to stump me."

"Hmm, I see a name-that-song war on the agenda. When I win, I want a date for my prize."

"I don't date."

"No? Then I guess you better win." Now that the idea was in her head, she really wanted a real date with him.

"And what do I get when I win? Because I'm going to."

"Don't count on it, but on the slim chance you do, what do you want?"

He glanced at Joseph. "I'll tell you later."

Was he thinking of something dirty? Something that would include turbocharged tingles? Lordy, she hoped so.

Joseph set down his guitar after finishing the song. Amusement was in his eyes as he shifted his gaze from her to Noah and then back to her. "Looks like you found your match, Miss Peyton."

Had she ever! She glanced at Noah. "Oh, I don't know. I'm confident he's going to have to plan a date." All she got on that was a grunt. Was she pushing him too hard? "Anyway, here's a burger." She set the container down, then pulled a five-dollar bill from her pocket and dropped it in his cup.

"Why don't you date?" she asked Noah as they walked to her loft.

"I spend half my life on deployment. It's not ideal for relationships."

"Good thing I'm not looking for a relationship then, but I do want my date when I win."

"If you win, princess."

She lifted her gaze to the sky. "Poor boy's delusional."

Chapter Eighteen

"You sure you don't want to come in? Have some dinner?"

Noah shook his head. "I'm sure. I think some one-on-one time with your father will do you both good. Call me when you're ready to go."

As soon as she got out of the car, Lucky jumped to the passenger seat. "I didn't tell you that you could get up here." The dog put his paw on Noah's arm and looked up at him with those two-colored eyes. "You think you're cute, don't you?" He was kind of cute, and Noah sighed. "Fine, you can stay there."

Since Peyton would be safe with her father, he had a few errands to run. His first stop was to buy condoms at the Walmart they'd passed on the way. By the time he and Peyton arrived back at her loft, she'd only had twenty minutes to change clothes before she needed to leave, so they hadn't had *the* talk.

Although the smart thing would be a firm no, he wouldn't agree to what she wanted, he accepted that saying no to Peyton was next to impossible. Besides, he was losing his desire to refuse her. As long as she could convince him that she wasn't looking for a relationship, he was in. So, he would prepare for the inevitable and buy condoms. He also bought a prepaid phone, and when he got back to the car, he programmed his cell number in it.

His second stop was to see Joseph. He hadn't wanted to ask earlier while Peyton was with them if Joseph had seen Dalton still hanging around. When they were close to Joseph, Lucky's ears perked up, his tail wagged, and he strained at the leash.

"Easy, goofball. We'll get to him." So far, the only person Lucky hadn't liked was Dalton. If nothing else, the dog had discerning tastes.

"There's my favorite boy," Joseph said, opening his arms to Lucky, which was all the invitation the dog needed to slobber Joseph's face with kisses. Once Lucky settled down, Joseph said, "Got you something." He pulled a treat out of his pocket.

Noah chuckled. "No wonder he loves you."

"Gotta keep my boy happy." He lifted his gaze to Noah. "Where's Miss Peyton tonight?"

"She's having dinner with her father." Noah squatted. "You see her ex hanging around today?"

"This morning. Across the street from her place for about an hour. I didn't want to say anything this afternoon and upset her. I figured as long as you're with her, she's safe."

"You have my word on that."

"He's looking a bit raggedy. That's unlike him. He always dressed to the nines."

"That's not a good sign." It likely meant the man was getting desperate.

"You still military?"

"Yeah," Noah automatically said. He grinned. Crafty old man. "I never told you I was in the military."

"Didn't have to. You got that look. A Marine here. I was in Desert Storm. Was never so glad to get out of that place when my time was up. Got messed up for a while with drugs and liquor. Lost my wife and home. Least I don't have any kids I'm missing."

The few times Noah had been around him, he hadn't seen any hint of red eyes or a slurred voice. "You're clean now?"

"For nine years. And if you're thinking you should do something to help me get off the streets, you can take your do-gooder thoughts and find someone else to save. I like my life just as it is." He patted his guitar. "Lucille and I make people happy, and we earn all the living we need."

Noah had been thinking something like that.

"Let's get back to talking about you, Mr. Alba. Army?"

"Shut your mouth, man. Navy." And because he couldn't resist bragging a little to a Marine, he added, "I'm a SEAL."

Joseph's grin stretched from ear to ear. "Well, la-tee-da. Don't that make you special?"

He knew Joseph was teasing, but in the blink of an eye, his horror show flashed in front of his eyes. He was not fucking special. Because of him, a young translator and a damn good dog were dead. "I have to go."

"Suppose you do. But first, my apology for bringing up bad memories. I have some of those, too. Why I tried to drink myself into oblivion. My best friend died because of me, and no, I'm not going to tell you the story. I don't talk about it ever. But, Mr. Alba...can I call you Noah?"

Unable to speak past the baseball-size rock in his throat, Noah only nodded. He got not talking about shit that gave you nightmares and made you want to drown your memories in drugs or alcohol, whichever worked.

Joseph dropped his hand to Noah's knee. "It was war, frogman, and nothing makes sense in war. So don't beat yourself up so hard that you don't see what's right in front of you."

"And what's right in front of me, Marine?" He really needed to know the answer to that from a street-living man who was probably wiser than the head doc Noah had to see in the morning.

"A beautiful, kind, pure-hearted girl, but if you hurt her, this Marine still knows how to send a SEAL to hell."

"She deserves better than me." And wasn't that the truth?

"She deserves whatever makes her happy. Bring that dog back to see me after you get over your snit," Joseph said as Noah stood.

He was not in a snit. He was just…antsy. Talking to Joseph was putting thoughts in his head, like what if he could be the kind of man Peyton deserved? What would it take to become that man? What if he tried, failed, and did hurt her in the process? They were questions he wasn't ready for, didn't have the answers to.

"I need to go." He pulled the prepaid phone from his pocket. "Got you this. My number's in it. Her ex comes around again, call me."

"You know, we could make him disappear, you and me. We have the know-how."

Noah barely refrained from rolling his eyes. "Let's assume it won't come to that." Hatching a murder plot with a homeless Marine was the last thing he needed. He grabbed Lucky's leash, then stood.

"Well, if it does, I got your six, frogman."

"Good to know."

His errands done, he headed back to Peyton's father's house. He'd already left her unprotected too long. When he arrived, he parked across the street where he could keep an eye on the house.

While he waited for Peyton to call, he thought about her. If the timing was right, he'd want to see where a relationship with her could go. He could imagine a lifetime of waking up to her every morning, of listening in amusement when she went off on one of her tangents and then kissing her silly when she did. But along with not having answers to the questions rumbling around in his mind, the timing couldn't be more wrong.

Soon, he'd have to return to his team, and his time with her would be nothing more than an interlude from his real life. And if that was regret he was feeling, he'd get over it. The day would come when she'd meet a man who didn't have a head crawling with demons, and he'd be happy for her…even if he hated the idea of another man touching her.

His phone rang, his brother's name appearing on the screen. "Hey, brother from another mother. Sup?" Clint had started the silly other mother joke, and initially, Noah had resented it. He was over it and had come to see the humor in it.

"It's like you forgot you had a brother."

"Like you'd allow that to happen, and honest, I planned to call you soon. I'm just trying to get my shit straight." Clint knew he was on leave, but all Noah had told him was that he'd messed up.

"How's that going?"

"It's going."

"As talkative as ever, I see. That's okay. You can share all when I come to Asheville this weekend."

"You don't have to check on me. Jack's doing a good job of keeping me in line."

"I'm sure he is, and I'm not coming specifically to see you. That's just a bonus of the trip. You remember I told you about Nichole's brother Mark and the kick-ass games he creates?"

"Yeah."

"I have a contract offer on his newest one. It's big, and I want to tell him in person. He's going to be one rich boy."

"That's great. I haven't met him yet."

"Surprising since you're staying with Jack and Nichole."

"About that…" He didn't want to try to explain Peyton over the phone and why he was staying with her. "We'll talk when you get here."

"You bet we will. Mom wants to know when you're gonna come see her."

"I don't know. If I can make it happen, I'll make a detour before reporting back to base." Maine would be a hell of a detour, but he might be able to pull it off.

Clint's mother, after learning Noah's history, had as much as adopted him. She was another thing he'd resented at first, but Leah Barnes was as bull headed as her son. It hadn't taken long to understand she and her son were his father's victims as much as he and his mom were. Now they were his family.

"Tell her I'll expect a blueberry pie with my name on it."

"You know she'll have that for you without your asking. And you better be sharing that pie with me."

"You get pie all the time." He lived in the same town with her.

"Don't care. I want half of yours."

Noah laughed. Boneheaded brother. "Don't piss me off between now and then, and I'll think about it."

"Nothing to think about."

"How's Rafe?"

"As hot as ever. He said to tell you hi."

"Tell him hi back, and that I'll share my pie with him." Clint and Rafe had been together for three years, and Noah didn't think he could find a better man for his brother.

"Asswipe. You're not giving him my pie. Gotta go."

"You need me to pick you up at the airport?" He absently scratched Lucky's neck.

"Nah, I'm renting a car, and I'm staying at Mark's house, so I'm good all around. I'll see you Saturday, and brother mine, we're going to have a nice long talk. You're gonna tell me what this leave is all about and why you're in Asheville."

Maybe. Maybe not. "Later, dorkbucket." He tried to disconnect before Clint could respond, but he wasn't fast enough.

"Love ya, fartface."

Noah grinned at his phone. That was how they ended every call, trying to be the last one to insult the other. He wondered what Clint would think of Peyton. No, he didn't need to wonder. His brother was going to love her.

"Tell me why this Noah guy isn't here when I specifically invited him."

Peyton set her fork down. "He's not here because I

told him he didn't have to come. He's not a boyfriend you have to vet."

"A man I don't know is living with my daughter and I shouldn't be concerned?"

"You've never been concerned before." About anything to do with her life. "Why start now?" She didn't want to argue with her father, but his lack of interest in her had always hurt. What had changed?

"Eat your dinner."

Anger burned through her, and she took several deep breaths to calm down. Why wouldn't he talk to her, treat her like a daughter he loved? But he didn't love her, did he? She was only an obligation, and she supposed she should be thankful he'd given her a home when her mother decided being a mother wasn't for her. He didn't have to, and she'd never gone without food, clothing, and a roof over her head. She was grateful, truly, but she'd give all that up for a father who loved her.

Now he was possibly dying, and she'd hoped that would bring them closer. Since he obviously wasn't going to make an effort to fix whatever was broken between them, it was up to her. So, she'd let go of the anger and disappointment and the little girl wanting his approval. She'd pretend that none of that mattered, and she'd be the daughter he needed to get through what all was coming at him. She'd make sure he lived so that just maybe the day would come when he'd tell her what was lacking in her that he couldn't love her, and then she could fix herself.

Instead of coming back with a snarky retort, she dutifully picked up her fork. "This is good," she said of the manicotti.

"It was your favorite as a child."

Yeah, it was, and that he'd made it for her tonight made her want to hug him, but he'd never liked shows of affection. "It's been a while since you've made it for me. Thanks, Dad."

He gave her a rare smile. "There's enough for you to take a container home. Maybe that man you won't talk about would like some."

She laughed. "Maybe so." Leaning across the table, she put her hand on her father's. "I don't want you to die. I don't care how hard you try to push me away, I'm going to be in your face over this. I'll be at your doctor's appointment on Monday, and I'll be there for your treatments. I've never been sure you loved me, but I love you, so deal with it."

"You think I don't love you?"

Her heart tripled its beat. This was a moment of truth between them, and she knew, just knew, that the answers to all her questions were within her reach. All she had to do was say the right thing. What was the right thing? The truth. If that didn't heal the rift between them, nothing would. So, the truth it was.

"You gave me a home and all the material things a child needed, and I'll always be grateful for that. You don't have to love me, but I always wanted you to. I tried so hard to please you so you wouldn't give me away, too. And I thought that maybe if I pleased you enough, you might decide to love me. But you never did. There was a wall between us that I couldn't find a way to scale." There was more she wanted to say, but tears were burning her eyes, her throat was closing up, and her voice was trembling.

"It wasn't you that was lacking, Peyton," her father

softly said. "It was never you." He sighed. "I should have told you this a long time ago. Wait here."

While he was gone, she used her napkin to wipe away her tears. She would not cry. For the first time, she'd bared her heart to her father, and all she'd gotten back was the assurance that she wasn't lacking. That was better than nothing, she supposed.

Her father returned and handed her a photo. She studied it, then lifted her gaze to his. "Who are they?" Was this the photo she'd caught him looking at all those years ago? He was in the picture, his arm around a beautiful woman and his hand on the shoulder of a young boy. By their smiles, they appeared happy. She guessed her father was in his twenties when it was taken.

"My wife and son."

"What? You were married?" How did she not know that?

"Yes. Before you were born."

"I don't understand."

He took the photo and stared at it. "Her name was Laura and that's Robbie, our son. They were my world."

She'd never been his world, and it hurt that there was a child he'd loved. Then it hit her. "I have a brother?"

"Had, and yes."

There was so much pain in his voice in that one word. "Why didn't you ever tell me? What happened?"

He stood, walked to the dining room window, and looked out at the darkness. His shoulders slumped and he bowed his head. "When you first came to live with me, you were too young for a story about death and heartbreak. As time went on, I…I just never found the right moment to tell you.

"As for what happened, they drowned." He turned

and faced her. "I was a partner in a law firm, too damn busy to take a full week of vacation. Laura and Robbie went ahead to the beach, and I was to join them for a long weekend. They were playing in the water and got caught in a riptide. Laura's body was recovered. Robbie's wasn't."

"Oh, God."

A sad smile crossed his face. "I wasn't there to save them, and I'll never forgive myself for that. I blamed my job for not being with them and never returned to the firm. A few weeks later, I got in my car with no destination in mind and ended up in Asheville. On my third day here, I was mindlessly walking around downtown when I saw a for sale sign for the brewery. I didn't know a thing about beer other than I liked it, but I thought, why not. So I bought it."

He scrubbed a hand over his face. "There's not a day that goes by that I haven't missed them, that I haven't regretted I put work ahead of my family. I often wonder what kind of man Robbie would have grown up to be."

She wanted to go to him, to comfort him, but she stayed in her seat. If he rejected her, he would crush her, more than she already was. He didn't love her because his heart belonged to his dead son. Had he seen something of Robbie in Dalton? Was that why he'd wanted her to marry Dalton? Tears burned her eyes again, and she squeezed them shut.

Since coming to live with him, she'd tried so hard to win his love and approval so he wouldn't give her away. He'd kept her while emotionally starving her. At least she now knew the reason, but she didn't feel any better for it.

"I'm sorry I'm not your son," she whispered.

He visibly shuddered, then he came and kneeled in front of her. "Don't ever say that. I don't regret you, I never have."

"But you don't love me."

He took her hands in his. "I tried hard not to. When Laura and Robbie died, they took my heart with them. Six years after the worst day of my life, your mother brought you to me. You had nothing but the clothes you were wearing and a ragged teddy bear."

"I remember that bear."

He smiled. "For months, you clung to that thing like it was your lifeline. I was so angry at your mother for your obvious lack of care." His gaze lowered to the floor for a few moments, then lifted to hers. "I'm going to be honest with you. I didn't want the responsibility of you, but she said if I didn't take you, she'd turn you over to child services."

Peyton hadn't thought her heart could be more broken than it already was. She was wrong. The two people who were supposed to love her hadn't wanted her. "If nothing else, I guess I have to thank you for not letting me grow up in foster care." She hadn't been able to keep the bitterness out of her voice, and she didn't care that her words made him wince.

He stood, then moved back to his seat. "You have the right to be both hurt and angry, Peyton. I haven't been much of a father to you. I didn't want to love you. If I let myself do that and something happened to you…" His chest rose and fell as he inhaled a deep breath. "I died inside the day I lost my family. I couldn't bear to experience that kind of loss again, so I kept you at a distance. I'm sorry for that."

The tears she'd tried to hold back fell down her

cheeks. "I am, too." There wasn't room in his heart for her, so she'd never have his love. Maybe over time it would help that she now understood why, and maybe she would be able to forgive him, but all she felt right now was disposable. She'd been the little girl no one wanted. A few years on a therapist's couch might be in her future.

"But that's not the end of the story." He leaned toward her, resting his arms on the table. "I said I didn't want to love you because I was afraid of what it would do to me if I did, but here's the thing. I worried about you being alone if something happened to me. I thought Dalton was an honorable man, one you could be happy with, so I encouraged the relationship between the two of you. If something happened to me, he would be there for you."

He shook his head. "The day I saw the bruise Dalton put on your arm and you told me he'd done that and had tried to force you to marry him, I've never known such a rage. I wanted to kill him for hurting my daughter."

What was he saying? She'd spent too many years hoping for him to notice her and love her, and she was afraid to hope again.

"That was the day I realized my heart hadn't died after all, that as hard as I tried not to love you, I failed. I can't think of anything I'd rather fail at than that, Peyton."

"Daddy." The tears were freely falling now as she let the words she'd never thought to hear from him flow through her.

He pushed his chair back, then opened his arms. "Come here, sweetheart."

When she was four, then five, then six, and for a part of seven, she'd longed to crawl onto her father's lap and be held by him. To know that she mattered to him. Somewhere in her seventh year, she'd accepted that wasn't going to happen, so she'd stopped wishing. It wasn't her adult self who crawled onto his lap but the little girl who'd wished for it ever so hard.

Chapter Nineteen

"You've been crying," Noah said when Peyton got in the car. Her father stood on the front steps, and he gripped the steering wheel to keep from storming over to the man and telling him off for making her cry.

She shrugged as if tearstains down her cheeks didn't matter. Well, they did to him. As he backed out of the driveway, he realized he was humming the Ray Charles song "Baby Don't You Cry." He stopped. For one, the man in the song was singing to the woman he loved. Maybe he felt something for the princess, but it sure as hell wasn't love.

For another, he didn't sing anymore…and that included humming songs. His penance for his sins. Even thinking about that day and his mistake put him in a dark mood. Lucky stuck his head between their seats and whined.

Peyton leaned her face against his. "Hey, sweet boy. You lonely back there?"

When the dumb dog tried to climb onto her lap, Noah pushed him back. "Stay." He glanced at Peyton. "You okay?"

She smiled. "Actually, I am."

"I don't like that he made you cry. You want to talk about it?" Before he could think better of it, he reached over the console and wrapped his hand around hers. Her gaze darted to his, and before he could take his hand away, she turned her palm up and linked their fingers.

Holding hands with a woman wasn't something he did. It was too intimate of an act. He left his hand where it was, and that he was willing to do that was something he'd think about later.

"I'll tell you everything when we get home." She squeezed his hand. "Thank you for not coming with me after all. I wouldn't have finally learned my father's secrets if you'd been there."

When we get home. Something in his chest loosened, allowing him to breathe easier than he had since the day he tried his damnedest not to think about. He hadn't had a home since his mother died. Not really. His aunt and uncle's home had never been his. He'd only had a small corner where a cot had been placed to call his own. That was the best they could do, and they didn't have to even give him that much, so he didn't begrudge them.

He shared his apartment in Virginia Beach with two other SEALs. Both were assigned to different teams, so it was rare that the three of them were ever there together. It was a bachelor pad, not a home. Both Jared and Ker were players, the apartment's front door a revolving one for women. That had never bothered him, but for reasons he blamed on a princess, he thought it would when he returned. Might be time to look for his own place.

As he pulled into the parking garage, his phone chimed a text notification with the tone he'd assigned

Joseph's prepaid phone. "Stay there. I'll come around and get you," he told Peyton. He grabbed the plastic bag with the condoms, then logged into his cell as he walked around the back of his car.

ex is here

Noah typed a reply. Noted.

He opened Peyton's door, then held out his hand. "Allow me to escort you to your castle, princess." Lucky scrambled over the seat, following her out. Noah glanced down at the dog. "You couldn't wait for me to open your door, dog?"

She punched him with her elbow. "Lucky."

"Whatever." He knew she'd react to that, and he hid his smile. As they crossed the street, he scanned the area, locating the ex attempting to hide in the shadows of a building.

What was he hoping for? To catch her alone? Then what? It wasn't a crime to hang out on the sidewalk, even if you were up to no good, which Noah was positive the man was. He'd already warned Dalton off, and another confrontation, although tempting, wouldn't accomplish anything. Since the man was watching them, Noah decided to push his buttons. Maybe the fool would do something that would get him arrested.

"Did I tell you that you look pretty tonight, princess?" Noah said, putting his arm around her and pulling her next to him.

"Um, no." She glanced up at him, surprise in her eyes.

"Well, you do. So pretty that I have to do this." He stopped and turned her to face him. Then he kissed her.

It was meant to be a taunt to the man watching them, but seconds into the kiss, he forgot about ex-boyfriends and taunts. He forgot they were on a public street until someone yelled that they should get a room.

That was a great idea, and there was one just minutes away. He grabbed Peyton's hand. "Your loft. Room. Bed."

"Finally," she said.

As soon as the elevator door closed, he stepped in front of her and put his hands on the wall behind her head. He stared into the blue eyes looking up at him, and what he saw messed with his heart, making the damn organ bang against his chest.

"We're supposed to talk before this happens," he said. "I'll condense it down to one sentence. Don't fall in love with me." Hearing the words come out of his mouth…well, wasn't he an arrogant son of a bitch? All she knew of him was that he was a moody, grumpy asshole who refused to share with her what was going on in his life. What was there to fall in love with?

She smirked as she saluted him. "Copy that, SEAL boy. All I want from you are mind-blowing tingles."

"Those I can give you, princess." The elevator door opened, and he grabbed her hand again.

The second they were inside her loft, he dropped Lucky's leash, then scooped Peyton up, grinning when she screeched. She wrapped her arms around his neck, and when she sucked on his earlobe, he grunted.

"We're not going to make it to the bedroom if you keep doing that."

Her response was to lick the shell of his ear. He walked faster. When he reached her bedroom, he kicked the door shut before Lucky could follow them in. He stopped at the edge of the bed and dropped her on it, smiling when she laughed. The box of condoms got dropped on the nightstand.

How to start? Where to start? He'd never been nervous before when taking a woman to bed, but he was with this one. Peyton wanted him to show her what she'd been missing. He didn't doubt he could do that, but he wanted this to be special for her. That wasn't something he'd ever worried about before. Someone like her should be romanced, but that kind of stuff... he was clueless.

"Not sure how I'm supposed to get tingles with you just standing there, staring at me," she grumbled.

He choked down a laugh. "I'm thinking." This was the first time he'd been in her bedroom, and he glanced around. Spying a bookshelf similar to the one in the living room, he switched on the lamp, then walked over to it. "How many vinyls do you own?"

"Not sure of the exact number, but over a thousand."

"I have over two thousand."

"Braggart."

He glanced over at her and grinned. "Just saying." As was his collection, hers were in alphabetical order by the artists' names. Perfect. Each album should run about thirty to forty-five minutes, so he flipped through the collection, pulling out four: Marvin Gaye, Usher, Al Green, and Sade. After putting them on the turntable, starting with Marvin Gaye, he returned to the edge of the bed and held out his hand.

"Come dance with me."

Her eyes widened in surprise, then she smiled and put her hand in his. When she was on her feet, he kneeled in front of her. "Shoes off." He unbuckled the ankle strap of her sandals, then slipped them off.

After removing his boots and socks, he reached over and turned off the lamp, then took her hand and brought her to the center of the room.

As Marvin Gaye sang "If I Should Die Tonight," Noah wrapped his arms around her waist and pulled her against him. The window shades were up, and the lights of downtown Asheville gave the room a soft glow, enough to see her. And he wanted to see her.

They swayed to the soulful magic of Gaye's voice, and when she rested her head on his chest, Noah sighed. Peace covered him like a warm blanket on a cold night. It wouldn't last. He knew that. But he was going to hold on to it as long as he could.

The next song came on, and he trailed his hand along the back of her dress. To his delight, he discovered a zipper. He found the pull and slowly lowered it. The end of the zipper stopped at the bottom of her spine. Perfect. Her dress was sleeveless, making it easy to remove her bra. He unhooked the clasp.

She lifted her head and peered up at him. "You want me to take it off?"

He put a finger over her lips. "Shhh. Put your head back on my chest, close your eyes, and let the magic in." He smiled against her hair. For a woman who usually had a lot to say, she obeyed without a word.

"I'm going to take off your bra now, princess. You don't have to do a thing except bend your elbow when I tell you to." He found the strap on her right shoulder and pulled it down. "Elbow." After that side was done, he moved to the left strap.

"You're very good at that," Peyton said after Noah tossed her bra away while leaving on her dress. It was both sexy and intimidating. How many bras had he re-moved? For sure, the women he'd been with were experienced, knew what they were doing. All she knew of sex was that it was boring. How was she supposed to compete?

"Stop thinking, princess."

Easy for him to say, but she needed to unless she wanted to ruin tonight. And she so did not want to. How did he know where her mind had gone, anyway?

"Relax," he murmured in her ear.

He was right, she had tensed up when thinking of him taking off the bras of all those stupid women. She pushed their faceless faces out of her mind. This was her night, and she wasn't going to let them mess it up.

She let her body go soft against his and breathed him in. He smelled so good, like musk and man and spices. She wanted to lick him. Would he think she was weird if she did that? He trailed his fingers over the skin of her back, and his doing that sent tingling heat straight to her sex.

Mercy and heaven help her. She'd never been so wet and aching, and if just baring her back, taking off her bra, and his fingers dancing along her spine made her feel things she never had before, she might die when they got to the main meal. Literally.

He rocked his hips against her. "Feel that? That's what you do to me. I'm so hard it hurts. But before we take care of me, I'm going to taste every inch of you."

Her legs turned to jelly.

"And I'm not going to stop until you're screaming my name."

She moaned.

"That sound you just made, princess, that's just the beginning."

His voice as he spoke into her ear was soft and low,

his breath warm on her skin. When she felt his finger-tips along the side of her breast, she whimpered.

"You like that, don't you?"

"God, yes." Her body was one giant, endless tingle, and he'd barely touched her. She'd thought she'd known what he could do to her, but she hadn't really. She'd imagined that they would shed their clothes, fall into the bed, and go at it. Instead, he was seducing her with the sway of their bodies, the gentlest of touches, and words whispered in her ear. Her imagination had been woefully unimaginative.

It was…it was amazing and incredibly sensual. "Let's Get It On" came on, and Noah's voice joined Gaye's. She didn't think he even realized he was singing. He had such a beautiful voice and listening to him sing to her what was probably the sexiest love song ever recorded only added to the magic swirling around her.

His hand brushed over the side of her breast again, Noah and Marvin sang about getting it on, and her body melted bit by bit. She was no longer sure she'd survive the night.

"Are your panties soaked, princess?" he murmured when the song ended.

That was such a dirty question, yet, it sent a thrill through her that he would talk to her like that.

"Tell me," he said when she didn't answer.

"Drenched." It should embarrass her to admit that. It didn't. Not with him.

"That's my girl." He pushed her dress down her shoulders, letting it fall to the floor. "Much better."

"You need to lose some clothes, too."

He chuckled. "Yes, ma'am." He took her hand and led her back to the bed. "Sit." He pulled his T-shirt over his head. That got tossed behind him. He unbuttoned his jeans, pulled the zipper down, but left them on.

Never in her experience had she seen anything as hot and sexy as the man standing in front of her. Since the first time she'd seen him without a shirt, she'd wanted to touch him, to explore his body and all those muscles, to lick him. She lifted her hand to his stomach, pressing her palm to his skin. He didn't move, just stood there and watched her. Feeling brave, she slid her hand down, over the arrow of dark hair that led to the bulge in his jeans.

He wrapped his fingers around her wrist. "Not yet, princess. Later, you can explore me to your heart's content. After I've made you come on my tongue."

Mercy. It was official. She was so not going to survive the night. She was going to go down in glorious flames. She didn't care.

He dropped to his knees, put his hands on her legs, and spread her thighs apart. The way he looked at her girl parts, the hungry gleam in his eyes…it was just crazy. The only thing he was touching so far were her knees, yet she was tingling. That wasn't even right. She was past tingles. Tingles were for his kisses. What she was, was aching. Throbbing in places she never knew existed. His gaze lifted to her face, and her breath hitched at seeing the raw hunger in his eyes.

No man had ever looked at her like that, and with those eyes that ravenously ate her up, he ruined her for any other man who came after him. She might care about that after he left, but at this moment, there was nothing but him. Noah. A man with demons and hungry eyes.

He dipped a finger into the top of her panties, then slid it along the waistband. She shivered as his finger brushed across her skin. One side of his mouth kicked up in a half smile that told her he knew exactly the effect he was having on her.

"Noah. I need..." She didn't know how to put it into words, this desire for something she'd never had.

"I know what you need, princess." He reached over, grabbed a pillow, and placed it behind her. "Lie back."

"Are you sure you want to do this?"

"Oh, yeah."

No man, not even Dalton, had put his mouth on her sex before. She'd assumed it wasn't something men enjoyed doing, but she heard in Noah's voice that he wanted to. He wanted to! She might crawl right out of her skin.

"I can smell your arousal, princess. It's making my mouth water." He pulled her panties down her legs. "I need to taste you." He put his mouth on her.

"Oh, God." He'd barely touched her, and she was about to shatter into a million pieces. "Oh, God!"

Peyton fisted the bedcover as his tongue did amazing things. He'd primed her so well that she shattered in mere minutes of his first touch. She thought she heard herself saying, "Oh, oh, oh," but she honestly didn't know. She could have as easily been repeatedly screaming the word in her head.

When she could breathe again, she opened her eyes to see Noah watching her, and if that wasn't an all-male satisfied smile on his face, she'd eat her hat. Well, she would if she owned one. She gave him her own extremely satisfied smile. "That beat shelling beans hands down."

He blinked. "Say what?"

"Did I say that out loud? I only meant to think it."

She frowned. "I never once thought of beans when you were doing that. Did you know that's the first time a man has put his mouth on me like that? It was amazing. Amazing isn't even a good enough word. Will you do it again? You didn't think it was gross, did you? It didn't seem like—"

Noah smiled. "I'm like one of Pavlov's dogs. Every time you chatter like a magpie, I have to do this." He leaned over the bed, put his hands alongside her head, lowered his mouth to hers, and kissed her speechless. After stealing all her words, he lifted his head, and stared down at her. "Anything else you need to say?"

"More?"

"You want more, princess? Not to worry. There's so much more I'm going to show you. And just so you know, it will all beat shelling beans." Damn, she amused him.

"I've already admitted that much, but can you beat brewing beer? That's my ultimate challenge."

"I guess you'll have to be the judge of that." He stood, pushed his jeans down, then stepped out of them. Her gaze zeroed in on his boxers, or more accurately, his erection pushing against the material.

She pointed a finger at his crotch. "I want that."

"And you shall have it." This woman. She could easily be the one if he'd met her at any other time.

In a few weeks, a month at the most, he'd be gone. Until then, he was hers. He'd show her what she should expect—what she deserved—from a man, and then she'd never again settle for less. And if it felt like the sharp point of an arrow had just pierced his heart at the thought of never seeing her again, it was what it was.

Chapter Twenty

"Well, hello there," Peyton said when Noah shed his boxer briefs. "That's some impressive stuff you got there."

"Stuff?" He laughed. "The princess can't say cock?"

"Correct, she cannot." She loved hearing him laugh. He was so different tonight from the brooding man she was used to. He'd probably revert back to that man tomorrow, but if she could help him be happy once, she could do it again. And she would, for however long she had him.

"Up." He tugged on the pillow he'd placed under her.

"How do you want me?"

"So many ways."

"That wasn't what I meant, and you know it." The many ways intrigued her, though. She scooted up, giving him room on the bed. He stretched out beside her, and she waited to see what he'd do now.

"Close your eyes."

"Why?" She wanted to watch everything he did.

"Because I said so."

"What are you going to do?"

"Not a thing if you don't close your eyes."

She huffed an annoyed breath but obeyed. When nothing happened, she peeked through one slitted eye.

"No cheating. Here's what's going to happen," he said after she'd closed her eyes again. "You won't know where I'm going to touch you until I do. Your senses will be heightened, and you'll try to anticipate what's going to happen. You're going to like this, I promise."

"If you say so." She didn't see how it could be better than seeing him do things to her.

"Keep them closed even when you think nothing is happening or I'll stop."

He didn't do anything for what seemed like a full minute, and it was torture. Then he blew on her nipple, and she gasped. It was unexpected and really nice. Was that his tongue now swirling around that same nipple? That was more than nice. It was incredible. Just as she was getting into what he was doing, he stopped. She whined in protest.

"Oooh," she said when he pinched the other nipple, sending an electrical shock through her. "Do that again."

"Hush. I'll decide what to do when." She felt his mouth next to her ear. "I'm giving you a lesson in anticipation, princess."

"I don't know if I can survive your lesson." Even his warm breath tickling her skin heated her blood.

"Barely maybe, but you will."

He lightly trailed his fingers down her side, feather touches that raised goosebumps. He explored every inch of her, sometimes with his fingers and sometimes with his tongue. How had she not known she had so many erogenous zones…her belly button, behind her knees, a spot behind her ears. Honestly, any place he touched at this point.

"Please, Noah." He had her so far on the edge that she ached.

"Is this what you need?" He slid a finger inside her, slid it out, and then back in. While he did that, his thumb circled her clit.

She instantly climaxed.

"That's it, baby. Ride that wave." He gathered her in his arms and held her as she tried to find air. "How was that for tingles?" he asked when she could breathe again.

She grinned. "It's a start." It was freaking amazing.

"I see how it is. You're going to be a greedy girl."

For him, absolutely. "I think you're right. Now, it's my turn." She wanted to explore every inch of him the way he had her.

"Next time. Watching you come apart was the hottest thing I've ever seen. I need to be in you. Now."

"I'm good with that." So good. As turned on as he'd made her with all the things he'd done, what she wanted most was to feel him deep inside her.

"Let's see how many more tingles I can give you." He grabbed a condom out of the box, and as he rolled it on, he lifted his gaze to hers. "You like watching me put this on."

It wasn't a question, but she answered anyway. "I don't know why, but yes. It's like I'm a voyeur, seeing something I'm not supposed to and can't look away from." He stroked himself, and she whimpered.

"You're killing me with those noises you make, princess."

"I promise to make more if you'll stop torturing me and get down to business."

He stared at her for a moment, then he grinned, then he laughed. "I think you're good for me, Peyton. My new high is waiting to see what will come out of your mouth."

Right then, he took his first step toward stealing her heart. She'd been in like before, but she'd never been in love. She could love this man like nobody's business. *He'll never be yours to love.* No, he wouldn't, but she sure as heck was going to enjoy him for as long as she had him.

"Missionary style, side by side, or you riding me? Your choice since tonight is for you."

And he just took a second step by giving her a choice. Without trying, he showed her what could be. That was good and bad. Good because now she knew. Bad because she was sure there was only one Noah.

"I'm more than familiar with missionary style, so cross that one out. Out of the other two, which gets you hotter?"

"You get me hotter." He brushed his knuckles over her cheeks. "You really do. But I'll answer your question. Side by side." He rolled toward her. "Put your leg between mine."

With her leg between the two of his, he made love to her slowly and sensually. And while he loved on her, he stared into her eyes, not letting her go. She stared back, wishing the day never came when he'd leave her.

"I never expected you," he said.

She wasn't sure what to make of that. "Are you saying I'm a bad thing?"

He thrust into her. "Tell me you don't think that's what I mean." He thrust into her again. "I'll never forget you. Never."

With that, he took another step into her heart, and she freely gave him the space. He was going to hurt her without wanting to, and she was going to let him.

"Come with me, princess," he whispered in her ear.

"Okay." Such a mundane word for the earthquake inside her that followed his whisper. She put her hand on his chest, over his heart and the hummingbird tattoo, memorizing how it pounded because of her.

"I don't want to hurt you," he said as if he'd read her mind.

Still on their sides and facing each other, she rested her palm on his cheek. He was going to. She already knew that, but if she told him that, he would regret tonight. She smiled as she lied to him. "No worries there, sailor boy. Just keep me supplied with tingles and I'll be happy."

"Copy that."

She traced the hummingbird with her finger. "Will you tell me about this? I know it has special meaning for you."

"It's in memory of my mother. She loved hummingbirds."

"Thank you for telling me. I thought it was something like that. It's beautiful."

He put his hand over hers and squeezed. "Tell me about your dinner with your father. Why were you crying?"

"Because he finally told me why he'd never let me get close to him. He had a family before I was born." She told him about her father's wife and son and what happened to them. "All these years, he was a broken man and I didn't know."

"Does it help you now that you know now?"

"So much yes. For the first time since I came to live with him, he told me he loved me. That was why I cried. I never expected to hear him say those words to me."

"You didn't have any hint that he was married once?"

"No. He said that no one at Elk Antler even knew, so there wasn't any gossip to the fact."

"You had quite an amazing day, huh?"

"Definitely, and then it was followed up by an amazing night."

"Yeah?" He brushed his hand along the side of her breast. "Think you'd like a little more amazing?"

"Show me what else you got in your bag of tricks, SEAL boy." And did he ever.

"Don't leave the building unless you're with your father," Noah told Peyton when he dropped her off at Elk Antler the next morning. "Call me when you're ready to go home, and I'll come pick you up."

"Copy that, sir." She tapped her lips. "Do I get a goodbye kiss, honey?"

"Bring that mouth here, sugarbuns." He leaned over the console. After kissing her, he waited until she was safely in the building before heading to Operation K-9 Brothers.

As he drove away, he realized he was smiling. It felt both good and wrong. He'd given himself permission last night to temporarily put his guilt and dark thoughts away in a box. Fearing he'd have a nightmare, he'd planned to sneak out of bed after Peyton fell asleep. Funny thing, he'd fallen asleep wrapped around her body, and had slept next to her until morning free of nightmares. He'd existed on an hour or two of sleep here and there since he'd so royally screwed up. That he'd slept through the night seemed like a minor miracle.

Did he deserve even a minor miracle? He didn't think so. Yet, he wanted more of these good feelings, he wanted more Peyton. He didn't fool himself that one night with her and his nightmares were a thing of the past.

After dropping Lucky off with Jack, Noah went to the therapist appointment. He did not want to do this. If he thought he could get away with it, he'd be a no show. Resigned to his fate, he followed the GPS instructions to an office in a medical center.

"Here goes nothing," he muttered. As he entered the building, he wished he'd brought Lucky with him, and what a damn strange thought that was. They'd discussed whether or not Lucky should come with him, but had agreed that since Lucky wasn't trained yet, he could be disruptive. Not that he'd ever admit it to Jack, but he was calmer when the dog was by his side.

"I'm Noah Alba," he told the receptionist.

"Dr. Meadows will be right with you."

"Thanks." He headed for a chair, but before he could sit, his name was called. He turned to see an attractive woman in her forties or fifties. "That's me."

"It's nice to meet you. I'm Dr. Meadows, or if you prefer, Renee." She smiled. "If neither of those suit, just Doc also works."

He preferred not to be here at all, but she probably didn't want to hear that. He'd expected a male therapist, so a female was a surprise and not a welcome one. How could she relate to the event that was his personal hell?

Not having a choice, he followed her to an office. A couch was along the back wall, and no way was he stretching out on that. He chose a chair in front of a beautiful desk that he guessed was mahogany. The walls were a cream color with pastel landscape paintings on the walls. He assumed the room was designed to be relaxing, but he was far from relaxed.

"Do you prefer Noah, Mr. Alba, or Petty Officer Alba?" she asked as she settled in the chair next to him.

Why wasn't she sitting behind the desk? She was too close. "Noah's fine."

She smiled again. "Since you didn't make today's appointment yourself, am I right in assuming you'd rather be anywhere but here?"

"True story." He gave her points for addressing that upfront. "I was ordered by my commander to see a head doc…sorry, a therapist."

She laughed. "Head doc doesn't offend me. I caught the widening of your eyes when you realized your—" she made air quotes "—head doc was a woman. You wondered how I could possibly relate to your military experiences."

The woman was a spooky mind reader. He could deny it, but she was being direct with him, and he appreciated that. "I'll admit it crossed my mind."

"I served three tours to Afghanistan with the rank of captain in the army. So, been there. Done that. Got the T-shirt to prove it."

"Sorry for assuming." He was really starting off on the wrong foot here. It was going to get worse when he refused to talk about the second worst day of his life.

"Not a problem. You'll find I'm not easily ruffled. All we're going to do today is talk about what you can expect from our sessions. We'll meet twice a week. You can schedule your appointments with Beverly before you leave today. Are you familiar with cognitive processing therapy, CPT for short?"

"No, ma'am."

"Without thinking about it, give me one word for what you feel the majority of the time these days."

"Guilt." Sneaky woman. If he'd taken the time to think, he would have kept his mouth shut.

"CPT is one of the more successful therapies in treating PTSD. The primary focus of CPT is cognitive intervention. What that means is that I'll work with you to identify negative thoughts related to the event in question, help you replace those thoughts with positive ones, and show you ways to cope when the guilt feels like it's drowning you."

Good luck with that, lady.

"At the end of each session, I'll give you an assignment to complete before your next appointment. I cannot emphasize enough how important it is that you not avoid. I can't help you feel your feelings or challenge your thoughts if you don't come to therapy or if you avoid completing your practice assignments."

He eyed the door.

"You can walk out right now, Noah. Go drown in your guilt, drink so much you can't hold down a job, or maybe drugs will be your choice to wipe out your memories. It's your choice, but if you do, I'll be obligated to report to your commander that you refused treatment. Do you have a girlfriend or wife?"

No, there was just a black-haired, blue-eyed princess who talked too much that he liked kissing too much. "I don't like you," he said instead of answering her question.

She laughed. "You'll like me even less at times during our sessions. For your homework assignment, I want you to write about what happened in Afghanistan."

"Fuck," he muttered. "Sorry, Doc. That slipped out."

Avoid. That was her word, and he was going to avoid his very first assignment because no way in hell was he going to write about that day.

"There is no ban on any word in my office, even if it's that one." She leaned toward him. "And, Noah, when you come for your next appointment, you better have your fucking assignment ready for me to read. Schedule your appointments with Beverly on your way out."

He did not want to like the lady, but grudgingly, he did. He did not want to respect her. It was impossible not to. He did not plan to ever come back.

He scheduled his next four appointments with Beverly on his way out.

One hour and twenty minutes after dropping Lucky off with Jack, Noah was back at Operation K-9 Brothers. Lucky went bonkers at seeing him. "You're ridiculous, dog. I wasn't gone that long." He squatted and obligingly gave the dog a belly rub.

"How'd it go?" Jack asked.

"Fine."

"That's it? She came highly recommended. If you don't think she'll work for you, we'll find someone else."

"It's good, Jack, so stop worrying, okay?"

"A friend of mine, he was Delta Force, saw her after his honorable discharge because of a busted knee. He said she's great."

"This was my first appointment. Ask me again in

a week or two. I have to go on Monday and Thursday mornings."

"Great. By the way, you'll meet that friend Sunday. You know your brother will be here this weekend, right?"

"Yeah, talked to him last night."

"Nichole and I are cooking out Sunday, and you and Peyton, along with Nichole's brother, Mark, and Clint will be there."

"Peyton will like that. She's mentioned a few times how much she likes Nichole." Funny, a day or two ago, he'd look for excuses—even outright refuse, not bothering with an excuse—to avoid being around a group of people. Damn head doc was apparently in his head since his brain had decided *avoid* was no longer acceptable.

He was looking forward to taking Peyton to a cookout, and he was even starting to like the ridiculous dog.

Chapter Twenty-One

Peyton was over the moon happy about a lot of things. She'd returned to work yesterday, along with Eddie, who'd refused to come back until she did. Gosh, she loved that old man. Most of her day had been spent getting back in the swing of things in the brewery, but two hours of it had been with her father in his office. He was teaching her the business side of the operation, and the best part, it had been his idea.

His responsibilities weren't her favorite part of the brewery, but if she was to take over someday—and she prayed that wasn't anytime soon—she needed to learn how to run the business. The plus in that was she would be spending time working with her father each day. He was a different man from the one she was used to. The man who used to keep himself closed off from her and never smiled was gone. He'd even praised her quick mind a few times. She was still marveling at the change in him, had pinched herself to make sure she wasn't dreaming.

A miracle had happened all because she'd finally stood up for herself and refused to marry a man she didn't love. Being a runaway bride definitely had its benefits. Then there was Noah, whom she never would have met if she hadn't hightailed it away from her wedding.

He'd spent last night in her bed again, and, Lordy, the man curled her toes. Her bed was going to be a lonely place when he left. But she wouldn't think about that, not today. She was too happy to allow sad thoughts in her head. There would be plenty of time for that when he was gone.

Tonight, she was meeting his brother, and she couldn't decide what to wear. Clothes had never been all that important to her, her preferences were jeans and T-shirts for brewing beer, pencil skirts and blouses for client meetings, leggings or shorts for home, and a few fancy dresses for dinners or special events.

What to wear for dinner with the man she was afraid she was falling for and his brother? Noah wanted to stay in, and she'd offered to cook…something. Cooking wasn't something she was particularly good at. Why bother when she lived alone and had great restaurants surrounding her?

Surprising her, Noah had asked her to make her grilled cheese sandwiches. She'd thought that was too simple, but he'd assured her Clint would love them. She was so putting tomatoes on them, though, and she smiled at thinking of Noah's reaction. He was out now picking up a large order of pho to go with the sandwiches. She'd told him to also stop at the bakery and choose something for dessert.

"You moving out, princess?"

She yelped. "You startled me. I thought you were still gone."

"Obviously, I'm back." He leaned on the doorframe

and eyed the pile of clothes on her bed. "What's with the mess?"

"I don't know what to wear tonight."

He smirked. "I'd say nothing if it was just me and you, but if you wore nothing in front of my brother, I'd have to kill him."

"Drat, no clothes would be so much easier, but since I don't want blood shed on my clean floors, I'll wear something. I just have to decide what." She shoved the top items aside. "Not these. I should have gone shopping, but I'm not so good with clothes, you know? I mean, what does a girl wear when she's meeting the brother of the man she's sleeping with? Something demure, maybe something casual, but what? Plain old jeans and a T-shirt just don't—"

"Peyton, Peyton, Peyton," he said. "Every time you do that, I have to do this."

When had he moved next to her? His mouth covered hers, and she forgot about clothes. She, in fact, ended up without any on.

"This is amazing," Noah's brother said.

Peyton grinned at Clint. "Thanks. I see you didn't remove your tomato." She slid her gaze to Noah. "Your brother knows a good thing when he sees…well, I guess in this case I should say when he tastes it."

He leveled a searing hot stare on her. "Trust me, I know a good thing when I taste it."

She gasped. "You did not just say that." Heat spiraled up her neck and on her cheeks. If inexperienced, naive her understood what he was implying, his brother certainly would.

"Pretty sure I did, princess." He winked at her.

"Well…well…ah…" She needed to stop sputtering, but what was she supposed to say to that? In front of his brother? Noah had thoroughly tasted her on top of the pile of clothes on her bed not two hours ago. The man obviously had superpower talents because her girl parts were still tingling.

"Between this amazing grilled cheese sandwich and this beer you brew, I think I'm in love with you, Peyton," Clint said. "Will you marry me?"

"If you promise to whisk me away from your Neanderthal brother, I'm all yours."

Clint laughed. Noah growled, which thrilled her. Like maybe he was a little jealous? She glanced between the two of them. They had the same eye and hair color, and the same lush lips, but that was the only resemblance. Noah was bigger, both in height, weight, and muscles. There was an easiness—a comfortable in his own skin vibe—to Clint that was missing in his brother.

"Your husband won't be cool with you whisking away with a princess," Noah said.

Two pairs of eyes watched her, as if waiting to see her reaction. "If he's as cute as you, Clint, we'll take him with us."

Clint grinned. "He's cuter."

"Well then. It's a done deal." She glanced at Noah. "Sorry, sailor boy. Looks like you're out of luck."

He narrowed his eyes. "You're not going anywhere, princess."

No, she wasn't. She was his until the day he left, and because she didn't want to get depressed by that thought tonight, she changed the subject. "Noah picked up a chocolate cake from an amazing bakery nearby. I'll make us some coffee."

"On one of my visits, you should take me on a tour of your brewery," Clint said.

"I'd love to."

He asked her questions about brewing beer while they lingered over the cake and coffee. When they finished, they moved to the living room. She wasn't sure how long it had been since the brothers had seen each other, and she thought it would be good for them to have some time alone.

She yawned. "Sorry. I think I'll head off to bed. I guess I'll see you tomorrow afternoon at Jack and Nichole's?" she said to Clint.

"You sure will."

As she walked down the hall, she heard Clint say, "I really like her." She paused, curious to hear Noah's response.

"So do I. More than I want to."

What did that mean? Why didn't he want to like her?

"Then what's the problem, brother?"

It was wrong to eavesdrop, but she couldn't make herself walk away.

"Things are messed up for me right now," Noah said.

"What happened? Why are you on leave?"

Peyton slid down the wall. She shouldn't listen to their private conversation, but she sat there on her butt anyway. She needed to know what had happened to him.

"Because I fucked up. Bad." Noah knew Peyton was still in the hallway, listening, but he thought she was developing feelings for him. She deserved to know why that wasn't a good idea, but he just couldn't tell his story to her face and see her disappointment in him, maybe even disgust. It was easier to let her listen while he told his brother.

Clint lifted his chin toward the hallway, and Noah nodded, acknowledging he was aware Peyton was listening. Would she ask him to leave after she learned he wasn't the hero she thought he was? That would be the best for both of them, especially her. But then who would protect her? He took a deep breath, then started talking.

"I should have been suspicious of the bed and called for a teammate to help me move it for a thorough search," Noah said as he finished the story. "That was my job. Instead, I didn't want to disturb a sick old man more than I had to. A good man and our team's dog are dead because of me."

He'd started out sitting back in the chair but now perched on the edge. His elbows rested on his knees, his hands dangling between his legs. Afraid of what he would see on Clint's face—revulsion, pity?—Noah stared down at his clenched fists, then slowly unfurled them before he was tempted to put them through one of Peyton's walls. When Clint didn't respond, he lifted his gaze.

His brother leaned his head back on the sofa and closed his eyes. "I've never told a soul this. I knew I was gay by the time I was thirteen. I didn't broadcast it, but I never hid it, either. There was a boy I had a crush on my junior year, and I thought he liked me, too. I don't remember how we came to be there, but one day we were under the bleachers. A group of five boys caught us kissing. These same boys had bullied me all year, and I was afraid of them."

He opened his eyes and stared at Noah. "They went

for Fletcher first, and like the chicken shit I was, I ran away. I didn't go to a teacher and report my friend getting beaten up. I hid like a coward. I never saw Fletch again because he never returned to school, but I heard he spent two days in the hospital because I didn't do anything to stop it. Shortly after he got out, his family moved away. The boys got a measly month's suspension for fucking up his face."

"You were just a kid." It wasn't the same. He was an adult. He was highly trained not to make mistakes like the one he had.

"Doesn't matter. I knew when I ran that they were going to hurt him. I should have gone straight to a teacher or someone capable of stopping it. My point is, we all have *should have dones* in our lives. Granted, some are worse than others, but what are you accomplishing by beating yourself up over something you can't change? Yes, you made a mistake, a tragic one, but I guarantee you'll never make it again. And, brother, you aren't honoring Asim's life by throwing yours away."

"How did you get past it? Not doing what you knew you should have?" Clint had given him a lot to think about, but there was a big difference in feeling responsible for a boy getting beaten and knowing he was responsible for someone's death.

"When I finally forgave myself."

Noah didn't know if he could do that. "Did you have nightmares?"

"For months. Sometimes they were what actually happened, sometimes I was the one being beaten, and in a few of them, I ran and got a teacher. Those were the worst because if I could do that in a dream, why hadn't I been able to for real? How bad are yours?"

"I try not to sleep. When I do, I see Asim's eyes staring at me." He scrubbed a hand over his face. "They're full of blame. Even though I wasn't in the room when he died and that didn't happen, I still see them."

"Are you seeing someone you can talk to about all this?"

"Yeah, on orders from my commander. I had my first appointment yesterday. The head doc doesn't put up with bullshit. I'm kind of pissed that I like her."

Clint chuckled. "Since I know how pigheaded you can be, you had no intention of talking, eh?"

"I plead the fifth."

"Don't be an ass, Noah. Talk to her. She'll have the tools to guide you through this, to show you the way out of the dark tunnel you're in."

"I don't know if I can." He met his brother's eyes. "Forgive myself." He heard a muffled sob from the hallway, and then a moment later, the soft click of Peyton's bedroom door closing.

"You can if you choose to." He stood. "On that note, I'm outta here."

Noah rose. "It's good seeing you, douchenozzle."

His brother strode to him and pulled him into a tight hug. "Love ya, numbnuts." He stepped away. "I'll see you tomorrow at Jack's. You better have a princess at your side."

"We'll see. Not sure what she thinks about everything she heard."

"Don't underestimate your girl, brother."

When Clint opened the door to leave, Noah said, "You know I love you, too, right?"

His brother grinned. "Yep, even though you never say it."

"My bad," he softly said. He'd never told another soul he loved them since his mother died. He needed to do better, at least with his brother and adoptive mother, who were the only people in the world he loved, anyway. There were also his SEAL brothers. Couldn't forget about them.

As for a princess... He shook his head. *Don't go there, Alba. You're just her bodyguard, and after tonight, she might not even want you for that.*

He took Lucky out. "You were a good boy tonight." He'd curled up at the side of his chair, and as if understanding there had been a serious talk happening, he'd stayed quiet.

When Noah returned to the loft, he walked down the hall to Peyton's door. No light shone under the bottom. She wasn't awake, waiting for him. He gently turned the knob, and as he suspected, it was locked.

"Smart girl," he whispered.

Chapter Twenty-Two

Peyton stood in the shower, letting the water wash away her tears. Both Noah's and Clint's stories had broken her heart. Like Noah had said, Clint had just been a scared boy. Those awful boys were to blame for what was done to his friend.

As for Noah, dear God. Now she understood the haunted look in his eyes. How did one forgive oneself for a mistake that cost a life? She didn't think she could if it had been her. Yet, it hadn't been intentional, and she couldn't begin to imagine what war was like or how anyone could make snap decisions in such stressful situations. Noah's mistake was trying to be kind and respectful to an old man, and that was forgivable even considering the tragic result.

He wouldn't want her pity, thus the shower cry. She needed to get her tears out of her system before she went to him. In a way, it hurt that he could tell Clint what had happened but not her. Yet, it was better this way. She would have burst into tears as her heart hurt for him, and he would have hated that.

After drying off, she put on leggings and his T-shirt, the one she'd never given back. It was huge on her, but it gave her both comfort and strength. She found him on his back on the sofa in the living room, and although he had the TV muted on some sports show, he stared at the ceiling. Lucky was sprawled over his chest, his eyes closed as Noah combed his fingers through his fur.

"Are you here to tell me to leave?"

"No." Not even. She perched on the edge of the sofa at his feet. "I listened to you and Clint talk." It was only right that she tell him.

His eyes met hers. "I know."

"Oh."

He looked so sad. She was glad she'd cried in the shower. If she hadn't, she'd be crying for him now. He'd told Clint he didn't sleep, something she already knew. But he had with her.

She stood and reached for his hand. "Come with me." Without commenting, he pushed Lucky off, then let her lead him to her bedroom. She was operating off the cuff, letting her instinct guide her. The warm water of the shower had helped her feel better, and she thought it would him. By the time she finished, she was going to be squeaky clean.

"What are we doing?" he asked when they reached the bathroom.

"Taking a shower."

"Peyton, I'm really not up for sex tonight."

"Not asking for that." She turned on the water. "Strip." While he was removing his clothes, she took off hers. She followed him in. "I'm going to take care of you, okay?"

"It's your party."

His voice was listless, his shoulders were slumped, and his face and eyes looked weary, as if he carried the weight of the world on his shoulders. Before tonight, even with his haunted eyes, there had been a strength and confidence radiating from him that was gone as he stood in her shower with his hands braced against the tile and his head bowed.

There were so many things she wanted to say to him, but he was lost in his memories and wouldn't hear her. She hoped with her loving care and some sleep, he'd be back to himself tomorrow. Then they could talk.

She poured bodywash on her hands, then started at his shoulders. When she pressed her thumbs into his skin, massaging the tense muscles at the bottom of his neck, he grunted. She thought it was a good grunt. From his shoulders, she moved down his back, scraping her fingernails over his skin. He shivered.

Because she didn't want this to turn into anything that felt sexual to him—that would cause him to feel like she wanted that sex he wasn't up for tonight—she grabbed a washcloth. After pouring more bodywash, she dropped the cloth over his shoulder.

"Here. Finish up on the places I missed." Although, she'd love to clean those particular places, too. Next time.

She stepped out of the shower, and while he was finishing, she quickly dried off, then put her leggings and his T-shirt back on. By the time she was dressed, he was coming out. She grabbed another towel.

His eyes dropped to hers. "I'm sorry I'm not—"

"Shhh." She put her finger over his lips. "No talking. Not tonight. Just let me take care of you, okay?"

"You don't have to."

"True, but I want to." She dried him off. "Put some boxer briefs on, then get in bed. I'll be back in a minute." He'd slept naked the past nights, but a naked Noah was too much temptation. As if he read her thoughts, he smirked. That smirk made her happy. He wasn't completely lost in his head.

Lucky raced into the bathroom as she came out. He hated being separated from Noah, and she was sure that Noah was finally growing fond of the dog, whether he wanted to or not. She smiled thinking how much Noah hadn't wanted anything to do with Lucky in the beginning.

Maybe she could be like Lucky and worm her way into Noah's heart. She stilled in the middle of the hallway. No, she couldn't think like that. The days were counting down to Noah's departure. She had to keep him in the box marked "On loan from the U.S. government. Enjoy him while you have him but return him as soon as possible."

She hated that box.

Doing anything about it was out of her power, though. All she could do was appreciate the blessing of having Noah in her life, however short that time was, and learning how it could be, should be, with a man. She padded to the kitchen, poured a healthy three fingers of whiskey, got a treat for Lucky, and returned to her bedroom.

"Treats for my boys." She tossed Lucky's, and he caught it out of the air. "You swallowed that whole," she admonished him. He looked back at her with eyes that hoped for more. "Sorry, sweet boy. That's all."

Noah was sitting up against the headboard, the cover pulled up to his waist. She was glad for that, even though she wanted to pull it down to admire what was hidden. His mighty fine chest was in view, though, and as much as she wanted to spend much time admiring that, she only allowed her eyes to skim over it. Then she lifted her gaze to his to see him watching her.

"Drink this." She held out the glass.

"Yes, ma'am."

She walked to her side of the bed and climbed in. Normally, she slept in boy shorts and a camisole. With Noah these past nights, she'd slept naked like him, and that had been an odd feeling at first, but she'd grown to like it. For tonight, she kept on her leggings and the large tee. Less tempting this way.

When he finished his drink and set it on the night table, she rolled over to face him. "Come down here and put your back to me." He raised his brows but didn't say anything, just did as she asked.

She wrapped her body around his. "I've got you. Go to sleep."

"Thank you, princess," he whispered sometime later.

She squeezed the arms she had around him. As she held him, she listened to his breathing slow as he fell asleep. Once she was sure he was out, she pressed her cheek to his back, closed her eyes, and joined him in dreamland.

"No! No. No. Fuck no."

Peyton jerked awake. She was still wrapped around Noah, felt his body jerk, then tremble.

"God, no," he said, so much pain in his voice.

Lucky jumped up, putting his paws on the bed. He looked at her, then at Noah and whined. "I'll take care of him, sweet boy," she quietly said. "Go back to your bed." He lowered his chin, resting it on his paws, his gaze staying on Noah.

"I guess you're staying, huh?" She slid her hand over Noah's chest and then down his arm. "Shhh, baby. It's okay. I've got you." Now that she knew what had happened, she didn't doubt the nightmare was of that day. "You're not there, Noah," she said, keeping her voice soft and low. "Sleep, baby."

She kept caressing his arm, up to his shoulder, down to his wrist. He settled, and his breathing slowed again. If he had these nightmares every night, no wonder he refused to sleep. But he couldn't go on like that, and she could only hope his therapist could help him. And just maybe, Peyton thought, she could play a part, however small, in his healing.

A few minutes after Noah quieted, Lucky disappeared from view, his nails clicking across the wood floor as he returned to his bed. "He loves you," she whispered against Noah's back. And maybe she did a little bit, too.

Noah woke wrapped around Peyton's warm, soft body. Sometime during the night, they'd changed positions with him now holding her. What she'd done for him last night…he had no words for what it meant to him.

For the first time since arriving in Asheville, regret settled over him that he would leave her. It was selfish to not go now so she could get on with her life, find a good man who would love her the way she deserved. Although it was wrong of him, he was going to be selfish.

He glanced at her bedside clock. Even though it was only five in the morning, he was now wide awake, but damn, he was tired. So tired of the guilt, the nightmares, and the PTSD, which the head doc had assured him he had. He'd never thought those letters would apply to him. Hell, he'd watched his mother's murder. It couldn't get worse than that, right? He should be able to deal with this without falling apart.

When he'd found Peyton's door locked to him, and although he'd expected it, the disappointment and hurt had taken him by surprise. He wasn't supposed to have feelings for her. And in that moment of being locked out of her life, he'd had a meltdown.

Because that was what had happened last night. Then when he'd expected Peyton to tell him to leave, she'd surprised him. No one after his mother had taken care of him like that. She couldn't possibly comprehend what that meant to him. She was one special princess.

Also, sexy as hell. Since he'd given in to the inevitable and spent that first night in her bed, he couldn't get near her without wanting her. It would have been easier to leave her when the time came if he hadn't allowed that to happen, but he didn't regret it.

He trailed his hand over her arm, then slipped under the T-shirt she'd kept. He liked her in it, something that had belonged to him. She sighed when he brushed his fingers under the curve of her breast. Those noises she made…they were his undoing. Every single time. More than anything, he wanted to bury himself inside her and make slow, sleepy love to her. But she'd been up half the night taking care of him, so this morning, he'd take care of her.

While she slept, he'd take Lucky out, and while they were out, he'd see what time the bakery opened. Unable to resist copping one more feel, he stroked a finger around a nipple, smiling when it peaked at his touch. Even in sleep, she responded to him, and wasn't that a turn-on? His erection jerked against her ass, and before he forgot she needed her rest, he eased away.

"Don't go," she drowsily said.

He buried his face in her hair, breathing in the fresh,

citrusy scent he would forever associate with her. "Go back to sleep, princess."

She reached for his hand, bringing it back under her shirt to her breasts. "You were playing with these. I liked it."

"Did you now?"

"Hmm-mmm."

He loved that sleepy voice. They hadn't made love in the morning, and mornings were one of his favorite times for sex. There was always a soft, dreamy feeling to it. He danced his fingers down her stomach, slipped them under her leggings, and toyed with her clit for a few seconds before sliding one and then two fingers inside her.

"So wet for me," he murmured into her ear.

"Only for you."

God, how he wished that could be true forever. He stilled, realizing he really meant that. Still half-asleep, she probably didn't even realize what she'd said or the implication. He wanted to be her only for as long as she would have him, but it couldn't be.

"Noah?"

He took his hand away. "Turn over and put your leg over mine." He needed to be inside her, wanted to be buried deep while she was still drowsy. "Wait. Clothes off." For both of them. He pushed his boxer briefs down, then kicked them off. After helping her out of her clothing, he reached over to the nightstand and grabbed a condom out of the box.

Once the condom was on, he pulled her against him. She was waking up and looking at him. He didn't want her awake. "Close your eyes and let yourself drift off."

"But—"

"Do it." That came harsher than he'd meant for it to, but he had this burning need for sleepy, lazy morning sex, something he couldn't remember the last time he'd had. "Close your eyes, princess. I'm going to make love to you and sing you back to dreamland." Where the hell had that come from? He didn't sing anymore.

"Ooooh," she breathed out. "I want that. All that." She closed her eyes. "Sing to me, Noah."

So he sang. He didn't even think about what song. As he softly sang Foreigner's "I Want to Know What Love Is," he wondered if she understood that because of her, he did want to know.

When her body relaxed, he eased into her. Inside Peyton Sutton was where he could live forever. It was where his demons weren't able to torture him because she'd drive them away if they dared to try. Somehow, he knew that about her.

Thinking that, a hazy memory hovered. He'd thought he was in the beginning of a nightmare during the night because he had a hazy memory of telling himself to wake up. But it had slipped away, so he must be thinking of some other night. Yet, he could almost hear her soothing voice, but he must be imagining that.

As he moved, slow and easy, she made a noise that made him think of a purring kitten. He decided it was his new favorite sound.

"Feels so good," she sleepily murmured.

"Yeah, it does." He closed his eyes, letting himself get lost in the moment. She was soft and warm, a haven for his troubled soul. "That's it, baby," he said when she clenched around him.

"Good. So good, Noah."

It was, and as they climaxed together, he held this

woman he could never have in his arms, committing everything about her to his memory. After he was gone, there would be sleepless nights when he would relive his time with her, and he wanted to remember everything.

Chapter Twenty-Three

"Strike!" the umpire exclaimed.

Jack slung the bat over his shoulder and turned to glare at the umpire, disbelief on his face. "Dudette, you need glasses. That was so not a strike."

Peyton laughed when the umpire got in his face, and the two of them argued over the call. "She's a riot." Nichole's friend, Rachel Denning, visiting from California, was the umpire. She was also a stunt double, and that was just crazy cool.

"I love her." Nichole cupped her hands around her mouth. "Hey, ump. Don't put up with his crap. Eject him from the game."

"Hush, woman." Jack scowled at his girlfriend. "Whose side are you on, anyway?"

The guys, Noah, Jack, Clint, and Nichole's brother, Mark, were playing ball—Noah and Clint against Jack and Mark. Jack's friend, Deke, was the designated pitcher. Apparently, he had a bad knee, hurt when he was in the military, and didn't want to risk messing it up by running the bases.

The four dogs, Dakota, Rambo, Maggie May, and Lucky, were in the middle of it all, stealing the ball whenever they could snatch it. Dakota was the only one who brought it back to Jack. The other three had to be chased down.

"Strike three," Rachel yelled, poking Jack in the chest.

"What? That was only strike two."

She smirked. "Strike three is for arguing with the official."

"What? You can't do that." He put his hands on his hips and turned his glare on Nichole. "Tell your friend, the one that also used to be my friend, that baseball is sacred. She can't make up new rules."

"Sure, babe. Rach, baseball's sacred, so apparently you're not supposed to mess with the rules, but I say go for it."

Noah jogged up. He put his hand on Jack's shoulder. "I thought I taught you better, son. Never face off against two women. You're not gonna win."

"You're just trying to butter up the ump so she won't call your balls strikes," Jack said.

"Is it working, ump?" He winked at Rachel.

"Let's play ball, people," Clint yelled from centerfield.

Peyton, sitting in a lawn chair on the sidelines with Nichole and Deke's wife, Heather, marveled at the difference from last night's Noah to today's. He was actually laughing and joking around with everyone. It was a beautiful thing to see.

Speaking of beautiful, her gaze roamed over the guys. "Man, they're hot. Every single one of them." Even Nichole's brother, a good five or six years younger than the rest of them, was a cutie.

"Amen, sister." Nichole held up her hand for a high five.

Peyton slapped her palm against Nichole's. "Not to start a who's the hottest debate, but my vote's on Noah."

"Puh-lease." Nichole rolled her eyes. "Your hottie's hot, but my Jack would win."

"You're both delusional," Heather said. "It's Deke hands down."

"Says you," Peyton and Nichole said together, then grinned at each other.

Peyton was loving her new friends. As she sat in Nichole and Jack's backyard laughing with these amazing women over which of their men were the hottest, she wondered if they'd still spend time with her after Noah left.

Don't go there, Pey. Not today.

There would be plenty of time to be sad after Noah was gone. There was too much laughter here with his friends to get teary eyed. The group was interesting. Deke was a detective with the Asheville Police Department, Heather was a physical therapist, Nichole a potter, Rachel a movie stunt double, Clint and Mark were gamers. Then a SEAL, and a former SEAL now training therapy dogs. She felt that as a beer brewer she could hold her own in such an eclectic bunch.

"Over the fence!" Noah said, drawing her attention back to the game to see him running around the bases with Lucky chasing after him. As he passed Jack, standing behind second, he turned and ran backward and smirked. "Hey, Whiskey. You see Double D hit a home run?" At Jack's raised middle finger, Noah laughed.

"What's Maggie May doing?" Heather asked when the dog dragged the bat up the stairs to the deck.

"Oh, jeez. Silly dog." Nichole stood. "Give that to me, Mags." She wrestled the bat away. "Maggie May's a kleptomaniac. She'll steal anything not nailed down."

Heather laughed. "That's funny. What does she do with the stuff?"

"She hoards anything she can filch in her bed. Cell phones, the remote, shoes, bras, panties, you name it. She never chews the stuff up, just wants the goodies."

"Like a dragon with his treasure," Peyton said.

"Where's the bat?" Clint looked around home plate with a puzzled expression on his face.

Nichole waved it in the air. "Maggie May decided y'all are done. It's about time to put the burgers and hot dogs on the grill, anyway."

After the meat was cooked, everyone filled their plates and found seats on the deck.

"This is really good beer," Deke said. "You have a new customer."

"Awesome!" Peyton had brought two cases of assorted Elk Antler beers as her contribution to the cookout, along with an Elk Antler logoed beer bucket. On their way over, Noah had stopped at a convenience store and bought four bags of ice. Everyone but Heather had grabbed a bottle from the bucket.

Heather leaned toward her husband. "Put a drop on my tongue so I can taste it."

"I have a better idea." Deke took another swallow, then kissed her.

"That is good," she said with a dreamy smile on her face that Peyton assumed was more from the kiss than the taste of beer. "As soon as this baby pops out and I can drink again, you'll have another customer."

Peyton smiled. "Also awesome." It never ceased to thrill her when someone loved one of her beers.

"I told her the first time I had one that I'd marry her

if I wasn't already a fool in love." Jack grinned at Nichole who blew him a kiss.

Noah made a growly sound. "But you are."

All the men's gazes zeroed in on Noah, as if some kind of understanding passed between them.

Noah frowned. "What?"

"You'll figure it out," Jack said, smirking.

Clint chuckled, which got a glare from his brother.

What was all that about? Whatever it was, Peyton sensed Noah didn't like the attention on him. "If any of you ever want a tour of the brewery, all you have to do is ask," she said to get everyone's attention away from Noah. "It's pretty interesting."

"We'll definitely take you up on that," Deke said.

Mark, who'd been quiet through most of dinner, raised his hand. "Me, too. Do we get free samples?"

"Absolutely." As the attention was off Noah now, his body seemed to relax.

"Deke needs to get my fat pregnant butt home, but before we go, you promised to show me your pottery studio, Nichole," Heather said.

"Your pregnant butt is a beautiful thing." Deke turned heated eyes on his wife.

Peyton leaned around Noah so she could see Heather. "How can you say your butt is fat? I wouldn't have known you were pregnant if you hadn't said something."

"I'm practicing getting used to a fat butt in my near future. So far, I'm okay with it. Ask me again when I look like a whale and I'll probably have a different answer."

"I think whales are beautiful creatures." Nichole stood. "Ladies, let's go for a tour of my studio while the guys do clean-up duty."

As Peyton dutifully followed the girls, Rachel stepped next to her. "All that bottled-up guilt isn't good for Noah," she quietly said.

Huh? "Has Noah said something to you?" It was true, but how else could Rachel know?

Rachel put her hand on Peyton's arm, stopping her. "I'm an empath. Do you know what that means?"

"Not really."

"It's not any kind of woo-woo, nothing magic about it. I just feel people's emotions, like if they're happy, sad, or in Noah's case, drowning in guilt. I don't know the reasons for their feelings. I can't read their minds or anything like that."

"How does that work?"

She shrugged. "I have no idea. It's just something I've been able to do as far back as I can remember. My grandmother could, too, so I guess I got it from her. I'm only telling you this because you're good for him. I felt that, too. You calm him. I just thought you should know."

"Thank you for telling me. I wanted to believe I was." Rachel had just given her a precious gift.

Jack stood. "I guess these dishes aren't going to march their selves to the dishwasher."

After the kitchen was clean and the leftover food put away, they returned to the deck to wait for the girls to return.

"Peyton's ex giving her any more trouble?" Jack asked.

"Other than hanging around, no. I don't trust the dude. For whatever reason, I think he wants control of the brewery, and apparently, he believes he'll get that if she marries him. That might have been true if she'd gone through with the wedding, but not anymore. Her father fired him as soon as he saw the bruise on her arm that Dalton put there. I worry that he'll pull a stupid stunt."

Deke frowned. "Are you thinking he might make a grab for her if he gets a chance?"

"I don't know, but I don't have a good feeling about him. I think he's desperate now. He told her he was going to take her to Vegas where she would marry him. If he thinks he can get away with grabbing her, I wouldn't put it past him."

"She should report him to the police if he's hassling her, especially if he's already hurt her."

Noah took out his phone, found the picture of her arm, and showed it to Deke. "I wanted her to report this, but she just wants him to leave her alone."

"That might have gotten him a night in jail." Deke handed his phone back. "But not much more than that, if that. The problem is, until he actually does something, there's not much the police can do. If you really think there's a chance he could do something stupid like kidnap her, put a tracker on her. Better safe than sorry."

That was a great idea. They could pick one up on the way home.

Deke took out his wallet and pulled out a card. "This has my cell number on it. Call me if her ex does try something."

"Thanks. I will." When the girls returned, he said, "You ready to head out, princess?" They had a tracker to buy.

"I am." She gave Jack a hug, then Nichole a longer one. "I really enjoyed today."

"I'm glad. Let's get together for lunch or something."

"I'd love that."

Peyton's smile was pure happiness, almost knocking Noah on his ass. Had he ever made her smile like that? He didn't think so, but suddenly, he wanted to be the one to put that kind of joy on her face.

He and Jack did the man hug thing, and surprising him, Nichole hugged him. Not a hugger, he felt awkward, but…it was nice.

"See you in the morning," Jack said.

"I have an appointment with the head doc first thing, so I'll see you right after that." Which reminded him he still had his homework assignment to write. Or not. The last thing he wanted to do was write about that day. He wasn't even sure he could.

"Let's go, boy." Lucky jumped up and followed them out. Maybe he could claim the dog ate his homework.

Chapter Twenty-Four

"There's something I have to tell you before we go inside."

Peyton paused in unbuckling her seatbelt. "What's that?"

Although they were parked in front of the doctor's office with the car engine off, her father hadn't moved to get out. His fingers were wrapped so tightly around the steering wheel that his knuckles were white.

"Oh, God. It's worse than you told me."

His gaze jerked toward her. "No, that's not it. You're not going to be happy with me, though." He expelled a breath. "Your last year of college I had a lobectomy."

"I don't know what that is." It didn't sound good, though.

"It's surgery to remove a lobe in the lungs."

"Wait. What? You were sick—" she couldn't even say the word *cancer* "—had an operation, and didn't think that was something I should know? That's how little you thought of me?" Did he even have a clue how much that hurt?

"It wasn't like that. You were halfway through your last year of school, and I knew you'd quit and come home."

"Of course I would have. I would have wanted to be with you when you needed me."

"It was only the early stage of lung cancer. I had the surgery, then chemo. It worked. I went into remission, so I figured, no harm, no foul. You were able to graduate without disrupting your last year."

"No harm, no foul?" The words tasted bitter in her mouth. Hell, she was furious. Bitter and furious. "Did Dalton know?"

He stared at his hands as he nodded. "Yes."

"Who took care of you after the surgery? Who drove you home afterward?" She knew the answer, but she was so angry that she wanted to make him say it to her face.

"Dalton."

She'd had to strain to hear him say Dalton's name. "I see." Betrayed. That was how she felt. "Tell me this. How did the idea of me marrying him come about?" She had her suspicion on that, too.

"Does it matter anymore? You're not married to him. He's out of your life now."

"Yes, it matters."

He sighed, but she didn't care if this was hard for him. "Dalton moved into the guestroom while I was recovering. He started talking about you, how much he respected you, how smart he thought you were. I didn't see it then, but looking back now, I can see that he was playing me. He would ask about your future if something happened to me, like the cancer coming back. Over the two weeks he stayed, he made me promises."

"Let me guess. That he would take care of me, that he would keep the brewery going?"

"Yes, things like that. He also said that he cared

deeply for you, and that he hoped the day would come when you'd feel the same about him. He told me he was in love with you, and I believed him. He subtly, and I admit shrewdly, planted the idea that if I died, you'd be alone. I started worrying about you having someone to take care of you if I wasn't around. He promised he wouldn't push you into a relationship if that wasn't what you wanted, but he asked permission to court you."

"Dalton's devious. He knew I'd do anything to get your approval."

"I hate that you felt that way." He scrubbed a hand over his face. "You almost made a terrible mistake because of me. I'm sorry, Peyton. I'm sorry for a lot of things where you're concerned. I know you can't forgive me right now, but maybe someday you will."

Her pride took a blow that he hadn't thought she could take over the brewery, but in his defense, this had happened when she was still in college. She could hold on to her hurt, but what would that get her? After a lifetime of not having a close relationship, they were finally finding their way to each other. That was more important than her wounded pride. Even more important was saving his life.

"I forgive you." And she meant it. She poked his arm. "Just don't do anything like that again, okay?"

Her father smiled at her. "I promise." He glanced at his watch. "I guess we better go in."

Forty-five minutes later, Peyton stared out the car window as her father drove back to the brewery. Words she'd never used before bounced around in her head. *Recurrence* was the term for the cancer coming back. It was such a benign word. There should be a stronger word for it…an uglier one. The doctor had said her father had non-small-cell lung cancer. Treatments were discussed: chemotherapy, radiation therapy, a combination of treatments. How was one supposed to know what was right? The oncologist said they'd caught the recurrence early, and he'd given her father's odds of surviving at around seventy percent. That was a number she was going to embrace. She wouldn't allow him to be in the thirty percent group.

"It's going to be okay, Peyton," her father said, breaking the silence. "I'm going to fight this with everything I have."

"We're going to fight it. We're a team now, Dad."

He reached over and squeezed her hand. "A kickass team."

"You got that right."

"I want you to promise me something. Stay positive. Keep smiling. You're too young to carry the weight of the world on your shoulders."

"I'll keep smiling and stay positive if you will." The doctor had stressed how important it was for her father to keep a positive attitude, and she meant to see that he did.

"Deal." He held up his hand, and she high-fived him.

Dr. Meadows peered at Noah over the top of her glasses. She waved the two pages he'd written. "The facts are here, and that's it. Where's the emotion? What you felt in here—" she tapped her chest "—as you saw the building explode knowing Asim and Snoop were in there? How did you sleep that night? Did you even sleep? When did you have the first nightmare?"

Noah pressed his lips together to keep his rage from

pouring out. How did he feel? Was she kidding? The pages she held in her hand had been torture to write, even though they were only the facts of the event. As for his emotions, they were locked down tight. If he let them out, he'd destroy everything in sight. He'd slipped out of Peyton's bed at four in the morning to do his assignment, and what he had managed to put on paper had slayed him.

He must have zoned out when he'd finished, lost in a waking nightmare. Lucky had brought him back to the present by whining and licking the tears rolling down his cheeks. He didn't even know he'd been crying.

"I can't do this," he rasped. The damn ants were biting.

"You can." She put down the papers, then removed her glasses, and set them on the desk. "You can't slay your demons until you face them. You're not a coward. If you were, you'd never have made it as a SEAL. Let's see some of those SEAL balls you guys have in abundance."

"It really pisses me off that I like you, Doc."

She laughed. "It's my bedside manner you can't resist."

He snorted. "If you say so." He rubbed the back of his neck, massaging against the developing headache. She wasn't at all what he'd imagined his head doc would be. Not even close. He'd envisioned a soft-spoken, bookish-appearing doctor who would silently study him until Noah blabbed all.

What he got was a mouthy, no-holds-barred doc who wasn't going to put up with any bullshit from him. She'd challenged him with her coward comment, and he might be a lot of things, but that wasn't one of them.

"Your assignment this week is to write this again, but with your feelings included, both the day it happened and in the following days. Get those demons out of your head and on paper so we'll know what weapons we need to destroy them."

"What I said about liking you… I changed my mind."

The woman had a full-bellied gusty laugh, which strangely calmed the biting ants. "You'll like me again by the time we're done," she said after she stopped laughing.

He wasn't so sure about that if she kept making him write about feelings.

Noah returned to Peyton's kitchen table after making a second pot of coffee. He'd had to walk away from his assignment three times already, but he was determined to finish without stepping away again. He was almost finished, but he'd reached the part most difficult to write…his damn feelings.

You want feelings, Doc? Here's mine… Asim's dead because I didn't do my job. That's a fact. In my nightmares, even though this part never happened, I see Asim's eyes right before the bomb goes off. He's looking straight at me with blame in them.

You asked me three questions. Did I sleep that night? That's a joke, right? Do I even sleep? Not so much. When did I have my first nightmare? Two nights later…the first time I couldn't keep my eyes open.

One other thing for you, being a head doc and loving this kind of shit to analyze. My guitar has

*always been my escape when the ants start bit-
ing. It has been since my mother...nope, not going
there. I'm not giving you more parts of me to dis-
sect. All I want to say is that the last person to
play my guitar was Asim. I can't bring myself
to touch it now, but I miss my escape when the
ants bite.*

*I'm done! If you tell me I haven't put enough
emotion and bullshit feelings in this one and tell
me I have to write it again, we're done, you and
me.*

Noah put his pen down. He didn't read it over. He
couldn't. If the doctor didn't like this one, that was too
damn bad. It was three in the morning, but he was too
wired from coffee and feelings to sleep. He'd sent Peyton to bed hours ago, telling her he'd join her as soon
as he finished the assignment from his doctor. But he
couldn't go to bed. Couldn't bear to see Asim's eyes.
Not tonight. He was too raw.

Lucky put his chin on Noah's knee and whined. Noah
had noticed that the damn dog sensed when the ants
started biting and would get that worried look he wore
now. So, instead of crawling into bed with Peyton, he
clipped Lucky's leash to his collar. The two of them
walked the streets of downtown Asheville until the gray
light of dawn.

In a few hours, he'd show up for his Thursday morning appointment, where he'd have to watch Dr. Meadows read what he'd written and then talk about it. He'd
rather pull his fingernails out with pliers.

He and Peyton were a sad pair. He'd been moody
since his Monday appointment, and although she was

putting up a brave front, she was worried about her father. They'd slept together in her bed Monday night…well, she'd slept while he—too afraid to close his eyes and see Asim's accusing ones—had spent the night watching her.

Although he'd wanted nothing more than to lose himself in her sweet body and forget for a while, she'd come to bed wearing leggings and the T-shirt she'd stolen from him. Clothes that said sex wasn't on her mind.

She'd told him about the doctor visit with her father, cried while he held her, and had fallen asleep in his arms. He'd felt almost content just holding her snuggled against him. Almost wasn't quite there, though, but it was there enough that he knew it was one feeling he could get used to. Damn doctor and her *feelings*.

He was going on two nights without sleep now, and he was tired. So fucking tired.

As the sun rose over the buildings, he returned to the loft, showered, dressed, and then made another pot of coffee. Like he needed more caffeine after all he'd already consumed.

It would be another hour before Peyton stumbled out searching for coffee, and he didn't know what to do with himself until then. The ants had stopped biting, but they were still crawling under his skin, regrouping for another attack.

Coffee in hand, and with Lucky at his heels, he went to the guest room, closing and locking the door behind him. He set the cup on the nightstand, then stood in front of the closet door for a good five minutes, his heart beating double time. He lifted his hand and opened the door.

The black guitar case mocked him as he stared at it. "You're a coward," the case said, or was that Dr. Meadows messing with his head?

It was his second guitar, the first a cheap one his aunt and uncle gave him the Christmas he was eleven. It was the only thing he'd asked for. This one he'd bought when he was sixteen with money he'd earned mowing yards in the summer and shoveling sidewalks in the winter. The one he'd set his sights on hadn't been cheap. It had taken him three years to save enough to buy it. The instrument was a part of him…or it had been.

"I'm not a coward," he murmured. Then he said it louder. "I'm not a coward."

He picked up the case and took it to the bed, setting it next to him. Then he stared at it some more. His fingers itched to touch it, to slide over the strings, to make music. If he opened the case, would it make him happy to see the guitar, to play it, or would it send him two steps back from the little progress he'd made? He flipped the latch open, then closed.

Open. Close. Open. Close.

Lucky sat at his feet, watching him.

Open. Close. Open. Close.

The dog stood and put his paws on the bed, then put one paw over Noah's hand.

"I'm not ready, am I?" Was that what Lucky was telling him? If he opened the case and saw death, he'd never open it again. He didn't think he could live with that. He returned the case to the closet.

"Noah?" Peyton knocked on the door. "Are you up?"

"Yeah. I'll be out in a minute." He took a minute to clear his head, then walked out.

"Good morning." She eyed him over the top of her coffee cup. "You never came to bed. Did you sleep at all?"

Not wanting to lie to her, but not wanting to admit he'd roamed the sidewalks all night, he grunted. Let her make of that what she wanted. He glanced at his watch. "You ready to go?"

"Yeah, just give me a minute. Are you okay?"

"I'm fine, Peyton. Do you have the tracker on you and still have the other one in your purse?"

She grinned. "Yep to both. I feel like I should be in a Bond movie."

"This is serious business. You won't be joking if your ex pulls something."

"Well, excuse me for daring to see the amusing side of this, Mr. Grumpy Pants." She set her half-full cup in the sink. "I'll just get my lazy butt in gear. You know, I can walk to the brewery. It's daylight and there are people out and about. Dalton wouldn't pull—" she made air quotes "—*something* in broad daylight with people watching. That way, I won't be an inconvenience."

She kneeled in front of Lucky. "Good morning, sweet boy. You're way more fun to talk to."

"You're not walking to work alone. Let's go." He was being an ass, but existing on too much coffee and no sleep didn't make for a good mood. Still… "Look, I'm sorry. I just have a lot on my mind this morning. Why don't we plan to go out tonight?"

"You mean like a date?"

"If that's what you want to call it, sure." He'd come back early and try to grab some sleep before picking her up.

"That's what I want to call it. But work on your attitude before tonight, okay?"

He almost smiled. "Yes, ma'am." It was hard to be a jerk to a princess.

Noah forced himself not to squirm in his seat while Dr. Meadows read his assignment. He'd resented having to write it, but sitting here, waiting for her verdict, all he wanted was her stamp of approval so they could either move on or he could walk out if it wasn't good enough for her. He wasn't sure which he was hoping for.

She glanced up at him while she was somewhere in the middle of reading it, then continued. What part was she reading, and what was that look for? He rolled his pair of dice around in the palm of his hand.

"It appears we have a lot to talk about," she finally said as she set the pages down on her desk. "The good news, you don't have to write about it again, but we're not done, you and me."

"Bummer," he muttered.

She laughed. "I know you don't mean that, so I won't take it personally. What's that you're playing with?"

"Just an old pair of dice." He opened his hand to show her.

"What do they mean to you?"

He shoved them back into his pocket. "Who says they mean anything?"

"Hmm," she murmured, letting him know she knew better. She tapped the pages with her index finger. "What do you want to talk about first? Your guilt, which is misplaced, by the way, but we'll address that at some point. Or how important playing your guitar is to you, yet you can't bring yourself to touch it now? The ants that bite you? Or your mother? Or we could talk about the dice that don't mean anything."

"I'm not talking about my mother." Had he put something in there about her? Too hyped up on his damn feelings and coffee, he didn't remember. He was stupid for not reading what he'd written before giving it to her. And he wasn't talking about the damn dice because that would lead to talking about his father.

"I'm guessing you want to, even if it's subconsciously, but we'll move talking about your mother down the list. That leaves your misplaced guilt, ants, a pair of dice, and your guitar. You choose."

He didn't want to talk about any of those choices. His guilt *was not* misplaced, and if she decided his assignment was to open the case and take out his guitar, then she might as well tell his commander that he was a lost cause. As for the biting ants, he didn't see how she could do anything about them.

"Which one of those, Noah?"

There was nothing she could say to take away his guilt or control the ants, so he said, "My guitar." And then he cursed himself. He couldn't talk about that, either, couldn't verbalize the storm raging inside him at losing the one thing that made the ants go away.

"Yes!" She gave him a fist pump. "I was hoping that would be your choice."

"Are you sure you're a licensed doc? Like, is fist pumping a thing you learned in head doc school?"

That made her laugh. "You're funny. I really like you. To answer your question, absolutely it's a thing when I think you're making progress. And you are making progress, even if you don't feel like you are."

Didn't feel like it at all.

"How old were you when you learned to play?"

"Eleven."

"And playing a guitar makes…" She picked up his assignment and scanned the pages. "What you call biting ants, it makes them go away."

"Yes."

"Do you think Asim would be happy to learn that you don't play anymore because you associate the guitar with him?" After a moment, she said, "Not going to answer?"

"What I think is that Asim is dead and he'll never learn to play the damn thing."

"So your self-imposed punishment is to never touch it again? What does that accomplish? It's not going to bring Asim back."

Damn ants. He scratched his arm, then put his hand on his knee to stop his bouncing leg. He needed out of this room.

"Think about that. Remember in our first session we talked about how important it is that you not avoid? Ask yourself what you're achieving by avoiding something that not only you love but seems to calm you. You have to forgive yourself. No one else can do it for you."

She glanced at her watch. "Our time is up for today. Your assignment this week is to play one song on your guitar. Also, bring it with you to your next appointment. I need to know if you can really play it or if you're blowing smoke."

"I hate you," he said.

She grinned. "No, you don't. Think about my questions. We'll talk about your answers next Monday. And you better show up with your guitar."

If he showed up at all.

Chapter Twenty-Five

Peyton left work early and went shopping. She had a date! A date with a sexy, mouth-watering, eight-pack abs SEAL boy who knew how to make a girl tingle. She wasn't even sure *tingle* was the right word anymore.

She wanted something sexy to wear for her date. Something that would have Noah crossed-eyed and drooling. Nothing caught her interest in the first downtown store, but as soon as she walked in the second one, she stopped in front of a mannequin.

"There you are," she whispered. The off-the-shoulder sundress had a cream-colored background and vines with green leaves and pink and blue flowers swirling around the fabric. The hem was low in the back—a good six inches below the knees—and would hit her about midthigh in the front.

"That's called a high-low hem," a saleswoman said, stepping next to her. "Very sexy without being raunchy."

Peyton fingered the material. "It's so soft and silky. I'll try it on." By the time she was done, she left with the dress, a pair of high-heel, strappy cream sandals, and dangly pink and blue beaded earrings. Also in her bags were a pale pink, lacey bra and matching panties. She was going to knock a certain SEAL boy's socks off!

When she let herself into her loft, Lucky greeted her with his usual enthusiasm. She was going to miss her sweet boy when Noah left. She would miss her grouchy pants boy even more. But she wasn't going to think about that. Not on her date night.

The TV was on, the sound turned down, and Noah was on the sofa, sound asleep. She eased her shoes off, then padded to the end of the sofa. She was happy to see he was getting some sleep. He actually looked peaceful, a look she liked on him.

Leaving him to his rest, she took her packages to her bedroom. She hung the dress on a hanger, then took the bra and panties to the bathroom with her. She had just washed the conditioner out of her hair when her shower door banged open.

"What the hell are you doing here?"

She shrieked. "Good gravy, Noah. Give me a heart attack why don'tcha?"

"What. Are. You. Doing. Here?"

A fire-breathing dragon had nothing on SEAL boy. "Um, washing my hair?"

"Let me rephrase that. How did you get home?"

"My feet. They do this thing called walking. Neat trick, huh?" Okay, he wasn't amused.

"What happened to you wait for me to come get you?"

Oops. Excited over going shopping for something to wear tonight, she hadn't even considered she wasn't supposed to go anywhere by herself. "Ah…"

His gaze roamed over her, his eyes heating for a brief moment before he blanked them. "We'll talk when you finish."

"You can talk to me while I shower." Aaaannd, she

was talking into thin air. The man could sure move fast when he wanted to.

She finished her shower, and after drying off, she rubbed lotion over her freshly shaved legs. She put on her new bra and panties. Not wanting to wear her dress until it was time to go, she slipped on her robe and belted it. She dried her hair and then went looking for Mr. Grouchy Pants.

He was in the living room, staring out the window. "Come here, Peyton."

Did he have eyes in the back of his head? She was barefoot, hadn't made a sound, hadn't even stepped into the living room yet.

"Come here."

She left her spot at the end of the hallway, coming to a stop next to him. "I'm sorry, okay? But it really isn't a big deal. As you can see, I'm fine."

"Look out there and tell me what you see."

There was something in his voice that put her on guard, that he wasn't just enjoying the view out the window. She reluctantly turned her gaze to the window. It took a moment, then she gasped. "Dalton!"

"So taking off by yourself isn't a big deal?" He leveled a hard stare on her. "This was your lucky day. He showed up after you came inside, but what if he'd been there when you arrived? You think he's harmless? Think again. He's desperate. Otherwise, he wouldn't still be hanging around. Desperate people do desperate things."

She thought she might be sick. "How do you know he wasn't there when I came home?"

"Joseph called when your ex showed his face."

"How? Joseph doesn't have a phone."

"Wrong. I gave him one."

She gaped at him. "Like Joseph's your spy?"

"If that's what you want to call him. He wants to keep you safe as much as I do. Imagine my surprise when Joseph wakes me up from my nap and I hear the shower running. I thought to myself, Noah, that can't be Peyton in the shower because she knows better than to be traipsing the streets all by her lonesome." He chuckled, and the sound wasn't a pleasant chuckle. "But what do I find? A princess in the shower."

She had no excuse, so she didn't try to offer one. "Why? Why can't he leave me alone?" She'd honestly forgotten about him. As far as she knew, he hadn't been around for...she wasn't even sure. A week, maybe?

"Because you're the means to get what he wants."

"He's delusional." There was no way her father would turn over the brewery to him now. She'd been so excited about her date with Noah, and Dalton was ruining it. No, she wasn't going to give him the satisfaction.

"It won't happen again." She stepped back from the window. "I was just excited about our date and wanted to go shopping for something that would knock your socks off. I forgot all about stupid Dalton."

"Knock my socks off, huh?"

"You bet your hot butt I'm going to." When Noah chuckled, she breathed a sigh of relief. Crisis averted. Yes, she'd been stupid to forget that Dalton was out there, maybe not a threat, but maybe he was. It wouldn't happen again.

"You think my butt is hot?"

"Hotter than my grannie's hot cross buns."

Noah did his fast-action thing and had her pressed against the wall in...well, she wasn't good at time and distances, but it just happened really fast. His gaze locked on hers. "What the devil are hot cross buns?"

"Do you really care?" She sure didn't, not with the way he was looking at her, like he might devour her any second. She'd never once wanted to be devoured by a man, but this man could eat her alive and she wouldn't file a complaint with…well, she didn't know what agency she could file a complaint with, and honest truth, she wasn't going to complain about him to anyone.

"Don't care," he said. "What are we caring about, anyway?"

"I don't know. Global warming?" What were they even talking about?

"Are you drunk, princess?"

"Drunk on you, SEAL boy."

He grunted in the sexiest way she never thought a grunt could be grunted. When he picked her up and headed for her bedroom, she panicked. "You can't see my underwear yet."

"Says who?"

"Says me. Put me down." She heard his sexual frustration, but until she had her date, he was not seeing her in the bra and panties that she'd bought just to make him go crossed-eyed and drool. He didn't have to like it, but that was the way it was going to be.

"Have I told you that you make me crazy?" He dropped her feet to the floor.

"If you think you're crazy now, just wait until you see what's under my robe." She danced away when he tried to grab her. The light was back in his eyes, and she wanted to keep that light in them. "Date, remember? What you're taking me out on. I hope you planned something worthy of seeing my panties." She laughed as she backed up to her room. "You won't be disappointed, SEAL boy." She slammed the door when he tried to follow her.

Noah stared at the door she'd just closed in his face. He glanced down at Lucky, who was also staring at the door. "She make you crazy, too?" He took the dog's bark for a yes. "Guess I better get ready for date night."

He couldn't remember the last time he'd had an actual date, hadn't even been sure what to plan for tonight. Before he'd napped, he'd researched romantic restaurants in Asheville and thought he'd found the perfect place. He'd only packed one pair of pants and one dress shirt before leaving Virginia Beach, so those would have to do. After a shower in the guest bathroom, he dressed, and then went to the living room to wait for Peyton.

The princess was beautiful in all her forms. The disheveled, barely dressed version he'd first met at the waterfall, the at home in her leggings and little tops one, the jeans and T-shirts she wore to work one, but... Noah blew out a breath when she walked into the room.

What was it she'd said she wanted to do to him? Right, socks. He strode to her, stopping a foot from her. Any closer, and he'd have his hands on her, and they'd never make it to the restaurant.

"You said you were going to knock my socks off. Mission accomplished. You're beautiful. That dress. Those shoes. I'm going to spend the night glaring at all the men drooling over you. Might have to knock a few upside the head."

That smile, that shy, pleased smile. She had no clue how incredible she was, how beautiful and sexy. She slayed him without even trying. He might have to bang on his own head just to get his brain to working again.

He thought about telling her to wear a different dress. One with more material in the front of the skirt. One that didn't stop midthigh, baring her gorgeous legs for every man to fantasize having them wrapped around him. Probably not a good idea to act like a jealous caveman, so he managed to keep his mouth shut. Barely.

"What about the women drooling over you? Can I pour their drink over their heads?"

He grinned. "The kitten has claws." Normally, he would hate a woman being jealous over him. It showed a possessiveness that he didn't want any part of. Why he liked it from Peyton he couldn't explain. "Let's go. We have a reservation for six."

"Where are we going?"

"You'll see." He hoped the restaurant he'd chosen was all it had sounded like online.

The Grove Park Inn was all and more than he'd hoped for. The sprawling hotel was over a hundred years old and sat on Sunset Mountain. The exterior of the hotel was uncut granite, harvested from the same mountain the hotel sat on, giving it an old-world look. The main lobby was massive, a huge fireplace the focal point.

There were several restaurants in the hotel, and he'd chosen to make reservations at Sunset Terrace. The mountain views were amazing, the evening perfect, warm enough to sit on the terrace.

As incredible as the views were, though, it was the woman sitting across the small table from him that he couldn't take his eyes off of. The sun hadn't set yet, but it was low in the sky. A candle burned on the table, casting a soft glow on her face.

She was happy. He could see that in her eyes as she tried to take in everything around them. The ants were quiet, and it occurred to him that they usually were when he was with her. He didn't know what that meant, and if he tried to analyze it, he was afraid he'd come to the conclusion that she meant more to him than was good for either of them. So, for tonight at least, he wasn't going to examine this contentment settling over him.

"I've never been here for dinner before," she said, her eyes finding his. "I do come sometimes at Christmas. You should see the place then. It's amazing. They have a national gingerbread contest that people from all over the country enter. There are hundreds of gingerbread houses. It's incredible, the details and how intricate they are. I wouldn't have the patience for it, but I'm in awe of the people who do. They have a kids' category, and even those are amazing. The finalists are announced on TV, on *Good Morning America*, I think."

He smiled as she babbled on. There probably wasn't another woman on the planet who chattered the way she did that he could tolerate for long. When she did it, though, it turned him on. Maybe it was Pavlov's dog syndrome. He was now trained to kiss her when she got on a roll.

"I wonder if I could make a holiday gingerbread beer. Does that sound like it might be good? I don't know. It could be really bad, but then—"

"Come here, princess." Suddenly glad it was a small table, he leaned across it. When she just blinked at him, he crooked his finger at her. "Bring that mouth here."

"Oh." And then she smiled as she met him halfway.

Although he wanted his tongue inside her mouth, they were in a classy restaurant with other diners around them, so he satisfied himself with a closed-mouth kiss. When she made one of those sighing noises he loved, he sat back before he did forget where they were.

"Why are you grinning?" she said.

"Just thinking. You're probably the only princess in the world who tastes like spicy beer instead of wine."

"Is that bad?"

"Hell to the no. It makes for a perfect princess." There was that shy, pleased smile again. It took so little to make her happy. The men in her life had been fools. Her father for not seeing what an amazing daughter he had before it was almost too late, and her ex…he wasn't going there. Not now while he was with a beautiful woman on a perfect night. The man was a fool, though.

Later, after a delicious dinner—his, a mouthwatering steak, and hers, Chilean sea bass, which she'd declared was the best thing she'd ever tasted—they strolled the grounds of the hotel. Terraces with firepits were scattered about, and fairy lights were strung in the trees and bushes.

"When I've come here, I've just gone straight inside to see the gingerbread houses. I've never seen all this before," she said, as they admired the manmade waterfall.

Her hand—soft and warm—was in his, and as they stood there, watching the water flow over the rocks, he never wanted to let go. But he would when the time came for him to leave.

A few years ago, one of his SEAL brothers pushed the woman he loved away because he didn't think he deserved her. At the time, Noah had thought that was stupid. But wasn't that how he'd been thinking about Peyton? He didn't see himself as a prize catch, but maybe he did deserve to be happy as much as the next guy. Something to think about.

But before he could even consider a future with Peyton—did she even want more from him than those tingles?—he had to get his head on straight. If that was possible, and just maybe it was if he could learn how to forgive himself. He wanted to. So fucking much.

Or would it be best for both of them, especially her, if they ended things with fond memories of each other? He'd seen too many relationships sour because of long deployments, love replaced by anger and hurt feelings. The kind of hurt that turned to hate. He didn't think he could bear her hating him.

"Penny for your thoughts," she said.

"Not worth half that." He squeezed her hand. "You ready to go, or do you want to walk around some more?"

"Walk around some more, but not here. Let's head back downtown. With the street performers, that's a more fun place to stroll. When we get tired of walking around, we can get a fancy coffee and sit at a sidewalk table and people watch."

"Your wish is my command, princess."

Chapter Twenty-Six

Peyton poured ginger ale into a glass for her father when they returned to his house. "Here you go." She set the glass on the end table. He'd felt good after his chemo treatment, but two hours later, his stomach was unsettled.

He'd wanted to go back to the brewery, but she'd put her foot down, and amazingly he'd only argued a little. He'd also tried to talk her into going to work, but he hadn't won that battle, either. This was his first treatment, and she refused to leave him without knowing how he would be affected.

"You don't have to babysit me. I'm going to drink this and then go lie down for a while."

"I'm not babysitting you. I'm spending time with you. Besides, I'm not allowed to traipse around by myself." The last time she'd done that, Noah hadn't been happy. If she did it again, he'd probably never speak to her again.

"Sorry. I shouldn't have forgotten about that. Have you had any more trouble from Dalton?"

"No." Other than his hanging around, which definitely made her uncomfortable, but she didn't want to worry her father. Not with what he was going through.

"Good. Where's your bodyguard?"

"At Operation K-9 Brothers. His friend's teaching him how to train therapy dogs." Maybe he would like it so much that he'd rather do that than go get shot at. But she couldn't see him being satisfied with spending his days with dogs forever, so that was wishful thinking. He wasn't even gone yet, and she was missing him.

After her father went to his bedroom, she got out her laptop. They were planning to increase production, and she had some questions, so she called Eddie. They talked for a good twenty minutes about inventory, distribution, and staffing. When they finished their conversation, she stood and stretched.

Thirsty, she went to the kitchen to get some water, and came to an abrupt halt. Her father's house wasn't an open floor plan like her loft, and she hadn't been able to see Dalton before she came into the room.

"What the hell are you doing here?"

"Language, Peyton."

"If me saying *hell* bothers you, you're not going to like this. Get the fuck out of my dad's house." As far as she could recall, that was the first time she'd dropped the F-bomb, but if ever it was appropriate, it was now.

"I don't think so. I worked too hard to get what I want to give it all up now."

"You were paid to do a job and paid well I might add." She needed to keep him talking while she tried to think of a way to get him out of the house. If her father heard them talking, would he stay in his room and call the police, or would he come out?

Dalton smirked. "Do you know how much ass kissing to your father I had to do, how I had to pretend you were wonderful and swear that I'd take care of you after he was gone? He promised the brewery would be mine after he died."

"The promise was that it would belong to us if we married." She pointed between them. "*Us.* Guess you're out of luck, because I'm not marrying you. Not ever." She'd never hated anyone in her life until now.

"Me. Us. Semantics."

"He'll never sign any papers giving you the brewery."

"Oh, I think he will."

"You're crazy." She took another step back, intending to go to the living room and get her phone. "I'm calling the police. You don't want to be here when they arrive."

"I don't think so." He showed her the hand he'd been hiding behind his back.

"Seriously, Dalton. A gun? What are you going to do, shoot me?" She wasn't exactly scared. There was no way he'd shoot her, but then she looked into his eyes. Now she was scared.

"Yes, if you don't do exactly as I say."

"You wouldn't."

He laughed, and it wasn't a good one. "Do you really want to try me? Move another inch, and I'll make your father watch me put a bullet in your brain."

"You won't get away with this. Walk out right now, and I won't tell a soul you were here." For as long as it took her to call the police and then Noah. "How did you get in, anyway?"

He reached into his shirt pocket and pulled out a key. "Your father gave me a key when I was staying here, taking care of him the first time he had cancer. Like I said, kissing his ass. You think I enjoyed listening to him retch after his treatments? Cooking dinner for him, pretending I gave a shit?"

"You're a bastard."

He tsked. "Not a nice thing to call your future husband. I'm tired of talking to you. You're going to do exactly what I say if you want to see tomorrow."

"You don't have it in you to kill anyone." She prayed that was true.

"No? You might want to ask my late wife about that." He chuckled. "But you'll have to go to the bitch's gravesite to do it."

God help her. He wasn't lying. The truth was in his eyes. How had she not noticed before how cold and dead they were?

"Thought that would shut you up." He pointed the gun at her. "Here's what you're going to do. Write a note to your father. Tell him that your bodyguard picked you up and you'll see him tomorrow. I'll read it, of course, so don't try anything stupid."

"And then what?"

"Then we get married."

"No. You've lost your mind if you think I'm leaving with you."

"So be it." He walked past her.

"Where are you going?"

"To get your father."

"That's your fifth yawn this morning," Jack said.

Noah yawned again.

"Late night with a princess?"

"Shut it. And wipe that stupid smirk off your face." It had been a late night spent in Peyton's bed and then an early morning when she had woken him with her mouth wrapped around him. Best way in the world to wake up.

Jack laughed as he slapped Noah on the back. "You're

a happier man these days. I had my doubts about you getting involved with Peyton, but I was wrong. She's been good for you. Don't screw it up, brother."

"There's nothing to screw up." The lie tasted bitter on his tongue. Peyton had been…was good for him. After she'd fallen asleep last night, he'd actually tried to think of how they could maintain a relationship. He just couldn't see it. Her home was here, the job that meant everything to her was here, her father was here. She couldn't move even if he asked her to, which he wouldn't.

He'd tried to imagine making his home in Asheville, and he couldn't see that, either. The mountain town was charming, and he'd be happy living here except for the simple fact that there was no work for him.

This was Jack's home, where he'd grown up, and he'd found a way to create an organization doing what he loved. Noah couldn't see himself training dogs for the rest of his life, and he wasn't about to mooch off Peyton. No matter how agreeable she might be to that.

So, no. There was nothing to screw up. He would leave. They would both miss each other. She would eventually forget him. He would never forget her.

"We gonna do something besides stand here and *not* talk about my love life?"

"Yeah, so pay attention." Jack crouched in front of Lucky. "Who's a good boy?"

The silly dog tried to climb up him. "What kind of training is that?"

Jack laughed. "You're a happy dog, aren't you, Lucky?" He glanced up at Noah. "He's got a great temperament for a therapy dog. He just needs to understand what his job is. It's much easier to train a therapy dog than it is a service dog. Basically, he has to learn all his commands. Heel, Sit, Stay, et cetera.

"Then we have to get him used to noises so he doesn't try to run away if he hears a car backfire or thunder or whatever. He'll have to learn to ignore distractions, strangers wanting to pet him, a cat running past him, and other dogs. We'll take him places like the mall where there are people. Right now, he wants attention from everyone, and we have to teach him to ignore other people. His purpose in life will be to give comfort to his owner, especially when he or she is suffering from a PTSD episode. He'll learn to recognize the signs."

Noah wasn't sure how he felt about someone else getting his dog. "How will he learn that?"

"To recognize signs of depression?"

"Yeah."

"Dogs are sensitive to their owner's emotions, and many pick up on that on their own, but the owner can also help that learning along by cuddling with the dog when they are experiencing symptoms of depression. That helps the dog learn the tell signs of that particular owner. Another way is to give the dog a treat when you feel an episode coming on. That teaches the dog to respond to the tells. Since people experience PTSD in different ways, responding to the signs part of a therapy dog's training will be done by the owner with guidance from us."

Noah almost let all that pass without comment because that would be admitting that he was one of those people Jack was talking about, but wouldn't that be avoiding? *Don't be a coward*, Doc Meadows said in his head.

"He knows when I'm having a…um, a black moment, I guess you could say. He'll do something like put his chin on my leg and look at me with worried eyes."

"Not surprised. He's an intelligent dog. He'll make someone a good therapy dog once he learns his manners."

Yeah, he would, and Noah was going to miss the silly dog when he returned to his team.

A woman emerged from the office, running toward them. "Who's that?" He'd not seen her here before.

"My new office manager. Just started today." He frowned. "Does she look like she's freaking out?"

"Yeah, she does."

"Trudy, where's the fire?" Jack said when the woman skidded to a stop in front of them.

"The man on the phone said it's a life or death emergency." Her gaze darted between him and Jack. "Are you Noah?" she said when her eyes landed back on him.

"Yes." The hair on the back of his neck stood straight up. Trudy hadn't gotten to what the man on the phone had said, but he knew, just knew that Dalton had somehow gotten to Peyton.

"He wants to talk to you."

Noah didn't know who *he* was, but that didn't matter. Whoever it was had intel, even if it was Dalton. "You have him on the phone?"

"Yes, in the office."

Noah raced past her. Jack's boots pounded the ground behind him. When he reached the office, he skidded to a halt, looking for the phone.

"Here," Jack said, picking up the receiver of a desk phone.

"This is Noah Alba."

"Noah, this is Gerald Sutton, Peyton's father. Is she with you?"

"No, she isn't. Talk to me, sir."

"Damn it, I'm going to kill him."

"I assume you mean her ex?" And Gerald Sutton wasn't going to kill the man, because he was.

"Yes. She left a note saying you picked her up, but it's all wrong."

"Wrong how?"

"Well, first, she addressed me as Father. Peyton's never been that formal with me. But the other thing was the reason I knew she'd been forced to write the note. She said Robbie picked her up. Robbie was my son. That's not a mistake she would have made unless she was sending me a message."

Clever girl. "But you didn't see Dalton take her?"

"No. I was taking a nap. When I woke up, she was gone, and I found the note."

"Mr. Sutton, how long do you think she's been gone?" It was hell standing here, asking his questions. He needed to be out there, doing something.

"I don't know. I wasn't feeling good after my treatment, and she insisted I rest. I've been asleep for about two hours. You have to find her, Noah."

"Oh, I will, sir. You can be assured of that. Give me your phone number." He grabbed a pen and wrote down the number. "Is that your cell?"

"Yes."

"I'm going to message you so you'll have my number. If you hear from her, you call me immediately."

"I will. Please, just find my daughter."

"You can count on it. That's a promise." He dropped the receiver on the desk.

Jack picked it up and put it in the cradle. "Details."

"Lacking." He keyed Sutton's number into his phone, then sent a brief message. He glanced at Jack. "All he knows is that she wasn't there when he woke up from a nap. She left him a note that Robbie picked her up."

"Who's Robbie?"

"His dead son. That's how he knows she didn't leave willingly."

"Shit."

"You got that right." Noah gave himself a few seconds to let the rage burn through him, then he locked it away. Like any mission, he had to have a clear head and a plan for a successful completion. When he found the son of a bitch, he'd free the rage and rain it down on the man.

"You mentioned getting trackers. Did you?"

"Affirmative. One she wears in her bra and one in her purse. And she better have them on her." Otherwise, he was going to paddle her pretty ass when he found her. He pulled up the app he'd put on his phone. "I also have an app to track her phone."

"I'm calling Deke."

"No. He'll have to report it and then SWAT will get involved since it's a hostage situation. That could end up being a shitstorm, especially if her ex has a weapon, and I think there's a good chance of that. There's no way Peyton would have willingly gone with him."

He knew the man was getting desperate. Had told Peyton so. This was on him. He never should have left her side.

"Okay, guess it's you and me." Jack squeezed his shoulder.

"You're not invited on this operation, Whiskey. I don't

promise I won't end up in jail when I'm finished with the asshole. You don't need to be involved. Nichole would never forgive me if you ended up in the cell next to me."

Jack snorted. "I'm inviting myself. Besides, I already have a cell with my name on it. It'll be like old home week." At Noah's raised brows, Jack said, "Story for another time. Let's find your woman."

"That's the plan."

"You seem pretty calm about this."

"If you think I don't want to tear the town apart with my bare hands to find her, you'd be dead-ass wrong. Let's take your truck. You know the area better and that will also free me up to track her."

"Is there any chance of him hurting her?" Jack asked as he turned the truck onto the highway.

"I don't think so, and that's the only thing keeping me calm right now. His only goal is to marry her so he can get access to the brewery. I don't know how he thinks he can pull that off now that her father has turned on him, but I'm not sure he's got all his marbles these days."

"Where to?"

Noah studied the phone screen. "You know where Hendersonville is?"

"Yep. Depending on I-26 traffic, we're about thirty minutes from there."

"We need to swing by your house and get—"

"My guns. Already headed there."

"Look, it would be best if you didn't come with me." Jack had a good life going with his girlfriend and the dogs. He didn't need to risk losing everything if this went south.

"Negative." He glanced at Noah. "I've got your six just like you'd have mine if I needed you."

True story, so he didn't try to argue. He'd be wasting his breath. Although he'd understand if Jack opted out of this party, he was glad to have his friend at his back. They were two of the military's highest trained warriors. The bastard had no clue what was coming for him.

Chapter Twenty-Seven

"You're out of your ever-loving mind. I'm not putting that on." Peyton stared in horror at the wedding gown... *her* wedding gown. He'd gone back to the waterfall and fished it out? Had it repaired and cleaned? He was wacked! He had to be on drugs if he thought she was going to put that on and marry him.

Dalton shrugged. "Makes no never mind to me. Thought you'd rather look pretty in your wedding pictures. But if you want to get married in—" he ran a critical gaze over her "—shorts and a T-shirt, you will get married."

"Get this through your head. I am not marrying you. I'll refuse."

"The man marrying us doesn't give a damn if you refuse, not with the money I'm paying him."

"It won't be legal."

He sighed as if she were trying his patience. "Wrong. He's totally legit." He chuckled. "Just easily bought."

"My father won't turn over Elk Antler to you, not after this stunt."

"He will if it means you get to live. After he's gone, who knows what your future will be, if you even have one." He walked to the door. "Think about that. Do you want to live, Peyton? I'll be back. Put the gown on. I want my bride looking pretty for me."

"Why are you doing this for just a few shares of the business? It doesn't make sense."

He paused. "I guess there's no reason not to tell you. Consider it my wedding gift to you. Two reasons. For one, I'd gotten myself in a bit of a jam money wise and had a few gambling debts hanging over my head."

"Since when do you gamble?" She'd never seen any sign that he wagered on anything.

"Does it matter?"

"I suppose not. How much do you owe?"

"Enough that there were people you don't want to mess with demanding payment if I fancied continuing to breathe."

"Okay, so we'll figure something out, a way to pay them." That was an outright lie. She had no intention of helping him in any way, shape, or form, but if he believed her, he'd let her go.

"Such an innocent little thing you are. It's too late for that. Thomas Guillain has paid the debt."

"Why would he do that?" Thomas Guillain was a slime ball liquor distributor. There were rumors that he had ties with the mob and that he laundered money through various businesses he had a stake in.

"Because when I own Elk Antler, he'll be a silent partner."

"You can't be serious. You've heard the rumors about him. He'll force you to do illegal things, like launder money through Elk Antler." The thought of Thomas Guillain getting his hands on her father's brewery, a business he'd put his lifeblood into, made her sick to her stomach. "I won't let you do this, Dalton."

He laughed. "You don't have any say in the matter. As for the second thing, you were promised to me by your father, and I mean to have you."

"Why? You don't love me, so way does it matter?"

"It's a matter of principle, sweetheart. You're mine, and I keep what's mine. Besides, no one will question my ownership of the brewery if you're my wife."

"You're crazy."

"Put the damn dress on."

She flinched at the sound of the door slamming behind him. She went to the door and tried to open it. The jerk had locked her in. Fury poured through her that Dalton would let someone like Thomas Guillain get his hands on Elk Antler. Not on her watch. First chance she got, she was going to poke his eyes out, and then she was going to do as much damage as she could to his baby-making parts so there would never be a child with his DNA.

Where was she? Dalton had blindfolded her as soon as she'd gotten in his car. Leaving with him was probably the biggest mistake of her life, but it was hard to argue with a gun. Afraid that if she fought him, it would wake her father, and what if Dalton shot him?

She glanced around. The room was about the size of her walk-in closet. Where was she? She had her tracker on her, but Dalton had made her leave her purse, which had her phone in it, in his car.

Noah would find her, she was sure of it, so she needed to buy time. There were two windows, but they were boarded up from the outside, so no escaping through them. She searched for something to use as a weapon, but other than a faded futon, there was nothing else in the room.

She glared at the gown. She should have burned it

instead of just throwing it in the water. What about the coat hanger? It was a wooden one, and she could do some damage with it. He'd notice it was missing, though, if she wasn't wearing the gown when he returned.

As she saw it, she had two choices that would keep Dalton from noticing the hanger was gone. "Nope, not putting you on, stupid dress. Didn't like you the first time around, hate you now." Second option then.

The gown wasn't as easy to rip apart as she would have thought, but she finally had it torn in strips. She stuffed one of the thicker ones in the pocket of her shorts. If she got a chance, she would cheerfully strangle Dalton.

Next, she went to work on the hanger. The metal hook was easy to unscrew, and she stuck that in her other pocket. It would come in handy if she got a chance to poke his eyes out. Pulling apart the hanger was harder, but she managed to break it in two parts. Where to hide it? She needed it on her, where she could get to it. She slid the smaller piece inside her shorts and panties, along the outside of her hip. After a few practice steps, she nodded, satisfied that it would stay in place. Hopefully Dalton wouldn't notice the slight bulge at her side.

Weaponized, however paltry, she waited for Dalton to return so she could make him sorry for kidnapping her. How could he even think she or her father would go along with his ridiculous scheme?

The door opened, and she backed up to the wall, pressing against it. When should she attack? Not in the room. If he managed to overpower her and take her weapons away, he'd lock her up again. Better to wait until she was where she could escape from the house or whatever this place was.

Dalton entered, carrying a champagne bottle and two flutes. His gaze swept over the floor, taking in the destroyed dress. "Guess that means you're getting married in your shorts." He held up the bottle. "I thought you'd like to celebrate our marriage."

"Not. Marrying. You. You won't get away with this insanity, Dalton."

He laughed. "I already have, love. Tonight, after we're married, we'll pay a visit to your father. I have the papers transferring the brewery to you and me ready for him to sign."

She was so tempted to pull out her hanger stick and beat some sense into his brain. Not yet, though. Timing was going to be everything, along with surprise. When she was out of this room and he was distracted, she would strike.

Then there was Noah. She didn't know if he was aware she was missing yet, but when he did find out, he would come for her. She didn't doubt that for a minute. Dalton should be shaking in his boots, but she wasn't going to warn him.

She was positive her father would know something was wrong as soon as he read her note. She'd banked on Dalton not knowing Noah's name or who Robbie was to her father when she'd written that Robbie had come for her. Dalton hadn't questioned Robbie's name, and she'd breathed a sigh of relief.

The one thing she was counting on was that as soon as he read the note, her father would remember that she'd told him about Operation K-9 Brothers, and he'd call there and ask for Noah.

So, while she trusted that her father would understand her message, that he would find and tell Noah, and that Noah would come for her, she wasn't going to wait around for a rescue that might never happen.

Dalton glanced at the champagne bottle he held. "I guess I get to enjoy this myself." His gaze lifted to hers. "You know, we really could have had it all, you and me." He shook his head as if he was disappointed in her. "But you didn't follow the plan and now it's too late for you to reap the rewards. I have to go pick up the preacher. Be a good girl until I get back, *wife*."

"First chance I get, I'm going to hurt you where your future children live." That was a promise she made herself as he walked out, trailing laughter behind him.

Noah frowned. "The tracing device on her is stationary but her phone's on the move."

"Which one do we track?" Jack said.

"I don't know. Has he found the one on her or the app on her phone?" He had a fifty-fifty chance of being right, and he had to get it right. "He might think to check out her phone, but I don't think it would occur to him to search her for a tracking device." He hoped to God that was true. "Let's go to the stationary one." He entered the location on the truck GPS. "You know if he's hurt her that I'm going to kill him, right?"

"Let's see what the situation is before you go off half-cocked. Jail's not a place you want to end up, trust me on that."

"More of that story you're going to tell me some-day?"

"Yeah. When you can listen instead of bouncing around in your seat. I'd drive faster, but you don't want the police, so we don't want to get stopped. Especially since we're packing."

"I keep telling myself that he won't hurt her, but I think he's living in La La Land. He's blown any chance of her father agreeing to anything Dalton wants, so what does he gain by pulling this stunt?"

"Revenge?"

"If it's that, then he has nothing to lose, and she's in danger. When we kicked him out of her loft, he'd told her they were going to Vegas to get married." Did he still think that would get him what he wanted? "It could be revenge, but my gut tells me that he's still out to get the brewery." He prayed that was the man's plan.

"We'll find out soon."

"Is where we're going close to the airport?"

"Closer than Asheville is. Maybe he's hiding out with her until it's time to catch a flight."

"The problem with that plan is that he'd have to drug her to get her on a plane. Otherwise, she'd be kicking and screaming. And carrying a drugged woman through the airport and trying to get her on a plane would invite too many questions." Unless he'd chartered a private plane, but according to Jack, the GPS location wasn't at the airport, so all they could do at this point was go to the designated location and pray that Peyton was there.

"We're about thirty minutes or so away." Jack glanced at the GPS map. "It looks like a rural area outside of Hendersonville."

"What the hell? Her phone is moving back toward the location of the tracking device. They're only a few miles apart now."

"That's weird."

"Yeah." He considered explanations that would make sense. "I think the stationary tracker is Peyton, and her phone's in a vehicle. So, who's driving it? Dalton or someone else? If it's someone else, why do they have her phone?"

"Either Dalton left and now is coming back, or someone else is joining the party," Jack said. "My preference is for the first. Another player complicates things."

"No shit." But if it was someone else, how did her phone get in the vehicle? All they could do at this point was guess, and he didn't like not having intel. Going in blind was never good. Too much chance for an operation to go south.

Not that he was worried about dealing with Dalton. He could deal with the man by himself with one hand—hell, both hands even—tied behind him. Considering who he and Jack were, the bastard didn't stand a chance. But throw another player in the mix, and not know who that was or what he was capable of, could definitely complicate things. Not that he was worried he and Jack couldn't take down Dalton and anyone else involved, he just didn't like not knowing.

He especially didn't like Peyton being in the middle of a shitstorm, and he didn't want to think of Dalton having his hands on her. Made him want to put a serious hurt on the man.

"What's the man's name again, her ex?"

"Dalton. Never asked what his last name was." He should have paid more attention to the man. There were a lot of things he should have done, like not leave Peyton alone for a minute, or convince her to file a report with the police when Dalton put bruises on her arm, or convince her to get a restraining order.

He'd promised to keep her safe, and he'd failed. Just like he'd failed his team. After he rescued her, made sure that Dalton was arrested…or dead, he'd leave. His medical leave was about up anyway, so time to go. Peyton would get her life back, and it would be even better now that she was back at the brewery and had repaired her relationship with her father. She wouldn't need him anymore. That thought was a punch to the gut but true.

"You ever going to tell me the story about those dice?" Jack said, glancing at the pair of dice Noah was rolling in his hand.

"Who says there's a story?" Jack was the only one of his teammates who'd ever asked why he carried them. He'd always shrugged off the question.

"Are you telling me there isn't?"

"Not saying that." He eyed the GPS. "I'll tell you why when you tell me your jail story. We're almost there. Her phone and tracker are back in the same location. I think we should find a place to park and walk in. Scope things out before Dalton knows we're there."

"Copy that."

"You will reach your destination in five hundred feet," the feminine voice from the GPS said. "Your destination is on the right."

Jack drove slowly past, both of them scoping out the dirt lane. Four mailboxes lined the entrance to the road. There was no way of knowing which was their target house or how soon they would come up on it.

"Find a place to park," Noah said.

"Here looks good."

Noah eyed the spot. There was just enough room to get the truck off the road without driving into the ditch. The truck wouldn't be hidden, but that shouldn't be a problem. Dalton didn't know what Jack drove.

After parking, they slipped into the woods that bordered the dirt road. Two children were playing in the yard of the first house they came to. He and Jack stayed hidden as they passed by. An old man was sitting in a recliner that was on the porch of the second house, and a teenage girl was hanging up clothes in the backyard of the third house.

"The last house it is then," Jack said.

"Let's just hope she's actually there." She'd better be, and she'd better be unhurt.

They halted at the edge of the woods. The house on the other side of the road looked abandoned, but there was a silver Mercedes parked in front. "That's his car." Noah blew out a breath, his heart racing in relief that he'd found her.

"Let's circle around and come at the place from the side," Jack said.

Noah nodded his agreement, but as they took a step back, gunfire sounded from inside the house. "New plan." He raced across the street. There had better not be so much as a scratch on Peyton, or Dalton was a dead man.

An older man stumbled out of the house. "I didn't sign up for crazy," he said as Noah ran past him.

Noah skidded to a stop inside the doorway. "Peyton?"

Chapter Twenty-Eight

Dalton returned and dragged her out of the room. He pulled her down a dark hallway, his fingers digging into the skin on her arm. He was going to leave bruises again. This time, she was definitely going to report his abuse to the police, like she should have done the first time.

Turned out they were in a house, one that looked like it had been vacant for a long time. Ugly wallpaper was peeling from the walls, and the carpet was so nasty that she didn't want to walk on it even wearing shoes.

He brought her to the living room, where a man who appeared to be drunk propped up a wall.

"Who's that?" When should she try to escape? She glanced out the dirty front window. Dalton's car was parked in the yard. She'd borrowed it once to run away. Looked like she was going to have to borrow it again.

"That's the magistrate who's going to marry us."

She scowled at Dalton, then glared at the other man. "I'm not marrying him, so you can just be on your way."

The man belched.

"Get on with it," Dalton said.

The man looked puzzled. "Get on what?"

"The wedding, idiot."

"Oh. Right. Ahem, dearly beloved, we are here today—"

"I'm not marrying this jerk!" Peyton screamed. Was this even legal? She was pretty sure the law required two witnesses. Knowing Dalton, he'd probably forge the witness signatures. But she wasn't taking a chance on whether or not any of this was legal.

"If the lady doesn't want to get married, I can't force her," the man said.

Peyton wholeheartedly agreed.

"Hey, now," the man said, his eyes going wide when Dalton pointed a gun at his head. "Put that thing away before you hurt someone."

Dalton kept the gun pointed at the magistrate. "Finish the damn ceremony."

It was now or never, before she ended up married to the biggest jerk in the world. She slid her hand down the inside of her shorts and wrapped her fingers around the coat hanger stick.

"Dearly beloved, we are gathered here today to join…" Bleary eyes peered at her. "What's your name, dear?"

"Well, in about ten seconds, Dalton here is going to call me bitch, so feel free to go with that." She tightened her grip on the stick, then pulled it up and out. Before Dalton realized she had a weapon, she aimed the pointy end at his junk and slammed the stick into him with all her strength.

"Bitch!" Dalton yelled as he doubled over. Unfortunately, he didn't drop the gun.

She didn't have time to take satisfaction in her perfect aim or that she'd called it. Yep, she was a bitch, and at the moment, proud of it. But there was still the matter of the gun that he was now raising toward her. She brought the stick up again, then slammed it down on his hand as hard as she could.

The gun fell between them, and they both dived for it. She got her hand on it first, but Dalton slapped his hand over hers. He got the gun away and pointed it at her as she backed up.

She stared into the barrel of the gun and knew she was going to die without ever seeing Noah again. That pissed her off. She saw in Dalton's eyes that he was past reasoning with, and she fell to the floor as a bullet whizzed past her head. That was a sound she never wanted to hear again for as long as she lived.

Having nothing to lose, she pulled the hanger hook from her pocket as she rolled toward him. If it was she last thing in her life she did, she was going to make him sorry for what he was trying to do to her and her father. She raised the hook, intending to rake it down whatever part of his body she could reach. She wanted to see him bleed.

Instead, it caught the trigger guard of the gun, and the gun fell to the floor between them. They both dived for it again, and miraculously, she got to it first. Before she could get away with the gun, Dalton's hand slammed down on hers. He squeezed her hand so hard that pain shot up her arm, but she refused to let go. He was furious enough now to shoot her if he got it away.

Desperate, she clamped her teeth down on his hand. He grunted and his grip loosened, and she had possession of the gun. Dalton looked at her with hate in his eyes, then he lunged at her. She had no idea how it happened, but the gun went off, and she was so startled that she almost dropped it.

Dalton screamed as he wrapped his hands around the tip of his shoe. "My toe! You shot my fucking toe off."

"Oops." Not wasting her chance to get away, she held on to the gun as she scooted backward until she hit the wall. Her heart was pounding against her chest, and she gulped air into her lungs. She stared at her hand. She'd never held a gun before, didn't want to be holding one now. What was she supposed to do with it?

"Peyton?"

She glanced up, relief slamming through her at seeing Noah. "Um, hi there." She turned her attention to the gun in her shaking hand. "Ah…you want this?" Please want it before she shot someone else's toe off.

"Yeah, princess, I'll take it. Just keep it pointed at the floor while I come get it, okay?"

She nodded. She could do that. He kneeled at her side, and she almost giggled that he was keeping well out of range of the gun's muzzle. Couldn't blame him for that, nor did she want to see him lose any toes because of her.

He wrapped his fingers around the barrel. "I got it, baby. You can let go now."

"O…okay." She wanted to, she really did, but her fingers refused to cooperate.

Apparently realizing that her hands were frozen in their grip position—hopefully not permanently because that would suck—he brushed his lips over hers. "Put your hands on my face, princess."

Yes, that was a much better place for her hands than the hard metal of a gun. Her hands agreed and after letting go of the gun, moved themselves to Noah's face. She sighed. Noah was here, and she wasn't marrying Dalton. Good, that was good.

The gun disappeared from sight, and he put his arm around her back, lifting her to her feet. Dalton's screams penetrated her fuzzy mind. How long had she tuned out, not even hearing him?

"I shot his toe off."

Noah laughed. "Yeah, you did. Couldn't have happened to a nicer guy."

"I didn't mean to. We were fighting over the gun, and I don't know, it went off. Maybe he was the one who pulled the trigger, shooting his own toe off. Yeah, I like that version. He was going to make me marry him, but I armed myself with weapons, if you can call a piece of wood from a coat hanger and a metal hook weapons, but it was all that was handy, so I improvised. I also have a strip of my wedding dress to tie him up with, or maybe use it to strangle him. Didn't get a chance to—"

Noah kissed her. He smiled against her mouth. Yeah, she had him well trained. Hearing that gunshot, fearing that he'd find her hurt or worse...hell, he'd never been that scared even in the middle of a firefight. She was shell-shocked, but she was all in one piece. Nothing else mattered.

The asshole was still screaming, and Noah reluctantly pulled his mouth away from Peyton's. "Can you shut him up?"

"I don't think so," Peyton said. "I'm pretty much done with having anything to do with him."

"Not you, babe."

She peered around him. "Oh, hi, Jack. Didn't know you were here, too."

Jack grinned. "Peyton, you're my new hero." He glared at Dalton. "Will you shut the hell up? It's just a little toe."

"I shot his pinky?" Peyton said. "His little pinky? That's it?" She marched over to her ex, bent over, and scowled. "Oh, boo hoo. You're lucky it was only your little toe. I was aiming for your junk."

"Bitch," he growled.

"Never *your* bitch, though. Ha-ha. To show you that I'm a better person than you, here." She pulled the long strip of white, lacey material from her pocket. "I was going to use this to strangle you, but I'll give it to you to wrap your stupid toe."

"I think she's high on adrenaline," Jack said.

Noah chuckled. Yeah, she was a bit manic. Jack was grinning like a fool. He knew the feeling. Peyton tended to have that effect on you. If you weren't smiling because of her, you were kissing her. Well, he was. No one else better be kissing her.

"Can we go now?" She wrinkled her nose as she glanced around. "I really need a bath."

"Sorry," Jack said. "We have to wait for Deke to get here." He glanced at Noah. "I called him while you were getting the gun away from her."

Peyton shifted her gaze to Jack. "Oh, right. I'm not thinking real clear right now."

Noah moved next to her. He gently trailed his fingers over the bruises on her arms. "How?"

"When we were fighting over the gun."

"You can't kill him," Jack said.

But he could accidently step on the bastard's wounded toe, taking satisfaction when the man's screams intensified.

Peyton tugged on his arm. "Can I at least go outside? It smells in here, and Dalton's whining is giving me a headache."

"You bet." He wrapped his arm around her shoulders and walked her out. He'd raced here thinking he was going to have to rescue her, but she'd rescued herself. Was he proud of her? Damn straight. "You did good, princess. Half the guys in boot camp wouldn't have been as clever as you in devising makeshift weapons."

She beamed at him. "I was clever, wasn't I? At first, I was really scared. I knew you'd come, but I wasn't sure how long it would take or if you'd be able to find me. So, I decided not to be helpless. How'd you find me?"

"The trackers. Your father called Jack's place and asked for me. He told me about the note and how you'd gotten a message to him by saying you'd left with Robbie. He immediately knew you were in trouble. Using his son's name was brilliant."

"It wouldn't have been if Dalton knew about Robbie, but Dad had said he hadn't told anyone here about his previous life. I counted on Dalton not catching that."

"Clever, clever girl." She smiled and he smiled back and what the hell was with his jittery heart? Felt like jumping beans were bouncing around in it. "Who was that man that came tearing out of here right before I came in?" he said to get his feet back on solid ground.

"That was a drunk magistrate Dalton paid I don't know how much to marry us."

Noah glanced around. "Guess he took off. Do you know his name?" He'd like to give it to Deke. The magistrate had been prepared to marry an unwilling woman to a man with a gun.

"No, he wasn't introduced to me." She glanced at the Mercedes. "Oh, I need to get my purse and phone out of Dalton's car. He wouldn't let me have them when we got here."

"I'll get them for you." He grabbed the purse from the front passenger seat, noticing a large envelope was also on the seat. He picked it up and pulled out the sheets, frowning when he realized what they were.

She took her purse and slipped the strap over her shoulder. Her gaze fell on the envelope. "What's that?"

"Looks like a contract agreement, turning the brewery over to your ex."

"He said my father would sign it if he wanted me to live. I should have shot all his toes off, although I still think he was the one to pull the trigger when we were wrestling for the gun."

Noah still might kill the man.

"I need to call my father. He's probably worried sick."

"Yeah, do that. He is worried."

While she was talking to her father, Noah stepped back inside. Jack was on his phone, and Dalton had moved from the floor to sit on a filthy couch. He had his shoe off and was rocking back and forth while holding his foot.

Dalton glared at him. "I need an ambulance, and when the cops get here, I'm filing assault charges on Peyton and cruel and inhumane treatment on the two of you."

"Shut your face." Noah turned his back on the man. Maybe he'd get lucky and the bastard would come at him.

Jack finished his call, then shoved his phone into his back pocket. "That was Nichole. She's as bloodthirsty as you, Double D. Said we should have taught him a lesson when we had the chance." He chuckled. "Damn, I love that woman."

"Believe me, that we didn't is my regret for the day. When's Deke supposed to get here? I'd really like to get Peyton home." He glanced around the nasty room. "I don't think what happened here has really hit her yet, and when it does, she's going to need some TLC."

Jack smirked.

"What?"

"Nothing. I'll let you figure it out for yourself."

"You said that once before. If you're implying there's something between us, sure, we like each other. At the end of the day, though, I'm leaving, and she'll go on living her life."

Jack snorted. "Uh-huh."

"Besides, there's nothing for me to do in Asheville even if I wanted to stay."

"You could work with me."

"Thanks, but dogs are your thing, not mine."

"Assholes, I'm bleeding out here."

Noah glanced over his shoulder. "Good, but hurry it up, will you? I'm tired of listening to you."

"Here he is," Jack said at the sound of a car arriving.

"Great." He walked to the window. A typical detective's car was parked next to the Mercedes, and a patrol vehicle pulled in behind Deke.

Deke was already out of his car and talking to Peyton…rather, Peyton was talking a mile a minute, her hands moving around just as fast. He shook his head and chuckled.

"What's funny?" Jack moved next to him and peered out the window. "Ah, she's doing her rambling thing."

"He just better not kiss her," Noah muttered.

Jack laughed. "The bug has bit you, brother." He

slapped Noah on the back, then went out to join Peyton and Deke.

So what if it had…not that it had, or if it had, that it would make a difference. He wouldn't know what love was if it stood in front of him waving a red flag. He'd certainly never learned about love from his father. Maybe his mother had loved her husband once, but in the years that Noah could remember, she'd only stayed because she had nowhere to go or the means to leave. And when she'd finally tried, she'd paid with her life.

Foreigner's "I Want to Know What Love Is" played in his mind again. What would his head doc say about that? That his subconscious was trying to tell him something? Maybe, and maybe he really did want to know what love was, but…

He wasn't even sure what the "but" was anymore.

There was nothing for him in Asheville other than a princess who might or might not want him to stay. She'd never given any indication that she did, and he wouldn't put her in a difficult position by asking. Funny thing, though. He couldn't imagine ever kissing another woman.

"It was nice of Deke to let me wait until the morning to sign my statement," Peyton said when they arrived home.

Noah inwardly snorted. There was nothing nice about it. He'd pulled Deke aside and told him flat out that Peyton was done for the day. She, along with him and Jack, had given their statements to Deke and the police officer, which Deke had recorded. What Noah wasn't willing to do was make her go to the police station today and wait for her statement to be typed up so she could sign it.

Deke hadn't been happy, but he hadn't pushed the issue. Deke also hadn't been happy that he and Jack hadn't called him as soon as they knew Dalton had taken Peyton.

"And have SWAT show up and escalate the situation?" Noah had said. "Would you have called the police if Heather had been taken and you had someone like Jack and me available to help you rescue her?" When Deke didn't answer, Noah nodded. "Thought so. Besides, Peyton saved herself without my and Jack's assistance. So no harm, no foul."

Deke's gaze shifted to Peyton. "She told me that Dalton admitted to killing his wife."

"Seriously?" He was glad he hadn't known that while the bastard had Peyton. He wasn't sure he could have kept a clear head with that knowledge.

"Believe me, we'll be taking a hard look at that. What she managed to do today was pretty amazing."

It was, and now he had her home where he could take care of her. At the moment, she was still on an adrenaline high, but at some point tonight, she was going to crash. He'd be here to catch her.

He filled her tub, added bath salts he'd found, and stripped her of her clothes while listening to her recount her day for the second time. He didn't think she even noticed he was undressing her.

"Seriously, did he really think I'd just go along with his plan like a good little girl?" She put her hand on his shoulder and stepped out of her panties when he lowered them to her feet. "At first, I thought my only hope was for you to find me. But I was pissed. Is it okay if I say pissed? Dalton wasn't okay with it."

Why hadn't he killed the bastard when he'd had the chance? He stood, cupped her cheeks, and lifted her face so she was looking at him. "Princess, anything you say, any word you use is okay with me." She smiled that smile that did weird things to his heart.

"Cool beans."

He laughed. "Yeah, cool beans. Get in the tub. I'm going out to get us dinner, but I won't be gone long. Anything special you want?"

"You."

This girl. "You'll have me all you want tonight." He tapped her butt. "In the tub with you."

"Where's Lucky? I want Lucky."

"He's at Jack's. We'll go get him in the morning. In with you."

"I don't want to be alone. Take a bath with me."

The offer was too tempting to refuse. Dinner could wait. "Scoot up," he said after removing his clothes. He eased in behind her, his legs on the outside of hers. Fortunately, her tub was an oversize Jacuzzi, easily accommodating both their bodies. He turned the jets on low, then leaned back and pulled her against his chest.

"How are you doing?" She'd been unusually quiet on the trip home, and he'd missed her chatter.

"Okay. I just want to forget today happened."

He rested his chin on the top of her head. "I get that." He'd felt the same way after his screwup. "You'll have to talk more about it tomorrow when you sign your statement, but for tonight, just relax and don't think about anything but how nice this feels." He picked up a washcloth and poured some of her bodywash on it.

"Will you sing to me?"

"Ah…" No, he didn't sing anymore.

"It's okay. You don't have to."

He trailed the cloth down one of her arms, and then the other. She purred when he moved to her breasts, then lower. What would never singing again accomplish? It wouldn't bring Asim or Snoop back. It wouldn't change anything, but it would make her happy. He liked making her happy, so he sang.

And as he softly sang "Pretty Woman," Dr. Meadows's words came back to him.

"You have to forgive yourself. No one else can do it for you."

Maybe he could figure out how to do that.

Chapter Twenty-Nine

"So, what happens now?" Peyton asked after she signed her statement. She'd never been in a police interrogation room before. It was intimidating, and she wasn't even the one in trouble.

Deke slid her statement into a folder. "Now you and Lucky are free to go."

"I mean with Dalton." She curled her fingers in the fur on Lucky's head. She'd wanted Noah with her, but he hadn't been allowed. Another detective had taken him into a different room to go over his statement. Deke had let Lucky stay with her, and for that, she was grateful.

It was over, and she should be relieved. She was, really, but she was…unsettled or something. What if Dalton went free? Would he come after her again? If he did, what if she wasn't as clever the next time?

"He'll spend another night in jail at least. Tomorrow he'll go before a judge. I'm sure he'll plead not guilty. He's making noises, trying to blame you for everything, but the evidence doesn't support that. Not even close, Peyton, so you don't have anything to worry about."

"Will you keep him in jail?"

"The DA will try to get no bail on him. He'll argue that Dalton is an ongoing threat to you. I think there's a good chance bail will be denied, especially since he confessed to you that he killed his wife."

"Do you think he really did, or was he just trying to scare me?" She almost wished for the latter because what woman wanted to think she'd come close to marrying a murderer? But if that confession kept him locked away, that was a good thing.

"All I can tell you is that I've talked to a detective in Dalton's hometown, and she's going to take a closer look at his wife's death. At the time, it was ruled a suicide."

"I think he did it. If you could have seen his face, looked into his eyes when he said it, you'd think so, too."

"That's not something you just make up off the top of your head. I think he's guilty as hell. We just have to prove it."

"What about Thomas Guillain?"

"We've passed his name and what little we know on to the FBI. It's in their hands now." He leaned back in his chair. "We're finished here unless you have more questions."

"No, I just want to…" What did she want to do? Not go to work. Her father had already told her to take the day off. She wanted to spend the day with Noah, even if it was at Operation K-9 Brothers loving on some puppies. Her first choice, though, would be at home with Noah, doors locked to the outside world, where she could have her way with him.

When they walked out of the interrogation room, Noah was leaning against the wall, waiting for her. Gosh, he was beautiful. He smiled, and she walked right into his arms.

"You okay, princess?"

She nodded against his chest. She was now.

* * *

Nichole had arrived at Operation K-9 Brothers with a large picnic basket in tow, and the four of them were having another picnic. Dakota and Lucky were already here, and she'd brought Rambo and Maggie May with her.

Noah had needed to come here after they left the police station, and although Peyton's first choice was for both of them to be naked in her bed, she'd been okay with getting some puppy love. She'd gotten a good hour of puppies licking her, tugging on her clothes, and smelling their milk-sweet breath before Nichole had shown up.

Rambo and Maggie May were playing tug of war with a rope Jack had tossed them. Peyton smiled at their antics. Dakota and Lucky had positioned themselves at her end of the picnic bench, their alert gazes sweeping the area. They reminded her of sentries.

"What's up with these two?" she said.

Jack glanced at the two dogs. "They're picking up on your tension, so they're guarding your six."

"My six?"

Noah wrapped his arm around her waist and tugged her against him. "Means they're watching your back."

"I'm not tense."

"Yeah, princess, you are. But you've earned being tense. I get Dakota picking up on that, but I'm surprised about Lucky." He glanced at Jack. "Wish I could take that dog home with me."

Jack chuckled. "The dog you didn't want any part of?"

"Yeah, that one, you sly bastard." His gaze still on Lucky, he shook his head. "But deployments."

Peyton was sure her heart seized when Noah talked about going home. She knew that was coming, and sooner rather than later. But even thinking she was prepared, tears burned her eyes. And deployments? Where he might be killed? She couldn't…she just couldn't.

She didn't want Noah to see her eyes watering, so she looked around. "Where's the bathroom?" She needed to get away from the three pairs of eyes suddenly focused on her before they stripped her bare, before they…no, before Noah saw that she wasn't so okay with him leaving. She couldn't remember, but she thought she'd promised him she wasn't looking for…well, she couldn't remember, so maybe she'd made him promises she'd thought she could keep and maybe she hadn't.

Whatever. He wasn't staying, not even for her.

"You okay?" Noah said.

"Why wouldn't I be?" she said, sounding snarkier than she'd intended. Or maybe she had intended to be a bitch. Again, whatever.

"I'll show you where," Nichole said, edging next to her. "Come with me, sweetie."

As she walked alongside Nichole, she glanced back. Noah was watching her, and she didn't like seeing the worry on his face. Worry that she'd put there. He had enough to deal with without her adding to it, so even though she was worried sick thinking of him on deployment, she had to hide it.

"He's leaving, and I promised that was okay when the time came," Peyton blurted as soon as a door closed behind them. She glanced around and frowned. "This isn't the bathroom."

"Did you really need a bathroom or just a place to rant on how stupid the male population has a knack for being?"

Peyton snort laughed. "That last part. So, where

are we?" It was like being in someone's living room. There was a leather sofa and two leather recliners, a TV mounted on the wall, and game controls were on the coffee table. Not a space she would have expected a dog therapy place to have.

"This is the family room. Sometimes a family member will come with the person going through training with their new dog, and they can come in here while the training session is happening."

"That's really thoughtful, having a room like this for them." She was impressed with what Jack was doing.

"So, you're not okay even though you promised you would be?" Nichole sat on the sofa, then patted the seat next to her.

Peyton nodded as she took a seat. "Yeah, I'm not okay. Not even close, but I can't let him see that. I'm going to miss him so much when he returns to his team, but I'm going to let him go. I don't really have a choice."

"He'll miss you, too. Don't you see how he looks at you? Like you're the air he needs to breathe. He just hasn't admitted it to himself yet."

Was Nichole right? Not that it mattered. As much as she wanted to hold on to him, she had to let him go. If he felt the same way she did, he'd come back. If he forgot about her, then she didn't want him…*shouldn't* want him. That was what she told herself, what she tried to believe.

Noah disconnected the call with his commander. He stared at the phone for a moment, then lifted his gaze to Jack. "That was Jacobson."

"I gathered. When does he want you back?"

"Monday morning. I was kind of hoping he'd forget about me."

"Do you mean that?"

"Honestly? I don't know." Until things had gone so wrong on his last mission, he'd thought he'd be in the navy, that he would be a SEAL until the day he couldn't pass the physical requirements. Meaning another ten, fifteen years. Now… Now, he couldn't fill in the blanks of what tomorrow looked like.

"What about your appointments with Dr. Meadows?"

"He said he talked to her this morning. She signed off on me returning on the condition that I continue seeing someone when I get back. Gave him a recommendation for a therapist she thinks will be a good fit."

"That's good." Jack stood. "Let's take a walk. We got things to talk about."

"What things?"

"Your future, brother, and we don't need interruptions if our women come back before we're done."

Our women. There was nothing more in the world he wanted than to claim Peyton as his and for her to put her claim on him. But he didn't have that right until he got his head straight. He thought he was finding his way to that happening, but what did he know?

"I've been thinking about something." Jack picked up a stick and threw it. Lucky, Rambo, and Maggie May took off after it. Dakota stayed at Jack's side.

"About?"

"I want to create a place for our brothers and sisters to come. A place where they can just get away for a few weeks. I'll call it Operation Warriors Center. I want two sections, the first for individuals, and eventually a place for our brothers and sisters to come with their families."

"What will they do there?"

"All kinds of activities. Fishing, rock climbing, hiking, a shooting range, stuff like that. Maybe down the road, equine therapy. I've been reading up on that, and I think it has potential. I want a full-time therapist or two on staff."

"Sounds like a big investment financially." He was aware there were some places like that around the country, but Asheville would be an awesome location for the kind of activities Jack had in mind.

"I've got an investor group lined up. If you sign on, I'll tell you who they are."

"Sign on?"

"Yeah, I want you to head it up. That means working with me on finding a suitable site, making recommendations on how we need to build it, and hiring staff. Your job title will be center director."

"I don't—"

"Don't give me an answer now. I get that training dogs isn't your thing, but this might be something you could sink your teeth into. You have what, another month before you have to re-up or opt out?"

"About that."

"Okay, take that time to think about it. If it's re-up, let me know as soon as you make the decision so I can look for someone else."

"It's a lot to think about for sure." Did he want to leave his team? Or was the better question could he go back? What if he screwed up again? Got someone else killed? Being a SEAL had been everything until the day he wished he could erase from his memory. Now? When he let himself think about returning to his team, he had to push the panic away.

If he took the job, it would mean no more deployments, one less obstacle standing between him and Peyton.

"Let's go out to dinner. If we sit at one of the sidewalk restaurants, we can take Lucky with us." At hearing his name, the dog's ears perked up. Noah was going to miss the silly thing. Not a fraction as much as he was going to miss a princess.

"That would be nice." Her smile didn't reach her eyes. "It's going to be a beautiful night, perfect for patio dining."

He was delaying the inevitable. She wasn't going to be so happy when he told her he was leaving on Sunday. Then again, maybe she'd be glad to see the last of him. It would be best for her if that was true.

Him, though? He was going to miss the hell out of her. He'd intended to tell her on the way back to her loft, but she'd seemed preoccupied, maybe a little sad about something. She'd said nothing was wrong when he'd asked, but she wasn't her chatty self.

She glanced down at herself. "I've got dog hair all over me. Give me a few minutes to shower and change."

"Take your time." He'd almost offered to join her in the shower, but she seemed off, almost as if she was distancing herself from him. Maybe she was tired of him, and now that Dalton was no longer a threat, she didn't need him. That thought hurt more than he'd expected it to. He rubbed his chest, at the ache there.

Since he smelled like dogs, he headed for the shower in the guest room. While he cleaned himself and then dressed, he thought about Jack's offer. It was intriguing. But he was a SEAL and was everything that defined. Was he ready to walk away from the only thing he knew?

Since he didn't have an answer to that question, not today, anyway, he filed it away for later consideration. Tonight, he had a dinner date with his princess. They had a few days before he'd leave. After he told her that he'd been called back, he'd give her the choice of spending his last days with her or he'd get out of her life if that was what she wanted.

He rubbed his chest again. Lucky whined as he peered up at him, his eyes full of worry. "What?" How did the dog know there was a rock sitting in Noah's chest? "What do you think I should do?" Lucky had no words of wisdom for him. He finished dressing, then went out to the living room to wait for Peyton.

When she walked out, he blew out a long breath. She had on white jeans that hugged her curves like no one's business, a sleeveless red top, and red sandals. With her black hair, red was her color.

"You trying to drive me crazy, princess?"

She frowned. "What?"

"You're sexy as hell." He stalked to her. "I'm going to be glaring all night at the men checking you out."

"Oh." She smiled. "You want me to change into a potato sack or something?"

"Wouldn't make any difference. They'd just be fantasizing on how to get you out of it." He curled a lock of her hair around his finger. "The song that's rumbling around in my head right now is Clapton's 'You Look Wonderful Tonight,' but *wonderful* isn't even good enough."

"You could sing it to me if you want."

"Maybe I will later…if you still want me to."

She gave him a funny look. "Why wouldn't I want you to? I love when you sing to me."

"Come, dinner awaits." Ignoring her question, he held out his hand. He grabbed Lucky's leash as they headed out.

In the time he'd been here, he'd come to love Asheville. The city was diverse, eclectic, and funky. Like the woman outside Peyton's building playing spoons.

"That's different," he said, after they listened to her for a few minutes. "Good different."

"She's a regular. Most of the street performers are."

"Pretty cool." He took her hand again. "Let's stop and say hi to Joseph."

As soon as Joseph saw them, he segued from the song he was playing to Ed Sheeran's "Perfect." As Joseph played the song, the words filtered through Noah's head. It felt like they had been written for him. He had found a girl, beautiful and sweet.

He'd never been in love, didn't know how that was supposed to feel, but something was going on with him. Was he in lust with Peyton? Or was he falling for her? Maybe. He wished they had more time to explore what was happening between them, but he was leaving on Sunday. As much as he wanted to stay, he couldn't disobey orders. He had the unsettling feeling, though, that he'd be walking away from his one chance at real happiness.

The problem was, it wouldn't be fair to her to give her hope—if she even wanted to hope—that he wanted more than the fun they'd had while he was here when he didn't know what his future held. If he reenlisted, and he probably would, he wouldn't ask or expect her to wait for him.

"That ex of yours still messing with you, Miss Peyton?" Joseph said when he finished playing. "Haven't seen him around for a few days."

"Nope. Right now, he's in jail right where he belongs." She grinned. "The jerk tried to kidnap me, but I showed him. I shot his baby toe off."

She sounded so proud of herself that Noah couldn't help but chuckle. "That she did."

Joseph's eyes widened, then he burst out laughing. "You got game, Miss Peyton, I'll tell ya that. Got a song for you." He played Nancy Sinatra's "These Boots Are Made for Walking."

Peyton clapped, clearly delighted. "I'm so badass."

Yes, she certainly was. After leaving Joseph, Peyton took him to her favorite sidewalk restaurant. When Lucky had first been put in his care, the dog would have been trying to crawl onto his lap, would have been going for the food on the table. Now with one word—*down*—he was on his belly under the table, watching the people walk by.

Peyton peeked under the table. "He's such a good boy."

And she was beautiful, perfect. He kept his news to himself through dinner, but when they returned to her loft, he couldn't put it off any longer. He walked to the window and stared out. The sidewalks were still filled with people enjoying a nice summer evening. Damn, he was going to miss this city…and her. Especially her.

He turned to face her. "I have news."

Chapter Thirty

Peyton stilled, one sandal in her hand and one still on. Something in Noah's voice was off, so much so that she wanted to slap her hands over her ears and refuse to hear whatever he had to say.

Always, the first thing she did when coming home was to take off her shoes. Then she'd go to her bedroom and change into something comfortable. Leggings and a T-shirt, or since Noah had been living with her, a pair of sexy panties and a soft cotton camisole. He liked when that was all she had on.

She needed to keep to her routine, not listen to words she didn't want to hear. "I'll just go change."

"I'm leaving on Sunday."

"Oh." As in oh God, her heart was breaking. She'd known this was coming and she should have prepared herself. But how did one prepare to say goodbye to the man she loved? She'd known she loved him since he'd taken care of her after Dalton had kidnapped her.

Okay, an even bigger truth, she'd probably fallen in love with him even before that. Maybe the night he'd arranged their romantic evening at the Grove Park Inn. Or one of the times he'd kissed her. Or when he sang "Pretty Woman" to her. But what did it matter? He was going to leave her. He was going to do that and never look back.

She wouldn't cry. She'd told Nichole she had to let him go, and she would do it without tears. She squared her shoulders, looked him in the eyes, and said, "Well, we knew this day was coming. Let's make the most of the time we have left." There was a slight tremble to her voice that she hoped he hadn't noticed.

He stared at her for a few moments, and she got lost in the emotions at war in his eyes. She wasn't sure what to make of what she was seeing. Regret? Sadness? Relief that she wasn't making a fuss?

"The time we have left," he murmured, then strode to her. He trailed his knuckles down her cheek. "How do you want to make the most of it, princess?"

"Naked," she whispered. She had her memories of him and their time together stored in her mind to relive after he was gone, but she wanted more. Enough to last her a lifetime.

Fire burned in his eyes, hot need in their depths. "Naked's good." He put his hands on her hips, backed her up to the wall, and pressed his body against hers. "Real good."

She dropped the shoe she held. "I thought so. Especially when you're the one without clothes. You have an amazing body, all hard and muscley, a work of art."

"Oh, I'm hard all right."

Like she hadn't already felt that. "I—"

His mouth landed on hers, and she forgot what she wanted to say. He slid his hands up her arms, over her shoulders, and then tangled his fingers in her hair. Kissing Noah was high on her list of favorite things.

Something was different with this kiss. It felt like

he was trying to ruin her for any man's kiss but his. She had news for him. He'd done that the first time he'd kissed her.

There was also a feeling of desperation radiating from him as his tongue demanded dominance over hers. As if he wanted to remember everything about her, too. Or maybe that was just wishful thinking.

She would wait a thousand years for this man to come back to her if only he'd ask it of her. He wasn't going to, though. She knew that about him. The tears she'd been keeping at bay burned her eyes, so she closed them, not wanting him to see that her heart was breaking.

The fingers he had tangled in her hair tightened as he rolled his hips over hers, his erection hard on her stomach. "Noah. Please."

"Please what?" His mouth left hers, and his lips peppered hot kisses across her face to the place below her ear that he already knew was one of her sensual hot spots.

"What?"

He chuckled, and she felt his smile on her skin. "You said, 'Noah. Please.' Please what, princess?"

"I don't know. I knew and now I don't know what the what was. Maybe if you stopped scrambling my brain, I'd know."

"Not gonna stop. I like your brain scrambled when I'm the reason for it." The hands he had tangled in her hair dropped to her hands. He linked their fingers, then brought her arms up to the wall. He wrapped one hand around both of hers. His other hand found its way into her panties.

He made a strangled sound when he slipped a finger inside her. "Fuck me." He lifted his head and stared hard at her. "When I'm on deployment, I'm going to spend my nights thinking of you, all wet just for me."

When he was on deployment. She hated the sound of that. He'd be on the other side of the world from her. He'd be in dangerous situations. He could die. What would the world be without Noah Alba in it? She couldn't bear to think of it.

"Naked, Noah. We're supposed to be naked, and we're not," she said to remind him, but even more, wanting him to get thoughts of him being in danger, of him leaving, out of her head.

"We'll get there. I promise."

His finger stroked deep inside her, his mouth crashed down to hers again, and he consumed her. There was no other word to describe what he was doing to her. He still held her hands above her head, against the wall, and she growled in frustration, wanting to touch him. He tightened his grip when she tried to pull her hands free. As much as she wanted to touch him, it was hot the way he held her prisoner while pleasuring her.

"Noah," she gasped into his mouth as pressure coiled low in her belly.

"That's it, princess. You're so beautiful when you come for me." He let her hands drop and gathered her in his arms, holding her close as the last of her shudders traveled through her. "Let's get you to the bedroom. I need to be inside you."

"Yes, please." She sighed when he scooped her up. How was she supposed to live without him, without this, the way he made her feel, and not just the amazing sex?

He chuckled. "Someone wants more, huh?"

"Someone sure does." She was doing her best to keep

her voice light, to keep the tears out of her eyes, to hide how much she was hurting.

When he reached the bed, he let her legs slide down his body. He undressed her, his eyes growing darker with each piece of clothing he removed. As she stood naked before him, he skimmed his hands over her, each place he touched sending those delicious tingles through her.

"Noah, please." She needed him inside her, needed them to be skin to skin.

Much faster than he'd undressed her, he had his clothes off. "My sweet, sweet princess," he softly said.

In his words, she thought she heard longing, that maybe he really was going to miss her. She wanted to tell him that she loved him, but if they were words he didn't want to hear, she didn't want to ruin the moment by saying them.

He wrapped his arms around her, then twisted, falling on the bed so that he was under her. "Now I've got you where I want you." He reached to the nightstand for a condom, then handed it to her. "Put it on me."

Who knew sheathing a man was such a turn-on, or that his watching her hands while she covered him was? When she had the condom in place, his gaze lifted to hers, and they were eyes she could happily drown in. He adjusted her so that she straddled him, his erection pressing against her sex.

"Ride me, Peyton."

She grinned. "With pleasure." She wrapped her hand around him and guided his shaft until he was buried deep inside her. When she lifted, then sank down on him again, he put his hands on her bottom, cupping her butt cheeks.

As she moved over him, their eyes locked together, she wished she could read his mind. Did their being joined in the most intimate act between two people mean something to him? Did he feel it, too? The way their souls touched, because that was how it felt.

The pleasure built inside her, the pressure of an oncoming climax growing, and while that was happening, she watched his face, searching for some hint that this…what was happening between them meant more to him than just fun times. As if he didn't want her to see into his mind, he closed his eyes.

She wanted to tell him to open them, to let her see, to give her a glimpse of his feelings for her, to allow her to hope. Instead, he flipped them over, taking control, angling deeper with each thrust. She got lost in the feel of him, in the waves of pleasure taking over her body, and she stopped thinking.

"Noah. Oh God, Noah."

"That's it, baby. My princess. So damn beautiful."

Maybe it was knowing that her time with him was ending and that had her greedy for all that he was giving her, or maybe it was the first time when making love with him that she absolutely knew she was in love with him, but whatever the reason, her world shattered, and she soared to the stars. It was like nothing she'd ever experienced before.

It was profound.

Make the most of the time we have left.

Sunday came before Noah was ready. He'd hated those words coming out of her mouth, as if all she wanted from him was sex, or "tingles." He'd expected tears or at least regret in her eyes, had been surprised at how much he wanted a sign that she didn't want him to go. Was she even going to miss him? He wasn't sure he'd ever be ready to leave her.

He hadn't told her about Jack's job offer, mostly because although he was considering it, he'd probably re-up. Why get her hopes up—if she was even hoping—that he might be back, emphasis on the *might*.

She'd asked if Jack could take him to the airport, and he'd hidden his disappointment. Was she that anxious to get rid of him? He tossed his toiletry kit into his duffel, picked up the bag and his guitar case, and carried them out to the living room.

Peyton stood at the window looking out, and he wondered if this was the last time he'd ever see her. That damn sharp-edged rock in his chest grew into a boulder. He swallowed past the lump in his throat.

"Guess that's it then." Was that the best he could do? He'd been inside her body, his mouth had loved every inch of her. He owed her more than a few meaningless words. He dropped his duffel and guitar case on the sofa, then walked over to her. "I'm going to miss you, princess."

"I'll miss you, too."

And that was the extent of any discussion on his leaving. It seemed like there should be more to say, but for the first time since he'd looked into the sky-blue eyes of a runaway bride, he couldn't read her. Her usually expressive face was blank, her thoughts hidden from him.

Was she ready to be back on her own and get on with her life? Because he didn't know, he didn't tell her what was in his heart. Truth, he wasn't even sure, another reason he stayed quiet. He thought he was falling in love with her, but what if once he was away, he realized it was just lust?

Equating his feelings for her to nothing but lust didn't sit well, though. She deserved better than that, so he shut down trying to analyze whatever this was or wasn't between them. His phone buzzed with a text.

"That'll be Jack. He said he'd message when he got here."

"Okay. Well…" She put her palm on his cheek. "Be safe, Noah."

"Always." He wanted more of her chatty words, the babbling that only ended when he kissed her. To hell with it. He lowered his mouth to hers. If this was the last time he'd get to kiss a princess, he wasn't going to let the opportunity pass.

Her body melted against his and her mouth opened, welcoming him in. How the hell was he supposed to leave her? His tongue slid over hers, and at hearing her sigh, he knew he couldn't leave without asking if she'd wait for him. Then…

She pushed against his chest, taking her mouth away. "Jack won't be able to double park for long. You better go."

Ask me to stay.

She didn't, so he left.

Chapter Thirty-One

Peyton had pulled off a miracle. She hadn't begged Noah to stay. *Please don't go* had been on the tip of her tongue. By sheer willpower, she let him go. It was the hardest thing she'd ever done.

She walked to the window. Noah came out of the building, Lucky at his side, and after opening the back door for Lucky to jump inside Jack's car, he lifted his gaze to the window. He didn't smile, didn't mouth words to her, didn't lift his hand to wave. He just looked at her, and then he walked around the front of the car, got in, and they left.

"Don't go," she whispered. *Please don't go.* The tears she'd managed to hold at bay in front of Noah fell down her cheeks. She crumpled to the floor, brought her legs up, and pressed her face to her knees.

It was too quiet, the silence in the loft thick and heavy. She tried to draw air into her lungs, but it was hard to breathe. He hadn't even said he'd call her. Her throat burned, her chest hurt, and the tears burned her eyes.

Even the dog was gone, back in Jack's care. She should have asked if she could keep him. God, she was a sad country song. Maybe she should get one of her beers to cry into.

She swiped her hand across her cheeks, pushed up, and went to her bedroom. If she was going to be a sad country song, she was going all out. In her bottom drawer was the T-shirt she'd never given back to Noah. She brought it to her nose and inhaled. It didn't smell like him anymore, and that brought more tears. Wasn't fair that he'd even taken his scent with him. She put it on anyway.

All she'd wanted were tingly kisses and someone intimidating enough to keep Dalton from hassling her. She'd gotten both those things along with a broken heart. She should have made Noah promise not to make her fall in love with him, but hindsight and all that. She crawled into her bed, pulled the covers over her head, and cried herself to sleep.

When she woke up, the sun was setting. Jeez, she'd slept the day away. Now what? This broken heart thing was new, something she'd never experienced before, and she didn't know what to do with herself. In the romance books she'd read, brokenhearted women drank wine and ate ice cream. She didn't have any wine in her kitchen and cheese beat ice cream any day, so there it was. Her one-woman pity party…beer and cheese.

She was headed for the kitchen when her doorbell rang. Noah? Her heart tried to dig its way out of her chest and race her to the door.

"Oh. Hi," she said at seeing Nichole.

Nichole smiled, sympathy in her eyes. "Sorry I'm not Noah." She held up an oversize bottle of wine and a brown bag. "Wine and ice cream, the go-to for all broken hearts."

"Come in." She wasn't up for company, and she really wanted that beer and cheese. Yet she'd never had the kind of friend she could pour her heart out to. Nichole was here, offering that to her, and it was nice.

"This is a cool place." Nichole set the wine on the kitchen island. "You doing okay, sweetie?"

"Yeah. No. Not really."

"Well, I'm here to talk about how stupid men can be while we pig out. What's your pity pick?" She took five different pints of ice cream out of the bag. "I didn't know what you liked, so I got a variety."

"Let's give all five a go." She got two spoons, handing one to Nichole.

"I like how you think. You got a wine opener?"

"Somewhere." She found it, poured wine into wine-glasses she'd never used before, and they settled on stools at the island, the pints lined up in front of them.

"I fell in love with him," she blurted.

"Of course you did. It's what we do. Fall in love with men who can't get their heads out of their asses long enough to see the perfect woman right in front of them."

Peyton giggled. "Ain't that the truth?"

An hour later, a bit buzzed after finishing the bottle of wine and devouring half the ice cream, they'd compiled a list of all the ways men were stupid. "Even so, he has the sexiest butt," Peyton said.

Nichole sighed. "He sure does."

"Hey, you're not supposed to be looking at Noah's butt."

"What? I thought we were talking about Jack."

"Huh? Why would I be looking at Jack's butt?"

"You better not."

"I might have once, but it was on the way to searching for Noah's butt when they were playing baseball." She picked up the bottle and peered into it. "All gone. I need to go to sleep. You can't drive home, 'cause of us drinking and all, so you can sleep in Noah's room 'cause he's gone and doesn't need it anymore." Why did she say his name? Now she was thinking about him again.

"Nope, Jack brought me so I wouldn't be driving home after drinking this." She picked up the wine bottle, waving it in front of Peyton's face.

"Smart thinking."

"I didn't think it. Jack did."

"Yeah, I meant him."

"Oh. Well, I'll call him."

Peyton wasn't sure how much time it took for Jack to arrive after Nichole called him. What she did know was that she wasn't going to feel so great in the morning, and that she really, really liked her new friend.

She leaned over and hugged Nichole. "Thank you for sharing my first ever pity party with me."

"My pleasure. There's the doorbell. Think that's Jack?"

"Well, it's not the pizza delivery guy. Know why?"

"No, why?"

"'Cause we didn't order pizza."

That cracked both of them up, and she was laughing so hard that she barely managed to get the door opened. "You're not the pizza man."

"You've got pizza coming?" Jack said.

"Nope. That's why you're not the pizza man." She glanced back at Nichole. "Told ya." That set them off again.

"I take it you two lovely ladies finished off the wine." Nichole snorted. "Guilty."

"Guilty. Me, too." Peyton leaned toward Jack so she could whisper. "I like beer better, but don't tell Nichole, okay?"

"Mum's the word," he whispered back with a big grin on his face. He glanced between the two of them. "I understand one of you needs a designated driver?"

"That would be me," Nichole chirped, raising her hand. She stood, then grabbed hold of the island counter. "Whoa. Who's moving the room around?"

"Easy, babe." Jack rushed to Nichole's side and scooped her up, then turned to Peyton. "You going to be okay?"

"Sure." Not. Noah wasn't here to carry her so she could nuzzle his neck like Nichole was doing to Jack.

"Okay. You have our number. Call if you need anything."

"Thanks. That means a lot."

At the door, he paused, seemed to consider something, then said, "He'll come back. I don't know when, but he will."

She didn't know what to say to that, so she just shrugged. "Be careful driving home, okay?"

"Always. Lock up behind me."

"I will." The buzz she'd had going was gone, the loft was back in silent mode, and as she locked her door, she squashed the hope that Jack was right. Noah was gone and she might as well get used to that. If that was possible.

God, she missed him with an ache deep in her heart and bones. Was he missing her? Thinking about her?

"Come on, man. Let's go out. You've been home for a week and all you do is train and mope."

Noah shifted his gaze from his phone screen to his roommate. "I don't mope." He hit delete on the text message, one of many he hadn't sent Peyton. It was better this way. A clean break so she could get on with her life.

"Go look in a mirror. That's a total mope face. What happened in Asheville? Some chick break your heart?" Jared laughed as if the notion was absurd.

No, he broke hers. Maybe. Was she missing him the way he missed her?

"You got indigestion or something? You keep rubbing your chest."

Because the damn thing hurt.

"Come on. I need a wingman and, dude, you need to get laid bad. I guarantee that'll cure that mope right off your face."

Like he could touch a woman who wasn't Peyton.

Jared scowled when Noah didn't respond. He plopped down on the other end of the sofa. "Okay. Talk. Who is she that's got your panties in a knot?"

"A princess."

"No shit, man? An honest to God princess?"

"What?"

"You said she's a princess."

He'd said that out loud?

"You're playing with your dice, Double D. You only do that when you're stressed. Talk to me. Get whatever has you sulking like a kid who lost his favorite toy off your chest. You'll feel better for it. I guarantee."

Noah stared down at the dice in his palm. He hadn't realized he'd taken them out of his pocket. How many times in his life had this pair of dice led him down the right path simply because he'd held them and asked, "What would my father do?" Then, whatever the answer was, he'd do the opposite. He silently asked that question now, and the answer...his father wouldn't think twice about stomping all over a princess's heart.

Had his father ever loved Noah's mother? Did he even know how to love? Noah didn't know the answer to that question. As far back as he could remember, the old man had only cared about gambling and his booze.

Then he thought of his mother. Although he was young when he lost her, he remembered her smiles, her hugs, and how much she loved him. He knew that because it was the last thing she said to him every night. "I love you, my sweet boy," she'd say, then she'd pull the covers up to his chin and kiss his forehead. She had taught him everything he needed to know about love.

Was he really going to walk away from the woman he loved, throw away his chance to be happy?

"Dude, either talk to me or get dressed so we can go out."

"Can't." With his fingers wrapped tight around the dice, he stood. "I got some things to do."

Chapter Thirty-Two

Peyton leaned her cheek against the window as she watched Asheville wake up on an early Saturday morning. Before Noah, she'd rarely been up early enough to see the sun come up, to watch her town come alive. Now, she wasn't sleeping well, so this greeting the sunrise was a new thing. She wasn't even sleeping in her bed anymore, which was just stupid, but it was lonely there without him. The sofa was her new place to crash. She'd doze off watching TV, sleep for a few hours, and then wake up with a body full of kinks.

She stretched her neck to the left and then to the right. Three weeks—three long, miserable weeks—had passed since he had left, and she hadn't heard a word from him. Not even a text message that he was alive and well. A thousand times in the past weeks, she'd typed out text messages to him and then had deleted them.

Hey. Just checking in to make sure you got home safely.

Do you miss me, because I miss you like crazy.

This one I'll definitely delete, but I want you to know that I love you.

You're a rotten dog, Noah Alba. You broke my heart, and you don't even care enough to check in on me.

I wish I'd never met you.

Okay, that last one was a lie.

And on and on and on. Well, as of today, that was stopping. She was done crying over unsent messages and messages never received. The only things keeping her going were her father and their new amazingly wonderful relationship, her job, and Nichole and Jack. She talked to Nichole a few times a week, and the couple had had her over for dinner several times. Lucky was always there, and it was great to get to see her furry friend.

Noah was never mentioned, not by her or them. That was another heartbreak, that he'd become *persona non grata*. She wanted to talk about him…no, she didn't. If only she could stop thinking about him.

The past two weekends she'd spent on her sofa, numbing her brain with mindless TV. That was going to stop, too. But what to do with herself? The brewery was her happy place, so she could spend the day there, play around with her recipe.

There wouldn't be a Wicked Witch Brewery now, but she liked the name, so she was working on a new beer she planned to call Wicked Witch's Broomstick Mocha Stout. When she lost herself in creating a new beer, she didn't think of anything else, and that was exactly what she needed today…no Noah thoughts, no tears, no temptation to call Nichole and ask if Jack had heard from him. It would kill her to know Noah was keeping in touch with Jack when he'd ghosted her, a clear message that she didn't mean beans to him.

Yep, got the message loud and clear, SEAL boy.

She wanted to hate him but couldn't make herself do that. He hadn't made promises he hadn't kept, he'd never lied to her or given her reason to hope he'd stay. He'd done everything she'd asked of him...the tingles being her favorite, and could the man ever make her tingle.

He might have ruined her for any other man. Or, he might have taught her what she should expect and deserved from some future man. It was impossible to imagine loving anyone other than Noah, but with time and determination to find him, maybe someday a man could walk into her life the way Noah had and win her heart.

He'd have to work damn hard at it as he'd have big shoes to step into, but it could happen, right? Because, seriously, she didn't want to end up being a crazy cat lady, lamenting to the end of her days of her one and only lost love. That would just suck lemons.

Had anyone ever created a lemon beer brew? Okay, now she was just getting silly. She pressed her forehead against the window. For her own sanity, she had to let him go.

"Goodbye, Noah. Have a great life."

She waited to feel better. It didn't happen. Time... that was what she needed. Given enough time, he would be nothing more than a favorite memory, a smile on her lips the few times she thought of him. Meanwhile, she'd go make the best beer in the history of Elk Antler Brewery.

Sunday she was on a cleaning frenzy in an effort to keep he who shall not be named out of her mind when the doorbell rang. She'd talked to her father earlier, and he'd been home, so it wasn't him. Since her friends list was woefully lacking, she couldn't think of who else could be calling on her. That reminded her that she'd vowed to find herself some girlfriends. She'd started with Nichole, but she wanted more. She should call Heather and invite her to lunch.

"Oh, hey." She didn't want to let on how happy she was to see Nichole.

Nichole's gaze landed on the yellow rubber gloves on Peyton's hands. "Ah, busy cleaning whatshisname right out of your life, huh?" She grinned. "Been there. Done that. Didn't work."

"Well, drat. Didn't want to hear that." She stepped back. "Come in." It was too early to offer wine…or beer, so what did you offer a new friend you were happy to see when it was too late for coffee and too early for booze? She needed to research girlfriend etiquette. "Um, can I get you something to drink?" That worked, let Nichole guide her in this new territory.

"Thanks, but I'm here to kidnap you. Jack's waiting in the car. We're going to take a ride on the Parkway and we're taking you with us."

"Oh, well, I don't want to be a third wheel if you and Jack are—"

"Girlfriend, just go with the flow, okay?" Her gaze returned to the rubber gloves. "But ditch those. Also, it's a beautiful day out, a cute pair of shorts and sexy top kind of day."

Peyton blinked. "Are you speaking in some kind of weird code."

Nichole laughed. "If you only knew. Come on. Take me to your closet and I'll help you decide what to wear.

We need to get a move on since Jack is double parked. You don't want him hauled off to jail, do you?"

"I feel like no is the right answer to that question."

"You are correct. Show me your closet so we can get this show on the road."

One new thing Peyton learned was that Nichole was a force of nature, especially when digging through Peyton's closet. In less than ten minutes she was dressed in a pair of white shorts and a sleeveless red top.

"I feel like I've fallen in a rabbit hole and nothing makes sense anymore," she said as Nichole pulled her into the elevator.

"Curiouser and curiouser," Nichole said with a suspiciously secretive smile on her face.

"What's going on?"

"Nothing. It's a beautiful day for a ride on the Parkway is all."

It was a beautiful day, and because the temperature up on the Blue Ridge Parkway was a few degrees cooler, they rolled down the car windows. This was what she needed…the breeze, the pine-scented mountain air, the incredible views, and time with friends.

Jack had a classic rock station playing on the radio, and they were all singing along to the Eagles' "Take It Easy." Not one of them could carry a tune, but they were rocking it at the top of their lungs.

Noah would love this.

Stop it. No thinking of him, no being sad today. When the song ended, Nichole high-fived Jack, then reached behind her with her palm up. Laughing, Peyton slapped her hand against Nichole's.

Gosh, it felt good to laugh. She hadn't been sure she ever would again. But as they drove along the Parkway, thoughts of Noah kept creeping into her mind. How much fun it would be if he were with them, how much she wanted to hear his voice chiming in with theirs. When Jack reached across the console and rested his hand on Nichole's leg, she unsuccessfully tried not to wish Noah was here to touch her.

She turned her gaze to the window and blinked against the stupid tears prickling her eyes. This tearing up over any reminder of Noah was getting old. If she was still missing him this much ten years from now, she was going to be seriously peeved.

"Why are we going here?" she said when Jack turned into the parking lot of a waterfall. *The* waterfall. Oh, no. She did not want to walk down that path.

Jack glanced back at her as he opened his door. "Nichole wanted to go to a waterfall. What Nichole wants, I give her."

"True story," Nichole said, giving Jack a goofy grin.

Well, she could act like a brat and stay in the car and pout, or she could grin and bear it. Since she couldn't bring herself to get bratty with her new friends, she pushed her door open.

As much as she liked Nichole and Jack, it was hard being around them, seeing the love they had for each other. She really thought she and Noah could have what they did if he'd only given them a chance. She would have waited for him for…well, forever if that's what it took.

Jack told her to go down the path first and Nichole walked behind her with Jack bringing up the rear. With each step she took, her heartbeat increased until she wondered if she was having a heart attack by the time they neared the bottom.

In less than a minute, she'd see the rock they'd sat on while sharing her bottle of champagne. She'd remember looking up and seeing the most beautiful man her eyes had ever beheld as he watched her. The smile curving her lips surprised her, but it was from remembering the wariness in the stranger's eyes as he no doubt wondered why a crazy woman was sitting half-naked on a rock, chugging a bottle of champagne.

Yet, he hadn't bolted, although she was sure he wanted to. No, he'd taken cautious steps toward her, had climbed up on that boulder next to her, had listened to her sad story, and had rescued her when she'd needed rescuing.

She sighed. Maybe coming back here would be therapeutic. Either that, or it would be like a knife to her heart when she stepped into the opening of the waterfall pool and laid eyes on *their* rock.

Ten more seconds, and she would see it.

Nine…eight…seven…six…five…four…three… two… She blew out a long breath, then took that last step, and there it was.

She blinked. She blinked again. "Noah?" she whispered.

It couldn't be, so she squeezed her eyes shut to clear them, but when she looked again, he was still there.

On. Their. Rock.

How? She glanced behind her.

"Go on," Nichole said. "Go to him." She slipped her hand in Jack's, and the couple walked back up the path.

Her feet still rooted to the spot, Peyton shifted her gaze back to Noah.

"Are you going to kidnap me?" he said, and she laughed at hearing him repeat the first thing she'd ever said to him.

Noah's hungry gaze roamed over the woman he

loved, the woman he'd missed with every beat of his heart. "Well?"

"Do you want me to?"

"Hell, yeah." Her smile, her beautiful smile sliced right through him. How had he ever thought he could leave her behind?

"Then I think I will."

"Thank God." Beside him, Lucky whined as his tail excitedly swept over the boulder, his gaze fixed on Peyton. Noah unclipped the leash. "Go. Go get our girl."

Lucky—considerably better behaved than he'd been when Noah had left—flew off the rock like he was Superman and hit the ground running. Peyton laughed as she knelt, her arms open.

"There's my sweet boy." She buried her hands in Lucky's fur, but her eyes stayed on Noah.

He gave them a minute to greet each other, then took his guitar out of the case. Her eyes widened, and she stood but stayed silent and where she was. His heart pounded. The last person to touch his guitar had been Asim. For Peyton, he would play it again.

Would she welcome him in her life? Holding her gaze, he strummed the intro to Elvis Presley's "Can't Help Falling in Love," and then he sang it to her. No other song expressed what was in his heart like this one did.

As he played and sang, she slowly walked to him. By the time he finished, she stood a few feet in front of him, tears streaming down her cheeks. His eyes burned, too. Still holding her gaze, he set his guitar back in the case.

"Do you mean it?" she said, her words a mere whisper.

"With everything that I am." He held out his hand. "Take my hand, princess. Take my whole life, too."

He needed to touch her, needed his mouth on hers… Hopefully, she'd allow that.

"I'm mad at you."

"Figured you would be."

"You could have texted me at least once, letting me know you'd arrived safely."

"I should have, and I'm sorry. If you'll come up here, I'll tell you everything."

She put her hand in his, and if he'd been standing, the happiness roaring through him like a tsunami would have brought him to his knees. He helped her onto the rock, pulling her next to him.

"Hey, you," he murmured, keeping her hand in his.

"Hi." Her smile was both shy and beautiful, and it about melted his heart. "You came back."

"I did."

"For how long?"

He heard the tremor in her voice, knew she thought he would leave again. "For as long as you'll have me."

"Do you mean that?"

"Yes." He rubbed his thumb over the top of her hand. "I'm opting out of the navy."

"I would never ask you to do that."

"It's time. For several reasons." He reached behind him and picked up the champagne bottle he'd already uncorked. "I have a lot to tell you. The first time I met you, we shared your champagne. Thought we could re-create that day a little." He waggled his eyebrows. "If you want to really reenact that day, feel free to strip down to your underwear."

She punched his arm. "That was a one-time show in public, SEAL boy."

"Pity." He handed her the bottle, then took his own

drink when she gave it back. "I missed you, Peyton. So much."

"If you missed me so much, how come I never heard from you? It hurt, that you could just walk away without a backward look."

"You were in my thoughts every minute of my days." He brought her hand to his chest, pressing it over his heart. "And here. You're in my heart. You are my heart. When I left, I thought I had who knows how many deployments ahead of me. I didn't want that for you. I wanted better for you than a man as messed up as I am."

"Shouldn't I have had a say in that?"

"Absolutely, and as for the messed-up part, I'm better than I was when I first arrived, but I'll continue to see Dr. Meadows. In all fairness, though, you never gave me any indication you wanted more from me than guard duty and the tingles I could give you." He smiled. "They were pretty incredible tingles if I do say so myself."

"Can't deny that. I wanted to ask you for more, to tell you that I'd wait for you, but I was afraid. You never gave any hint you wanted more, either."

If she had told him she'd wait for him, at the time he left, he wasn't sure it would have made a difference. He likely still would have thought he was doing what was best for her by walking away. Maybe he'd needed to do that for both of them to realize what they meant to each other.

He'd told her he loved her, and she hadn't said it back. He thought she did, and he badly needed those words from her, but he wanted them to come because she wanted to say them.

"When did you get back?"

"Late last night. Jack picked me up, and I stayed

with him and Nichole. We had things to talk about, like my new job."

"You have a new job? Here?" There was so much hope in her voice.

"Yep. That make you happy?"

"So happy. What kind of job?"

He told her about Jack's plan for the center for their military brothers and sisters, and his role in making it happen. The more he and Jack had talked about it last night, and the things they wanted to accomplish, the more excited he got.

He'd always thought they'd have to drag him kicking and screaming from his SEAL team, but a future he'd never expected and never dreamed he could have was his for the taking. A job that would give him tremendous satisfaction—one where he wouldn't risk being the reason someone was hurt or died because of him—and a beautiful, amazing girl at his side. It didn't hurt that she could brew some damn fine beer.

"That's awesome, Noah. Not just that it means you're moving to Asheville, and I can't tell you how happy that makes me, but that you'll be doing something that I think will mean the world to you."

"You mean the world to me," he said. "The days I was away from you—"

She kissed him.

Well, that was supposed to be his move, but he wasn't about to argue with a princess.

"I love you, Noah. So much." Then she claimed his mouth again.

In his mind, he sang Faith Hill's "This Kiss."

Epilogue

Eight months later...

"I do."

The minister turned from Jack to Nichole. "Do you, Nichole Masters, take this man to be your lawfully wedded..."

Noah tuned out as his eyes locked on Peyton standing on the other side of Nichole, and he smiled at the woman now wearing his engagement ring. In the near future it would be them exchanging vows. He shifted his gaze back to Jack and Nichole, and when the minister nodded at him, he handed his best friend Nichole's wedding band.

His attention returned to Peyton. How had he gotten so lucky? She was everything he hadn't known to wish for. Things were going unbelievably well. Their relationship was stronger than ever. A big part of that was thanks to his head doc. Dr. Meadows had helped him learn how to forgive himself, and for that, she would always have his gratitude.

As for the other things that were good, Peyton's father was in remission, her ex was out of her life for good, having been found guilty to the charges against him, and he and Jack had started construction on Operation Warrior Center. Jack had accepted Noah's offer to invest in the center, so he was now a partner instead of an employee.

The wedding was taking place on the land he and Jack had bought for their new venture. A white trellis with pink roses woven through the slats had been erected next to the river that flowed through the sixty acres.

The guest list had been kept small, only family and close friends. Rachel, Nichole's friend, had flown in for the ceremony, serving as the maid of honor. And, of course, the dogs were here, obediently sitting where Jack had commanded them to park their butts. Dakota, Rambo, Maggie May, and Lucky formed a semicircle in front of the bride and groom, their gazes fixed on the minister as if soaking in his every word. How Jack got these dogs—any dogs—to obey the way they did still amazed him.

Jack's only disappointment was that their former SEAL team was on deployment and unable to attend his wedding. The team had pooled their money and sent Noah a thousand bucks to cover the cost of Jack's bachelor party with the instructions to get him good and drunk and then send them pictures. Jack had refused to get wasted and Noah wasn't about to push him. However, Jack had faked being drunk and Noah had emailed the team some pretty funny photos.

As it had all during the ceremony, his gaze returned to Peyton. She was Nichole's only bridesmaid. He smiled again, thinking about how excited Peyton had been when Nichole had asked. She and Rachel had bonded over their duties as maid of honor and bridesmaid. His girl had been like a kid in a candy store, and he'd been thoroughly amused by her excitement and determination to help make Nichole's wedding perfect. He was more than ready for his own wedding, though.

Life was good.

Afghanistan

As he had each time he'd been interrogated by his Taliban captors, Dallas Manning answered their questions as required by the military's Code of Conduct and the Geneva Conventions: name, rank, service number, and date of birth. Nothing more, nothing less.

For his insolence, his captors broke another finger. That made three now. On the positive side, he still had seven that worked. Back in his cell, he tore another strip from his tattered and filthy navy-issued T-shirt and wrapped the finger as tightly as possible.

The burns worried him more than the broken fingers. Plus, they hurt like a son of a bitch. He used a little of his precious water—he was only given a cup a day—and dirt from the floor to make mud. He couldn't reach some of the burns on his back, but on the ones he could and on the ones on his arms and legs, he covered with a layer of the mud to keep the sand flies out of the open wounds.

When he finished his doctoring, he slid his index finger along the dirt floor, then lifted the paper-thin pallet and marked another day. He stared at the dirt lines. Nine days of hell on earth. When he'd first been thrown into the cell, he'd marked the days on the wall with a line of smudged dirt. The bad guys hadn't liked that and had punished him. They wanted him to lose track of the days, to lose hope that his team would find him.

Well, to hell with them. He would never lose hope

that his team was not only looking for him, but that they would find him. They would. It was just a question of how long. What his mental state would be, that was the question. The assholes were getting entirely too creative in devising ways to torture him.

He was the Ghost. He sure wished he was literally his call sign so he could float through the walls, right out of this hell hole. As he did at the end of each day, he dropped to the floor and did one-arm push-ups while repeating his name, rank, service number, and birthdate over and over until his trembling arms couldn't take any more. It was worrisome that the number was fewer each day.

Lack of sufficient food and water, the tortures, and the interrupted sleep each night—the bastards loved waking him up every twenty to thirty minutes—were taking a serious toll on both his body and mind. There wasn't much he could do about that other than to try to stay strong with the exercises, but he absolutely had to keep his mind sharp. He couldn't allow himself to go to that dark place his brain seemed to want to travel to the last few days.

As he did each night, he closed his eyes and imagined that he was at his family's Montana ranch, riding his favorite horse over the hills until sleep took him. He was awoken by a guard banging on the cell bars with a metal pipe.

"Fucking asshole."

The man laughed.

The one thing he knew and held fast was they weren't going to be laughing when his team got here.

Until then, life sucked.

* * * * *

Acknowledgments

Here I am, again writing an acknowledgment after finishing a book…and this one makes number twenty. I
have truly been blessed on this journey and have so
many people to thank for their love, support, and help
when I needed it.

First up, Sandra's Rowdies. My Facebook reader
group is awesome! Thank you, ladies, for the love and
the laughter (and the hot guy pictures, especially those).
I love every single one of you and look forward to many
more years of fun.

To my readers, thank you all for loving my books,
for the reviews, for sharing my book news on social
media, and for recommending them to your friends! All
of that is so much appreciated. I've met some of you,
wish I could meet all of you, and consider many of you
my friend. Just so you know, my favorite question is
"When's your next book coming out?"

To all the great book bloggers, thank you for reading my books, reviewing them, and talking about them.
Y'all rock!!!

To Jenny Holiday, my friend and critique partner,
remember when? We've come a long way, baby, since
sharing our dreams of being published one day, and

there's no one I'd rather have taken this journey with than you. Love ya!!!

AE Jones and Miranda Liasson, my Golden Heart sisters, I was beyond thrilled to get that phone call in 2013 that I was a Golden Heart finalist. I wasn't expecting to find two awesome friends because of that phone call, but that's exactly what happened. I love that you're just a phone call away to plot talk, give encouragement when needed, and to talk about the business side of writing. Love you both!

Editors…those people authors love most of the time. Ha! Just kidding. I always love you, even when you tell me I need to kill my darlings (a favorite scene). To my Harlequin/Carina Press developmental editor, thank you Deborah Nemeth for showing me how to put a beautiful shine on my story. To my acquiring editor, Kerri Buckley, thank you for believing in the Operation K-9 Brothers series.

To my agent, Courtney Miller-Callihan, what an amazing eight years it's been! A huge thank-you for all you've done for me. You're a rock star!!!

Last, but definitely not least, a big thank-you to my husband, better known to my readers as Mr. O. Thank you for your love and support. You're a funny guy, so also thank you for all the laughs. Love you, babe!

About the Author

Bestselling, award-winning author Sandra Owens lives in the beautiful Blue Ridge Mountains of North Carolina. Her family and friends often question her sanity but have ceased being surprised by what she might get up to next. She's jumped out of a plane, flown in an aerobatic plane while the pilot performed death-defying stunts, gotten into laser gunfights in aerial combat, and ridden a Harley motorcycle for years. She regrets nothing.

Sandra is a Romance Writers of America Honor Roll member and a 2013 Golden Heart Finalist for her contemporary romance *Crazy for Her*. In addition to her contemporary romance and romantic suspense novels, she writes Regency stories. Her books have won many awards including The Readers' Choice and The Golden Quill.

To find out about other books by Sandra Owens or to be alerted to cover reveals, new releases, and other fun stuff, sign up for her newsletter at bit.ly/2FVUPKS

Join Sandra's Facebook Reader Group:
www.Facebook.com/groups/1827166257533001/
Connect with Sandra:
Facebook: bit.ly/2ruKKPl

A woman on the run.
A wounded SEAL who wants to become invisible.

Two strangers, one mountain cabin.

Keep reading for an excerpt from
Mountain Rescue, *the upcoming third book*
in the Operation K-9 Brothers series
by Sandra Owens.

Chapter One

The passengers on the red-eye from Salt Lake City to Atlanta were asleep. All but Dallas Manning. He didn't trust his nightmares. They were persistent fuckers, rarely allowing him to sleep through the night. The three weeks he'd been home at his family's ranch in Montana, his screams had disturbed his family's sleep, too. He wasn't about to chance scaring the hell out of a plane full of strangers.

Unable to take another day of his family alternating between smothering him and tiptoeing around him, he'd jumped on his friend's invitation to come to Asheville, North Carolina. Not that he blamed his family for their worry. He was damn lucky to be alive after enjoying a two-week stay at Hotel Hell on Earth as a guest of the Taliban. He snorted. *Enjoying.* Yeah, right. But he'd survived the torture, the starvation, and the mind games.

His body was a bit messed up, and he'd have permanent scars, but he'd held strong, never giving his captors more than his name, rank, service number, and birthdate. If his SEAL team hadn't found him when they did, he didn't doubt for a minute that he'd be dead by now. His captors, frustrated and angry that he wasn't spilling his secrets, had been growing more creative by the day in their efforts to make him talk. The bastards' last gift to him was the damn nightmares. After the first one his family witnessed, they'd treated him differently.

He couldn't take their pity, their need to baby him, never mind that he was the youngest. He was a damn SEAL, not a baby needing coddling. He loved his family, would willingly die for them, but when his friend and former teammate issued the invitation to come for a visit, he'd grabbed on to what felt like a lifeline.

Jack Daniels had started a foundation, Operation K-9 Brothers, training therapy dogs for their military brothers and sisters suffering from PTSD. Another former teammate was also in Asheville, working with Jack. If anyone could understand what he'd gone through and what he was dealing with now, it would be his SEAL brothers. One thing he could count on, neither man would try to baby him.

In Atlanta, he changed planes, cramming his body into the seat of the commuter plane that would take him to Asheville. Fortunately, the last leg of his trip only lasted an hour since he had difficulty being in small places thanks to the two weeks he'd spent in a cell where he could stand in the middle and reach all four walls. After deplaning and getting his suitcase, he headed for the short-term parking lot. The Jeep was where Jack had said he it would be. When he had refused Jack's offer to pick him up, since he was arriving in the middle of the night, Jack had insisted on loaning him one of Operation K-9 Brothers' vehicles.

After tossing his suitcase and carry-on in the back, he got in the Jeep, then reached under the seat for the envelope with the keys and address to the cabin. That was another thing. Jack had invited him to stay with him and his new wife, but Dallas needed a place of his own, where he could get away from people when he needed to.

Turned out Operation K-9 Brothers owned a cabin, and Jack had said he could stay there. He programed the cabin address in the GPS, adjusted the seat and mirrors, then headed out.

Thirty-five minutes later, he pulled to a stop in front of a small log house. He couldn't see much of it in the dark, but he didn't care what it or the surrounding area looked like. It was a place to crash and hide out for a while.

Inside, he dropped his suitcase, found a light switch, and glanced around. It was an open floor plan, living room, dining room, and kitchen. The place wasn't as rustic as he was expecting, and he was kind of disappointed. A stone fireplace on one wall with floor-to-ceiling windows along both sides was the best part of the place. The furniture was sturdy and basic. Brown leather couch, two leather recliners, TV, and coffee table in the living room, and a dinette with four chairs around it next to the kitchen. Deciding he'd unpack in the morning, he left the suitcase where he'd dropped it, and taking his carry-on, he headed down the hall.

The first room he came to was a bathroom, and he made a pit stop, then checked out the next room. The bedroom had twin beds, a dresser, one chair, and a TV mounted on the wall. He didn't think it was the main bedroom, so he continued on to see if there was a room with a bigger bed.

He'd taken two steps into the next room and was reaching for a light switch when something came at him. Instinctively, he dropped his carry-on and put a hand up, wrapping his fingers around what felt like the rough bark of a tree branch. He pulled it to him, bringing his attacker with it, and found himself with an arm full of enraged wildcat in possession of a woman's body.

She went for his eyes, and he grabbed her wrists, gentling his hold so that he didn't bruise her. When she tried to knee him, he flipped her around and wrapped his arms around her, her back to his chest.

"I'm rather fond of that part of me, sugar."

Robert's people had found her, and this was the day she was going to die. Rachel Denning refused to make it easy on Robert Hargrove's henchman, though. She stomped on his foot, but because she was barefoot and he wore boots, that was about as effective as slapping his face with a feather.

A fight scene from a previous movie where the villain had her in a similar hold flashed through her mind. In the scene, she'd gotten away by slamming the back of her head into his nose.

The problem with that scenario was that this man was a good head taller than her, so no way she could reach his nose. His chin, maybe, but it was worth a try, better than doing nothing. She leaned her head forward, then slammed it back as hard as she could, taking satisfaction when he grunted. Unfortunately, the stunt worked better in the movie.

"Easy, wildcat. I'm not going to hurt you."

Yeah, right, and unicorns existed. "Let go of me." He wouldn't, she knew asking was futile, but it was all she had. He was stronger than she and had her in a hold she couldn't escape.

Keeping one arm around her, he reached for the light switch, and she blinked against the sudden brightness. Then he lifted her right off her feet as if she weighed less than a bag of potatoes, carried her to the bed, and dropped her. Facedown on the rumpled cover, she waited for the blow…or whatever he planned to do to her. Oh, God, what if he raped her?

No, she wasn't going to wait around to find out what he planned to do. She flipped to her back, her gaze searching for a weapon. When she'd arrived at the cabin, she'd gone out and found a tree branch, wanting something handy to protect herself if she had to. She should have brought the whole damn tree in.

She had a knife from the kitchen under her pillow. She hadn't started with that because she'd thought she would have a better chance with the branch. Her plan had been simple. Bash him upside the head and when he was out cold, tie him up, then disappear.

If she could get to the knife, maybe she could hurt him enough to escape. Keeping her attention on the man, she inched her hand toward the pillow. His gaze followed her hand before shifting back to her.

"You got a knife under there? Go ahead, wildcat. See if you can get to it before I have you in my arms again." A smirk curved his lips. "Been a while since I've had this much fun."

Something wasn't right. The man wasn't acting like a killer. The men who worked for Robert were as cruel as he. They didn't tease, and if they called her anything besides her name, it would be *bitch*. They especially didn't smile as if they really were having fun. If he was one of Robert's men, wouldn't he just kill her and be done with it?

Now that she could study this man, he…well, first to get it out of the way, he was gorgeous in a rough bad boy kind of way. A trimmed beard, more like a few days of scruff really, covered his face. A fresh scar ran from the corner of his right eye and down his cheek before disappearing into his beard. She almost cringed at seeing how close he'd come to losing an eye.

No, she wasn't giving him her sympathy, not when he was here to hurt her. Yet his eyes weren't mean or cold. The only thing she could see in them was curiosity as he stared back at her. They were pretty eyes, though. Hazel, the kind that would change with the color of shirt he wore or his emotions. His dark brown hair in need of a haircut scraped across the neck of his T-shirt. Then there was a body worth drooling over.

Stop it, Rachel. Stop noticing how hot he is. She was totally stupid for letting her mind wander when there was danger in the room. Because, while he was a feast for the eyes, she had no doubt the man could be dangerous when he wanted. Still, he wasn't emitting dangerous vibes at the moment, and that confused her.

"What do you want from me?"

His gaze slid over her body, those hazel eyes heating. "I have some ideas if you're interested in hearing them."

There was that smirk again, and she had the distinct feeling that he was toying with her, that he was amused. Not at all how a man Robert would have sent would be acting. Also, that heated stare reminded her that she was wearing nothing but an almost transparent white T-shirt and purple panties. She grabbed the corner of the quilt and pulled it over her. Certain it would take at least a week for Robert to find her, and she planned to be long gone by then, she'd worn her favorite sleep shirt to bed. She should have slept fully dressed, and she wouldn't make that mistake again.

He laughed. "Too late, wildcat." He pointed to his head. "Pretty in purple is already imprinted in here."

Best to ignore that comment. "Did Robert send you?"

"Who's Robert?"

It was weird, but she wasn't feeling threatened by him anymore...well, still a little, but not like when he'd first walked into the room in the dark. It was her first night here, and used to the night noises of LA, she'd been unsettled by the silence. It hadn't bothered her when she'd stayed here while attending Nichole and Jack's wedding, but she hadn't been someone's target then. This time, every creak the cabin made shot her nerves through the roof.

When she'd heard the front door as he'd closed it behind him, heard footsteps coming down the hallway, she'd thought her heart was going to stop. She hadn't known how Robert had found her so fast, but she wasn't going to go easy. That was what she'd thought, anyway, but in seconds, the man had shown her how unprepared and helpless she'd been.

His answer penetrated her mind. "Robert. The man who sent you."

"I don't know a Robert, and no one sent me."

"Who are you?"

He lifted his brows. "Who are you, and what are you doing in Jack's cabin?"

"You know Jack?"

"The question is, do you?" He glanced around. "You needed a place to stay…" Shrewd eyes landed back on her. "Maybe a place to hide out from this Robert person, so you broke in?"

"I did not break in," she said, affronted. Well, she kind of had, but not in the way he was insinuating. "Tell me something about Jack that proves you know him."

"Easy. He has a dog, Dakota. Jack was his team's dog handler until he and Dakota were hurt by a roadside bomb."

That was true. She supposed Robert could have found that out, but there would be no reason to pass that particular information on to his men. She still wasn't going to turn her back on this man, but she didn't believe he was here to hurt her.

"Now, back to you. If I call Jack and ask if he knows…what did you say your name was again?"

"Nice try, cowboy." There was that amusement again. Why? Because she'd called him a cowboy? He did make her think of one with those cowboy boots and that belt buckle with a bucking horse on it.

"I'll tell you mine if you tell me yours, wildcat."

"That's fair, I guess, but only first names. I'm Rachel."

He tipped an imaginary hat. "Dallas at your service, Miss Rachel."

Jeez, the man even had a sexy cowboy name. "Okay, Dallas, if Robert didn't send you, why are you here?" *And please don't say you're planning to stay.*

"Same game. I'll tell you why if you reciprocate." Dallas sighed when she pressed her lips together, clearly having no intention of sharing.

He didn't know what to make of the woman. She

was obviously afraid of this Robert person. An abusive boyfriend, he guessed, and that didn't sit well. She'd also obviously broken into Jack's cabin, but he wouldn't kick her out in the middle of the night or report her to Jack…at least, not yet. Tomorrow, he'd figure out what to do about her.

What he didn't appreciate was that the image of her in those purple panties and a T-shirt so thin that he could see the outline of her nipples *was* imprinted in his mind. Long legs, honey-blond hair and golden-brown eyes the color of Macallan—his favorite whiskey—did nothing to dim the desire that had shot through him as his gaze had roamed over her.

The intent had been to unnerve her, but the joke was on him. Purple might be his new favorite color, and that pissed him off. He didn't need an irresistible wildcat in his life, not now. He eyed the king bed she'd claimed, then sighed because it appeared it was going to be a twin for him.

"Where are you going?" she said when he turned to leave.

"To the other room unless you want to invite me to get in that nice big king with you."

She snorted. "Dream on."

"Was afraid you'd say that." He should have brought his cowboy hat on this trip so he could tip it to her. She had no clue she'd nailed it calling him cowboy. He tipped a nonexistent one. "Goodnight, wildcat."

"Wait. You didn't say why you're here."

"Visiting a friend for a while." He'd give her that much. "You?"

"You aren't going to call Jack, are you?"

So she was going to ignore his question. "Not tonight. I don't make any promises for tomorrow. Depends on what bullshit story you give me."

"You can't stay here."

He laughed. The woman really was amusing. "You're a funny girl." He stepped over the tree branch, picked up his carry-on, and closed the door behind him, pausing long enough to hear the click of the lock on her bedroom door. "Good girl," he murmured. He retrieved his suitcase—not that he didn't trust her, but why take a chance—and headed for the other bedroom where he'd probably spend most of the night staring at the ceiling in a bed that was too short for him.

Who was wildcat Rachel, and how much danger was she in? The last thing he needed was a female in distress. Yet, he'd felt more alive for the little bit of time sparring with her than he'd felt since the day he'd been captured.

Not good that females in distress were his kryptonite.

The next morning, after a sleepless night—no surprise there—he sat in a rocking chair on the porch and watched the sunrise. He liked that the cabin was isolated, surrounded by woods on three sides, with a clear view of the valley below from the front. No nosy neighbors wondering who he was or wanting to chat, a definite plus to his mind.

The Blue Ridge Mountains were the complete opposite of the mountains in Montana. Jack had stocked the kitchen, and as Dallas drank his coffee, he debated which he preferred, the beautiful lush green and gentle slopes of the mountains here, or the rugged and desolate beauty of the ones at home.

From mountain comparisons, his mind turned to the woman in the king bed he coveted…the bed, not the woman. *Uh-huh. Keep telling yourself that.* He'd half expected her to take off after she thought he would be asleep, but she was still here. Thanks to his captors, he'd gotten good at sensing the presence of others even when he couldn't see them. That skillset was apparently still active.

Little did she know if she'd tried to skip out on him, he would have been on her tail, something he would have cursed himself nine ways to Sunday for. But he would have done it anyway. He knew what it was like to be afraid, and she was one scared wildcat in need of protection, in spite of the bravado she tried to wrap around herself.

Also, she made him feel alive. That was as enticing as sugar water to a hummingbird for a man who was dead inside. Would she tell him the truth today, or had she spent the night thinking up a bullshit story? He was looking forward to finding out.

He was on his second cup of coffee when his mystery woman walked out. She went straight to the railing without even a glance at him. "Morning, wildcat."

"Oh." She faced him, leaning back on the railing. "You're still here?"

"As you can see. Wasn't sure you would be, though."

She looked away, shielding her eyes, but not before he saw the fear in them.

"You don't have any other place to go, do you?"

Determination was in those whiskey-colored eyes when her gaze returned to him. "I was here first. You find some other place to go."

"Give me one good reason I shouldn't tell Jack he has a squatter."

"How do you know Jack?"

He chuckled. "You're good at that, avoiding answering questions. Here's the deal. I'll answer a question for each one you do." He set the rocking chair in motion, sipped the last of his coffee, and waited her out. Not like he didn't have all the time in the world. Besides, she was keeping him entertained.

A full minute passed, then she sighed. "You're right, I don't have any other place to go. Not at the moment."

It was a start, but there was a whole lot of additional intel he intended to get out of her. "Okay, my turn. Jack and I were on the same SEAL team." Her eyes widened at that. *Surprised you, huh, wildcat?* "Who's Robert? An abusive boyfriend you're running from?"

"No. You could stay with Jack."

"Hurts my feelings how hard you're trying to get rid of me. Answer the rest of the question."

"You said one for one. I answered the second one."

"A technicality, but go ahead. Ask me something else." She was making him work for that intel he needed, and he liked that. She was no pushover, this one.

"Should I be afraid of you?"

Now, that was a question he wasn't expecting. "No, ma'am. My mama would skin my hide if I ever hurt a woman. What's the story on this abusive boyfriend of yours? Is he looking for you?"

"You're devious. You keep asking two questions."

He swallowed a smile. "My apology. Choose one." The last thing he'd expected from this trip were all the smiles his mouth wanted to do around this woman.

"Robert isn't my boyfriend." She crossed her arms,

which resulted in pushing her breasts up, and being a man who happened to love breasts, his eyes fell to her chest before he could stop the rascally things.

"Eyes on mine, cowboy."

Heat flamed in his cheeks at being caught out. What was up with that? So he'd checked out her breasts. It was what men did with a woman who interested them, and she definitely interested him. She had on jeans and the same thin white T-shirt from last night but had added a gray hoodie. Still no bra, and no complaint from him on that.

"Are you a cowboy?"

"I guess I can claim the title. Grew up on a working ranch. Rode some bucking broncs when I was young and reckless."

Her gaze fell to his stomach. "Is that a championship belt buckle?"

"Yep. Don't know if you've noticed, but you're two questions ahead of me now. If Robert isn't your boyfriend, then what is he to you and why are you afraid of him?"

"I'm tired of this game." She turned her back to him and stared at the mountains.

"No problem. I'll ask Jack if it's okay if you hang out here for a while."

She spun around. "No, please don't."

He thought that would get her attention. She didn't need to know that he'd already decided to keep her existence here a secret, at least until he found why she was hiding and how much danger she was in. It concerned him that her trouble wasn't a boyfriend. Asshole boyfriends were easy to deal with.

"Then give me a reason not to."

"You're a jerk, you know that?" She glared at him, and he was glad she didn't have that tree branch in her hands.

He swallowed another smile. Damn, if he didn't like that fire in her eyes. "I've been called worse." Recently, in fact. His captors had had a long list of insulting names they'd thrown at him.

"Fine. Here's your reason. Jack's wife, Nichole, has been my best friend since third grade. I didn't break in." She pulled a key out of her pocket and held it up. "I stayed here for their wedding because her house was full of family. I forgot to give it back, and when I needed someplace to go, I came here."

That didn't make any sense. "If Nichole's your best friend and you're in trouble, why wouldn't you turn to them for help? Believe me, Jack's capable of protecting you. He's not a man to mess with."

"That's exactly why. He'd want to get involved, and I'm not about to put the man Nichole loves on the radar of a man who's a ruthless son of a bitch. Robert wouldn't see much difference in killing Jack from stepping on a bug."

Dallas was seldom at a loss for words, but she'd left him speechless. What the hell had she gotten herself involved in? While he was scrambling for a response because he suddenly had a shit ton of questions, she walked past him, going back into the cabin. Then she popped her head back out.

"If you care about your friend, you won't tell him and Nichole I'm here." Then she was gone again.

He thought about the little she'd revealed and decided she was under his protection, Ruthless Robert be damned. After giving her time to cool down, he went inside to see if he could sweet-talk a wildcat into making him breakfast.

Don't miss Mountain Rescue,
*coming soon from Sandra Owens
and Carina Press!*

www.CarinaPress.com

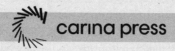
Navy SEAL Jack Daniels is back home after a bomb left him scarred with only his dog, Dakota, for company. Nichole Masters is on a losing streak with men and her rescue puppy won't get in line. Jack offers to help her with her dog, but when Nichole feels like she's being watched, he's the only person she can turn to.

Read on for a sneak preview of
Operation K-9 Brothers *by Sandra Owens,*
available now from Carina Press.

"The first rule to remember is that you're the pack leader."

"Okay. How do I do that?" Nichole asked. Jack was standing next to her in her backyard, and his masculine, woodsy scent was a distraction to the point it was hard to pay attention.

He'd followed her home, and they had ordered a pizza. While eating, she'd told him what Trevor had done, and she had the feeling Jack regretted letting Trevor off so easily. She'd never expected to have a real-life warrior on her side, but here one was in the flesh. And what nice flesh it was.

What impressed her the most was that Jack hadn't used his fists to get his point across to Trevor. If it had been Lane there today, her ex-boyfriend wouldn't have been satisfied until Trevor was bleeding and begging for mercy. Because of Lane's violent tendencies, she had grown to despise any kind of fighting. But Lane was history that she had no wish to revisit, so she pushed thoughts of him away. If only the man himself would stay away.

"I'll teach you that as we go along."

"Teach me?" What were they talking about?

A smile curved his lips and amusement lit his blue eyes. "Where's your mind, Nichole?"

On how good you smell. Those blue eyes of yours. Kind of wondering just what things you could teach me. She gave herself a mental shake. "Um, my mind wandered a bit. Sorry."

"Mmm-hmm," he murmured, his smile morphing into a sexy smirk.

"Ah, you were saying?" She was sure she was blushing, which only confirmed that he was right as to where her thoughts had wandered to.

"Since my mama taught me it's impolite to embarrass a lady, I won't ask what's going on in that beautiful head of yours."

Oh boy. Another sexy smirk like that and her panties were going to melt off without any help from her. Jack Daniels was lady-parts lethal, something she'd best remember.

Don't miss what happens next...
Operation K-9 Brothers *by Sandra Owens.*
Out now from Carina Press!

CarinaPress.com

Love Harlequin romance?

DISCOVER.

Be the first to find out about promotions,
news and exclusive content!

Facebook.com/HarlequinBooks

Twitter.com/HarlequinBooks

Instagram.com/HarlequinBooks

Pinterest.com/HarlequinBooks

You Tube YouTube.com/HarlequinBooks

ReaderService.com

EXPLORE.

Sign up for the Harlequin e-newsletter and
download a free book from any series at
TryHarlequin.com

CONNECT.

Join our Harlequin community to
share your thoughts and connect
with other romance readers!
Facebook.com/groups/HarlequinConnection

HSOCIAL2021

HARLEQUIN

Heartfelt or thrilling, passionate or uplifting—Harlequin is more than just happily-ever-after.

With twelve different series to choose from and new books available every month, you are sure to find stories that will move you, uplift you, inspire and delight you.

SIGN UP FOR THE HARLEQUIN NEWSLETTER
Be the first to hear about great new reads and exciting offers!

Harlequin.com/newsletters